4/11

The Great Night

CHRIS ADRIAN

FARRAR, STRAUS AND GIROUX   NEW YORK

The Great Night

Farrar, Straus and Giroux
18 West 18th Street, New York 10011

Copyright © 2011 by Chris Adrian
Printed in the United States of America
First edition, 2011

Library of Congress Cataloging-in-Publication Data
Adrian, Chris, 1970–
    The great night / Chris Adrian.— 1st ed.
        p.   cm.
    A retelling of Shakespeare's A midsummer night's dream.
    ISBN 978-0-374-16641-0 (alk. paper)
    I. Shakespeare, William, 1564–1616. Midsummer night's dream.
    II. Title.

PS3551.D75G74 2011
813'.54—dc22

2010047603

Designed by Jonathan D. Lippincott

www.fsgbooks.com

1   2   3   4   5   6   7   8   9   10

FOR COLIN

And I do love thee: therefore, go with me;
I'll give thee fairies to attend on thee,
And they shall fetch thee jewels from the deep,
And sing while thou on pressed flowers dost sleep;
And I will purge thy mortal grossness so
That thou shalt like an airy spirit go.

—William Shakespeare, *A Midsummer Night's Dream*,
III, i, 163–68

Part One

1

One night in the middle of June, three brokenhearted people walked into Buena Vista Park at nearly the same time, just after dark. One came from the north, out of the Haight, another climbed up out of the Castro from the east, and the last came from the west, out of the Sunset and Cole Valley: this one was already going in the wrong direction, and shortly all three of them would be lost. They were going to a seasonal party of the famously convivial Jordan Sasscock, at his home at 88 Buena Vista West (Molly was headed, mistakenly, to 88 Buena Vista East). Jordan's parties were as famously convivial as he was, and the invitations, while prized, were not exactly exclusive, because it was in the nature of his conviviality never to leave anyone feeling left out. There were swarms of people who trudged up the hill in the middle of every summer to drink Jordan's beer and wine and stand on his roof and dance in his expansive garden. He was a lowly resident at the hospital nearby, but his grandmother had died five years before when he was still a medical student, leaving him the house and the garden and all the treasures and garbage she had stuffed into it in the eighty-nine years she had lived there: ruined priceless furniture and money under the mattresses and case after case of fancy cat food in the basement, and fifteen cats, only five of which were still alive on the night of the party, because, affable as he was, Jordan didn't much like cats, and he didn't take very good care of them.

Henry, like the other two people entering the park, was late. He was not even sure he was entirely invited, though it seemed that everyone at the hospital was invited, just as he wasn't sure that Jordan Sasscock liked him, though Jordan seemed to like everybody. They happened to be working together that month on the Pediatric Oncology service, and here and there a flail or a mistake had occurred that was almost certainly Henry's fault, and yet somehow the blame had spilled onto Jordan. Henry generally sought out blame, being comfortable with it, having been blamed for all sorts of things his whole life long and having accepted responsibility for all sorts of crimes he had only barely committed, at ease in the habit of culpability because he had an abiding suspicion, fostered by an unusual amount of blank history in his childhood, that he had once done something unforgivably wrong.

Three months before, he would have stayed home on a night like this, in the context of an invitation like this, entertaining potential scenes of confrontation or humiliation or trickery: Jordan telling him quietly to leave, or asking from the middle of a group of encircling unfriendly faces if he could see Henry's invitation; didn't Henry know an invitation was necessary to come to the party? But Henry had turned over a new leaf since his lover had issued his latest and most final rejection. He was spending less time imprisoned in imaginary scenarios, and through no recognizable effort of his own he was becoming, day by day, a better man. It was a shame, really, that all the faults and neuroses and quite considerable pathologies that had helped spoil the relationship were finally lifting from him just in time to be too late. The timing was ridiculous, and it added significantly to his heartbreak that it had done no good to demonstrate his renaissance to Bobby, who had been out to San Francisco for a month to work (and expressly not, he said, to visit Henry). Bobby had issued his most detailed, hope-abolishing rejection on the day before he left, and they hadn't talked in all the months that had passed since then. It was a dismal discovery: there were so many different intensities of rejection, and every successive "no!" could feel worse and worse. It had put Henry into a state of what felt like perpetual agony, and yet he wasn't exactly depressed, or at least he was depressed in a totally different way than he had been all his remembered life up until then. Dull, quotidian misery had been replaced with a brighter sort of suffering, and he felt more connected to everything and everyone around him than he had for twenty years. Each day for weeks he had given up some neurotic quirk: excessive hand washing; fear of doorknobs and the ground; a reluctance to touch the sick children of smokers; fear, most recently, that having a single drink of alcohol would transform him into a monster. "People like us shouldn't drink," his mother had told him, over and over and over, "because of the horrible things that have happened to us." With one hand she would mime throwing back a shot and with the other draw an imaginary knife across her throat. "Ack," she'd say, as her invisible lifeblood poured out. "Instant addict." Never mind all that. He had already decided to drink a lot of beer at the party.

There remained, of course, the fear of the park itself, part and parcel of his old habits of bleaching and hand-washing and hand-wringing. The place had used to make his skin crawl, and the whole city and even the state around the park had made him uneasy even before it became intolerable to imagine being there. He had lived in San Francisco as a regular child, and then as a child abducted, and those unremembered years between the ages of nine and thirteen had cast a pall over the whole city. The story, as little of it as he had reconstructed, was as weird as the behaviors he had manifested when it could not be contained any longer in unmemory, and the strangeness of it had attracted Bobby in the beginning, as much as it had ultimately tortured him and driven him away in the end.

It's just a park, he thought, standing at the entrance, just a collection of trees and bushes artfully planted to approximate a wild wood on a hill. The worst thing about it, in fact, was that Bobby had brought him here to tell him to fuck off forever, to leave him alone for all eternity, to *never bother him again*, and part of Henry was still sensitive to the imagined residues of physical and emotional trauma, though he wasn't controlled anymore by his aversion to them. He would take a break and sit on the very fucking bench where Bobby had said goodbye, just for the sake of doing it, and he would consider how atrociously sad and ridiculous the collapse of their relationship was, how all the pieces of an extraordinary partnership had come together in just the wrong way. Then he would set the timer on his phone and spend a full five minutes demonstrating to the uncaring world and his unwatching lover that he was not who he had been.

Henry stepped off Haight Street onto the first step up into the park, thinking again that his was as magical a transformation as to have woken up one day to find he had become a pony. And he had a little daydream about Henry the pony, because even though he had been liberated from the obsessive prisons of his imagination, he was still an inveterate day-dreamer. He was sure it must be an escaping wisp of the daydream when he thought he saw a face in the stone wall beside the step and thought he heard a voice say, very clearly, "Poodle!" He stopped and peered at the wall; it was getting dark, so when he stared all he could see was a rough suggestion of the texture on the stone. He shook his head and did a little pony step and kept walking into the park.

A little farther north, Will was trying to find a way in. He had come up the steps from Waller Street, expecting to find another staircase, but there was only the sidewalk that encircled the park and then some not very passable-looking brush separating him from a path that wound up the side of the hill. He thought he saw someone moving on the other side of the brush and took that for an indication that there was an entrance nearby. He was frustrated and late and anxious about entering the park so late in the day, because the chances of getting afflicted with an uninvited grope rose exponentially if you went in after sunset. He lived in the Castro in a sea of homosexuals, and loved his neighborhood and his neighbors, and judged no one. If anything, he felt a kinship with those lonely souls drifting through the muffling darkness, rubbing up against one another, accidentally burning one another with the tips of cigarettes. It wasn't so long ago that he had been engaged in parallel pursuits. He had rooted in a different trough, but he knew what it was like to be lonely and to commit intimate acts that only made you feel lonelier still. The horror of it, and what made him a sorrier sort than even the most hideous troll in the park, was the fact that he had done such things while in the company of the most wonderful woman on earth. He had burrowed all through that relationship, making slimy tunnels, and at last it collapsed when his deceit and his unwarranted unhappiness were revealed.

Will sighed, and realized he had been standing on the sidewalk not moving at all, distracted by unprofitable thoughts, and it was getting very dark. He looked at his watch and became anxious again at how late he was. Jordan Sasscock was friends with both Will and Carolina, the only mutual friend he hadn't lost when she left him, and one of the only people in his whole circle of friends who sort of sympathized with him, both disgusted and understanding in a way that made Will think that at least one person in the world had forgiven him for what he had done to her. It was entirely possible—Jordan had hinted at it—that Carolina would be there tonight. And Jordan had hinted further that she knew Will might be there too. It was the closest thing Will had had to good news in a year.

He put his head down and pushed through the bushes, slipping and trying to catch his balance on a handful of leaves. With a little more scrabbling he was up the rise and on the path. He heard a whisper, very distinct, as he was wiping his hands off on his pants, that said something like "Poodle?"

"No . . . get away!" Will shouted, assuming it was someone asking him if he *wanted to poodle*, and he was ashamed even to know what that might mean. He hurried along the path, walking up the side of the hill toward a place where he was almost totally certain there was a road that cut straight across the park and led directly to Jordan's block.

On the other side, and farther up the hill, Molly, having wandered a little around Ashbury Heights in the fog, came at last to the high western entrance to the park. Had she known that she was going in the wrong direction and that she had already passed within a few blocks of Jordan's house, she might have given up entirely on going to the party. She already felt painfully self-conscious—she felt that way whenever she left her house, and imagined everywhere she went that people whispered about her, saying, "There goes that poor girl" and "The poor thing!"—and lately she had learned to avoid all sorts of lesser disasters and heartbreaks and misfortunes by recognizing them from far away; getting lost on the way to a party you didn't want to attend, on the way to a date you were neither interested in nor ready for—that was a sign from somebody that you really should turn around and go home.

She sat down on the curb and put her hands over her face—it felt like she'd spent most of the last eighteen months in this pose but lately she did it really more because it helped her gather her thoughts than because it was a good position in which to cry—and considered things for a moment. She could feel her couch pulling at her from way back at Sixteenth and Judah, but she knew she'd come too far, in both her own and other people's estimation, to go back now. If she didn't show up, people would think she still couldn't move on from Ryan's death. The truth was, she couldn't, but she didn't want that to be obvious to the gossipy old ladies who seemed to live in the hearts of all her friends. "Everything is not ruined," she said, repeating a mantra that had started off as a joke, pulled from a ridiculous guide to getting over the suicide of your boyfriend. The guide had been sent to her by a distant aunt, part of the small subsection of her extended family not crazy for Jesus, and though it was less ridiculous than any of the countless Christian manuals of survivorship that flocked her way, Molly had still chortled over its obvious and unconvincing lessons in the first few months: Everything is not ruined; it wasn't your fault; you will be loved again someday by a nonsuicidal person. But as she degraded over the months it became her secular Bible and her best friend, and once she even dreamed sexually about the author, a great big lesbian with tight gray poodle hair, swathed in purple from head to toe in her gigantic back-cover author photo.

Her date tonight was with Jordan Sasscock himself. The honor of this was lost on her, as she barely knew him. He had come into her shop to visit one of her coworkers, and then had returned again and again, buying increasingly pricey arrangements of flowers and then increasingly pricey design pieces, a process that culminated in the purchase of an exorbitantly expensive Scandinavian foam couch cunningly crafted to look just like a boulder. "I've been looking for one of these for years!" he said, lounging in it. He looked very appealing with his hands behind his head; the swell of his biceps pleasingly echoed in the contours of the fake rock.

Everyone else in the shop—boys and girls alike—swooned over him, but Molly hardly noticed him at first, and for the longest time assumed he just really liked flowers and good design, until he finally asked her out. That was a strange moment. Time seemed to stop and everything seemed to tremble, not just the flowers but the colors in them, the air itself, and the porcelain bells above the door, which seemed just on the verge of ring-ing, everything so very gently disturbed. "I'm having a little get-together this Thursday and I want you to be my guest of honor," he had said. When she only stared, marveling at the odd ripple that stole over his face and body, he added, "Or you could just show up at some point. You don't have to be guest of honor, if that's too much responsibility. Anyway, think about it." He told her his address, which she misremembered immediately.

"Sure," she said, without thinking about it at all. "See you there." She had packaged up his latest purchase, a transparent piece of china with a hand-painted rim of little blue flowers, and now she handed it to him, not smiling. Sensing perhaps that to do so would push his luck, he didn't say anything else but just smiled and nodded. When he left, her boss let out a shriek of delight. "You've got a date with Jordan Sasscock!" she shouted, grabbing Molly's shoulders and jumping up and down like a fool.

"It's not a date," Molly said. "I'm just going to his party." It would be another hour before she fully regretted the decision to say yes, and then it would seem like the stupidest thing she'd ever done. She spent the next few days telling herself that she wasn't ready for this, and that she was, and that she wasn't. Now, sitting on the curb with her face in her hands, she felt sure that she wasn't, and only because she was still in love with Ryan—or still in *something* with him. The feeling that dominated her day and night was not the same lovely invigorating obsession she had felt every day before his death, when he seemed like the very beginning and end of her perception, his mind and body and spirit each an occasion of persistent joy. Ever since she had come home to find him hanging by his neck from a tree in their garden, only the character of the feeling had changed, not the strength of it. She had married him the instant she met him, and now he still attracted and owned all her parts.

"Jordan Sasscock!" she shouted, lifting her face out of her hands, and somehow that made her feel better. She was sure a voice answered her, but instead of saying, "Shut up!" or "Yes, dear?" it said, very quietly, "Poodle."

"Leave me alone!" she said, not sure whether she was addressing Jordan or Ryan or sardonic voices that, while they weren't exactly hallucinations, weren't voices that anyone but she could hear. "It's just a party," she said to herself, when nothing and no one else answered her. "What's the worst thing that could happen?" She got up, not considering the worst things, turned around, and found she had missed the entrance in a shadow and had sat down very close to it. She put her arms around herself and bowed her head and walked into the park.

2

*A*t the top of the hill, just beyond the threshold of ordinary human senses, a door was opening in the earth, letting out a light that was as lustrous and thin as autumn sunshine. The light spilled down the hill and seemed to calm everything it touched: branches stopped their trembling despite the wind, and little creatures paused in their snuffling, as if leaf and shrew both were waiting and listening for the sound that shortly came drifting up out of the hole into the earth. It was a noise of bells, at first extremely faint and then not much louder but somehow more obvious, perhaps because, though the noise was soft and the individual tones quite pleasant, there were odd harmonies and overtones unnerving to animal ears. Shadows appeared in the light, reaching down the hill, followed by a variety of figures.

They came in twos, matched by height (because that was pleasing to their Mistress) though not by form, so lovely creatures were paired with homely ones and wizened faces with young ones. Opposite and antagonistic natures were paired together as well, though this was harder to tell simply by observation, except where the smiles (also mandated) were obviously forced and where, instead of just holding hands, each partner held the other's wrist in a mutual, clawing clutch. It was as stately a procession as a bridal march, though a very keen observer, or one who had seen the faeries pour out of the hill in the days before their King was lost and their Queen went into mourning, would have noticed a tired, shuffling quality to it. In other days, decorum restrained a joy at the dusking of another night; now it propped up tired, depressed spirits, some of whom would have preferred to stay under the hill, dreaming of better times.

Soon dozens and dozens of them had come out into the night, the first few no taller than a thimble. The last few, as tall as streetlamps, were followed by eight more, all of a middling height, who bore a litter upon which their Queen reclined, propped up with coarse black pillows, blackbirds fluttering in her hair and two black cats, entirely uninterested in the birds, asleep on her lap. She yawned as she went through the door, carried after the rest of the procession in a half loop that took her to the flat top of the hill. There her bearers set the litter down on the thick, soft grass and danced around her in a ring. Every step was choreographed for the Queen's pleasure, though it had been years since she had taken an interest in the design of the dance and many months since she had really paid any attention to them as they performed for her.

Still paired, the faeries danced five turns around the litter, twisting and dipping, one now leading and then following, one lifting the other partner when the bells rang a particularly discordant note, the lifted dancer now doing a split and now a curtsy toward the Lady, until the bells rang faster and the couples disengaged, everyone dancing alone, increasingly frenzied yet precise, as the bells rang ever louder. It was a sight to nauseate and entrance any human observer, though the dance was not what it once was, and the dancers, for all the ways they leaped high and threw their bodies low, looked as bored, in their frozen, smiling faces, as their Queen.

In waves the bells reached toward a crescendo until they broke, and then a hundred different unsettling overtones hung a few moments more in the air over the hill. The frenzy of the dancers broke as well, and they stopped, scattered in heaps around the litter but not sweating or out of breath. Smiles vanished, finally no longer required, and they all stood and bowed toward their Queen, who was idly stroking one of the cats and entirely ignoring the other, though it pressed its face into her belly. The birds in her hair had flown away. She flicked one hand absently at her court, and they rose, their unsmiling faces now showing every sort of emotion except happiness. A frog-sized gnome with very curly brown hair was glaring furiously at her, and a feathered, pony-sized woman was staring at her with a combination of sadness and desire, while another lady, tall and pale and barked like a birch, was silently weeping.

They stood around like that for a time, silent conversations passing from face to face; the host had grown accustomed to such long, boring silences, for the Queen had the privilege of speaking the first words of the night, and this was especially true tonight, the Great Night, the midsummer holiday when all their customs were most formal. Some nights it was halfway to dawn before she called for a game or named the clouds or sang a song (always sad ones, these days). Tonight she seemed to nap a little, clutching now at both cats, who did not squirm like ordinary cats would but suffered her tight embrace, staring into each other's eyes, panting and gasping a little at the pressure around their necks and chests. The darkness had hardly fully settled under the trees before she started and sat up and spoke.

"Where's Puck?"

A collective sigh escaped from the host, and they dropped their stiff poses, some of them reclining on the grass while others turned away from their enforced partners to seek out their real friends and lovers. Some of them retired in twos and threes to the edge of the summit of the hill, not quite brave enough to leave entirely, but so sure no Great Night festivities were coming that they were already conspiring to make their own party. But three individuals stood by the litter. Formerly Oberon's closest servants, they had given up or forgotten their names when he disappeared and borrowed others from the human world.

"Up to no good," said Fell, who was beaver-sized and somewhat beaver-faced.

"Out in the city making babies cry," said Lyon, one of those faeries whose appearance mirrored his disposition but not his name; he looked to be made of tightly spooled string and was seven feet tall at his shoulder.

"Searching for our Master, and ever faithfully," said Oak, who might be mistaken for a human boy if you missed his rabbit's feet and thickly furred face and bottom. He was the nearest thing Puck had in the entire faerie company to a friend since Oberon had disappeared.

"Summon him," said the Queen, holding out the cats. Oak and Fell each took one, holding them at an odd angle, and began to squeeze them not quite in succession, so they let out an overlapping series of shrieks and yowls. Despite the abuse, the cats remained docile, not clawing or spitting but only making noise, as dutifully as any instrument. The cats sounded for nearly five minutes, the company around them drawing farther away from the players, not because they didn't enjoy the music but because of how much they feared Puck. There was a tune in the wailing of the cats, not very obvious at first, but it was actually a very short bit of song they were playing, repeated again and again, something that shared a lot of notes with "Danny Boy," though to anyone who knew that song it would seem as if notes of violence and threat had been inserted at random into the music. It was those elements, as much as the mandate of obedience laid by Oberon upon the wild spirit who had nearly destroyed them a thousand years before, that drew Puck into the presence of the Queen. Before he appeared, walking quite unremarkably up the hill, a whistling was heard, an echo and exaggeration of the song of the cats. Puck's whistling grew as loud as and then louder than the cats, until he stopped a few feet before the Queen and bowed.

People and faeries, animals and spirits—any observing entity—each saw Puck a little differently. What you saw depended on how you were feeling; he was often the image of one's worst fear or most troubling anxiety. To some of the faeries he looked like a naked boy with a luxurious Afro, and only the height of the boy or the width of the Afro changed from eye to eye. But some saw him as a sliver of flame, or a blackness heavier and darker than the black air, or a fluttering pair of dark wings, and some saw him as an image of their Queen only even more depressed, disheveled, and defeated-looking. In every form he wore a chain, sometimes made of tiny silver acorns or leaves of twisted silver grass. Sometimes the chain was made of thick links of silver manacle, and sometimes it was just silver glints upon the air or the fire. The chain had been placed there by Oberon a very long time ago, so long ago that no one but the Queen remembered the true particulars of the binding, though the battle was a story they all had once sung under the hill and one they celebrated every Midsummer's Eve.

"Where is your Master?" Titania asked him.

"Still hidden," he said.

"But the last report was so . . . promising," she said. She had been trying to discover the King by reports of unusual events in the city, because she was sure he had not quit the world but only sunk himself in it, putting on a mortal face and a mortal life because she had wounded him when his heart was already broken, like hers, over the death of their son. She never went out to look for him herself anymore, even though she was sure she would have recognized him no matter how expert his disguise; as lost as he might be to himself right now, he would never be lost to her if she could only stand before him. And she only barely trusted Puck, even under his world-heavy bonds, because all love of his Master was forced on him, and what did he care, really, if her King and husband and lover never returned? But lately she could not abide the sight of mortal boys; everyone looked like their Boy, and so she, Queen of the Night and Empress of the Air and Suzeraine of the Autumn Moon and the bearer of a hundred thousand other lofty titles, some of which could only be expressed in hours of music, ran sweating and shaking from blue-socked babies in their strollers and baseball-capped toddlers and little hoodlums on skateboards, and cried for days under the hill after each time she ventured out. Once, a few dim but well-meaning sprites had scouted out a poor replica of her Boy and called him up to the hill, singing him out of the Mission, warding him as he crossed the street, turning buses and bicycles out of his path as he walked in a daze, not quite awake but compelled toward the park, held fast by the certainty that every good thing he ever had wanted was waiting for him there. When he presented himself in a stupor at the bald top of the hill, mouth agape at the faeries, who were only partially hidden from him, it roused the Queen from her own stupor. In an instant she understood the nature of the spell and knew who had cast it. In another she had punished them, as swift in her vengeance as she ever was in the good old days when every night was great, when the host spent the hours on the hill from dusk to dawn consumed in masques of jealousy and violent, elevating, rejuvenating lust. With a mere gesture, she tore the wings from the do-gooders and forced them to bear the boy upon their wounded backs, crawling under him in the dirt as he dozed and drooled until they deposited him on the Haight Street sidewalk.

Often, but not always, when her subjects assumed she was lost in sad reverie, she was actually listening to the city where her husband had hidden himself, though it wasn't any ordinary sense of hearing that she deployed. As she lay on her litter or her bier, startling little flashes of wonder would flare up beyond the hill, sometimes so intensely that she could feel them like a warmth against her face. These showed her where to direct her attention, and it was not much longer before she could discern the particulars of the event: a child floats away with his kite; a dog suddenly grows flowers in its coat; a hideous transvestite stumbling down Eighteenth

Street at 2 a.m. actually becomes, for twenty paces, a beautiful woman. This was magic, and it must indicate the presence of her lost love, because for a long time now magic had been absent from the city and the country beyond the hill. In his hidden state, unknown to himself and unaware of his power, the magic would seep from Oberon and temporarily change the world around him, at random or according to the changeable and petty wishes of the mortals with whom he slummed. The latest report had been the most promising: A white bull, cock a-swagger and head held high, had paraded through a coffee shop in Noe Valley and then strolled down Twenty-fourth Street toward Diamond Heights.

This was a sign like none other. The white bull was one of his aspects; a form to wear in battle or in passion but also one he liked to wear after a bitter quarrel with her, because she could never stay angry at him when he was a creature so warm and breathy, and she could never detect any duplicity in Oberon's apologies in those giant brown eyes. So it was a sign and a signal. He had become his most distinctive beast because he was ready to put back on his power and become her King again, and because he was so sorry for leaving her, for hurting her more than he'd ever done before in all the years of their marriage.

"I never saw the bull," Puck said, "though the wonder of him was written still on the faces of all the mortals who beheld him. I followed his scent for a quarter mile and found a flowering bush wet with his piss. See? I brought you a flower from it." From somewhere on his naked person he produced a small blue flower with thick hairy petals that glistened as if they were still wet. He took a deep whiff and presented it to her with another bow and flourish. "It is his stink!' he said with a wide smile. A light came off his teeth too bright for most of them to look at long, though Titania was never cowed by it. She snatched the flower from him and brought it hesitantly to her face. Puck had frozen it in time, but his spell came apart in her hand. The petals softened and felt moist instead of glassy, and when she shook the flower a few drops fell onto her dress as the salt and iron odor rose up and transported her into a rapture of nostalgia. It was pathetic, she knew, to weep over the scent of her lost lover's piss, but it was the first time in a year she had been able to partake of his odor, since all his clothes had disappeared on the same day he did, and the sheets on his side of their bed, too. It wasn't an unpleasant smell, though she would have cherished it even if it were. It smelled powerful and ancient and sad, and she thought she could apprehend in it some trace, a compacted seed, of the extraordinary love he bore her.

Her courtiers yawned, and here and there they muttered "There she goes again" and "I thought tonight would be different" and "Some Great Night this is going to be!" A few of them wandered off in small companies down the hill, more faithful to their holiday than to the Queen who didn't have the heart to celebrate it. Most were too timid to spurn her presence, but bold enough to sit without leave and complain to one another loudly and at length. But the three who had been nearest to her husband, and who now were nearest to her, closed on her, taking liberties with her person, stroking her hair and kissing her hands and her feet, uselessly attempting to comfort her. Puck, still smiling, remained where he was.

"Wicked thing," the Queen said to him. "You are failing on purpose to find him."

"You know I cannot willingly fail at anything you set me to. Your word is his word, and I am bound to obey." He shook his silver chain, and the tinkle and rattle and chime stilled a few complaining conversations. It made the host nervous when Puck rattled his chain, and none of them were really comfortable having him around now that the King was gone. "He outmatches me. But perhaps if I were unbound?" He fell to his knees and slid closer to the Queen, offering her the back of his neck, where a thumb-sized block of rough silver bound the ends of the chain. They had this conversation every night, after every report of failure, Puck always bolder in his requests for freedom.

"I would sooner put out the sun," she said, her usual response, and it sounded to all but the most discerning ears the same as it did on any other night, but Puck and her three closest courtiers heard overtones of resignation in her voice. The three courtiers reacted by stroking and kissing her more frantically, whispering to her that she shouldn't listen, and calling on Puck to be silent.

Puck said, "Maybe someone should put it out." The thought had actually occurred to her, when she was in her deepest troughs, that there would be a certain satisfaction in putting out the sun or banishing the moon or pulling down the sky, taking away from the world something commensurate with what had been taken from her. But these indulgent fantasies always passed in a moment; she cried them out along with all the resurgent bitter anger she felt toward her husband, and when her nightly tears were done she only ever felt a deep sadness that had a small quality of peace to it. She tried to weep herself down there now, because she was more bitter and angry and hopeless than ever, all because of the bull, prancing outrageously down Twenty-fourth Street, and now through her mind's eye wagging its ass, teasing and mocking her for having been stupid enough to drive him away in the first place and for being too weak now to call him back. She took her hands away from her courtiers—two of them were rubbing her palms—and covered her face and wept harder, so the circle of the host widened even more, because it was bad enough for the Queen to be languid and depressive on the festival night, but to indulge in histrionics was frankly poor taste. Even the cats, who had formerly been licking at her arms and breasts and face, slunk off the litter and disappeared over the edge of the hill with another dozen faeries. Titania took no notice of them. She was on her way down to the saddest place in her memory, Oberon's leave-taking, when she had made her awful mistake. It had seemed like the only thing to say at the time, the only sensible response to the horrible new world she had woken into after the long dreamlike demise of their Boy. Grieving furiously, she had set about destroying everything left to her.

"You do not love me anymore?" her husband had asked her.

"I do not," she had said.

"You do not love me?"

"I do not love you. All my feelings have been false."

"Then I am undone. Behold, I never was Oberon, nor you Titania, and never was the boy our Boy. I undo it all with a word, *no*, and pass away." And then he walked away, from this very spot where she lay every night on her bier, down the hill and out of the park and into the mortal world. In memory she watched him, and instead of turning her face away from his receding back (as she actually had done), she propelled herself after him. Even in her imagination she could not capture him, but this exercise usually sent her into the deeper and more peaceful sadness that she sought. Tonight it eluded her, and seeking it she had a thought, terrible and surprising. Puck was staring at her when she looked up, wearing Oberon's face, sad but disdainful, looking at her just the way she most feared he might look at her.

"Milady," said Lyon, "best not to look into his eyes!" He tried to cover her eyes with a fan, but she batted it away.

"Maybe someone should put it out," she said to Puck. "What does it illuminate for me, except everywhere my love is not? And does it see him and not tell me where he is? Shouldn't it be punished?"

"I have always hated the sun," said Puck.

"The sun is our friend, " said Fell nervously, sensing the direction in which the conversation was turning and not liking it at all. "It makes the green things grow."

"What worth is the world with him not in it?" It wasn't the first time she had considered destruction as a remedy for her ills. Before she had become confined to the hill, she had made a study of mortal suicides. No faerie had ever done such a thing, or even died at all, though in remote legend some great grief had turned one to stone, or caused a sleep of ages. Mortals' deaths always only reminded her of how different she was from them. She was ageless and immortal, and the only creature ever to threaten her life or those of her subjects had been overcome a whole age before, his wild magic contained by a bond that was as frail as it was strong, so that anyone might break it with a single word, though only Titania and Oberon knew the word, which changed from year to year. The magic in the chain prevented any accidental utterance, so that lately Puck, in the city in the service of his Queen or his own constrained appetites, might hear someone forget the breed of their beloved dog when asked, or might hear someone say, "What a lovely dog. What is it? Of course I know . . . it's on the tip of my tongue! The lovely fur like hair, the distinctive hairdo. Hypoallergenic!" A person might work themselves into a fit trying to speak the word, but Oberon's magic would strike them dead before they ever uttered the first syllable.

"Do you think it would draw him out, Adversary, if I set you free?"

"Oh, most certainly," Puck said, visibly trembling.

"Milady!" said Fell.

"You can't be thinking of it!" said Lyon.

"He is my friend," said Oak, "but you would make him nobody's friend!"

"You are not that sad," said Fell. "No one is that sad!"

But I am, she thought, standing up and shaking them off. And though she told herself it was a reasoned choice, that freeing this monster would call her husband back more swiftly and certainly than her entreaties of love and remorse ever could, duty to his subjects, and care for all those

Puck would threaten being more important to him than her happiness, death was in her heart when she spoke the word. Her courtiers, liegemen first even though they had been her closest companions in the past year, tried to stop her. They leaped upon her with spells and claws and whirling bits of wire-sharp string. Oak came at her bottom first, his rabbit's tail exuding soporifics strong enough to put an elephant to sleep for a week. But she was their Queen for a reason. She brushed them aside in a moment. It was over so quickly that the rest of the host had barely marked the commotion before she leaned down and spoke the word to Puck.

"Poodle," she said, and the chain around Puck's neck shattered into countless pieces. She said the word very quietly, but it was heard loud as a klaxon all over the hill, and then a little softer all over San Francisco, so husbands turned to wives in countless living rooms and bedrooms and said, "Did you just call me a poodle?" and plays and movies and a single opera were briefly spoiled by the incongruous word, spoken softly but very clearly. Every faerie knew immediately what it signified, and they all ran screaming toward the edge of the hill as soon as they heard it, aiming for Tunisia or Ireland or Samoa, anyplace but here where the monster was. In a few seconds, only Puck and the Queen were left on top of the hill. He was rubbing gently at his neck and looked no different than before, except that he stood much straighter, as if a weight had been lifted from him. She no longer looked sad or droopy but had gathered all her power to herself, ready to fight the Beast she had freed and make a noise that her husband must hear. Her subjects, had any been around to see her, would have been proud. But Puck only bowed to her again.

"Milady," he said, "I am in your debt, and so I will eat you last."

3

It took them both a long time to understand that the boy was sick, though she would point out that she was the first to notice he was unhappy, and had sought to remedy his discontent with sweeter treats and more delightful distractions. She thought it was evidence that she loved him more, how she noticed first that something was wrong, and she said as much to her husband, when they were still trying to outdo each other in love for the child, before he became sick enough to demonstrate to them that they both loved him equally and immeasurably.

Neither of them had any experience with illness. They had each taken many mortal lovers but had cast them off before they could become old or infirm, and all their previous changelings had stayed healthy until they were returned to the mortal world. "There was no way you could have known," said Dr. Blork, the junior partner in the two-person team that oversaw the boy's care, on their very first visit with him. "Every parent feels they ought to have caught it earlier, but really it's the same for everyone, and you couldn't have done any better than you did. In fact, you did great. You did perfect." He was trying to make them feel better, to assuage a perceived guilt, but at that point neither Titania nor her husband really knew what guilt was, not ever having felt it in all their long days.

They were in the hospital, not far from the park on the hill under which they made their home, in the middle of the night—early for them, since they slept all day under the hill and had taught the boy to do the same—but the doctors, Beadle and Blork, were obviously fatigued. The four of them were sitting at a table in a small windowless conference room, the doctors on one side, the parents on the other. The boy was back in his room, drugged with morphine, sleeping peacefully for the first time in days. The doctors were explaining things, earnestly and patiently, but Titania was having trouble following along and found herself distracted by the notion that she should be delighted by the newness of this experience, for she and her husband had always been seekers after novelty, and yet already she did not like this at all.

"A boy should not be sick," she said suddenly to Dr. Blork, cutting him off as he was beginning to describe some of the side effects of the treatment they were proposing. "A boy should play . . . that is his *whole* purpose."

"It's hard to see him like this," Dr. Blork said, after a glance at his superior, "and I'm so sorry that your beautiful boy is so sick. It's going to be a long haul, and he may be sicker before he's better, but we'll get him through it." He started talking again about specifics, the drugs they would use—the names seemed rather demonic to her—and the timing of the treatments, which parts could be done at home and which parts must be done in the hospital. This was suddenly very boring. She waved her hand at them, a gesture practiced over centuries, and even though there was no magic in it, Blork was instantly silent.

"You will do your mortal thing," she said sadly. "I know all I need to know."

"Pardon me?" said Dr. Blork.

"Leukemia!" said Oberon, breaking the silence he'd kept all through the meeting. "Leukemia!" he said again, and it sounded as if he were somehow trying out the idea behind the word. He was smiling and crying into his beautiful beard. "Can you cure it?"

"Yes!" said Dr. Blork. But Dr. Beadle said, "Maybe."

She could not remember the quarrel that brought her the boy. A real or perceived dalliance or slight, a transgression on her part or her husband's—who knew? They had been quarreling for as long as they had been in love. She forgot the quarrels as soon as they were resolved, except for a vague sense, when they fought about something, that they had fought about it before. But the gifts her husband brought her to reconcile—even when she was at fault—she never forgot. The boy was one of those gifts, brought home to the hill, stolen from its crib in the dark of morning and presented to her by dawn. "That is not sufficient to your crime against me," she remembered saying, and remembered as well that she barely paid the child any mind during her restless sleep, except to push it away from her when it rolled too close. Oberon had rubbed poppies on its eyes to quiet its crying, so it was still sleeping soundly when she woke. For a while she lay on her back, watching the stars come out on the ceiling of her grotto, listening to the little snores. Oberon was snoring more magnificently. She turned on her side to better look at the child, and noticed for the first time how comely it was, how round and smooth were its face and shoulders and belly, how soft-appearing and lustrous was its hair. It made a troubled face as it slept. She put her hand out to touch the child, very lightly. Right away it sighed and lost the troubled look, but then it gave a little moan. She draped her hand over its shoulder, and when it did not quiet she rolled it closer to her. It stopped moaning only when she held it in her arms, and put her nose in its hair, and breathed in its scent—poppies and milk and warm earth. Oberon had woken and was looking at her and smiling, propped on one elbow with a hand against his ear, the other lost under the sheets, but she could hear him scratching himself. "Do you like it?" he asked.

"I am indifferent to it," she said, holding the boy closer, and squeezing him, and putting her face in his neck.

"This place is so ugly," Titania said. "Can anything be done about that?" She was talking to the oncology social worker, one of a stream of visiting strangers who came to the room, a woman who had described herself as a person to whom one might address problems or questions that no one else could solve or answer. Nonmedical things, she had said. You know—everything else!

"But you've made the room just lovely," the woman said. Her name was Alice or Alexandra or Antonia. Titania had a hard time keeping track of all the mortal names, except for Beadle and Blork, but those were distinctive and actually rather faerie-like. Alice gestured expansively around the room and smiled, not seeing what was actually there. She saw paper stars hanging from the ceiling, and cards and posters on the wall, and a homey bedspread upon the mattress, but faeries had come to carpet the room with grass, to pave the walls with stone and set them with jewels, and blow a cover of clouds to hide the horrible suspended ceiling. And the bedspread was no ordinary blanket but the boy's own dear Beastie, a flat headless creature of soft fur that loved him like a dog and tried to follow him out of the room whenever they took him away for some new test or procedure.

"I don't mean the room," Titania said, "I mean everything else. This whole place. And the people, of course . . . Where did you find them? Look at you, for instance. Are you deliberately homely? And that Dr. Blork—hideous! He is beyond help, but you . . . I could do you up."

Alice cocked her head. She did not hear exactly what Titania was saying. Everything was filtered through the same disguising glamour that hid the light in Titania's face, that gave her splendid gown the appearance of a track suit, that made the boy appear clothed when they brought him in, when in fact he had been naked. The same spell made it appear that he had a name, though his parents had only ever called him Boy, never having learned his mortal name, because he was the only boy under the hill. The same spell sustained the impression that Titania worked as a hairdresser and that Oberon owned an organic orchard and that their names were Trudy and Bob.

"You need to take care of yourself," Trudy said, thinking Titania was complaining about feeling ugly. "It might feel a little selfish, but you can't take care of him if you can't take care of yourself. Did you know we have a manicurist who comes every Wednesday?"

"You are so sweet," Titania said, "even if you are homely. Did you ever wish you had the eyes of a cat?"

"A hat? You can buy one downstairs. For when his hair falls out, you mean. That's weeks away, you know. But the baseball caps are awfully cute. But listen, not everybody wants to talk about this at first, and not everybody has to. I'm getting ahead of myself . . . of ourselves."

"Or would you rather be a cat entirely? Yes, I think that would make you lovely." Titania raised her hands and closed her eyes, seeking for words sufficient to the spell she had in mind. They came to her in an image, words printed on a little girl's purse she had glimpsed in the waiting room outside the surgical suites downstairs. She started to speak them—*Hello, Kitty!*—but Oberon walked in before she had the first syllable out.

"What are you doing to the nurse?" he asked her.

"She's the social worker. And we were only talking." Alice's head was turned to the side and she was staring at Titania with a mixture of curiosity and devotion. The glamour had slipped as Titania was about to strike, and the woman had seen her true face. "Her name is Alice."

"Stop playing," Oberon said. "He's almost finished. Don't you want to be there when he wakes?" The boy was downstairs getting things done to him; a needle in his hip to take the marrow from his bones and another in his neck to give him an IV that would last through the weeks and months of the treatment.

"I'll just stay here and wait," she said, sitting on the bed and idly petting the Beastie when it sidled up to her.

"He'll be looking for you," Oberon said.

"You'll be there."

"He'll ask for you."

"Tell him I'm waiting here with his Beastie." She lifted it into her lap, as if to show him the truth of what she was saying but also to demonstrate that she was settling in. Alice, still standing between them, was looking back and forth, catching glimpses of their majesty, as their mounting anger caused them to let it slip, and getting drunker on them.

"Did I give you your meal tickets yet?" Alice asked them. "The cafeteria is really not so bad, for what it is."

"You'd rather laze about than comfort him. Do you love him at all?"

"More than you do, and more than you'll ever understand. You like to see him undone and ailing, but I can't bear to look at him like that." She had drugged the child herself many times, when he was younger, but now she could not stand to see him in the vulnerable, unnatural sleep the anesthesia brought.

"Those are very normal feelings," said Alice. "I validate those feelings. Haven't I been saying how hard it is to see him like this?" She turned to Oberon. "Haven't I?"

"Heartless and cowardly," Oberon said. "A most unattractive combination."

"That's normal too," Alice said. "The anger. But don't you know it's not her that you're angry at?"

"You stupid sour cock," said Titania, and then they just called each other names, back and forth, getting angrier and angrier at each other while Alice turned back and forth so swiftly it seemed she was spinning.

"How can I make you understand how totally normal all of this is?" Alice cried aloud at last, just before collapsing in a heap. The Beastie, whose nature was to comfort, tried to go to her, but Titania held it back.

"Now look what you've done," said her husband.

At first he was like her own sort of Beastie, a creature who followed her around and was pleasant to cuddle with. It didn't take long before he stopped his agitated weeping, before he stopped crying for the mortal parents whom he'd hardly known, and then he smiled for everyone, even for Oberon, who barely noticed him for months. He was delightful, and she was fond of him in the way she was always fond of the changelings, and yet she had dresses and shoes of which she was just as fond. She liked to dress him and feed him, and took him to bed every night, even when Oberon complained that he did not like to have pets in the bed. He might get lost under the covers and migrate by morning to some remote corner, and she would half wake in the early afternoon, feel around for him, and not sleep again until she had gathered him up.

He grew. This was unexpected—she had completely forgotten even this basic fact of human physiology since the last changeling—but quite exciting. He wouldn't fit anymore in the footed pajamas in which he'd been stolen, and then she kept him naked. Many evenings she would stare at him, hoping to *see* him get bigger. She liked to feed him, initially just milk and dew and a little honey on her finger, but then she woke one morning to find him attached to her breast, and she wondered why she hadn't fed any of the other changelings this way. It was easy enough to make food come out of her nipple: not-quite-ordinary milk at first, but then less usual substances: weak wine and chocolate and peanut butter and yogurt.

It wasn't long before Oberon regretted his gift and started to hide the child somewhere on the hill, attended by faeries, so he could have his wife to himself. She tolerated that for weeks, but within a few months she couldn't stand to be apart from the boy, though she couldn't really say why. Perhaps it was because he smiled at everything she said and never argued with her; for months and months he never even said a word, but only babbled. It was different from talking to her husband, who could turn any conversation into an argument, or from talking to the members of her court, who always seemed to be listening for ways to curry her favor.

The boy grew, and changed, and became ever more delightful to her, and she imagined that they could go on forever like that, that he would always be her favorite thing. It would have been perfect, and maybe it would have been better if he had stayed her favorite thing—a toy and not a son—because now he would just be a broken toy. She ought to have had the foresight to make him dumb, or Oberon ought to have, since the boy was his terrible gift to her. But one evening the boy ran back to her, and climbed upon her throne, and giggled at the dancing faerie bodies leaping and jumping all around them, and put his face to her breast, and sighed a word at her, *molly* or *moony* or *middlebury*—she still didn't know what it was exactly. But it was close enough to *mommy* to ruin everything.

They poisoned the boy exquisitely. Beadle and Blork had reviewed it all with them, the names and the actions and the toxicities of the variety of agents they were going to use to cure him, but of that whole long conversation only a single phrase of Blork's had really stuck. "We'll poison him well again," he'd said, rather too cheerily, and he had explained that the chemotherapy was harder on the cancer than on the healthy boy parts, but that it was still hard, and that for the next many months he would act like a boy who had been poisoned. "Sometimes we'll poison him a little," he said, while Beadle frowned more and more vigorously at him, "and sometimes we'll poison him a lot." And indeed in that first week it seemed to Titania that they were poisoning him as vigorously and enthusiastically as anyone ever poisoned anybody, for or against their own good. The chemotherapy came in colors—straw yellow and a red somewhere between the flesh of a watermelon and a cherry—but did not fume or smoke the way some of her own most dramatic poisons had. There was nothing in them she could comprehend, though she peered at the bags and sniffed at the tubes, since there was no magic in them. She was only reluctantly interested in the particulars of the medications, but Oberon wanted to know all about them and talked incessantly about what he learned, parroting what Beadle and Blork said or reading aloud from the packets of information the nurses gave them. He proclaimed that he would taste the red liquid himself, to share the experience with the boy, but in the end he made a much lesser faerie do it, a little brownie named Doorknob, who smacked his lips and proclaimed that it tasted rusty in the same way that blood smelled rusty, and went on to say he thought he liked the taste of it and was about to sample it again when he went suddenly mad, tearing at his hair and clawing at his face and telling everyone his bowels had become wild voles, and perhaps they had, since there was an obvious churning in his hairy little belly. Oberon knocked him over the head with his fist, which brought him sleep if not peace, and though he had previously been one of the meekest spirits over the hill, every day after that he was angry and abrasive, and more than anything else he liked to pick a fight.

The boy had a very different response. Right away the poisons settled him down in a way that even the morphine did not. That put him to sleep, but in between doses he woke and cried again, saying that a gator had his leg or a bear was hugging him to death or a snake had wound itself around the long part of his arm and was crushing it. Within a few days the poisons had made him peaceful again. Titania could not conceive of the way they were made except as distillations of sadness and heartbreak and despair, since that was how she made her own poisons, shaking drops of terror out of a wren captured in her fist or sucking with a silver straw at the tears of a dog. Oberon had voiced a fear that the boy was sick for human things, that the cancer in his blood was only a symptom of a greater ill, that he was homesick unto death. So she imagined they were putting into him a sort of liquid mortal sadness, a corrective against a dangerous abundance of faerie joy.

Then he seemed to thrive on it. If she hadn't been so distracted by relief it might have saddened her, or brought to mind how different in kind he was from her, that a decoction of grief should restore him. His whole body seemed to suck it up, bag after bag, and then his fever broke, and the spots on his skin began to fade like ordinary bruises, and the pain in his bones went away. She watched him for hours, finally restored to untroubled sleep, and when he woke he said, "I want a cheese sandwich," and the dozen little faeries hidden around the room gave a cheer.

"You heard him," she said, and ordered them with a sweep of her arm out the door and the windows. The laziest went only to the hospital cafeteria, but the more industrious ventured out to the fancy cheese shops of Cole Valley and the Castro and even the Marina and returned with loaves under their arms and wheels and blocks of stolen cheeses balanced on their heads and stuffed down their pants, Manchego and Nisa and Tomme Vaudoise, proclaiming the names to the boy as if they were announcing the names of visiting kings and queens. The room filled rapidly with cheese and then with sandwiches, as the bread and cheese was cut and assembled. The boy chose something from the cafeteria, a plastic-looking cheese on toast. Oberon, asleep on the narrow couch beneath the window, was awakened by the variety of odors and started to thank the faeries for his breakfast, until a pixie named Radish pointed and said in her thin high voice, "He mounches! He mounches!" Oberon began to cry, of course. He was always crying these days, and it seemed rather showy to Titania, who thought she suffered more deeply in her silence than he did in his sobs. He gathered the boy in his arms, and the boy said, "Papa, you are getting my sandwich wet," which caused some tittering among the faeries, some of whom were crying too now, or laughing, or kissing one another with mouths full of rare cheese. Titania sat down on the bed and put a hand on the boy and another on her husband, and forgave Oberon his showy tears and the boy the scare he'd given her.

Just then Dr. Blork entered the room, giving the barest hint of a knock on the door before he barged in. The faeries vanished before his eye could even register them, but the cheeses stayed behind, stacked in sandwiches on the dresser and the windowsill, wedged in the light fixtures and stuck to the bulletin board with pins, piled in the sink and scattered on the floor. He stared all around the room and then at the three of them, looking so pale and panicked that Titania had to wonder if he was afraid of cheese.

"He was hungry," Titania said, though the glamour would obviate any need for an excuse. "He's hungry. He's eating."

"You have poisoned him masterfully!" said Oberon, and Titania asked if they could take him home now.

He was never a very useful changeling. Previously Oberon had trained them as pages or attendants for her, and they learned, even as young children, to brush her hair just in the way she liked. Or they were instructed to sing to her, or dance a masque, or wrestle young wolves in a ring for the entertainment of the host. But the boy only hit her when she presented him with the brush, and instead she found herself brushing *his* hair.

And she sang for him, ancient dirges at first, and eldritch hymns to the moon, but he didn't like those, and Oberon suggested that she learn some music more familiar to him. So she sent Doorknob into the Haight to fetch a human musician, but he brought her back an album instead, because it had a beautiful woman on it, a lovely human mama. She looked at the woman on the cover of *Carly Simon's Greatest Hits*, golden-skinned and honey-haired with a fetching gap in her smile, and put on her aspect, and spun the record on her finger while Radish sat upon it, the stinger in her bottom protruding to scratch in the grooves, and Titania leaned close to listen to the songs. Then she sang to the boy about his own vanity and felt a peaceful pleasure.

Oberon said she was spoiling him, she had ruined him, and he had no hope of ever becoming a functional changeling, and in a fit of enthusiastic discipline he scolded the boy, ordered him to pick up some toys he had left scattered in the hall, and threatened to feed him to a bear if he did not. Weepingly, the boy complied, but he had gathered up only a few blocks before he came to a little blue bucket on the floor. "I'm a puppy!" he said, and bent down to take the handle in his mouth. Then he began to prance around the hall with his head high, the bucket slapping against his chest.

"That's not what you're supposed to be doing at all!" Oberon shouted at him, but by the time Titania entered the room, warned by Radish that Oberon was about to beat the changeling, Oberon had joined him in the game with a toy shovel in his teeth. Titania laughed, and it seemed to her in that moment that she had two hearts in her, each pouring out an equivalent feeling toward the prancing figures, and she thought, *My men.*

They were not allowed to go home. It was hardly time for that, Dr. Beadle told them. The boy was barely better at all. This was going to be a three-year journey, and they were not even a week into it. They were going to have to learn patience if they were going to get through this. They were going to have to learn to take things one day at a time.

"I like to take the long view of things," Titania said in response, which had been true as a rule all through her long, long life. But lately her long view had contracted, and yet it was no comfort to take things, as Dr. Beadle suggested, as they came. Even without looking ahead into the uncertain future, there was always something to worry about. Oberon suggested she look to the boy and model her behavior after his, which was what he was doing, to which she replied that a child in crisis needed parents, not playmates, to which he said that wasn't what he meant at all, and they proceeded to quarrel about it, very softly, since the boy was sleeping.

Still, she gave it a try, proceeding with the boy on one of his daily migrations through the ward. Ever since he had been feeling better he went for multiple daily promenades, sometimes walking and sometimes in a little red buggy that he drove by making skibbling motions against the ground. He had to wear a mask, and his IV pole usually accompanied him, but these seemed not to bother him at all, so Titania tried not to let them bother her either, though she was pushing the pole and had to stoop now and then to adjust his mask when it slid over his chin.

The ward was almost the ugliest place she had ever seen, and certainly the ugliest place she had ever lived. Someone had tried, some time ago, to make it pretty, so there were big photographs in the hall of children at various sorts of play, and some of these were diverting, she supposed. But the pictures were few. In other places on the wall, someone had thought to put up bas-relief cartoon faces, about the size of a child's face, but the faces looked deformed to her eye—goblin faces—and they seemed uniformly to be in pain.

The boy was not allowed to wander beyond the filtered confines of the ward, so they went around and around, passing the posse of doctors on their rounds and the nurses at their stations and the other parents and children making their own circumnavigations. The boy called out hello and beeped his horn at everyone they met. They called back "Hello, Brad!" or "Hello, Brian!" or "Hello, Billy!" since he answered to all those names. Everyone heard something different when they asked his name and Titania replied, "Boy."

She walked, step by step, not thinking of anything but the ugliness of the hall or the homeliness of Dr. Blork or the coarseness of Dr. Beadle's hair or the redness of the buggy. *There is no past and no future,* she told herself. *We have been here forever, and we will be here forever.* These thoughts were not exactly a comfort. She considered the other parents, staring at them as she passed, remembering to smile at them only when they smiled at her. It seemed a marvel to her that any mortal should suffer for lack of love, and yet she had never known a mortal who didn't feel unloved. There was enough love just in this ugly hallway, she thought, that no one should ever feel the lack of it again. She peered at the parents, imagining their hearts like machines, manufacturing surfeit upon surfeit of love for their children, and then wondered how something could be so awesome and so utterly powerless. A feeling like that ought to be able to move mountains, she thought, and then she wondered how she had come to such a sad place in her thoughts, when she meant to live entirely in the blank present. They went back to the room where Oberon was playing a video game with a brownie perched on his head.

"I hate this place," she told him.

They always called the good news good news, but for the bad news they always found another name. Dr. Blork would say they had taken a little detour on the way to recovery or had encountered a minor disappointment. Occasionally, when things really took a turn for the worse, he'd admit that something was, if not bad news, not very good news. It was an unusual experience, to wait anxiously every morning for the day's news and to read it—in the slips of paper they gave her that detailed the results of the previous day's tests and in the faces of the people who brought the news, in the pitch of their voices and in the absences they embraced, the words they did not use, and the things they did not say.

Oberon said the way that good news followed bad news, which followed good news on the tail of bad news, made him feel as if he were sailing in a ship on dangerous swells or riding an angry pony. Titania was the only one among them ever to have ridden on a roller coaster, but she didn't offer up the experience as an analogy, because it seemed insufficient to describe a process that to her felt less like a violent unpredictable ride and more like someone ripping out your heart on one day and then stuffing it back in your chest on the next. There was very little about it that she found unpredictable, and it was as much a comfort to know that the bad news would be followed by good as it was a slumping misery to know that the good news was not final. She was starting to believe that, more than anything, they had only lucky days and unlucky, that some cruel arbiter, mightier than either she or her husband, was presiding over this illness, and she wasn't always convinced, when Beadle or Blork told them something was working, that something they did was making the boy better.

His leukemia went away, which was good news, but not very quickly, which was bad news. His white blood cells would not grow back, which was bad news, and yet it would have been worse news if he had had too many of them. He had no fever, which was good news, until he got one, and that was very bad, though Blork seemed to intimate, in his stuttering way, that there were worse things that might happen. It meant they could not go home, though Beadle and Blork were always promising that a trip home was just around the corner. On the third week the fever went away and the white blood cells began to come back, but then Dr. Blork came to them with a droopy slip of paper documenting that the white blood cells were the evil, cancerous sort, and Titania could tell that there was not much worse he could think of to be telling them. They shuffled the boy's poisons, and brought him shots of thick white liquid that they shoved into his thighs. The shots made him scream like nothing else had, and she could not bear to be in the room when it happened, because she could not bear the look the boy gave her, which asked so clearly, *Shouldn't you kill them for hurting me like this?* The new poison turned him around again; the evil cells began to retire from his blood and his bones. But then his innards became irritated, and they decided, though he was always ravenous, that he couldn't eat.

"It's a crime," Oberon said. "Damn the *triglycerides*, the boy is hungry!" The nurses had hung up a bag of food for him, honey-colored liquid that went directly into his veins. Oberon slapped at the bag, and said it didn't look very satisfying. He fed the boy a bun, and a steak, and a crumpled cream puff, pulling each piece of food from his pocket with a flourish. Titania protested and threatened to get the nurse and even held the call button in her hand, almost pressing it while Oberon laughed and the boy shoved steak in his face. He threw it all up in an hour, the steak looking practically unchanged when it came back up, and became listless and squash-colored for three days. When they were asked if the boy had eaten anything, Oberon only shrugged.

But as soon as he had recovered, he was crying again for food, pleading with them all the time no matter how the nurses fiddled with the bag that was supposed to keep him sated. One morning the whole team showed up: Beadle and Blork and the junior-junior doctors whose names Titania could never remember and Alice and the nurse and another two or three mortals whose function, if it was something besides just skulking about, she never did discover. When Dr. Blork asked him how he was doing, he pleaded with them, too.

"Can't I have one tiny little feast?" he asked, and they laughed at him. They chucked his chin and tousled the place where his hair had been, and then they went out, leaving her with this dissatisfied, suffering creature. "Mama, please," he said all day, "just one little feast. I won't ask again, I promise." Oberon was silent and left the room eventually, once again crying his useless tears, and Titania told the boy he would only become sick if he ate, that even one feast might mean another week before he could eat again. "Don't think of eating," she said, "think of this bird, instead." And she pulled a parrot out from within the folds of her robe. But the boy only asked if he could eat it.

He wore her down toward evening. Oberon had still not returned, and when she sent Radish to fetch him she said only, "He's still weeping. See?" And she held a thimble up, brimming with tears. Titania sighed, wanting to run from the boy and his anxious, unhappy hunger, which had seemed to her as the day dragged on to represent, and then to become, a hunger for something else besides food. He didn't want food. He wanted to be well, to run on the hill under the starlight, to ride on the paths in the park in a little cart pulled by six raccoons. He wanted to spend a day not immersed in hope and hopelessness. She could not give him any of that right now.

"All right, love," she said, "just one bite." And she brought out a chocolate from her bag, but before she could give it to him Oberon returned, calling for her to stop because he had something better. He cleared a space on the bed and put down a little sack there, and very delicately, pinching with his thumb and his forefinger, removed all the ingredients of a tiny feast and laid them on the bed.

"It will be faster if you help," he told her, as he squinted to chop up a mote-sized carrot. So she picked up a bag the size of her thumb, emptied out the beans from them, and began to snap. The boy kept trying to eat things raw at first, but Oberon slapped his hand away and told him to be patient, and eventually he helped as well, twisting the heads off the little chickens when Oberon handed them to him, and laughing when they danced a few seconds in his palm. It took a long time to prepare the feast, though they had more and more help, as more faeries popped up in the room, some of whom were sized better for the work. Still more of them gathered round in an audience, stuck to the walls, crowding the shelves, perched on the lintel, all of them muttering opinions as the preparation went on, that they would have baked the fish, not seared it, and salted the cabbage but not the asparagus, and chosen caramel over fudge for the cake.

When it was done the boy ate the whole thing and did not share a morsel, which was exactly as it was supposed to be. Aside from the size of it, there was nothing magical about the food. It shouldn't have sated him any more than half a dozen peanuts, but even the aroma calmed him down as they were cooking, and by the time he had finished off the last tack-sized pastry and dime-sized cake, he was very quiet again. He looked around the bed and around the room, as if for more food, so when he opened his mouth wide Titania thought he was going to shout or cry. But he burped instead, a tiny little noise, commensurate with what he had eaten.

She had lost him once, just for a little while. He liked to hide but didn't do it very well, too giggly ever to make his location a secret. But she woke one morning to find him gone from his customary place underneath her arm, and she couldn't find him in the usual places, in a lump under the covers at the foot of the bed, or on the floor next to the bed, or even under the bed. "Is this a game?" she asked her husband, shaking him awake, and she demanded, "Where have you hidden the boy?"

He had not hidden him anywhere, and no faerie had made off with him or used his parts in a spell or put him in a pie to eat. But all through the early part of the evening he was nowhere to be found, though she commanded the whole host to search for him under the hill. She began to suspect that his mortal mother had stolen him back and not even done her the courtesy of returning the little hobgoblin that had been left in his place. Oberon could not convince her of how extremely unlikely this would be, so she strapped on her armor, greave by greave. For a while Oberon was able to get it off her as fast as she could put it on, nuzzling her and speaking ever so soothingly about how the boy would be found, but eventually she outstripped him. She placed her helm on her head and called the host to war, and all the peace-loving faeries of Buena Vista Park reluctantly put on their silver mail and took up their ruby-tipped spears and made ready to stream out into the Mission to slay the woman who had stolen their Mistress's child. But Doorknob found him before they could march out of the woods. He was under a cupboard, sound asleep, and one had only to sniff at him to understand that he had wandered thirsty from bed to the kitchen, drunk at length from the wine bowl instead of the water bowl, and perhaps had had a solitary toddling drunken party all his own before hiding himself away to sleep. Titania wanted to kiss him and hold him, of course, but it occurred to her that there were other things she could do right then as well, shrink him down enough to carry him around in her mouth, or make him a hump on her back, or chain him to her, foot to foot. He woke as she was considering these things, and blinked at her and then at the faeries all attired for war, and turned on his side, and went back to sleep.

"What a terrible gift you have given me," she said to her husband. They were sitting at the boy's bedside, not holding hands, but their knees were touching. There had been bad news, and then worse news, and then the worst news yet. The bad cells were back in his blood, and he had a fever, and there was an infection in the bones of his face. Dr. Blork said a fungus was growing there and had admitted that this news was in fact bad, and he had looked both awkward and grave as he sat with them, twisting his stethoscope around in his hands and apologizing for the turn of events, though not exactly accepting responsibility for the failures of the treatment. Oberon had said that mushrooms were some of the friendliest creatures he knew, and he could not understand how they could possibly represent a threat to anyone, but Dr. Blork shook his head, and said that this fungus was nobody's friend, and further explained that the presence of the new infection compromised the doctors' ability to poison him anymore, and that for that reason the leukemia cells were having a sort of holiday.

The boy was sleeping. They had brought back the morphine for his pain, so he was rarely awake and not very happy when he was. Titania moved from her chair to the bed and took his hand. Even asleep he pulled it away. "A terrible gift," she said.

"Don't say such things," Oberon said.

"Terrible," she said. "Terrible, terrible." She sat on the bed, taking the boy's hand over and over again as he pulled it away, and told her husband she was afraid that when the boy died he would take away with him not just all the love she felt for him but all the love she felt for Oberon too, and all the love she had felt for anything or anyone in the world. He would draw it after him, as if by decree of some natural law that magic could not violate, and then she would be left with nothing.

"Do not speak of such things, my love," her husband said, and he kissed her. She let him do that. And she let him put his hands inside her dress, and let him draw her over to the narrow little couch where they were supposed to sleep at night. She tried to pretend that it was any other night under the hill, when they would roll and wrestle with each other while the boy slept next to them oblivious. They were walked in upon a number of times. But everyone who walked in saw something different, and no one remembered what they had seen after they turned and fled the room. The night nurse, coming in to change some IV fluids, saw two blankets striking and grappling with each other on the couch. A nursing assistant saw a mass of snakes and cats twisting over one another, sighing and hissing. Dr. Beadle actually managed to perceive Oberon's mighty thrusting bottom and went stumbling back out into the hall, temporarily blinded.

One evening Dr. Beadle came in alone, Blorkless, and sat down on the bed, where the boy was sweating and sleeping, dreaming, Titania could tell, of something unpleasant. "I think it's time to talk about our goals for Brad," he said, and put a hand on the Beastie over the boy's foot, and wiggled the foot back and forth as he talked, asking them whether they were really doing the best thing for the boy, whether they should continue with a treatment that was not making him better.

"What else would we do?" Titania asked him, not understanding what he was saying but suddenly not wanting him in the room, or on the bed, or touching the boy.

"We would make him comfortable," he said.

"Isn't he comfortable?" Titania asked. "Isn't he sleeping?"

"Not . . . finally," Dr. Beadle said. "We could be doing more and less. We could stop doing what isn't helping, and not do anything that would prolong . . . the suffering." Then Oberon, who had been eyeing the man warily from the couch, leaped up, shouting, "Smotherer! Smother-doctor! Get back to Hell!"

"You don't understand," Dr. Beadle said. "I don't mean that at all. Not at *all*!" He looked at Titania with an odd combination of pleading and pity. "Do you understand?" he asked her. In reply she drew herself up, and shook off every drop of the disguising glamour, and stood there entirely revealed to him. He seemed to shrink and fell off the bed, and while he was not kneeling purposefully in front of her, he happened to end up on his knees. She leaned over him and spoke very slowly.

"You will do everything mortally possible to save him," she said.

The night the boy died there were a number of miraculous recoveries on the ward. They were nothing that Titania did on purpose. She did not care about the other pale bald-headed children in their little red wagons and masks, did not care about the mothers whose grief and worry seemed to elevate their countenances to resemble Titania's own. Indifference was the key to her magic; she and her husband could do nothing for someone they loved. So all the desperate hope she directed at the boy was made manifest around her in rising blood counts and broken fevers and unlikely remissions. It made for a different sort of day, with so much good news around it seemed hardly anyone noticed that the boy had died.

Oberon sat on the floor in a corner of the room, trying to quiet the brokenhearted wailing of the Beastie but not making a sound himself. Titania sat on the bed with the boy. A nurse had been in to strip him of his tubes and wires and had drawn a sheet up to just under his chin. His eyes were closed, and his face looked oddly less pale than it had in life and illness. The glamour was in tatters; Oberon was supposed to be maintaining it, and now Titania found she didn't really care enough to take up the work. No nurse had been in for hours, and the last to come had lain down upon the clover-covered floor and giggled obtrusively until some thoughtful faerie had put an egg in her mouth to shut her up. Before she had gone drunk, the nurse had mentioned something about funeral arrangements, and Titania was thinking of those now. "We should take him home," she said aloud, and no one stirred, but she said it again every few minutes, and by twos and threes the faeries crowding the room began to say it too, and then they started to build a bier for him, tearing out the cabinets and bending the IV pole and ripping the sheets and blankets. When they were done the walls were stripped and the furniture was wrecked. Twelve faeries of more or less equal size bore the bier, and they waited while another dozen brownies hammered at the doorway to widen the exit. When they were ready they all looked to Titania, who nodded her permission. Oberon was the last to leave, standing only when Doorknob tugged at his arm after the room had emptied.

There was no disguise left to cover them. People saw them for what they were, a hundred and two faeries and a dead boy proceeding down the hall with harps and flutes, crowded in the service elevator with fiddles and lutes, marching out of the hospital with drums. Mortals gaped. Dogs barked. Cats danced on their hind feet, and birds followed them by the dozen, hopping along and cocking their heads from side to side. It was early afternoon. The fog was breaking against the side of the hill and Buena Vista Park was brilliantly sunny. They passed through the ordinary trees of the park, and then into the extraordinary trees of their own realm, and came to the door in the hill and passed through that as well.

They marched into the great hall and put down the bier. The music played on for a while, then faltered little by little, and the players came to feel unsure of why they were playing. Then the hall was quiet, because they didn't know what to do next. They had never celebrated or mourned a death before. They were all looking to Titania to speak, but it was Oberon who finally broke the silence, announcing from the back of the room that the Beastie had died of its grief.

4

Besides Henry, Will, and Molly, there were five other people present in the park at the moment that Puck gained his freedom. None of these others were particularly brokenhearted, though neither were any of them entirely whole of heart or, for that matter, whole of mind. None of them were invited to Jordan Sasscock's party, or even knew him, though Jordan had scolded one of them once for scaring some toddler's mother in the ER on Parnassus Avenue. Bob had been trying to play with the little boy, the sight of whom transported him into ecstasies of sadness for no reason he could fathom, but his patty-cake made the mother shriek and drew a lecture from Jordan on the responsibilities of the drunken and the smelly. You were supposed to lie quietly on the gurney and leave the kids the fuck alone.

Huff, Bob, Mary, Princess, and Hogg: they were in the park to rehearse a musical, far away from curious ears and prying eyes, because the musical was a weapon whose potency depended on secrecy. People were disappearing from the streets of San Francisco, and the players knew why. It was not a very complex mystery, but because the disappearing people were homeless, no one was trying very hard to solve it, and in the halls of the homed people had barely noticed the problem at all. Each of them could count two different people who had disappeared: sometimes it was a friend, sometimes just an acquaintance, and sometimes it was someone they all knew, but every week there was always someone else who was suddenly not where he or she ought to be.

The disappearing was not the reason to perform. People disappeared all the time; everyone knew that. People passed through, or moved away, and, yes, people died—there were a lot of reasons a friend or a companion or a sister might not be on the accustomed corner. But it so happened that the disappearances coincided with a mysterious beneficence from the office of the Mayor: suddenly there was food everywhere, kitchens open in formerly abandoned buildings or in the corners of churches that had been closed for months or years for lack of funds. More sinister than the mysterious plenty was the change in people's attitudes. The ladlers and the carvers and even the lady who always wanted to test you for syphilis had become inexplicably cheery, as if the weight of their work had suddenly been lifted from them. A bounty of food was not a problem by itself, but a bounty and a sudden change in people such that they acted as if the homeless problem had been solved—and indeed both Huff and Princess had overheard conversations to that effect, in which one party congratulated the other on all their fine work and commented that at this rate the *problem* would be solved before the wildflowers bloomed again at Point Reyes—these pointed most obviously toward a gruesome plot. San Francisco was feeding the homeless to the homeless.

Putting on the musical was Huff's idea. He had seen the movie years ago and almost entirely forgot it, but then he saw it again at the beginning of the summer, projected on a giant inflatable screen in the middle of Dolores Park. He had fallen into a troubled sleep there, dreaming of his disappearing friends, and opened his eyes to find the sunny afternoon had been replaced by a foggy evening, and his isolated spot on the slope of the hill had become crowded with young folks, a sea of fuzzy fleece flowing down the hill to the giant screen. He lay unmoving and watched Charlton Heston have his dystopian near-future adventure, and when he proclaimed that Soylent Green *was people*, Huff knew what he had to do. He already suspected what was happening to his friends and colleagues; Charlton's message only confirmed it, and Huff lay stunned while the young folk rose and shuffled off in a soft herd. He considered the implications of what he had seen and suddenly conceived of the project by which he would bring down the coalition between the Mayor's office and whatever latter-day Soylent corporation was helping him turn people into food.

The first song came to him immediately. It was just a fragment, but it was lovely, and just having that one little bit come so easily made the enormity of the project less intimidating. He sang it in his head as he walked down the street, and then sang it to Mary when he found her in her customary spot at Noe and Seventeenth Streets.

People, he sang, *people who eat people* . . . That was all he had so far. If he followed the song from which he'd taken the melody, the rest of it would say that they were the luckiest people in the world, but that was not what he wanted to say. Still, he knew right away that this was going to be the signature theme of the whole musical, and it would be sung by all sides, both the people who believed that eating people was a sin and a crime, and those who believed that you ate people and you had to.

What about them? Mary sang back. She had a lovely voice, which was something Huff had not known about her, and discovering it seemed to be a sort of blessing upon the enterprise.

"I don't know yet," he said, "but it's coming."

And it did come. Over the next few weeks the music came in little snatches of melody, and lyrics came in pieces, blazing letters he would see across the back of his eyelids when he closed his eyes, and the choreography came in stretches of involuntary movement that would steal over him as he was walking down the street.

Mary was his first recruit. She brought in Princess, who happened to know that Hogg played the guitar and the cello and had perfect pitch. Bob showed up one day uninvited in the little room at the library where they gathered to watch a videotape of the movie over and over again. He was unobtrusive and easy to work with, and while he didn't talk much, when he did it was usually to say something very useful. It was he who suggested the park when they were ready to start rehearsing.

This was already their second night of rehearsal. The first had been particularly profitable despite some disagreement over the best place to do the work, with Hogg and Princess inclined toward the clearing at the top of the hill, while Mary and Huff pointed out that it was too dark to see anything at the top of the hill and too far to walk every night anyway. They preferred the tennis court, a nice flat surface. Bob offered no opinion except to say that the tennis court was nice footing for dancing. And he did a little dance, as if to prove his point, a rather complicated five-step maneuver, repeated five times. "That's brilliant!" Princess had said, and they had all learned it, more or less, right then, on the sidewalk outside the Duboce Street entrance to the park. They were all so pleased with how easy it was to get started rehearsing that they all went very merrily to the tennis courts and blocked out the first half of the first act in two hours.

On the second night they came back to the tennis court with no disagreements, but then an argument began, after they had briefly recapitulated the blocking they'd done the night before, about what should be done next. Princess happened to have come upon a set of jai alai baskets and was wielding them with both hands and demanding that they proceed immediately to choreograph the scoop dance.

"But that's three-fourths of the way to the end," said Mary. "Maybe even closer. It's the penultimate scene. The penultimate! If you know what that means, you'll know it's far too early to hash it out now."

"Here comes the scoop!" Princess shouted in reply, and proceeded to try to maul Mary with her jai alai baskets. Huff shouted, "Order!" and Hogg shouted, "Cut! Cut!" and someone else shouted, "Poodle!" Bob seemed not to be noticing that anything was happening but had cocked his head to the side and was staring into the dark beyond the tennis courts. Just then the tennis court lights went out. Princess stopped her swinging.

"That happened later last night," she said.

"We're out of time already," said Mary, "and you wasted it all."

"Do you hear that?" Bob asked them.

"Hear what?"

"Screaming," he said, and then the streetlights just outside the park did something odd. Without exactly going out, they became considerably dimmer, as if a not entirely opaque veil had been thrown over them.

"I don't hear it," said Mary, shaking her head. "But what's happening to the lights?"

"An eclipse!" said Princess.

"Jesus fucking Christ," said Mary. "Those don't happen at night."

"But look at the moon," said Princess. "It's all fucked up." That was one way to describe it, Huff thought. It was not discolored or misshapen, but the man in it had an unpleasant look on his face. He looked horrified.

"It looks fine to me," said Hogg.

"No, it's a sign," said Princess. "Go home. Scoop another night!"

"Never mind the moon," said Mary. "You're the one who's fucked up." But Huff was still staring up at the sky, and now the face was looking even more horrified and worried, and even as he watched the expression grew more distinct, and the face grew brighter. He realized in a moment that this was because the streetlights were now nowhere to be seen.

"What horrible shit," Huff asked all of them, "is the Mayor up to now?"

"Now do you hear it?" Bob asked them, and they did, very faint initially, sounding at first like a tiny siren wailing at a distance, then as it grew closer and louder it seemed a noise a cat might make if you did something truly horrible to it, and then as it got very close it seemed unmistakably human: something was afraid, and it was coming their way.

"Enough for tonight!" said Hogg, and ran for the gate to the tennis court.

"Get back here!" Huff shouted after him. "We haven't even started yet!" The screaming got louder, and in another moment the others were gone as well, all of them scattering in the direction of the street, though none of them would find it in the thickening dark. Huff stayed where he was, more angry than afraid. He was sure it was going to be the Mayor making the noise. He'd come riding up in a tiny open car, so small his knees would be touching his chest, and there would be a tumbling red light and a set of shrieking siren horns on the hood. "You are under arrest," he would say, "for conspiracy to disrespect me." Huff planted his feet and lowered his chin and squared his shoulders, feeling ready for what was coming, though it was true that there was something about the sound that made him feel sure he was going to throw up and shit in his pants at the same time. He wasn't ready for what he saw, though. A tiny person, no higher than his shin, came running by. He had an extraordinarily big nose and curly brown hair and blue eyes as big as tennis balls. He stopped in an odd way, as if he managed to go from running to being perfectly still without having to bother to slow down, and stared at Huff. "Better run," he said after he stopped his screaming. "The Beast is coming."

Part Two

5

*H*enry was lost. He had been walking for half an hour and had not only failed to exit the park again, he hadn't even found the top of the hill. He had been getting lost in all sorts of benign places ever since he was a child, when a trip to the supermarket inevitably involved an agony of separation from his mother, and he routinely lost his way in the hospital where he had been working for a year. It was hard to get lost in the boutique wilderness of Buena Vista Park, but he was not particularly surprised to have done it tonight. Since coming to the understanding that he had willfully, if not consciously, driven away the one person in the world who had loved him without any taint of sadness or rage or resentment, he had developed a whole new wary relationship with his subconscious, and though he had decided that going to Jordan Sasscock's party would be good for him, and even that cutting through the park would add another sort of correction, he knew some part of him still thought it would be better to stay home for another night of weeping and doughnut-feasting and masturbation.

It felt like he had been walking in a circle, always uphill. He had passed some landmarks that he recognized from the miserable outing with Bobby: the tennis courts, where some homeless people seemed to be settling in for an early bedtime; a willow whose droopy branches hung low enough to scrape the path. He passed the shin-high stone wall, made with old pieces of headstone, that wound along the path to the steep stairs that rose to the bald little crown of the park. He'd started up those stairs but never arrived at the top of the hill. Every hundred steps or so he paused, and looked around, and saw the same thing: a darkening vista of pale eucalyptus trees in the steep ravines, and through them a glimpse of the city below the hill and, beyond that, the bay and the bridges. But glimpse by glimpse, the city was obscured. It hadn't been particularly foggy when Henry had left his house, but it rolled in precipitously while he walked the steps, and soon he could only see a wall of fog beyond the trees, roiling and heaving as if it were breaking upon an invisible barrier.

The steps led to still more steps. He thought he must have taken some detour without noticing, because soon he was going straight across the hill and then down before he went up again, and then he was deposited in a little clearing, a flat field cut into the side of the hill and ringed by trees. There was a rock with a flat seat and a high back that looked, to someone who had been walking uphill for twenty minutes, a lot like a chair.

Henry sat down and kicked off his shoes and put his feet in the soft grass. This was a pretty ordinary gesture, but for him it was still something of an extraordinary accomplishment. Once he had a terror of the ground, because it was dirty in the ordinary sense of dirty, and because it was dirty in all the new, miserable ways he had learned things could be dirty since the threat of true love had turned him into a younger, poorer sort of Howard Hughes. He wanted to say, *Bobby, this is nice!* because it *was* nice. The grass was soft and cool and dry, and though he thought he could properly appreciate it through his socks, he took those off, too, and dug his toes into the tight spaces between the blades until he could feel the deeper cool and softness of the soil underneath. In the first days of his recovery, he had done things like this demonstratively, always showing off for his absent, rejecting ex-boyfriend, but soon he was doing all the formerly forbidden things for the joy of them, because it was lovely and interesting and sustaining to put one's feet in the grass, or to shake the paw of a strange dog, or even marvel over some pornographic vagina, formerly the abomination of abominations and the anathema of anathemas. Now, beyond any hope of reunion with old stay-the-fuck-away-from-me Bobby, Henry had nothing left to prove, and for the first time in forever he did things for no other reason than because it made him happy to do them.

He sat for a while appreciating his feet on the grass, and appreciating the feeling of his bottom and his back against the stone, and wondered if this could reasonably be considered the end of the night. He had already socialized more in twelve hours than he had done in a typical month of days in the past year, even though he hadn't made it to the party and the only interactions he'd had so far were smiling at some friendly men on Eighteenth Street and a short talk about the possibility of fog with a pierced-up fellow in a café on Haight and Scott, where he'd stopped just before heading up the hill. There were nights back when he lived in Boston when he would never venture out of his apartment, because it was too much effort to get out of bed, or put on his shoes, or navigate the gauntlet of contamination that the mailman, who might have touched a letter that touched a letter that touched a letter that his mother wrote, left around the front door and the stoop and the sidewalk. He had gone days without talking to anyone, and when he did talk to anyone it was usually Bobby, who happened to live next door for the whole first year after they broke up, and who, from Henry's kitchen window, could be observed talking on the phone, or eating cereal, or frolicking with his new dog. Some nights he closed every shutter in his house and left Henry to speculate miserably about what might be going on behind them.

It was almost enough, to have tried to go to the party and to have made an honest effort to be sociable. Giving up and going home, when the party was simply not to be found, did not make him a depressive recluse, did not make him what he was before losing Bobby had caused him to come to his senses. He could not be blamed for going home, and yet, when he really considered it, he decided that he didn't want to go home. Other people had become a whole lot more interesting since he had been freed from the labyrinthine solipsism of his self-enforced misery. He could not previously have imagined a more boring waste of time than to go and drink in the company of strangers and quasi-strangers, but now there was something decidedly intriguing about it, even if he was enough of his old self to feel that sitting alone on a rock in the middle of the park in the late evening was its own sort of good time. Rather slowly, he decided that the night had only just begun, and he was in no hurry to get home, and he would get to the party eventually. For now, he continued to sit on the rock.

It was pleasant to sit still, in part because there was a lot more to experience and feel, even sitting and doing nothing, than there had been when he was his old self, and also because he was chronically exhausted, both from the relentless succession of twelve-hour workdays he was suffering under in his new job and the relentless procession of doomed cancerous children who crossed his path. He had started thinking that he had picked his profession because it was guaranteed to provide an inexhaustible source of profound sadness, for how wonderful that must have seemed to the old Henry Blork, who thought sadness was his lot, and for whom it was a simultaneously sustaining and debilitating atmosphere. Any rest was to be cherished, though it left him open, like sleep did, to affectionate but utterly useless thoughts about Bobby. It did no good anymore, here beyond any hope of a reconciliation, to think of him, and yet Bobby was all Henry could think of when he wasn't forcefully distracted. There were other things to think about: dying teenagers on the Oncology Service at the hospital; whether or not his drug-addled ex-con sister was going to make it on her own now that their mother was dead; what kind of dog he would get when he got a dog. But he hardly touched his mind to any of these subjects when thoughts of Bobby intruded on them. He wondered if the teenagers would die without ever being in love, and any thought of love led back to Bobby. Thoughts of his sister led to thoughts of Bobby's brother, an analogously drug-addled beautiful soul who had died hardly two years before Henry and Bobby had met. And any thoughts of a dog led in prancing leaps to thoughts of Bobby's dog, a black Lab named Hobart whom Henry had come to love almost as much as he loved his master.

It ought to be possible, he thought, to will himself not to think about him. Back when he would still return his calls, Bobby had described, rather too proudly, a process like that, by which he had forcibly lifted himself out of love with Henry, into a place where Henry didn't cross his mind at all hours of the day, and distract him from every task, and invade his dreams, and loiter in his masturbatory fantasies. "It was a lot of hard work," he told Henry, implying that Henry had a lot of hard work himself to get to this loveless place. "That's the most horrible thing I ever heard," Henry had said, and Bobby had replied, "You say that now, but just wait." Henry had done just the opposite thing, it seemed to him, falling every day more deeply into love while Bobby lifted himself ever higher out of it, until they could not possibly have been farther away from each other. Henry sighed and closed his eyes, suddenly feeling lost and trapped, in the park, in his feelings, and in the world at large. He began to think about how strange and stupid it was that his love for Bobby had, too late, displaced a combination of guilt and shame and sorrow as the organizing principle of his life, and he considered how wonderful it would be to live under that organizing principle of love if Bobby could return it again.

He sighed again, more of a guttural huff of the sort that Hobart was inclined to let out every now and then when he met the rare thing that displeased him. This was not what he ought to be thinking about. There might not be any hurry to get to the party, but the night was going nowhere except in nostalgic spirals around Bobby. Even if he was never going to move on, it was time, for tonight, to get moving. He would have gotten up and started walking again right then, except that he knew his thoughts would be no different, while he finally made his way out of the park, while he knocked on Jordan's door, and even while he talked to the now-interesting strangers behind the door, even while making out with one of them, though that was an admittedly unlikely prospect. Bobby would still be everywhere all night long, a living ghost. There was really only one thing that seemed to banish him. Masturbation, Henry's regular companion since the age of thirteen, had used to extend and reinforce the depressive self-loathing under which he had labored on account of being gay, leaving him feeling simultaneously ashamed and wanting more of it right away, the way that sex had for most of his life. But lately it had become what he thought it ought to have become a long time ago, an innocent distraction that harmed no one, least of all himself. And it had become a way, even though the act issued imperious invitations to thoughts of Bobby, of forgetting about him. It blew the Bobby fuse, and it could be hours or days before the yearning brimmed again.

Opening one eye, he scanned the clearing. There wasn't anybody there, though at this time of night it would not have mattered much if there had been. People came into the park for such things, after all, though it hadn't really been Henry's style since he was in college to engage in furtive public park sex. Yet it was somehow of a piece with the pleasantness of his seat on the rock, and of the feeling of his feet in the grass, to reach down his pants and begin to grope himself a bit. At first his head was empty of anything except for the obvious sensations and a mild anxiety about getting caught, but he was very soon in the place that brought memories of Bobby swooping into his mind. And they weren't entirely the sort of memories one would expect, given what Henry was doing with his hand, and given that Bobby had come to dominate his sexual imagination such that he could barely imagine having sex with someone else, even when he actually was having sex with someone else. There had been enough hot sex, back in the good old bad old good old days, to fuel whole seasons of masturbation. Thoughts of the sex flitted, swift as darting birds, in and out of his head, too quick to properly consider them. It was weirder, and sadder, to beat off while submersed in more innocent nostalgia, in distinct memories of waking up in the middle of the night with Bobby in his arms and realizing that he could hear it snowing outside, or of Bobby offering him a Benadryl when he was poisoned by bad sushi, or of puzzling together over a hysterical middle-aged lady with syncope, randomly encountered in a vacation hotel. It was strange and pathetic enough to do it in his own bedroom, and seemed stranger and more pathetic here, outside and quite close to the geographic center of the city, but it was what worked.

He had hardly properly gotten going with it when he was suddenly aware, even though his eyes were still closed, that he was being watched. He opened his eyes and saw a little man—a very little man, not more than two and a half feet at his shoulder—standing about three yards off. The man was panting and his face was shining with sweat in the moonlight, which was falling down into the clearing from an open sky even though the park was surrounded by fog. Henry stared, cock in hand, feeling a unique combination of revulsion and surprise. It wasn't actually so surprising that there might be homosexual midgets in the park; the lonely and the desperate came in every shape and age and size and color. But there was something stranger about this man than diminutive boogly trolldom.

"That won't keep him away," the little man said. "He's not afraid of your little weenaloo."

Henry let go of his cock and pulled up his pants at the same time that he pushed himself back and over the rock. He fell over the back of it, got up, and started running, not at all sure about why he had to get away so quickly from this admittedly harmless-looking little man. There was an etiquette to this sort of interaction, a way to indicate that you didn't want to be watched, let alone touched, during your public escapade, without necessarily hurting anyone's feelings, which didn't involve running away in such a hurry that you forgot to put your shoes back on or failed to pull up your pants and your underwear all the way, so they tripped you. He kicked them off and left them behind and ran again. It made less sense than was immediately apparent, to flee as he was doing, and he realized as he was running that what he was feeling had a lot of the character of his old reasonless fears, and then he stopped. He had run into a stand of white trees, whose peeling bark gave them something in common with eucalyptus, but the grove reeked of cinnamon. He didn't know the park very well, but this looked like nowhere he had ever been.

"You're running the wrong way," said an already familiar voice behind him. "You should be running off the hill. You should go hide in a church. He doesn't like those. But there's no way out anyway, except maybe by going under. My Lord has warded the hill, to keep the Beast inside, and there's no way out, just bruises. See?"

He pointed at his own nose, and Henry could see that it was darker than the rest of his face. The man made a beavery sort of noise with his lips. Henry stepped back. "Don't touch me," he said, which was the first thing that sprang into his mind.

"I wasn't going to touch you," the man said. "I was just saying. I shouldn't bother at all with you, except my Master bade me be a guide and a keeper to lost travelers. He is gone, but his wards and his work remain, and my love for him remains. The world is doomed tonight, but my love for him remains. I will die before the dawn, but my love for him remains. So I would keep you, if I can, from running into the Maw instead of away from the Maw, since it is better to struggle against the Beast than to lie down for him, though best of all these things is to run away. I know your odor, though. Have I ever fixed your shoes?" He turned his head from side to side, taking a deep sniff from each of Henry's shoes, and then he smiled. His teeth were as pointy and black and wet as the spines of a sea urchin.

"Don't touch me," Henry said. He ran again but didn't get far. Feeling he should turn to watch and make sure the man didn't follow, and tell him again not to touch him, he had barely sprinted up to full speed when he collided with one of the slender white trunks, which felt a lot like running into a flagpole, and his head made it ring metallically like a flagpole. He fell backward, listening to the funny bell tone, and realized before he lost consciousness that the little man had caught him.

"There you go," the little man said. "I've got you."

Henry and Bobby talked for months online before they met, in part because they were afraid to meet each other, Bobby being relatively new to dating men, if not to having sex with them, and Henry already sensing, after a string of failed dating ventures, that this was something nice he would only fuck up if he let it go too far. And just as they were beginning to talk seriously about meeting, Henry got called away to his mother's house in Carmel, because she had tried to starve herself to death. This was something she had tried to do before, with considerably less success, but on those occasions Henry's father, who had squired her through her depression after Henry left home, had still been alive. Now he was nearly six months dead from lung cancer, after a swift decline that Henry had tried, most inexpertly, to manage. Henry's older sister, to whom the role of caretaker might also have devolved, was in jail for a drug offense.

Henry had a complicated relationship with his mother, who was a complicated individual; her habitual mask of depression hid aspects of her that were more terrible and more delightful than anyone might presume, even after knowing her for years. Her problem, grossly oversimplified, was that she was constitutionally incapable of looking on the bright side of life and wouldn't tolerate anyone around her doing so, though you sensed, if you really knew her, that she wanted as much as anyone, and maybe more than most, to be happy. Henry was her declared favorite, but only because he carried in him (he supposed that she supposed) the greatest potential for unhappiness, having had a greatly terrible thing happen to him as a child. His dramatic disappearance and reappearance, the empty years in memory reconstructed out of police reports, the presumed sexual abuse, had anointed him in his mother's eyes. There were tragedies in her own life, to her mind equivalently insurmountable if not equivalently news-worthy, upon which she frequently reflected. "They ruined you," she would tell him, when some bizarre cousin of nostalgia prompted her to break out the abduction scrapbook and review it with him at the kitchen table, while his father slept and his sister slipped out her bedroom window to visit her current boyfriend. Henry's mother would marvel at the strange details: the whole houseful of boys kept imprisoned in the Mission, the pet bear, the basement full of sex toys. "They ruined you," she'd say, though she was pointing at a picture of just one man, a portrait-in-death of the man who'd abducted them, dead on a dirty mattress after the police shot him when they raided the house. "Just like they ruined me."

Henry went back to California with Bobby filling up a little bit of space in his head, and they continued their conversation while Henry's mother languished in the hospital, two resident pediatricians discussing the bewildering world of adult medicine into which Henry had been unwillingly thrust, and two sons discussing the deeper downs of filial obli-gation. Henry remembered practically nothing of these conversations and wished, in his post-breakup nostalgia, that he had saved the e-mails.

His mother looked like an Incan mummy when Henry first laid eyes on her in the ICU, but with someone to make her eat and a new, forcibly administered antidepressant in her every morning, she became the better part of her old self, a mean, witty old lady. Henry was out there for nearly a month, visiting his mother during the day, and sitting at night on his mother's patio with her strange little dog at his feet, stealing the neigh-bor's wireless signal and talking to Bobby online. He found her old scrap-book and paged through it at her kitchen table, hearing her old narration in his head as he flipped past the newspaper clippings and the police reports and the notes from the therapists who could never get him to remember anything. After he closed the book, he spent a while at the sink washing dust and old ink off his hands.

When Henry kissed his mother goodbye and left the house, he felt perfectly fine. But two hours later, in the airport, he felt like his hands were still dirty, still covered with dust and ink even though they were clean enough to look at. He washed them in the airport and then three more times on the plane. It wasn't the first time he found something to be unaccountably dirty or scary. Certain things had always been scary since he was thirteen, which was to say his whole life, since he had no memories previous to that year: clowns, beavers, public parks, public bathrooms, bicycles, the numbers 14 and 28 and 40, magicians, dragonflies, black dogs. But none of these things had made him feel dirty or contaminated or potentially ruined, which was how he felt by the time he had gotten back home to Cambridge. He had the admittedly ridiculous sense that an almost irreversible process of cootification was under way.

He bought a new pair of shoes in the airport, being careful after he put them on in the bathroom not to step in the same place in the new shoes on the way out as he had in the old ones on the way in. Outside his apartment, he abandoned his bag underneath the deck and put his clothes in the trash by the door, then walked directly to the shower. He washed off once with soap, which was somehow not enough, so he did it again, and felt only slightly less dirty. He had been cleaning the shower before he left, so there was a tall bottle of powdered bleach on the side of the tub. He took a head-to-toe bleach bath, which stung his eyes and made him reek of chlorine and made him tremendously itchy, but it worked. He felt clean again.

That same night he waited outside a bookstore in Harvard Square, wondering if he would recognize Bobby, or if Bobby would know him from his pictures, which he had been considering in the minutes before he left the house, and thinking that he looked much older now than he did then, though the pictures were only a year old. As it turned out, Bobby might have walked right by him if he hadn't been wearing a vaguely troubled look that Henry recognized from Bobby's online picture, and the thought broke in Henry's mind, like a languidly rolling whale, that people who were troubled were more interesting than people who were not.

"You had me at dead father," Bobby would say later, only half-jokingly, and much later would present it as evidence that they didn't ever belong together, since they had cleaved to each other initially on the basis of common misfortune instead of shared joy. Within two hours they had discovered just how much misfortune they had in common: dead fathers and complicated addicted siblings and mothers who said really inappropriate things all the time. The only awkward moment of the night came when Bobby asked if Henry smelled an overpowering odor of bleach in the lousy Chinese restaurant where they were having dinner, to which Henry replied, "It's me. I was swimming." And at the end of the date, when it was time to say goodbye to Bobby or try to take him home, Henry chose to do the former, suddenly afraid of being perceived as an easy whore. Henry shook the lovely man's hand. He wandered home, and wondered if perhaps he should have been a whore—maybe Bobby liked whores, or at least liked a person not to pretend not to be a whore for the sake of mere heteronormative propriety. He had convinced himself by the time he got home that he would never hear from Bobby again.

Bobby called the next day, and they arranged another date, and there was another after that, and then another. Dinner, a walk, tea or coffee, and a stiff hug goodbye, Henry careful to keep his hips away from Bobby's. The awkwardness of the goodbyes increased, until Henry, on goodbye number four, blurted out, just as they were closing on what he sensed might be the valedictory hug of the whole relationship, "Would you like a cookie?"

"What?" Bobby asked, looking like the prospect of a cookie might be troubling.

"A cookie. Chocolate chip. I baked them this afternoon. Want to come up for one?"

"Sure," Bobby said, but he didn't smile.

Henry sighed with relief and then tried to pretend he hadn't done it. He walked in front of Bobby, trying to guide him past the places that had become increasingly contaminated in just the two weeks since he'd been home. Bobby solicitously removed his shoes inside the door and then got the three-minute tour of Henry's extremely small apartment, which was as fancy as it was small, having recently been renovated by a diminutive little couple with good taste, who had moved out when they had a third, very small, child. "I like small spaces," Henry said, which was true, though he was afraid of small people.

Bobby took a cookie and some milk and followed Henry the twelve short steps from the fridge to the couch. Henry was thinking that this was how pediatricians were supposed to seduce each other, with cookies and milk and stickers. Sitting there on the couch, cookie in hand, he had the feeling that there was something at stake and that the wrong move, the mistimed grope, the too-hasty blow job, could ruin everything. *I like him*, he said silently to his cookie. *Why do I already like him?*

Bobby was eating his own cookie, considering it a moment before taking a bite, then looking around the tiny bedroom/living room, which was empty except for the bed and the couch and a small bookshelf. He stuffed the last piece of cookie in his mouth and kept his finger in there to suck off some chocolate, and caught Henry looking at him.

"What?" he said.

"Nothing," said Henry, but he slid closer on the couch, so their legs were touching, and reached for another cookie from the plate, but Bobby caught his hand and put it on his belly, and put his own hand around Henry's neck to draw him in for a kiss.

6

Will had lost a shoe, and couldn't decide whether this was a disaster or a disguised stroke of luck. He had liked the shoe, but it would be a funny story to tell at the party, and if he were injured, or even appeared injured, that might be reason for Carolina to look his way, and maybe stare at him as he limped around, or maybe come over to examine his blue bruised foot, and maybe even say something to it, or to him, something not angry or wounding, possibly even some neutral utterance like, "Foot, you've been hurt," and maybe (though this was admittedly much less likely) something kind, or kindish, like "Are you all right?" And then he could tell her all the ways in which he was not all right.

He had to find the party first, though, before he could present his pathetic, hilarious foot and tell the story of his fall off the path when a crazy homeless lady came tearing along behind him and knocked him aside. He rolled down a ravine, ass over hips over head, sliding on his back and then somehow on his belly, and ending up face down on a shallow carpet of eucalyptus leaves. He wiggled his feet to make sure he had not broken his neck, and realized that his shoe was missing. He knelt, then sat, then stood, looking up the ravine at how far and deep he had fallen, and was suddenly grateful he hadn't busted his head open on one of the white rocks glowing softly in the moonlight where they poked out of the hillside ivy.

He had searched awhile for his shoe. That same bright moon that lit the stones in the ravine lit up the little hollow where he'd landed, but the fog was behaving oddly, streaming through the trees in thick discrete sheets that left him hardly able to see his hand in front of his face. Hunched over and feeling blindly under the carpet of leaves, he found an old plate, a seat cushion, and something that looked and felt very much like an old cabbage, which he dropped right away. And he found a shoe, though not his shoe—a tiny lady's shoe, a sparkly sequined pump that seemed a magical discovery when he held it up in the light. He found an empty condom wrapper after that, and took it as a signal to stop looking, since he was sure that the gooey condom would be the next thing his fingers wandered across. By then it had occurred to him that showing up cold, shoeless, and battered at the party could grant him a temporary celebrity that might get him a gram or two of favor from Carolina.

He started back up the hill, without his shoe and without any path to follow, though he wandered the length of the hollow looking for a stair or a little clearing. He pulled himself up hand over hand, grasping clumps of ivy, and pushed himself up from tree to tree. After ten minutes of this, he felt sure he'd climbed as far as he'd fallen, but there was no sign of that path the crazy homeless lady had knocked him from. He kept climbing, thinking it ever more miraculous, the higher he climbed, that he hadn't been seriously injured in the fall. Then, soon, it began to seem stranger and stranger that he hadn't found the path, and he wondered if he might be climbing sideways instead of upwards, and wondered also if some part of him was deliberately missing the path as it cut across the hill, because as much as he wanted to see Carolina again, he was terrified of her, too. He was terrified of her righteous anger, and her ferocious woundedness, and terrified of being rejected by her again, or rather by her continuing process of rejection, by the emanations of rejection that proceeded from out of her, which he could always feel, and by which he thought he could sometimes tell where she was in the city, in the same way you could tell which way the wind was blowing by sticking out your wet finger to feel the pressure. He imagined those emanations pouring down the hill from Jordan's house, and imagined that he was climbing directly into them, and that it was her rejection and not just gravity that made it such a weary chore to get up the hill.

Will had no easy days anymore, but threw himself off the morning and into the afternoon and evening the way he pushed from tree to tree, or clawed his way through the day the way he clawed through the ivy on the hill, head and shoulders always set into the steady stream of her eternally rejecting emanations. His whole world had become populated and dominated by metaphors of rejection and reconciliation; he could not eat a cream puff without considering how it was filled to bursting with cream the way he was filled to bursting with love for her. Meta-pastries like these were obvious, and even pathetic, and generated by the worst part of him, not the best. But he was generating something artful for her too, stealing time from his day job as a tree doctor to write her a story that had nothing and everything to do with them, with what she had suffered and with what he had done. It was a long apology, and an argument meant to convince her that, gross despicable appearances aside, he had loved her as truly and deeply and consumingly as anyone had ever loved another person. Most days he worried that it was only going to be as useful or affective as a pastry, and that it would ultimately only be about as artful as a pastry, but other days he was sure it was the closest thing to a miracle he would ever wreak and when she read it she would understand him— and understand them—in a way that might just possibly allow her to forgive him.

It would be a miracle if he could satisfactorily express, both to her and to himself, why he did what he did. "Why did you do that?" she had asked him, in the moment of calm that preceded her berserker frenzy. He might as well have squawked like a bird or moaned like a retard as said something like "I forgot how much I love you." But a novel could say such things, in between its lines and underneath what the silly wounded people said and did within its pages, in a way that made perfect sense and avoided the curse of squawking retardation because what was said was never actually said. He wondered if he shouldn't maybe give up on the elusive party and go home to work on the damned thing. But just then he pushed off a tree toward a trunk shape in the intermittent fog, went past it, and took a much gentler tumble, onto soft grass.

He rolled forward this time, for a slow stately while, each rotation somehow more pleasant and less alarming than the one before. The ground was not just soft but warm, and the grade not too steep, and though the fall felt like it lasted so long he thought he might roll out onto Haight Street before it was done, he found himself unworried, and when he finally stopped he just lay there a moment, feeling very peaceful, even though he was thinking that a person could overcome one fall on the way to a party but a second fall was a sign that you ought to go home. He did another twitching check of his extremities and then stood up and surprised himself with a long, luxurious stretch, throwing his head back and reaching toward the sky. The moon was so big it looked like it was about to land on him, and though the sky above the park was still clear above the fog-shrouded trees, there was something in the air that distorted the crater face, making it look very worried. He blinked and rubbed his eyes and looked again, but the moon still looked worried. That dispelled his peaceful feeling, and he remembered just how late and how lost he was.

He did not recognize the part of the park he was in. Worse and weirder now, he did not recognize the trees. As tall as poplars, their bark was too smooth to be poplars, and poplars didn't grow in the park, or in San Francisco for that matter. Will knew trees because they were his living and knew all the weird plants that grew in this weird city, tikotikis that could thrive nowhere else but here, and toothed azaras, one-of-a-kind things that looked like they ate children. These gray poplars reminded him of something, but they were utterly strange, covered with short branches that bore pale green leaves and white flowers whose petals had the thick consistency of mushrooms when Will pinched one. Scattered between the regularly spaced sort-of-poplar trunks were much smaller trees, junior versions of the sort-of-poplars that were as perfectly manicured-looking as bonsai, and it certainly looked as if someone had been caring for them, since some were decorated with tiny bells, thin ribbons, and little wind chimes.

He bent down to touch a bell. It sounded a high vibrating note that tickled his ear. There was something about the tickle in his ear that dispelled the thought that he might be dreaming even as it came to him; the bell sounded a note so irritating he couldn't imagine ever sleeping through it, and the discomfort from the noise felt real in the way that a sharp, cruel pinch feels real. There was something interesting about these trees that went beyond just how strange-looking they were, or that they were hidden in a secret dell, something so interesting it made him forget all about his party and his lost shoe, and it shamed him, a little, that he could not place what that was exactly until he crushed a bit of leaf and smelled the familiar odor, cinnamon and pepper, on his fingers. "Shit!" he said to the crushed-up leaf, and then "Shit!" again to the trees all around him, and "Shit!" to the worried moon. He started walking into the dell, looking for something now. The tall gray trees began to space out the farther in he went, but the little bonsai started to cluster together more thickly. The bells and chimes sounded louder and more insistent as he loped along in a one-shoe run; his sock was getting long in the front, and it waved around wildly as he went, threatening to trip him, but even before he heard the moaning he was in too much of a hurry to stop to fix it. It was a woman's voice, or a little girl's voice, or there was both a woman and a little girl up ahead, experiencing something unpleasant. Will ran faster and soon came into another sort of clearing, though this one was carpeted with the tiny trees instead of grass. They clustered in circles around a giant tree that had the form of an oak, but its bark was shining silver and its leaves, shaped like the hands of little children, were gold. "Carolina!" Will said when the woman moaned again, because this was her tree, and because it made perfect sense that he should be called to rescue her from some affliction, in a dreamy undream, in a park that was not behaving like itself, under a moon that was making faces that it shouldn't.

It didn't matter if this was some terminally weird reconciliatory setup engineered by Jordan Sasscock, or a wild kidnap coincidence, or just a really odd bit of fortune. What he should do now was as clear as what he should not have done back when he and Carolina were together. There was a table under the tree, big enough, it occurred to him as he rushed it, for sacrificing a Jesus-lion, and the moaning was coming from a little figure tied down on it. The littleness stopped him short—whatever was there was the size of Carolina's smallest purse—yet it moaned with a big voice.

"Death!" said the little woman. She was impossibly small; Will was sure she was actually smaller than Carolina's smallest purse, a hand-sized clutch made of fake pearls. Something unspeakable had been done to her. "O my death! Are you my death?"

"No," said Will. "I'm going to help you."

"Death!" she said again. "He said death was his gift to me, and his gift to the whole world. Are you a gift?"

"I'm Will," he said again, looking around for something—he had no idea what—that would explain this or make it less strange. "I'm going to help you."

"Radish was my name," the woman said, more calmly. "You cannot help me. If you are not my death, you should run away. If you are not my death, he'll not treat you kindly."

"I'm going to get you to a hospital," Will said, though he couldn't imagine what hospital would be able to care for her, given her unusual size and the extraordinary ways in which she was crumpled and twisted. He moved forward to pick her up off the table and felt a wetness all of a sudden on his head, a warm rain. He looked up and saw a naked woman in the tree, hanging from a branch with her legs spread, pissing on him. He wiped stinging urine from his eyes and shouted, "What are you doing?" And then, when he saw her more clearly and examined her face and recognized her, "What are *you* doing here?"

"What I do," the lady said, and climbed down the tree, head first like a lizard. She leaped onto the table, took the tiny lady in her hands, and tore her in half. "I am your host," she said to Will, as blood sprayed around his eyes and his head and against his open lips. It tasted quite strongly of rosemary.

"What . . ." Will said. "What . . ." He meant to ask, What *are* you? because even though it looked like the first woman he'd ever had sex with, popped up inexplicably naked in a park in the middle of the night, it felt like something even stranger and much more terrible.

"Run!" said half of the little lady. "Run, Not-My-Death! I will distract him!" She turned her little head and bit the lady on her thumb, which only caused her to laugh. Will turned and ran, not noticing his floppy sock or his single shoe, not considering that he was running away from the opportunity finally to solve the mystery of Carolina's tree. He wasn't thinking of anything except getting away from the horrible monster. He ran back the way he came, the little trees spaced themselves farther on the ground, and the silver trunks flew by. He ran and ran and ran but never came to the edge of the dell or found the slope he'd tumbled down, and though very soon he gave up hope of finding a way out, he didn't stop running.

Carolina was one of Will's clients: they met over a sick tree. She contacted him through his website, attaching a picture of her tree, a stately oak. He hadn't ever gotten a picture through his website before—you weren't supposed to be able to do that. It was a premium feature, and he could not afford premium features. Her note was short. *I love him. Can you help me?* It was the sort of note a freak would send, with the telling substitution of *him* for *it*. Will had discovered since becoming an arborist that there were crazy tree and shrub ladies out there just like there were crazy cat ladies (and sometimes they were men), people who preferred the company of nonhumans, or even nonanimals. They were perfectly pleasant people, just deeply strange and difficult to work with, since they acted like tree surgery was baby surgery, and acted like you were sawing off the limb of their child when you sawed off the limb of their tree.

So when he arrived at the house on Fourteenth Street, he was expecting a sixty-year-old lady in a housedress and slippers, or a divorcée in a caftan, or even a spritely twenty-year-old dressed in bark. He had actually encountered the twenty-year-old, in the treeless Outer Sunset, of all places, presiding over a secret garden at Thirty-fourth and Judah. She had turned him away even before showing him her problem tree, because of his vibe. It was a surprise to see who finally opened the door, a full five minutes after he started ringing the bell. Something kept him from giving up, though he had other work he could have been doing, other trees to check up on: there was a flax-leaf paperbark in Pacific Heights with cankers, a trident maple in the Castro with gall, a jacaranda in the Marina with chlorosis. But he sat there on his toolbox with his chin in his hand, looking out on the street and not understanding why he was waiting.

She was pretty close to Will's own age, with short brown hair and very large brown eyes that gave her the appearance of being pleasantly surprised by something, and Will thought perhaps she was favorably surprised by his appearance (though his picture was all over his website). But then she cast the same pleasantly surprised look at his toolbox, then down at the doorknob, and he realized that she looked like that at everything and everyone.

"I'm so glad you've come," she said.

"Sure," Will said, and followed her into the house, which was both grander and more decrepit than he could have guessed, just by looking at it from the outside. It was enormous, but the rooms were alternately fancy and dilapidated; lovely murals alternated with cracked plaster and bare lath, and though the kitchen was done up as snobbishly as any he'd seen in Seacliff, there was a hole in the floor. Big expensive rooms made him both a little anxious and a little bored. He had enough rich clients that any wonder at the dizzying extremes of wealth in this city had worn off a while ago, but it made him unsettled in some small way to see what he didn't have, and would never have, with his combination career of tree surgeon and ultra-obscure short-story writer. He wondered very briefly what she did, and did so well, that she could afford a place like this, even in its partially ruined state, and then he got distracted watching her walk and nearly ran into her when she stopped suddenly. They had proceeded through the foyer and the dining room and living room and the kitchen, and a couple of rooms whose purpose Will could not divine, and finally come into a sunroom empty except for five large pillows uncarefully arranged on the floor. To Will's left a whole wall was covered with photos of a man, a little younger than him, another Monchhichi-like creature with a fuzzy brown head and big brown eyes.

"My brother Ryan," Carolina said. "He's dead." Then she picked her way swiftly through the pillows and went outside. Will followed, wondering briefly if people came to kneel on the pillows and worship the pictures. Any other arborist might have dismissed her as crazy, but Will was in a position to sympathize with someone who had plastered a wall with pictures of her dead brother, and who paused conspicuously to draw the attention of strangers to them. He had a dead brother of his own and had thrown up his own sort of worshipping wall over the years since Sean's death.

"Come along," Carolina said, standing in the door to the garden. She went right to the tree, the oak that looked even worse in real life than it had in the picture, but Will's attention was captured by the sorry state of its neighbors, a peppermint willow and a carob tree and a Grecian laurel, all suffering some variety of rot, a tristania overgrown to the point of strangling itself as well as an adjacent pear tree, and a slimy koi pond, which wasn't even his responsibility, yet he longed to clean it as soon as he saw it.

"What do you think?" she asked. "Can you help?" She was standing next to her tree, one arm around the trunk. She looked like she was about to cry, and Will thought, dismissively and uncharitably, *She thinks the tree is her brother. She thinks he came back as that tree or went into that tree.* He shook his head at himself and considered that maybe she just wasn't ready for anything else in her life to die just yet.

"You can't?" she asked. "But you haven't even looked at him yet. Can you really tell from over there?"

Will realized he was still shaking his head. "No," he said. "I mean, yes. I can help. Probably. Maybe. Do you know what kind of tree this is, exactly?" He asked because, as he got closer, he saw that it was not an ordinary specimen. The bark was a silver color that the photograph had not properly represented, as it had not represented the heaping tarry excrescences that dotted it on every limb. The parts of the leaves that in the picture appeared discolored and diseased were in fact the healthy parts—he could only tell when he touched them that the silver and gold portions had the texture of health, while the green parts were rubbery or brittle.

"No," Carolina said. "It came with the house. It was planted a long time ago. It's an oak, isn't it?"

"Or something," Will said. He walked around the tree once, staring up into the branches and listening to the odd rustle of the leaves; there was something metallic just at the edges of the noise. "This whole place is a mess," Will said, not looking away from the odd oak. "Do you want me to fix them all up or just this one?" He turned to look at her and wished he had phrased the question differently, because her wounded posture and the sad expectant look on her face made him feel churlish and rude.

"Please," he said, unthinkingly, and then, "Sorry. This garden could be magnificent. But there are a lot of sick plants."

She straightened her back and frowned at him. "I don't really care about the rest of it," she said, "but you can do whatever you want. Just save this tree." Will stood there a moment, careful to be nodding instead of shaking his head, and then, trying to sound as solicitous as possible, offered to show her around her own garden.

As he expected, she didn't know a quarter of what was growing in her own yard. It turned out that she had only been in the house a few months; before that her brother had lived there for years. Will showed her the tristania and the pear tree and the laurel, crushing some leaves for her, but she acted like she had never smelled a bay leaf before. She nodded politely at everything he showed her. He was not exactly puzzled. He'd passed behind walls all over the city into gardens that were as sumptuously ignored as this one.

In the next few weeks he put a lot of work into that garden and that tree, eventually neglecting his other clients. That neglect was initially on account of the peculiar oak and the professional challenge of figuring it out and restoring it to health, but more and more, as the weeks passed, he went back for the peculiar lady. Initially, Will perceived her as a challenge as well—a challenge to figure out and a challenge to get to know and a challenge to befriend—and he didn't quite know why he should want to do that right away. He had other clients who were as pretty and as strange, whose gardens were as ramshackle, and yet he was only as interested in them as he was in their money. He supposed it must just be her wonderful tree that set her apart, the tree whose leaves appeared in none of his reference books and which were recognized by none of the experts he contacted.

Back then he was relatively celibate. He masturbated all the time, like everybody else in his neighborhood, it seemed—he had accidentally left his shades up one night as he sat reclining at his desk and whacking away to sensuous *Playgirl* porn, which was the only sort that didn't make him feel as guilty as it made him feel aroused, since the portion of his imagination that was always at work to spoil his boner inevitably pictured the women in the more patriarchal porn in poses of unsexy victimhood, black-eyed, methed-up, and crying every time they had off-camera sex. The soft light and misty lenses of the *Playgirl* porn left him imagining a lady with a monocle and a cigarette holder behind the camera, who arranged gift bags for all her starlets and provided day care. He didn't need the porn to get off, but every now and then it was fun, and he might spend hours at his desk, at the same place he wrote, shooting seven times in the course of a two-hour film. The seventh time was always a little difficult to manage: he had been working away vigorously for an hour before he realized that night had fallen and his neighbors were watching from across the courtyard, four men and a woman, each in their own window, arranged like a bunch of masturbating Hollywood Squares. Will laughed when he saw them, and thought, *What a fucked-up city I live in.* But he didn't close the curtains.

He was celibate but not asexual. He didn't get out much and had not, since college, met anyone who sustained his interest enough to date. If his literary imagination had been as active as his sexual imagination, he would have written a dozen novels by the time he was thirty, instead of just one little book of short stories. And yet it took a long time for Carolina to work herself into his solitary sex life. Again, he thought it must be the tree, because for a while she *was* the tree: he couldn't think of one without the other, and he wasn't one of those arborists who had sexual thoughts about trees, though he knew those men and women existed, people who discovered in preadolescence that it felt nice to sit on a tree branch and move your hips just so and then never recovered from the pleasure.

When she did make an appearance, it was a bit of a shock. He was fully immersed in *Pirate's Passion*, having adopted the role of the cabin boy, and was thrusting away when he opened his dreaming eyes and saw Carolina's face under him. They were at sea: there wasn't a tree in sight. She smiled at him, a carefree smile of the sort he had never seen on her actual face. He had stopped his vigorous pirate thrusting in the fantasy, and stopped stroking his cock in the real world, but he came anyway, a small but debilitating ejaculation that actually made him groan. He sat there with cum on his face, feeling immensely embarrassed. A neighbor across the courtyard gave him two thumbs-up.

By that time, he and Carolina had gotten to know each other fairly well. He was making visits to the garden two and three times a week. For the first week she had only watched him from the multiple doorways and windows that faced on the courtyard, but then one afternoon he turned around to find her standing behind him with a cup of water.

"Hi," she said. She hurried away as soon as he had taken the cup, but in the following days she brought other cups, filled with water, then tea, then blended juices and complicated smoothies that he could see her at work on through the kitchen window. The last time she brought him one of those, she had bits of fruit in her hair, and she stayed and talked to him while he drank it. The day after that, she brought out two bottles of beer and sat down with her back against the tree as soon as he had taken one. She patted a space to her left, between two roots. Will sat down, not too close, suddenly aware of how sweaty and smelly he was.

"How's it coming?" she asked, though it wasn't really necessary to ask. She could have just looked around to see how things were different. The tristania and the pear tree had been neatened up considerably, and the laurel was starting to recover from its blight. He had planted, here and there, in the places he had cleared, a new fern pine and a mayten and a bottlebrush that stretched over the pond. He had learned not to consult with her about any of it, because the first few times he had asked for her opinion about something she had shrugged her shoulders and said, "Do what you want. I trust you."

"Pretty good," Will said, "except for Mr. Peepers there." He jabbed a thumb over his shoulder at the oak, which was a bit neater-looking but not really any healthier. He had pruned it, marveling at the bright silver sap, and patched up a crack in the north side of the trunk, but none of the pastes he'd applied seemed to make any difference in the progression of its disease. The silver leaves were still turning brown and green, and even the leaves that retained their color were getting the rubbery quality that felt so ugly compared to their natural unnatural texture. "But I'm trying," Will said. "I have a couple of ideas. I'll do my best, anyway."

"Funny how that's never enough," Carolina said, and then she startled him by dropping her head onto his shoulder. She let it fall heavily. It hurt a little, and made him think of falling coconuts. He sat very still, clutching his beer bottle, suddenly feeling like it would be a bad idea to breathe. "Ryan loved that tree so much," she said, and went on to talk about him for half an hour, not taking her head off of Will's shoulder even to sip her beer.

It became customary, over the next two weeks, for her to bring out the two beers and to sit next to him and to put her head on his shoulder. She didn't only talk about Ryan, and he didn't always talk about Sean, but the conversation always seemed to come back to them, since they touched on everything and had to do with everything, something she seemed to have come to understand without his having to write a book about it. After the incident aboard the captured HMS *Pussywillow*, it became a different experience for Will to sit next to her with their shoulders and hips and legs touching, aware of the way his sweat was getting on her skin. Her head was a very particular weight on his shoulder, and he turned intermittently to talk into her hair.

The tree, in the meantime, began to do a little better. Will wasn't sure why. He had a new malathion spray, which he was putting down twice a week. And he had tried a fungicide from Davis, but that seemed actually to be killing an ironwood under his care in Laurel Heights, so he stopped using it. Still, one whole side of the tree, the one they sat against when they talked, was taking on the appearance of something like health. Will spent a number of hours walking around and around the trunk, or standing at the border of healthy and unhealthy, his hands clasped behind his head, whistling tunelessly and trying to figure out what he was missing. He had finally started to consider bringing in someone else to look at the thing, to see if someone could recognize it in person though no one had been able to recognize it in pictures, and to see what sort of ideas others might come up with since he had nearly run out of them himself. But for a while he had been feeling possessive of the oak, and of the whole garden, which by this time he had officially transformed. He didn't want to share it, or its owner, with anyone.

One evening, just as he had started to compose in his head a letter, not of resignation but of resigned incompetence, she brought out twelve beers instead of two, six in each hand, swinging the cartons as she went.

"What's the occasion?" Will asked as they sat down.

"Nothing," she said. "It's just a nice afternoon. And everything looks pretty."

"Yes," Will said. "It does." Before they had even finished the first beer, she was kissing him. He was pretty sure she had a plan, that the beers were premeditated and part of a plan they didn't need. He had been fucking her in his head for the past six weeks, in the shower at night, at two in the morning when he couldn't go back to sleep without whacking off, in the morning when he woke up on his belly with his boner almost jacking up his pelvis. The real thing was more awkward and he was ambivalent about

it, as it proceeded, in a way that he never was when he was just pretending. He kept kissing her and smiling, running his hands up and down her
back and holding on to her neck. She wasn't smiling. In fact, she looked
like she was on some sort of mission, and there was something very no-
nonsense about the way she tore his sweaty shirt up over his head.

"Oh, you have a nice *everything*," she said, exploring around in his
pants.

"Umm . . . yeah," he said, and she finally smiled, and laughed, and it
got a little less awkward. What came next came next. They both knew
what to do, even Will, and it had been years since he had had sex with
anyone outside of his imagination. *Oh*, he kept thinking, over and over,
that's what it feels like, while she sat on his lap and he pushed his hips up
off the grass, sure he was about to launch her up into the tree, and when
he turned her over and fucked her between the two roots. There was
something about the angle they made, and the way his forehead, extended
over her shoulder, pressed into the bark, and the way the tree seemed to be
leaning over them, that made him feel a little like he was fucking the tree.

It was only awkward again at the end, when he tried to pull out. She
held on to his hips and said, "Don't." He kept pulling back and said, "But
it's *rude*," and she said it again, "Don't, don't, don't," and amid the
pulling and the pushing he suddenly couldn't tell if she meant don't cum
in me or don't not cum in me, and so he ended up doing it half in and
half out of her, and between the two of them, and with all that and the
spilt beer and the way the churning motion of their hips had flattened and
torn up the grass, they made a lot of mud. "Holy shit," Carolina said, but
Will couldn't speak.

The next day the tree was in bloom.

7

The animals, Molly noticed, were behaving strangely. You weren't supposed to see animals at all in nighttime city parks. She had learned that on a nature program once, some special on the secrets of the urban wilderness, full of infrared footage of normally invisible creatures bustling in the semicultivated hedgerows of Golden Gate Park. And she was sure that most of the animals she'd seen so far tonight should have been asleep anyway. Owls and raccoons were one thing, but normal squirrels did not leap about on their hind legs in the dark, and she was reasonably sure that the birds lined up in unusually precise rows of four and seven on the ground and in the trees, singing their hearts out, were not nightingales.

She had been wandering for almost an hour, amazed at just how lost she was. She had been in the park before, always with Ryan. She had sat on a bench near the top of the hill, not reading the book in her lap, staring out at the northwest part of the city while Ryan sprinted vigorously up and down the narrow wooden stairs and the dirt paths below. It was a pretty extraordinary view. Ryan seemed a little obsessed with the park, but he loved every pretty place in the city and was always stopping with her in various places around town, standing behind her with his chin against her ear, lining up their heads so he could be sure that they were seeing the same thing. "We are so *lucky to live here*," he would say, and she couldn't disagree. They were lucky that the earth had conspired to heap up such startling beauty in one place, and they were lucky that it hadn't all fallen apart yet in a geological catastrophe. But she felt more lucky to get to share it with him—standing with him in Duboce Park, a whole variety of dogs hurtling around their shins, she could look at the daytime moon rising over the Oakland Hills, and appreciate how lovely that was, and then turn and look at his face, and appreciate how lovely that was, and she mostly felt lucky just to be with him.

Those times she waited for Ryan while he vaulted himself all over this park she had gotten a sense for how big it was. Most of the time she thought she could hear his heavy steps or catch his scent, and it never felt like he was very far away, even when she couldn't see him. For all its contained wilderness, this park was really just a big backyard, but tonight it seemed different, bigger and deeper and darker, and full of animals, who were all having crises of identity. Here and there, over the past two years, Molly had had little episodes of unreality, echoes or flashbacks to the way she had felt when she found Ryan dead. That had been the most unreal moment of her life, or else the most real—his dead body was either the most densely real thing she had ever encountered, and so everything else in the world seemed unreal in comparison, or else it was the most unreal thing she had ever beheld, and it sent out warping rays of unreality into the world, past and future, making everything feel fake. For weeks after he died she had felt detached and uncertain whether anything she was experiencing was actually happening. That got better, but the feeling came back now and then, at completely random and inopportune times, when she was arranging flowers at the shop, or trying to chose a loaf of bread, or struggling with the BART ticket machine at the airport. The flowers never wept, the bread never talked, the BART machine never handed her a ticket that said, *Who are you, that he did that?* But it would not have surprised her if they did, because in those thankfully brief moments, she felt suspended in a place where absolutely anything could happen. So the dancing squirrels and the insomniac budgies (or whatever they were) made her wonder if she was on her way into a more final sort of breakdown, precipitated by an effort to get to a party she didn't want to go to, for a date with a man in whom she had no interest.

But just as she was getting ready to see a little Volkswagen full of clowned-up raccoons trundling down the path, she came across a very familiar-looking stairway. She climbed it, thinking how Ryan used to take the stairs two and three at a time. There were four and seven frogs lined up on the top two stairs—they stared at her unblinkingly as she stepped over them—but beyond them was the bench where she used to sit waiting for Ryan to finish his run. She ran for it and sat down.

That's better, she thought, and, as if on cue, the fog parted, and the city opened up before her. She recognized St. Ignatius, lit up brilliantly, and that made her feel nicely settled. Her eyes wandered to the blinking lights on the bridge and the sleeping-elephant silhouettes of the Marin Hills, then east to the Lower Haight and Alamo Square, and she imagined Ryan standing behind her and saying it again. *We are so lucky to live here.*

Reminiscing was not the way to get over him, and it was exactly at odds with the mission of the evening to sit there on the bench and imagine herself in another day, holding her book unread in her lap and listening to her boyfriend throw himself all over the hill. She closed her eyes and imagined that when she opened them she would be in that day, that he would come up behind her and press his chin against her ear, that he would lean around to kiss her after she agreed that they were lucky to be together in this city, and then she would proceed to keep him from killing himself.

Molly opened her eyes. The fog had closed in again. She couldn't see anything beyond the eucalyptus trees just below her, and those seemed oddly to have gotten a bit taller while her eyes had been shut.

"I'm the luckiest girl in the world," she said.

Molly met Ryan in the shop. He came in one day, just like Jordan Sass-cock did a million years later. She had only recently quit school and had not been working very long at Root and Relish. Her reiteration as a shop-girl was a lucky break, which came thanks to her friends Gus and Tyler, who knew the owner, Salome, a woman entirely at odds with her name, since she was a blocky lesbian unlikely ever to do the dance of the seven veils, unless the veils were named Anxiety, Insecurity, Depression, Petu-lance, Micromanagement, Persnickitiness, and Need. She was actually a pretty good person, underneath her cloud of neurotic exhaust, and that came through often enough to make her just exactly bearable.

Arranging flowers and selling fancy knickknacks to the well-heeled felt like just the right thing to be doing, for now. She had dropped out of divinity school in Berkeley, after finally figuring out she never should have gone in the first place, the whole enterprise having been mostly a way to both please and enrage her parents, since she was studying to become a pastor but doing it in a Unitarian school where some people thought Jesus was a gay role model. She discovered during her first Field Education placement how terrible she was at pastoral care, though the idea of it—helping people with their problems by praying to gay Jesus and the Great Spirit and maybe a voodoo saint here or there—was most of what drew her to the profession. But she wasn't good with death, and that was all she saw in her ill-starred chaplaincy internship. She had no experience with it. Her many brothers and sisters were all alive and in good health, as were her parents, though it was years since they had spoken to her, and her grandparents and great-grandparents were lasting into extreme old age. She had never lost a childhood friend, had never owned a hamster or a fish, and her childhood cat was twenty-five years old. She had no experience with death and had discovered, on that horrible job, that she wanted none. She had nothing remotely useful to say to people who were afraid of dying, and nothing that she'd read or learned in school seemed to matter in those close, stifling rooms in Oakland where some dessicated old person whispered small talk at her. "Why am I trying so hard to believe any of this?" she'd asked her advisor, a red-haired lady with an ageless face who relied heavily on literature to answer just that sort of hard question, and who'd countered Molly's previous crises of faith with skillfully deployed Mary Oliver poems. But chaplaincy pushed Molly to such an extreme of nervous exhaustion and sadness that her advisor had no poem that could help her and finally suggested, when Molly failed to ask for one, that a break might be good for her. Molly was twenty-six years old, and it seemed to her that she could spend an eternity as a shopgirl at Root and Relish, where Salome suffered and shared her daily inconsequential agonies, but no one ever died and no one ever grieved except over the prices.

Ryan broke a set of china cups. They were beautiful—Molly had had her sensibilities refined in the weeks she had been working at the shop— translucently thin and so light it was hard to be sure, with your eyes closed, that you were actually holding one. She had one at her bedside with a candle in it, and she made a habit of watching the light burn down in it every night before she went to bed, which was something Salome had said helped her when she was feeling generally awful and had no faith anymore that the beauties in her life would ever measure up to the horrors. That was the only time she ever hinted at what she knew from Gus and Tyler about Molly's flight from graduate school, and it was followed immediately by a tirade that was both about how Molly would never even know bone china from porcelain, and how Salome's sister was still trying to make Salome look bad in their mother's eyes, even though the woman had been dead for a year and it required a medium to communicate the slander. But Molly thought it was about the nicest thing someone who expressed affection through china could have said.

The display, a Christmas tree of tiny cups, came tumbling down, and Ryan turned this way and that, trying to catch them. Molly had noticed him when he came in, because she was supposed to notice everyone and greet them—it helped to keep them from stealing things—but she didn't really remark him, or notice that he was remarkable, until she saw him in the midst of the collapsing display, catching a cup but then breaking it when he caught another. She learned in those first few seconds that she really looked at him that he had a lovely face, that he had big hairy forearms, that he was pretty nimble for someone who walked into displays of china, and that he was a quick thinker, since he managed to save three of the cups, with one balanced on his head and one in either hand.

"I'm so sorry," he said.

"It's okay," Molly said, though of course it wasn't. Salome was in the back, inventorying her disappointments, but she came out at the crash, and failed so utterly to be gracious that Molly was embarrassed for her. Salome cried, which Molly might have found excusable if this had been a dinner-party accident and it had been her grandmother's heirloom china that got destroyed, but it seemed like egregious behavior in a shopkeeper. She didn't have to demand that he pay for what he had broken; he offered right away. But that didn't stop her tears, and he kept buying things, accompanying her around the shop and listening with a sympathetic face when she turned the conversation to her sister's personality disorder. Molly watched him as she swept little scattered china bits—he tried to help but Salome wouldn't let him—looking down at the floor whenever he caught her eye. Salome rang him up herself, dry-eyed now, but Molly half expected her to start crying with joy at his truly grand total.

"What a nice young man," Salome said after he had left, and then said she was going to take a nap on the daybed that she kept in the back. She always said that big sales exhausted her, and Molly wondered if there wasn't something postcoital for her about their aftermath. Molly was alone out front when Ryan came back, and had settled into her shopgirl pose, with her elbows on the counter and her chin in her hands, watching the traffic go by on Hayes Street and feeling quite detached from the things that probably ought to have been bothering her just then. Some days her experience of life felt like one big shrug, but there was something as much contented as uncaring in that figurative gesture. Still, when he came back in, she stood straight and threw her hands up and said, "Hey!" And then she blushed because she thought it must have looked like she just gave him a high-school cheer.

"I actually meant to get flowers," he said. "But I forgot."

"We have those," she said, and then added, when he stared at her a little longer without speaking, "in abundance." She showed him around the roses and the lilies and the daises. He nodded at everything she presented, and spoke very quietly when he said one or the other of them was pretty, as if he was afraid too much noise would draw Salome out again from the back. "How many do you need?" Molly asked him at last. She had been handing the flowers to him as they walked back and forth among the stock, and now he was holding a bunch big enough to completely obscure his face.

"Oh, I don't know," he said, so she handed him a few more roses and a few orchids and a single dendrobium. She had worked long enough at Root and Relish to recognize a hideous arrangement of flowers when she saw one, but when she offered to fix them up for him he said he could do it himself when he got home. "I'm just going to scatter them around," he said. "A few in each room."

"Alrighty," Molly said, wrapping up the stems. She handed them to him with a smile. You were always supposed to hand things over with a smile; that was one of Salome's inviolable rules. The customers weren't always right, and you were even allowed to insult them, provided you did it in a way that they probably wouldn't understand as an insult, but you always, always, always had to smile at them. Molly had tried out the smile and the gesture at home and been reminded of rehearsing her band smile as a child, standing in a line with her sisters while her mother gave them feedback: Mary you are too stiff, Molly you are too loose, Malinda too much gum is showing, and Melissa don't close your eyes when you smile. What was on her face was practiced at first, but when he smiled back her face shifted uncontrollably, and she thought he smiled a little wider and looser himself, and then she blushed, even before he asked her out. She said yes without a second thought, which always, in future reflection, whenever her depressive nostalgic daydreaming led her back in time to the day they met, went to show what a different person she was back then, the sort who went out with strangers all the time, who took numbers from men in the laundromat and the grocery store and in line for the porta-potty at outdoor concerts. Even at her most burned out and frazzled, freshly on the run from her job and her family, she still hurled herself thrillingly and mostly unself-consciously into the adventure of getting to know somebody new, into the dinners and walks and conversations and the fucking, which all went to show, she ultimately decided, how much less ruined other people's tragedy left you, compared to your own.

They didn't even wait until the end of the date to have sex. That was a first for Molly, but it felt like the right thing to do, and she didn't worry at all about whether or not he was going to respect her later, or come back for a second date, though even before they had exchanged a dozen sentences, she knew she wanted to see him again. He came to her apartment in the Sunset and stood in her door with the giant haphazard bouquet of Root and Relish flowers in his hands. "Hi!" she said, and kissed him, meaning for it to be something really innocuous, a greeting less formal than but not really that much more intimate than a handshake. But she tripped over her threshold, and broke her fall against him with his lips. If she had been holding her head at a slightly different angle, it would have been a totally unsensual bonk, but there was something lucky in the way they were lined up. *Huh*, she thought, and she might have said it, too, as she pulled her head back but left the rest of her leaning against him.

It seemed like very good fortune, to lean against him like that, and when they seemed to decide together that dinner could wait, and started making out there in her doorway, it seemed lucky to her, too, for their desire to align as perfectly as their lips had, and for a collision that might have been disastrous to be a wonder, instead. She kept thinking, *Oh, that's nice* and *How fortunate*, when she discovered how meaty the high part of his chest was or how soft the hair was under his arms. *That's lovely*, she thought, as he started to heat up and put off an odor like warm bread and warm grass. By the time he came it smelled like someone had just mowed a lawn in her bedroom, but lovelier and stranger than that was the sense she had, as they rolled and humped and pressed their faces all over each other, of how nicely they fit together, however they combined. She had always been a little incredulous, back in college biology, that all the vital chemicals and enzymes that kept us alive and thriving just happened to run into one another all the time in exactly the way they needed to. Absent the Directing Intelligence, in which she no longer really believed, it seemed too good to be true. Suddenly it was easy to believe that two bodies could come together and together and together, over and over again from the dawn of time to the end of time, with barely a misstep. It wasn't the first time she had had really good sex, but it felt that night that there was as much an abundance of luck in her bed as an abundance of pleasure. Later she would always feel the luck as much as the love between them—it felt like the universe had showered good fortune on her in his person, and she felt luckier and luckier and luckier to be with him, until her luck was suddenly exhausted.

She fell asleep, finally wondering if she should explain that she didn't ordinarily do this sort of thing on a first date, let alone before dinner, and dreamed of her mother, who often made predictable visits whenever Molly had particular sorts of fun. They were having a girls-only session of home schooling, and she was quizzing them. "Who can tell me what a pussy face is?" she asked, and Malinda's hand shot up. "A pussy face," she said confidently, "is the face a weak man makes when he's crying."

"Exactly . . . wrong!" their mother said, and gave Malinda a smack with the back of her hand. "A pussy face," she said, "is the convergence of a face and a pussy." She went on to ask what you got when a pussy and a face converged, and Melissa answered, incorrectly, "A baby! A baby!" Honesty was the answer, and honesty was the subject of their lesson. It was like her mother's real-world lessons for there to be a little mystery, at first, about what the subject was, and for the posters and learning aids to be covered up initially, though it was never with such a fantastic multicolored cloth as what her mother swept away in the dream. The heart of the lesson, which seemed to go on for hours and involve an endless show of orgasmic faces, was that men were only honest when they were having sex, and that there was an ancient witch's art, to which she and her sisters were heir, of discerning a man's intentions by gazing into his eyes as he ate you out. Those squinting Kilroy-Was-Here portraits were a whole other set of faces to examine, and Molly asked a question in the middle of the show. "But what does it mean," she asked, because she remembered very clearly how in her darkening room Ryan's eyes had shed light upon her naked belly, "if his eyes are all glowy?" She woke up before her mother could answer, when the N Judah went rumbling past her building and made her apartment shake, and lay a moment in bed thinking of her mother's actual and eternal lesson about sex, which was that sex didn't matter, because when you met your true love and the Jesus in you married the Jesus in him, things happened on a higher level where penises and vaginas became irrelevant. For a few moments she pictured two blank-crotched Jesuses scissoring away in heavenly ecstasy, and then she realized that Ryan was gone from her bed.

He was sitting on her balcony in his underwear, perched on the railing. It was forty feet to the sidewalk, but he was slouched, seemingly without a care about his balance. She had a nice view east—past the hospital and the big hill of Buena Vista Park you could see all the way downtown to the Transamerica Building, a tiny and distinct little triangle. A bank of fog was spilling hurriedly down the hill behind the hospital and breaking in the distance against the park, lit up by a giant moon.

"Hello there," he said.

8

Titania sat alone for a while on her bier, listening to the shrieks of her subjects as they hithered and thithered all over the park. She was also afraid, but all her long life she had only run screaming toward things, and not away from them. She was not quite sure if it had been a mistake to release Puck, but she was entertaining the possibility. It had not really made her feel better to do it, but she felt different. She still missed and loved her husband and her Boy, and she was still extraordinarily sad, but this seemed to weigh a little less heavily. She realized all of a sudden that even her clothes felt less heavy where they hung on her. She raised her arms, and shrugged her shoulders, and opened her mouth as if to laugh, but didn't laugh. The difference, she decided, was that now there was something to be done. Hell would be raised, and Oberon would come or not, but at least there would be no more idle tears. The night would end in joy or ruin, and somehow that was easier to abide than an endless, static grief.

She went back under the hill, not to hide but to get ready. She was about to have the fight of her life and wasn't going to do it in a dress made of moss, rosebuds, and butterfly wings. There was an alcove in her grotto, darker and colder than it should naturally have been, where two ebony chests, each the size of a beefy ape, stood side by side. She opened hers and found a brownie inside. She lifted him out. "He'll find you here, too, Doorknob," she said.

"I'm not *hiding*," he said. "I'm looking for *the knife*."

"It will take more than a knife to slay the Beast," she said.

"Not *a* knife. *The* knife. As it is sung: *With a knife of rowan wood they spilled his blood and bound him fast.*"

"Ah," she said. "One can't do such things twice," which wasn't entirely true. She didn't actually remember the particulars of how Puck had been bound the first time. The knife had been involved somehow, but the song had come long after the fact and had almost nothing to do with the actual history.

"Poodle!" he said. "*Poodle!* Damn you, Milady. Damn you! I'll find your knife, wherever you hid it, and then you'll fix this!" He ran out into the long halls beyond the grotto. Titania listened a while as his tiny footsteps faded, then turned back to the chest, lifting out the contents and putting them on. First there was a thick white underdress of muslin and a veil of cobwebs, and a dress of mail, the links forged of abused silver, so hardened with magical insults by faerie smiths that it was harder than steel. Then there were stiff gloves of rhinoceros hide, and a fitted breastplate studded with afflicted pearls. Her silver ax was at the bottom of the chest. She lifted it and cradled it in her arms and whispered its name, always known only to her, feeling it stir. She smiled at it, thinking of all the creatures, inhuman and human, monsters and jealous wives, she had beheaded. The heads tumbled through her memory, lit softly by a nostalgia as tender as what she might reserve for old lovers. She swung the ax around her head, dancing away from the dark little alcove, and in seven strokes reduced the bed to kindling and feather fluff.

Huff was trying unsuccessfully to gather his players together. They had scattered to all corners of the park, if a round park can have corners, and now he was striding confidently along the slanting paths, trying to set the example by his bearing and his walk, that there was nothing to be afraid of, since the man who ran into their midst saying such alarming things had been very strange but also very small.

"Soylent Green is people!" he cried. "Soylent Green is *people*!" He had only just now decided that this ought to be their rallying cry. It was perfect, and it ought to have been all along the phrase by which they might distinguish each other from the Mayor's agents. He was thinking of such things as passwords, and the need for secrecy, because he could only conceive of deliberate reasons for the disruption that had been visited upon them. The little man had been an agent of the Mayor, and his unusual size had merely been a disguise. You were supposed to think he was from the circus, but really he was from City Hall.

It complicated things, to say the least, if the Mayor was on to them. It changed the whole purpose of the play, Huff thought, because it required the element of surprise, to prick a person's conscience. Without the element of surprise, it would only be a scolding on a hardened heart—it wouldn't change him or cause him to reverse all his cannibalistic social policies in an agony of regret. But it might still expose him. When he came down on them with his curious two-foot-high storm troopers and sent them all to jail for their activist presumption, people would ask,

"What's so threatening, what's so *illegal*, about *Soylent Green*?" And those questions would lead to other questions, which would lead to others until, brick by brick, the Mayor's little flesh-eating bungalow would be disassembled, and he would be exposed sitting inside at a table with somebody else's foot in his mouth.

"Soylent Green is people!" Huff shouted again, and he thought he heard a faint reply: "People!" It was like an echo, except it was a women's voice. He was not familiar with the part of the park he was in—he had run up when everyone else had run down. He generally never penetrated up into the higher parts if he could help it, not being a fan of steep hills and not caring much for views. He was on a wide path now, flanked by tall white eucalyptus on either side, and some thoughtful person had put colored lanterns high in the branches. There were thick wisps of fog blowing among the trees, and these combined pleasingly with the lanterns, so the reds and greens and blues and purples were softly muted. It was something to admire. Views made him dizzy and seasick, but he was not indifferent to beauty.

The woman's voice sounded again. "People!"

"Soylent Green!" he called back.

"People," came the voice again. Huff ran, as much as he could run, down the lighted road, which seemed to go on and on and on. He ran for a full minute, and still the scene ahead of him didn't change. He looked back, and the road stretched serenely into the dark. But when he turned around, there was a little something different up ahead after all: something was swinging over the road. He half ran—it was a sort of unwhimisical skip—calling out his coded greeting again, and the swinging package called back.

"Princess!" he said. "Is it you?" When he ran up closer, he got a better idea of what exactly was going on with her. She was tied by a long rope to a tree branch that arched over the path, swinging in a wide arc and gently striking the trunks on either side of the road, cursing each time she hit. Someone had wrapped her in a shroud, as if to bury her.

"It's me," she said.

"How did you get up there?"

"Shrug," she said.

"Shrug?"

"Shrug. I'm saying it, since I can't do it."

"Was it the Mayor's men?"

"Shrug. I was just walking, trying to get the fuck out of here."

"I'll get you down. This is all getting very serious, I think. Little people! Traps!" Perhaps it was ill-advised to say *traps*. Or maybe he was talking too loud. In a moment he was swinging off-tandem with Princess, wishing he had been more sneaky.

"Like that!" Princess said, and laughed.

"It's not funny," he said. "We are defeated, and we haven't even gotten through a full rehearsal yet."

"I have gotten where I am in life by learning to enjoy everything that happens to me," she said, but she didn't laugh again.

"I suppose they'll come get us down and then take us to jail. I don't want to go to jail. And we didn't even do anything. Not yet. But maybe it will generate some outrage, when they put us in jail for no other reason than daring to speak truth to power."

"I am really marveling at this technology," Princess said, stretching in her shroud. "I never saw it coming. Not even when I saw it happening to you."

"Well, this is San Francisco, isn't it? Who knows what sort of devices that man has at his disposal? He's probably watching us right now." He looked around for a camera, but of course it wouldn't be the kind that you could see. They swung there for a while, not unpleasantly, Huff thought. He liked spending time with Princess, when she was in the right mood—or right moods, since she often seemed to hold on to more than one of them at once, and combine them in sometimes sophisticated flavors that could be pleasant or unpleasant, depending, Huff believed, on the measure of tension in the combination. Sad envy made for a gentle Princess, while raging joy made her too much to handle, and anxious tristesse left her quiet and bemused. She almost sustained his interest sometimes, with her ever-changing personality, but he had never met a woman who sustained his interest, and indeed he had had a dream on the eve of his sexual debut in which an old hag had stood over his crib and declared that he would *never* meet a woman who could sustain his interest; there was something so awful and so great in him that he would never find a partner who could tolerate his potential. He was grateful to that old lady for bringing him that information. A lifetime of failed relationships might otherwise have been even more dispiriting. But predestination was a relief in this case, and he had always made a habit, in his foreknowledge, of enjoying the ladies while they lasted.

"I like you, Princess. I thought you should know that, here at the end."

"You're all right," she said, and spat at a squirrel that came out on a nearby branch to stare at them. *"Shoo!"* she said, but that only seemed to invite another squirrel onto the branch. It was joined shortly by a third and a fourth, and in very little time that branch, and all the branches, and the ground below them, were crowded with raccoons and owls and even bluejays and wrens, creatures that really ought to have been asleep. They all stared, much too quietly, and Huff stared back, totally unsure of what to say. One or two or three of them he might have confronted as agents of the Mayor, sophisticated animatronic squirrel-bots, but a whole silent *Snow White* symphony of woodland creatures was something else entirely. He liked to think that he tolerated more strangeness than most people, because he knew from experience that life was generally much stranger than most folks could imagine. But this suddenly seemed of a different order. This was all much stranger than anything else he'd ever lived through, and yet it didn't feel at all unreal. "My dear," he said, "we are *not* dreaming."

"Pinch," said Princess. The silent animals continued to stare, but now the ones on the ground, who had been crowding the path, started to shuffle to either side, making an aisle. A moment later a figure came walking down the path. Huff could tell right away that it was a lady, though she wasn't dressed like a lady. Something ladylike went before her, figuratively speaking, to which he was sensitive. Two of the Mayor's dwarves walked beside her, stepping very carefully—perhaps even timidly—down the path in a way that contrasted sharply with the lady's confident stride.

"My Lady," the two said in unison. They were both the size of schnauzers, and one had an old man's face while the other had an old woman's face. "It is not the Beast that we have captured."

"Are you with the Mayor's office?" Huff called down to the lady, who was close enough for him to examine in a little more detail. She was very tall, and her face was harsh, and the battle-ax resting in her arms, while it brought to mind certain ladies he had known, was decidedly unladylike.

"I am with the office of eternity," she said. "And the office of regret, and the office of love renounced, but of the Mayor I know nothing at all."

"It's just two mortals," said the dwarf with the old man's face.

"And not pretty ones, even," said the other one. Princess spat on her, but she didn't seem to notice.

"Still, they may come," said the lovely lady. "It wouldn't do, to leave them unattended on the hill. And the Beast is their enemy, as much as ours. Get them down." The little man and woman clapped their hands, then did a little do-si-do with each other, slapped each other on the cheek, and finally whistled, high and clear for a few seconds, but then the tone descended. Huff and Princess descended with it, not too fast, but still they landed on their heads and lay crumpled and bound among the animals and the goons.

"You had no right—" Huff began, but the animals and the little people and the tall lady were already starting to move down the path. The white ribbon that bound Huff's arms and legs was already unraveling, and the same thing was happening to Princess; they freed themselves and stood up at the same time. They took each other's hands and then each tried to lead the other in the opposite direction. Huff pulled Princess after the remarkable lady. Princess pulled him away from her.

"Where are you going?" they both asked.

"The fuck out of here," Princess said, and Huff said, "Where she's going." They pulled each other again, and then Huff let go.

"Fucked-up crazy shit!" Princess said. Huff thought there was something poignant in her tone, as if she were saying, *I want to go with you, but*—she hurried down the path, which actually ran deeper, that way, into the park. Huff turned and followed the last of the little animals, telling himself that he had to see what the Mayor was up to, but also understanding that there was something very special about that lady besides her ax. He was slower than the squirrels but faster than the raccoons, who ambled and sniffed on their way. The lady's armored head was shining under the moon; she was easy to follow even when the path twisted and turned and became overgrown with dark ferns.

It was a pleasant walk. Huff got used to things pretty quickly—it was a special talent, related to his tolerance for strangeness. It was good to be able to sleep anywhere, when you slept everywhere, and good to be an easily contented person (though not a person accepting of injustice), when your luck was bad and your life was hard. So Huff enjoyed the bright low-hanging moon and the wisps of fog and the noise and proximity of the animals as they went, and even the collapsing-pumpkin faces of the Mayor's little old man and woman. But most of all he enjoyed the sight of the lady, who was lovely and rather awesome even from behind, and he enjoyed her odor, something he had not appreciated from on high.

They marched for a little while, longer than ought to have been possible, given the size of the park, unless they were going around in circles, which Huff thought they were not. That was all right in the same way that the purposeful bunnies all around him were all right, though he could not tolerate it when he came upon a raccoon in the road worrying a pair of boxer shorts with his teeth. Huff shooed him away, and put the shorts, which were blue, and printed with little red Scotty dogs, on his head. The farther Huff proceeded down the road, the more he knew just where he was going as well: after the lady. It didn't matter if she was an agent of the Mayor or something else—possibly even more dangerous—he was still going to follow her and talk to her and figure her out.

The procession stopped at a rectangular clearing, the same size and shape as the tennis courts, and Huff thought it might actually have been the same place, since the trees that surrounded the clearing looked about the same as the ones that surrounded the tennis courts, even if there were no houses visible through the trees. The animals took up places at the edge of the field, giving a wide berth as they went to the figure standing in the middle. He was smiling hugely. Huff could see that even from yards and yards away, and it was that vain, shit-eating smile as much as the malicious aura that radiated off the man that made him easy to recognize, despite the darkness and the distance. It was the Mayor.

"Milady," he said. "I said I would eat you last. Would you prefer I do it now?"

"It's time," the lady said, "for us to fight again. Let's make a noise, Puck."

"Did you make walls out of the air?" he asked her. "I want ice cream and a little mortal blood, but my way is blocked." The lady shrugged. "No matter," he said. "I'll be through by dawn."

"Or bound again," she said. "Or dead." She swung her ax over her head and ran at him, and he laughed at her, which seemed unbearably disrespectful to Huff. He ran at him, too, though he wasn't a violent person and had always been someone who fought with his wits and not with his fists. It was the very last straw, though, and worse somehow than feeding his constituents to his constituents, for this smirking asshole to be rude to someone who was obviously the most wonderful woman in the world.

The Mayor slapped the woman down with one blow—her ax went flying and stuck in a tree—and then he caught Huff by his neck and lifted him up and sniffed at him. "Milady," he said, "did you bring me ice cream as well?" Huff had all sorts of things to say, now that he had an audience with the man, but he couldn't breathe to speak. The Mayor sniffed at him and smiled even wider—Huff could see the whole panoply of animals and goons reflected behind him in the man's teeth—and then his smile vanished. "What's this?" he asked. "Could this be?" He took a long draught off the underwear on Huff's head, and then he shook him. "Are you disguised, my friend?" he said, giving Huff a shake. "My old friend!" he said, taking another sniff. "My dear friend! Or is this a trick?"

"Maybe," Huff tried to say, not sure what answer would distress the Mayor more. He plucked the underwear from Huff's head, then dropped him, and dragged him to where the lady was standing again, rubbing a bruise on her face.

"Maybe not," he said, after smelling the underwear and smelling Huff again. "These do not belong to *you*. Milady, I wish I had time to torture you better before I eat you, but this will have to do. *Obey your husband.*" He took a ring from Huff's finger, tearing it away hard enough to hurt, and jammed it on her thumb. She was staring blankly at both of them, all the harshness drained from her face. Huff grabbed the Mayor by the arm. "I am making a citizen's arrest," he said. It was a giant arm, thickly muscled and as wide around as Huff's leg, but he couldn't seem to hold on to it.

"Abuse your wife," the Mayor said, and ran off away into the trees.

Her parents always gave the new kids a tambourine and stuck them back with Molly, because it was easy to play the tambourine, though there were intricacies to it that nobody else understood or appreciated, and because she was nice, though she was actually only about half as nice as everyone supposed her to be. The new boy was not very different to look at than any of his predecessors, the black foster brothers and sisters who came and went and came and went, circulating one at a time through her actual family until they were inevitably ejected. She had barely learned to re-member Jordan's name before he was gone, trundled off to a Job Corps assignment in Houston, and now here was Paul, at thirteen years old a lit-tle younger than his unmet foster brother once removed, and just as bad with the tambourine. Molly stepped closer to him in the garage and tried to keep the beat in a way that was more obvious and easier to copy, but he didn't catch on, and though he stayed in tune when he sang, he kept get-ting the words wrong. "I love you," Molly sang, coming in with the rest of the family for the chorus. "I love you a lot. I love you more than you can know, but Jesus loves you *more more more more!*" It wasn't the hardest refrain to remember, but still he kept singing, "I love you so much" instead of "I love you a lot," and "more than you can imagine" instead of "more than you can know." It boded ill when they couldn't get the refrain right on this song. It meant that nothing would be easy for them.

It was useless, though, to worry about them, even at this early stage, when you'd think something could be done to help them out, to make them fit in better, or to defuse the inevitable conflicts that would lead to their being sent back to the pound or shipped off to some other family, or to a trade school, or the Marines—or to any number of pseudo-opportunities that were the consolation prize for not actually becoming a member of the musical Archer family of Virginia Beach, Virginia.

Molly smiled at Paul, and he nodded coolly at her, which was something different. Usually, they just gave her a nervous smile on the first day, but he seemed to be appraising her somehow, looking her up and down with the nod. Then he turned, swinging his hips one way and his shoulders another, and he gave the same look to her sister Mary, where she stood tossing her hair back and forth at the keyboards, using one finger on each hand to play. He did one shake of the tambourine at her—it was off the beat—then turned around and did the same thing to her brother Colin, where he was playing the guitar, toward the front of the garage, near their parents. Colin was strumming and dipping from the waist, left and right and left, and hopping in place during the chorus. He was as pale as Molly and looked sickly all of a sudden, compared with the new boy. Molly held her breath and closed her eyes and with an effort—it was like squeezing something inside her head—she refrained from thinking something unpleasant about her actual brother.

The new boy did the same thing to Malinda, singing between their parents to Craig, on the violin, and Clay, on the bass. He turned around to do the thing—a salute? a shake of the fist?—to Chris, on the drums, and to her parents, and then to little Melissa, a moving target since she played no instrument and did not sing but just danced around enthusiastically, and finally to the life-size picture of Jesus taped to the back side of the garage door, where a different sort of family, or a different sort of band, might have taped a picture of a stadium crowd. It was two shakes for Jesus.

He closed his eyes then, and kept dancing in place and mumble-singing the wrong words. "Jesus Loves You More" did not rock very hard. None of their songs did, though their father, who wrote them with minimal input from Mary and Craig, the two eldest, would have said otherwise. Molly did what she could to shake things up. She and Chris had a thing going, where she accented his drumming just so, jingling grace beats that brought out the rhythm underneath their father's vanilla melody, which was always one of only four melodies. One could do only so much, though. If you shook it too hard, you only drew attention to yourself in a way that made it clear you had given up on the song or that you were trying to drag it someplace it just didn't belong. It was a subtle bit of tambourine lore, not something to be intuited the first time you picked one up. But the boy was stomping and shaking and spinning and clapping to a song that was the breathless, hopped-up cousin to the one they were actually playing. Chris and Mary and Clay frowned at him, but the others, standing in front of him with their hearts turned to Jesus, didn't notice for another minute. The song stopped, not entirely on their father's karate-chop cue, but the boy did not. His eyes were closed, his hands and his feet were flying, and he was smiling as he sang. "Jesus, he's my friend, sort of! He's my kind of sometimes friend. Jesus!" Melissa laughed and danced along until Mary grabbed her shoulder.

"Paul," their mother said. *"Paul!"* He stopped dancing and looked at her.

"When the music stops," their father said, "the song is over."

"My name," the boy replied, "is Peabo."

There was a time when they had just been the Archers, and not the Archer Family Band, but Molly could barely remember it. There was a time when her father had been a full-time instead of a part-time dentist, and her mother had been the dental hygienist in his office, when they had all gone to regular school instead of home school, when the family car had been a Taurus instead of a short bus, and when Melissa hadn't even been born. Then their parents woke up one morning—without having seen a vision or having experienced a dark night of the soul—with a new understanding of their lives' purpose. They both took up guitars, never having played before, and started to praise Jesus in song.

There was a time, too, before they had made albums or gone on tours or made Handycam videos produced and directed by their Aunt Jean, which aired (rather late at night) on the community cable channel and then eventually on Samaritan TV, when Molly actually liked being in the band and liked being in the family. She had had Melissa's job once, and had danced as enthusiastically as Melissa did now, and had felt the most extraordinary joy during every performance, whether it was a rehearsal in the garage or a school-auditorium concert in front of three hundred kids.

Then she had woken up one morning two months ago to find that the shine had gone off everything. It was a conversion as sudden as the one her parents had suffered. She had gone to breakfast feeling unwell but not sick, and was puzzling over how it was different to feel like something was not right with you and yet feel sure you were in perfect health, but she didn't know what her problem could be until she noticed at breakfast how unattractive her father was. It wasn't his old robe or his stained T-shirt or even how he talked with his mouth full of eggs; he wore those things every morning and he always talked with his mouth full; it was just how he was. She kept staring at him all through breakfast, and finally he asked her if there was something on his face. "No, sir," she said, and a little voice—the sort that you hear very clearly even though it doesn't actually speak—said somewhere inside her, *He's got ugly all over his face.*

Peabo sat next to her at dinner that first night. Molly had just been getting used to the extra room at the table, to being able to eat with her natural right hand instead of her don't-bump-elbows-with-Mary left hand. She had said goodbye to the empty seat the night before, when their father had announced to the family that they were getting another brother.

"Already?" Chris asked, because Jordan had been gone only three months.

"Already?" their father said. "You mean finally!"

"I miss Jeffrey," said Malinda.

"His name was Jordan," said Chris.

"What's his name?' asked Melissa. "Is it Jeffrey? Is it Elmo? Is it Sarsa-parilla?"

"Paul," said their father, and their mother said, "Paul Winner," and Chris said, "Yeah, I bet he's a real *winner*." Colin gave him a high-five, and they were both subsequently disfellowshipped for the rest of the meal, their chairs turned away toward the wall, their faces turned to their laps, and their desserts divided between chubby Mary and fat Craig.

Chris and Colin stayed in the corner while all the others got to speak their gratitudes. Mary went first and used up the obvious one: she was grateful for their new guest; she was grateful for the totality of his life and for his spirit. She was always saying things like that. Molly could tell by the way Colin's shoulders were moving that he was poking his finger in his mouth to gag himself. Clay was grateful for the tension in his guitar strings. Craig was grateful for the color alizarin crimson. Malinda was grateful for the note of D-flat, and Melissa was grateful for fur, but when pressed by their father to be more specific, she said "furry creatures." Molly had been feeling a little panicked lately when her turn inevitably approached. There was a lot to be grateful for; the whole point of uttering one's gratitudes was just that. It was meant to be easy, a nightly reminder that they lived their lives surrounded by visible and invisible bounty. But sometimes, out of sheer nervousness, Molly failed to think of anything, and sometimes the things that popped into her head were not the things she was supposed to be grateful for: the way her breasts were exactly the same size, while Mary's and Malinda's looked like they had traded four markedly different boobs between them; the way it felt when she rested all her weight on the tapering edge of her bicycle seat; the way Jordan's right eye had been ever so slightly out of sync with his left eye. And lately the voice would speak with her, so when she said out loud, "Dandelion fluff," or "The spots on the wings of a ladybug," the voice would say *Poverty* or *Measles*. She said, "This fork," and held it tightly, as if clutching it could keep her from saying "My asshole" instead.

Peabo was quiet during his first dinner. Colin had predicted that he would be ravenous and nose for scraps off other people's plates, but he hardly ate at all, tasting everything and finishing nothing but praising it all politely. Molly watched him, expecting him to pick up his plate and shake it at her, but he only cocked his head when he caught her looking. The family made the usual first-dinner conversation. On their mother's instructions, they were supposed to let lie all the presumed horrors and not ask him anything directly about his past, and so the gist of the conversation was something like "I like potatoes, Peabo . . . Do you like potatoes?" He answered these questions the same way every time, with a solemn nod of his head and "I do." Molly thought about the presumed horrors anyway. He had a burn on his left arm that she had noticed right away, and though she didn't stare at him she wondered how he'd got it, and there was a scar on the side of his neck that had healed all bunched up and thick.

It would have been tantamount to suggesting that they cast Jesus out of the household to say that an end should be put to the endless stream of foster brothers and sisters that had been coming and going in the seat next to her forever. But she wondered if it reduced the sum total of anybody's

suffering to keep them around for a few months in a situation that ultimately did nobody any good, that changed nothing in anybody's life and
only rearranged some things for a little while. But that was like wondering
if they should stop playing and singing because their songs did not in fact
enter into people's hearts and make them love themselves and each other
and Jesus, who mediated all love of any kind, the love clearinghouse and
the love circuit board. Looking at the new boy, she thought that it might
be easier for everyone if he just went away right now, and she waited for
the voice to add something snarky and cruel to that thought. She waited
and waited, but nothing came, and when he glanced her way again and
caught her staring she put a piece of broccoli in her mouth and looked at
her lap.

"What an unusual name," Mary said later, when the four girls were in the
bathroom getting ready for bed. "Peabo. Pea . . . *bo.*"

"It's a dog name," said Malinda. "Here, Peabo. Here, boy!"

"Here, kitty kitty!" said Melissa, then thought a moment and added,
"It has pee in it. I bet his middle name is Doody." She struck a pose in
front of Mary and stuck out her hand. "Hello, my name is Pee Doody.
How do you doo-doo?" Mary slapped her hand away, and Melissa
laughed. It was as typical and ordinary and expected as the dinner questions, or starting the new kid off on the tambourine—it had all happened
before, and it would all happen again, the touch of cattiness in the beginning, relatively innocent doo-dooisms that lacked any deep venom. These
would fade away little by little and the giggling denigrations would be
replaced by goggling admirations, a slow fade-up that might not be
noticed if it hadn't been part of the eternal foster cycle. Molly paused
while brushing her teeth to sigh expansively.

"What?" Malinda asked.

"Nothing," Molly said, because Malinda had become convinced in the
past few months that Molly thought she was better than all the rest of
them, and she had taken it upon herself to teach Molly just how un-
Christian and bitchy it was to go around heaving big sighs to let everyone
know you were bored by your own superiority. That wasn't it at all, of course.
Molly actually felt pretty lowly, compared with the rest of them—just because she was always unwillingly coming up with insults against them all

didn't mean she thought she was better than anybody else. But she didn't tell Malinda that.

"What?" Malinda said again.

"His middle name is Bo," Molly said. "I saw his papers on Dad's desk: B-O. Paul Bo. P. Bo."

"You like him," said Mary, smiling.

"You're not supposed to be looking at things on that desk," said Malinda.

"Molly and Doody," Melissa sang, "sittin' in a tree."

"He won't last a month," Molly said. She rinsed out her mouth, put her toothbrush back into her color-coded space—blue—in the holder, and went to her bedroom. It was hers that year by lottery; her sisters shared a room. Malinda said that having her own room had gone to Molly's head.

She turned out the light, neglecting both her regular and her special Bible study, neglecting to kneel at her bed to pray, and only very quickly (though not insincerely) asking a silent blessing on all the people in her family, flipping their faces through her head like a deck of cards instead of turning them over in her mind like little statues. She considered the new boy last, picturing him on a card all his own, in his tambourine pose, in midshake and midbenediction or threat, whatever it had been, and let her mind go quiet for a moment while she held on to that image, as if inviting the voice to say something cruel about him. But again nothing came. For the rest of her family, she prayed for happiness and a long life, and that they be gathered up in Heaven if they should all die that night in an earthquake or a fire (and she briefly imagined them all buried under the earth, and with burning hair). For the boy, she just asked that things work out for him here after all. Then she went to sleep.

When she saw him standing at the foot of her bed, her first thought was that it was strange to be dreaming about him, since he was interesting but not fascinating, and sad but not troubling. She stared at him for a while before she realized that she was actually awake. She sat up. "What are you doing here?" she asked him. In response he did an explosive move, throwing his arms up and out three times, slapping his heel, and spinning in place. She flinched but didn't cry out; he did it again, and then something more complicated and harder to follow, and yet she did follow it, and preserved every move, the pointing and the spinning, the way he made double guns of his hands and fired them all around her room and then blew the imaginary smoke from the tips of his finger-pistols, the splits in the air and the brief air-guitar solo and every blocky motion of the robot dance. He smiled at her when he was done. She stared back at him, not smiling, with the covers drawn up to her chin, and watched as he danced out of her room, doing a perfect curving moonwalk right out the door, which he left open. She stared at the open door for a while, considering it as evidence that he had actually been there since she made a point of closing it every night before she got into bed, and trying to think of what she should say to herself about what she had just seen. She didn't know what to say, so she waited, instead, for the snarky, dissatisfied voice in her to say something, fully expecting it to be something more cruel and more vile than anything it had yet dared to say. But the words, when they came, were *Nice moves.*

She considered those moves as she sat the next day with her mother and the other girls sewing the costumes for the new video. They were in the garage, the only place in the house with enough empty floor space to lay out the fabric, though today they were just sewing spangles on the jumpsuits, each of them sitting cross-legged on cushions nipped from the living-room sectional. She had wondered until she finally fell asleep if she should tell on him. It was probably her duty, after all, to get him whatever help he needed to keep him from entering relative strangers' rooms uninvited at night. And maybe she ought to tell on him for her own sake, since any variety of bad behavior might be dormant in him, and the little dance only a fluid, grooving prelude to a lifetime of deviance.

And yet it had only been a little dance. That was all he had done. There were Christian households where that was a crime, but this wasn't one of them. There had been some kind of infraction; she was certain of that. But what exactly it might be was not clear at all. Whatever it was, ejection from the household on only the second day of his tenure seemed a little too severe a punishment, but that was what would probably happen, since she knew her father would regard the situation with considerably less sophistication than she was currently bringing to bear. She found that she cared whether or not he stuck around, because it had been nice to hear something from the voice that she could actually agree with. Maybe, she thought, the reign of malicious sarcasm was over and she could be a good person again.

"Pay attention, honey," her mother said, because she was about to sew a spangle fish on backward to the sea-blue one-piece, zip-up-the-back pants suit. The girls had lost an argument with their father about how the fishes should be placed. "The fishes all swim the same way," he said. "Up, toward Jesus." It would have been more pleasing, Molly thought, to have them going every which way.

"Sorry," Molly said. Her mother handed her the seam ripper, and Molly began to undo the stitches, but she was imagining Peabo dancing in a suit of haphazardly swimming fish. Her mother was still staring at her when she handed back the seam ripper.

"Well?" her mother said.

"What?"

"You're the only one who hasn't shared yet," she said. "Cat got your tongue?"

"Huh?"

"What do you think about the latest addition to our family?"

Molly shrugged. "He seems nice," she said.

"And?"

Molly shrugged again.

"And she's too fancy to share her opinions," said Malinda. Their mother shushed her with a wave of her hand. "Mary," she said. "Tell your sister what sort of family she's living in."

"A Christian Democratic Union," Mary said, not looking up from her work.

"And what does a Christian Democratic Union rely upon?" She looked at Malinda now, but it was the voice that Molly heard answering first: *Every citizen being perfectly ugly and perfectly boring.*

"The open and honest loving communication of information equally shared among all participants," Malinda said. Molly sighed, and Malinda glared at her, but she was sighing at the voice, not at her sister.

"So," their mother said to Molly. "Once more, with feelings!"

"Did something bad happen to him?" Molly asked.

"Bad things happen to all of us," her mother said.

"Something especially bad," Molly said. "Something tragic?" She hadn't read any farther than the first page of the file on her father's desk, and didn't know anyway if they put that sort of thing in it, the list of his lifetime of problems: *dead mother, dead father, beaten by auntie, contracted out to a sweat-shop, punished with burns* . . .

"Not everybody can be lucky like you," said Malinda.

"Or like *you*," said their mother. "Or *you* or *you* or *you* or *you*." She pointed to all of them, then to Malinda one more time, and then she suggested that they take this as an opportunity to express their love for each other, so Molly turned to Mary and Melissa and said it, and finally suffered Malinda's stiff hug.

"I love you," Malinda said, and leaned close to whisper, "Even though you totally suck."

"I love you, too," said Molly, and she tried hard to mean it.

Later, during the afternoon rehearsal, she kept expecting Peabo to do the dance again. But today he was copying her exactly, doing the one-two, one-two shuffle in perfect time with her, and singing in tune on the signature piece of the new album, which was the reason they were rehearsing every day, and sewing costumes, and blocking out a video. They would start a tour in two weeks.

"The Ballad of the Warm Fuzzies" was the most complicated song her father had ever written. It didn't involve any more than the usual four chords, but it was seven minutes long, and the lyrics told an actual story, which her father had borrowed from a children's book of hippie ethics. Her father didn't like hippies, but had sent a note to California to the author of the children' book, thanking him for the inspiration and encouraging him to put Jesus in his heart instead of Charles Manson. The tale of the Warm Fuzzies and their battle with the Cold Pricklies unfolded in twelve verses, with half the family squaring off against the other in song. Peabo, along with Molly, was among the Pricklies.

All day, Molly had watched him as closely as she dared, given how closely she was being watched by Malinda for evidence of snootiness or lack of charity toward the boy. Her mother had told them that Jesus would help them along to a place where they couldn't even see that he was black, that with perfect love would come perfect color blindness, but every time Molly saw him standing next to one of her brothers or sisters it was all she noticed about him, how different he looked. *Black is beautiful*, the voice kept saying, which made her shake her head.

He talked to her in the same way that he talked to all the girls, politely and never for very long. He joshed and roughhoused with the boys and seemed to settle immediately into companionship with them in a way that belied the remote gaze he had trained on everyone during the first rehearsal and dinner. She watched him at play with her brothers. It was as if there were two boys, who didn't jibe with each other. There was the boy who had sneaked into her room to offer up the little dance for her interpretation, and then there was the boy who arm-wrestled with Craig and did algebra equations for fun with Colin. She could understand if there were two boys in him, since she had felt like there were two girls in her, one for the regular voice that said regular things about people and one for the other voice that spoke a language made up only of cruel insults. If she stared in the bathroom mirror long enough, she thought she could catch that other girl's features superimposed in brief flashes upon hers: her eyes were small, and her nose turned up like a pig's, and her mouth was a colorless gash in her face. Malinda caught her staring at herself like that once and said, "You think you're so pretty, don't you?"

Molly tripped up on the beat and came late to the chorus. At first, it seemed that no one had noticed that she'd messed up the rhythm—Chris was the only one who usually cared, anyway—until Peabo did the same thing, just one beat off, but didn't look at her. He did it again: another missed beat.

She missed one back, and then threw in an extra one at the end of the next verse, and then for the rest of the song they were trading omissions and additions, having a conversation above and below and around the song that no one else, not even the snarky voice in her, could understand, and it occurred to her, just before the song ended, that they were speaking tambourine.

"Off the charts!" their father said, because they all stopped playing at exactly the same time for once, and everyone had been on key and no one had forgotten any verses; even Melissa's flailing dance had been more graceful than usual. "He is risen! He is *risen!* Off the *charts!*" he shouted. Peabo was nodding soberly as they all put down their instruments and began to exchange hugs, something they usually did at the end of the rehearsal, though they were only half done now. It was one of those moments that Molly would really have appreciated a couple of months before. Everyone was hugging with breathless abandon, entirely caught up in how much they loved the music, one another, this day, and Jesus, of course. *Jesus, Jesus, Jesus,* Molly said to herself, but the voice said *Mariah Carey, Mariah Carey, Mariah Carey,* which lent a new emergent sense of alarm to her effort really to feel what they were feeling, and with her eyes shut tight she tried to feel it by sheer force of will. She strained, and there was a sensation in her like a bubble popping, and clear as day she had a picture in her head all of a sudden: a lizard sunning itself on a rock, staring rapt and remote into the distance.

They went to church that evening. Molly sat there, looking around without moving her head. It was worse here, surrounded not just by her family but by the whole congregation, hairy Mrs. Louque in the row in front of her and ancient Mr. Landry behind her. The church, which was as big as a warehouse because it had once been a warehouse, was full of good, normal people who put her to shame by their example. Up on the stage, Reverend Duff was a lightning rod for the voice. *There once was a reverend named Fudd*, it sang, and she tried to do the mental equivalent of sticking your fingers in your ears and singing *la la la*.

It was a different sort of Jesus time than the one they had that day at home, but Molly was failing at it just as badly. Her mother was trembling and ululating and her father was shaking and barking and her brothers were yipping and her sisters were mewling, and beyond them the whole congregation was similarly taken up, and Molly would have to listen, later, as they all talked about how wonderful it was for them when they spoke the spirit that way. She closed both eyes, then opened one to a slit to watch Peabo, who was standing quietly next to her. The limerick about Reverend Duff faltered and was silenced as she watched him. *He doesn't look stupid like the rest of them*, the voice said, at the same time that she thought, *He doesn't look stupid like me*. Molly looked forward at the back of Mrs. Louque's head. The lady was dancing in place like a little girl.

Their hymnbooks were touching and their elbows were touching and their knees were touching. But Peabo didn't look at her, and he sang the hymns without any extra notes or extra syllables that could be put together into a message. When it came time to exchange the peace, he turned to her mother and hugged Colin and Chris and Clay and her father, and he reached past her to hug Mary, but he didn't even look at Molly. That would have been too obvious, she told herself, and she tried to think of some clever way of communicating with him. All she could think was to tear a piece from one of the hymnals and fold it into the shape of a snake, which would signify something, though she wasn't sure what. Her failure to imagine just what that was made everything feel useless and dumb, and she was sure, all of a sudden, that she had imagined his unique advance. She closed her eyes and shook her head and found herself wanting to scream.

It would have been fine to scream. You were supposed to express the spirit however it came. This usually took the foster children by surprise, even though they were briefed about it before they came to church for the first time. But he seemed to take it all in stride. Molly did her usual thing, swaying back and forth with her eyes on the ceiling and muttering times tables in pig Latin to herself. She tried to distinguish the voices of her brothers and sisters from the cacophony. She heard Malinda saying something like "Edelweiss!" She heard her father saying "Omalaya!" and her mother saying "Paw-paw!" and then, finally, she heard Peabo, right next to her, saying something that sounded like "I love you I love you I love you I love you." There was an altered, electric quality to his voice. She did not open her eyes or look at him, but she slipped the words into her times tables: "I-ay ove-lay oooh-yay." She kept on with the oooh-yays until the very end, when folks were passing out and the last hymn was starting up slowly, rising from various places around the hall from those who had recovered enough to sing. When she opened her eyes, she saw Peabo standing straight and tall next to her, mouth agape with the hymn, shouting it as much as singing it.

She went to his room that night, after she was sure everyone else had fallen asleep. It was the little room they put all the foster kids in, not even really a bedroom, since it didn't have a closet, just a wardrobe. There was a dresser and a small chair, but no space for anything else except the single bed. The drapes were open, and by the light of the streetlamps Molly could see Peabo stretched out in bed, on top of the covers in his pajamas. She stared from the doorway for what felt like five minutes, but she couldn't tell whether his eyes were open or not.

She didn't say anything because he hadn't said anything, and it seemed like it would be cheating to use words. She didn't know what words she would have used anyway, though it was clear what she wanted to say. She did the message: reach, reach, dip, kick, leap, leap, leap, every time a little higher, though not too high, since his room was right above her parents' room. But she went high enough to kick her feet—one, two, three times—and when she landed softly she dropped into a squat and then exploded upward. This was a move from the video for "Jesus Loves You More." Her hands were supposed to stretch out and then fall, fingers fluttering, to her sides. But the same not–part of her that spoke with the voice that was not a voice took control of them just as she was stretching, and her hands opened up at the top of her reach into two perfect Fuck You birdies, aimed not at Peabo but at the whole world.

He didn't stir at all the whole time she danced, which wasn't very long. Her dance was shorter than his had been, and she regular-walked, not moonwalked, out the door. Back in her bed, she wondered if he had been awake at all, not sure if it would be disappointing to actually talk to him at length, now that they were communicating at a higher level. She imagined going on forever this way, through his successful fosterhood and eventual adoption, through weddings and family reunions and funerals, proceeding in parallel past family milestone after family milestone. She imagined them at Malinda's funeral, softly jangling their tambourines at each other, communicating shades of irony and grief not contained in the mundane verbal condolences of the others. She had nearly fallen asleep, and was sure she was about to enter a dream in which, knowing it was a dream, she could enjoy Malinda's death, and say things like "No, I don't miss her at all," when she felt a pressure on her mattress and awoke with a start. He was sitting on her bed. "Do you want to see my Jesus?" he asked her.

"Darkness," said Aunt Jean. "And light! Light . . . and darkness!" She was doing Molly's makeup for the video, painting half of her face black and half of it white for the concept portion of the shoot, which involved the family taking turns presenting their black faces and their white faces to the camera as they sang in a black-and-white checkered "dreamspace." (That was a sheet Jean had colored herself with a reeking marker.) Melissa, who had insisted on having her face done first, kept sniffing at it curiously. Jean had paused in front of Peabo, a tub of makeup in either hand, and said, "Why, the dark is built right in, isn't it?"

"Uh-huh," he said, and gave her a neutral stare. In the end, she painted him just like the rest of them, but his black side was darker and his white side more startling than everyone else's.

"Cold," Jean said, throwing her head back and raising her hand to make mouthy little singing motions with it as she showed them her black profile. "Warm!" She pivoted sharply on her heel to show them her white face. Molly felt sure that the total effect, with the checkered background and their swiveling Kabuki faces, would make people dizzy or possibly give them a seizure, but she didn't say so. And the voice didn't say so, either. It had been quiet all day. She didn't really care anyway if someone had a seizure. She didn't really care if she was playing well, during the fish-spangled band-shot portions of the video, when Jean roller-skated around the garage with the video camera to her eye. She didn't care if she kept the beat or not, and she didn't care if Peabo did, either. If he was throwing her grace beats, she ignored them.

"Everything will be different, after you see Him," he had said, and that was true. As Molly had tried unsuccessfully to sleep, with the Jesus swinging languidly in her mind in a five-second arc that measured the minutes until dawn, she tried to see how she could not have understood what he actually meant, and she pictured herself on trial before her family, with Malinda seated as judge and everyone else in the jury box, listening with impassive faces as she attempted to explain. "I thought he meant he was going to share his Jesus with me. His own personal Jesus. His *experience* of Jesus." And it had been true that part of her thought this was going to be the case, and that same part had wondered what it would be like to show him hers. She could only imagine the obvious thing, opening her chest to show him the very shape of her heart.

Everything looked the same. Her father looked the same, singing with his eyes closed and strumming those same four chords on his guitar. Her mother looked the same, shimmying in place. Chris and Craig and Colin looked the same, and Clay looked the same, thrusting his chin out while he played the bass. Mary was stabbing, as she always did, at the keyboard, and Malinda was managing to open her pinched-up little mouth just enough for her weak voice to slip out. Melissa was dancing around like a fool who didn't have a clue what was in store for her, and Peabo . . . it didn't even matter what Peabo was doing. They were all hideous, and she knew without a mirror to tell her so that she was uglier than any of them. As soon as the video shoot was done, she found her father in his study and told him.

They started their tour in the auditorium of the New Calvary School, which was where they started all their tours, because it was down the street from their house and because it could be relied upon to provide a crowd that was both sympathetic and constructively critical. Though the family had technically abandoned the institution, the principal was still a good friend of their father's and a member of their church, and he passed out evaluation forms, dutifully completed by all the students, which scored their performance from one to ten in areas like musicality and spirit and goodness of news. A week after Peabo's departure, there was still a shadow on the performance, though Melissa was the only one who said she missed him, or that they had played better with him around, or that the music sounded different without him. "Don't be stupid," Malinda said. "He only played the *tambourine*."

All their parents would say was that he had done something that demonstrated that it wasn't in God's plan for him to live with them, which was what they said about everyone who got sent back or sent away, but the children suspected it must have been something horrible, because no one before had ever been sent away after only one week. "I guess you were right about him," Malinda said to Molly. "He didn't last a month." She gave Molly a hard stare.

"I guess so," Molly said, finding it easy to stare back blankly at her sister as if she'd had nothing at all to do with Peabo's ejection. It was exactly as easy as it was to stare blankly at her parents, together and separately, when they asked if anything else had happened besides just a *viewing*. Aunt Jean took her shopping, though she wouldn't buy any of the things Molly had picked out for herself. The special attention almost gave away that something had happened to her, and Molly hid the condolence barrette that Jean had given her, after a weepy interrogation in the car. "It must have been so horrible for you!" she said, and Molly said, with perfect calmness, that it was.

They opened with "Sycamore Trees" and then played "Jesus Loves You More" before their father talked a bit to the audience. He wasn't a preacher, but he liked to give sermons and tell stories meant to throw the message of the song into starker relief. He was saying something about choices, which led into "The Ballad of the Warm Fuzzies," and Molly had a moment in which she thought she could hear the silence into which the voice should be speaking an insult to him. But it had been silent since Peabo left, as if it were sulking. She didn't miss it, but she didn't feel any better, now that it had shut up. She wondered where Peabo was. She had been succeeding fantastically at not thinking about him, though not about his Jesus, which accompanied her everywhere. It was not exactly that she could not stop thinking about it, or even that she saw it in cucumbers or carrots or bunches of bananas. It was with her in a way that was hard to describe, because nothing had ever stayed with her this way before, a permanent afterimage not perceived with the eyes.

The music started without her; she had missed her father's cue. She started in late and settled down into an unthinking rhythm. She looked around at the audience and found herself searching for Peabo, but there were only three black kids in the whole student body and they were all girls. "Don't you miss him?" Melissa kept asking them all. Molly could swear that she did not, but now she thought she might cry. That was okay. Her father approved of tears, though not sobs, during a performance. She missed the chorus the first time around, waiting for the tears to come, but not a single one fell, even though everywhere she looked she saw the shine and the blur of them. Her family were moving all around her, and she didn't know why until they squared off into their fuzzy and prickly sides. They sang at her, cocking their heads as they asked if she was going to be a Warm Fuzzy, but it was clear from their faces that they were really asking what was wrong with her.

I don't know, she tried to say, right into her microphone, but something else came out, not even a word but just a noise made in a voice that did not sound like her own voice, though it was very familiar. It was lost in the singing. The family stepped expertly back to their original positions and started the second verse. Melissa picked up a bag and started to throw Warm Fuzzies—really just plush kittens with their hair teased up and their legs cut off, bought in bulk from the five-and-dime—into the crowd. Molly spoke again, louder this time and clearer, so it might have been heard over the music if it hadn't been lost under the noise of the crowd. "Bitch!"

Malinda turned around to glare at her and raise her hand to her lips in a gesture denoting not "Shush" but "Shut up and sing." Molly shook her tambourine at her, two shakes off the beat. Malinda furrowed her brow and stamped her foot, which warranted another shake of the tambourine and a spoken response: "Bitch! Bastard! Bitch!" Then her mother turned around. She got a shake as well, and then Molly gave one to everyone in the family, one here and two there, and then a scattering of them for the audience. She imagined her family in the audience, and imagined herself in the audience, and imagined Peabo in the audience, and imagined his Jesus in the audience, and now she was singing to all of them. It was a whole audience of delicately curving, uncircumcised Jesuses, and each of them was asking her a question. "Fuck!" she answered. A twisted moan, it hardly sounded like the word, but it was the answer, as she shouted it, to every question she could ask. Where did he come from? Where did he go? Where had the shine gone when it disappeared off everything? What was wrong with her? The noise she was making—*"Fargh! Foo-ack!"*—was the answer, and then it was the question, too. She stood up straight and tall, shaking her tambourine and singing for a long time after the music had stopped.

Part Three

9

Molly was developing a relationship with the bench. She knew it pretty well already, compared to all the other benches in all the other parks in the city, because she had spent so much time on it while Ryan made his Buena Vista peregrinations, but tonight it felt like it was giving something back to her, which was what separated the really special benches from the ones you were merely friendly with. She sat on it, and then slouched, and then eventually reclined, and the longer she spent on it the more at ease she felt about never making it to the party. The more time she spent on the bench, the more it seemed like enough work—indeed, *a lot* of work—to have climbed this high hill, and the more it seemed like enough satisfaction to sit and enjoy the view, though the fog had closed it half an hour ago and she had spent the last fifteen minutes on her back staring up at the swirling white ceiling above the treetops.

More than that, Benchy seemed to be saying, in his utterly sympathetic and nonoverwhelming way, that there was work to be done, here by herself, equivalent to what would have been done if she trudged out of the park and found her way to the party, if she knocked on the door and drew attention to herself as the most late arrival, if she restrained the urge to talk to everyone except Jordan Sasscock and managed to sustain a conversation with him throughout the various great rooms of his fancy house on the hill, and even if by unspoken signals communicated to him that it would be all right with her, should they find themselves alone in the library or the summer kitchen or the sunroom, if they made out a little.

Jordan, Benchy said somewhat righteously, didn't really matter at all. He was just the handsome tricycle the world meant her to pedal a few yards down the road to recovery, and once she saw that she could see he wasn't actually necessary to the work. She could just lie here and transport herself, by force of will, those same few yards. Anyway, she wasn't at home, and not being home alone was as important as being at the party.

Benchy agreed, not exactly speaking in a recurrence of the voice that had talked to her as a kid. It was more that the habit of listening to such voices had recurred after Ryan died, though she had a very different relationship to them as a woman than she did as a girl. The purple lesbian spoke in soothing tones, but she accused more than she comforted. Getting over it, as she stressed in her last chapters, was hard work, and hard work looked a lot more like forcing a smile at Jordan Sasscock and his friends than it looked like lying on a bench with your fingers dragging in the grass. Her friends were even more accusatory, and went so far as to suggest that any activity that did not somehow aerobically denounce her attachment to Ryan was a wallow. "A wallow by any other name," said Gus, and Tyler added, more gently, that genuine recovery, whether it was from failed romance or grief or both, was always complicated, but a party would be good for her. "No Jesus, no peace," said her mother, and Molly reacted like she always did when her mother brought her intrusive thoughts of Jesus, and briefly imagined giving Him a blow job. The mother in her head kept in touch much more aggressively than her actual mother did and had to be managed differently, with shocking images that frightened her away into some stale gray heaven where everyone loved one another with a perfect absence of feeling, though Molly had once in a latter teenage rage actually said, to her actual mother, that Jesus could suck *her* dick.

"It's not safe here," said another voice, which Molly didn't recognize. She opened her eyes and sat up. It wasn't beyond her imagination and her irrational mind to gang up on her and introduce a voice before there was a face to go along with it—that had happened with Ms. Grimace, the goofy baritone preceding the big purple lesbian's entrance onto her mind's stage, though only by a few moments—but this voice had sounded real. Molly looked around, but she was alone with the trees.

"Hello?" she said.

"It's not safe here," the voice said again. "You must come with me."

She looked up in the branches, expecting to see a park ranger or a home-less person there, but they were empty. "I'm over here," the voice said, and then it was obvious that it was coming from one of the trees, not because there was someone lounging in the branches but because she had mistaken the speaker for a tree. He—it was a man's voice, though the person did not look particularly male or female—was at least seven feet tall, was dressed in leaves and twigs, and looked like he was made out of string. Molly had seen any number of unusual skin conditions in her brief foray into hospital chaplaincy, so she did not initially categorize him as an impossible creature. There were children that looked like gnomes and hobbits and goblins, and seeing them and talking to them was no slur upon a person's sanity, so he didn't, on first glance, make her worry about hers.

"Huh?" she said.

"It's not safe here. The Beast is loose on the hill, and we are trapped with him inside the walls of air which my Lord, in his lamentable absence and considerable wisdom, has thrown up on the borders. The Beast can't get out, and neither can we, and oh, he is very upset!"

"Actually, I was just leaving," Molly said.

"You cannot *leave*," the man said. "My Lord has thrown up impassable walls of air. We're all trapped. Trapped!" Molly peered at him. He was wringing his hands together and, looking closely at his arms, she could see how little stringy bits were coming off his forearms and elbows; he looked quite literally to be coming unspooled.

"It'll be all right," she said cautiously, because it seemed like the right thing to tell him, but also because it seemed like a good thing to tell her-self. A closer look at him had made her afraid, not of whatever beast he was talking about, but of her own mind. She had spent the last two years waiting for a breakdown that never properly came: a perpetual sneaky feel-ing that sandwiches were going to start talking to her never matured into an actual conviction that she could talk to sandwiches; the feeling that Ryan was still around, no less a part of her life than when he was alive, never became a feeling that he *really* was still around; and she was always only convinced that dead was dead. He wasn't watching her from some shining spirit abode. He wasn't in Heaven and he wasn't in Hell, and though she talked to him all the time she knew he wasn't listening. And while she very actively imagined scoldings from her mother and the big lesbian and even from Jesus himself, she never actually saw those people talking to her, and when they spoke she only heard them with her mind's ear.

On closer inspection, the thin man was a lot stranger-looking than she had taken him for initially. His eyes had a moldy glow about them, and she was reasonably sure he didn't have any ears, and his joints seemed all out of place—his waist was too low and his elbows were too high and his neck was much too long. As unreal as he looked, though, nothing about him suggested to her that she was dreaming. Still, when she stood up she did a little jump, trying to fly, because that was the way she always tested her sleeping dreams. She'd interrupted more than one unpleasant dinner with her family, or naked classroom presentation, or uncanny and terrifying reunion with Ryan by putting down her fork or her laser pointer or her doughnut and saying, "Excuse me, but I think I can fly." Then she'd leap up and fly away into wakefulness. She didn't excuse herself to the man now but made a little leap, which took her nowhere.

"The walls are round on top," he said. "They make a dome. Up is also no escape. But were you trying to fly? I've never met a mortal who could fly." He said this as if trying to fly were the most natural thing in the world.

"I wasn't . . ." Molly said. "I'm going to go now."

"Exactly!" he said. "Come along." He held a hand out to her. She didn't really look at it. "You might not be safe with me, either. But at least you won't be alone."

"Maybe we could just walk together for a while," Molly said, because she wanted to get moving but she didn't want to make him angry. She was afraid, all of a sudden, of what she had in store for herself. She had thought it might be a relief, when her break finally arrived, because the waiting would finally be over and she would be delivered from anxious anticipation into careless fancy-free psychosis. But this wasn't a relief.

"Very well," he said, "as long as it is this way and not that way." He pointed in opposite directions, crossing his arms across his chest. She started walking, across the hill to her left, and he followed beside her. "Pardon me for staring," he said as they went, "but it's been a long time since I've seen a mortal up close like this. You have very nice skin."

"Thanks," Molly said, not looking at him. He was very interesting to look at, but she didn't particularly want to see him close up. The closer she looked, the more real and unreal he seemed—noticing new details made her more certain she wasn't dreaming, but revealed him to look weirder and weirder and weirder. He was, she realized, a good candidate to escort her off into lunacy. She slowed down, pausing before every step, and he gave her a little push. "Don't . . ." she said, meaning to tell him not to touch her, but even as she said it she realized it was too late. She started running anyway, thinking that if she just tried hard enough, or concentrated hard enough as she ran, the trees would part and the fog would lift, and she would find herself shortly on Jordan's doorstep. She hurried away down a path that petered out before she'd drawn ten heavy breaths, and then she was running among trees, ducking branches and leaping over fallen logs. It was an unchanging scene—white trees and white fog and dark wet grass—and she felt as she ran as if she could do it forever and never get any farther than the next white tree. That was not so terrible. It was nice just to be running from the awful certainty of the touch of that weird man; it was one thing to see him and hear him, but to feel him was evidence that she had finally and truly lost it. She calmed but did not slow, and realized she was running from that certainty, and that it was okay to run because here in this state of flight she could inhabit a last liminal sanity. It was okay to run—she wasn't disappointed in herself and nothing anyone, real or imagined, could say would make her feel any differently— but sprinting through the woods made obvious just how much energy it took to run, and she started to feel tired, not just on account of the past five minutes of swift flight but on account of the whole past two years, on account of what seemed, in running reflection, like a titanic effort to stave off something she maybe ought to have just welcomed long before. What she had done over the past year had required an equivalent expenditure of energy to a year-long sprint, and when she thought of it that way it was obviously an unreasonable thing to do. Remaining sane—clinging and grasping at it, seeking to please a propriety constructed by people whose boyfriends had never killed themselves—was in fact the most insane thing she could have done, and anyone properly equipped by the right kind of experience would understand that. Funny, she thought, how all it took was a breakdown—or really just the beginning of a breakdown, since she had probably only dipped her toe in it so far—to make everything so clear.

"You are a very nimble mortal!" the man said, running next to her. "But you can slow down now. We're almost there!" That certainly seemed true to Molly. She was almost there. She had almost reached a place where everything would seem different, a place where her life would change again, in measure with the change that came with Ryan's death, and so what if that change came at the cost of her sanity? So what, really, if it was a change for the worse? She would be happy just to have a change. She sped up, hurrying toward it even though the man told her again to slow down, and shortly exhausted the trees. A clearing opened up in front of a flat face of rock in the side of the hill. She stopped running and stood there, too much out of breath to talk to any of the other people standing around. She leaned over with her hands on her thighs and craned her neck to look at them, a man and a boy.

"Welcome, brother!" said the boy, who was wearing a partial bunny costume, just the furry bottom and the tail and the feet, and was dressed in pair of baggy shorts held up with suspenders. "You found one too! I had two, but one got away. I win! I win!"

"I had three," said the man who had brought Molly. "But two declined to come with me. And no one wins."

"You look normal," said the other man in the clearing, who was not dressed in a costume and looked to be made of ordinary flesh, and was in fact quite normal-looking if you excused how obviously terrified he was, a tall pudgy dude in a plaid shirt. He wasn't bad-looking, and Molly could not think why her unhinged mind would have conjured him. He was missing a shoe.

"I'm not," Molly said.

"Did you see that thing?" he asked.

"Is this all we've collected?" asked Molly's escort. "Two mortals? There are more on the hill—I heard their voices. Our Lord will be sad with us."

"What thing?" Molly asked.

"Our Lord will be sad," said the boy, "as our Lady is sad. And sadness repels sadness. But shouldn't it attract?" He ran up and pulled on Molly's skirt. "Does like not cleave to like?"

"That thing," said the dude. "That lady. Except she wasn't a lady."

"You mean she was a trannie?" Molly asked. The dude shook his head and gave her a look—he seemed scared and solicitous at the same time, and Molly thought for sure that if he had not been standing ten feet away he would have taken her hand.

"Do you know what's going on?" he asked.

"Yes," she said. "I know exactly what's going on." Before she could give him the details—bad career choice, dead boyfriend, persistent failure of psychological recovery, and final florid breakdown—they were interrupted by the arrival of two more men. An old man, small beyond any reasonable shrinkage of age, came huffing and puffing into the clearing, dragging another, normal-sized man by the legs. The dragger was dressed in a perfectly pressed linen suit; the draggee wore nothing from the waist down. "Look," she said to the man in the plaid shirt. "Now it's getting interesting." And she tried to decide which was a more extravagant effort on the part of her demented imagination, a man with no pants or a tiny grandpa in a nice suit or a boy with a bunny tail—as he pulled on her skirt and jumped up and down beside her, she decided that his tail was not a costume.

"Look what I found!" said the tiny grandpa, who seemed to get smaller instead of bigger as he got closer. "I win. Smell him. He's special. I win!"

"I had two," said Bunny Boy. "I win!"

"I had three," said the Tree. "But . . ."

"Smell him! There's something special. Something *awful*. It's more points, when they're special."

"It's not!" said Bunny Boy. "Whoever gets two and loses one is the winner. Those are the *rules*."

"There are no rules!" said the Tree. "This is not a game. This is an *emergency*!"

"It's a game!" said Bunny Boy. "If we're all going to die anyway, I want it to be a game!"

"Will you please just smell him!" Tiny Grandpa shouted. The three of them glared at one another, but the other two went over and sniffed grudgingly at the man with no pants, who stirred a little at the pressure of the Bunny Boy's nose.

"I thought he was dead," said the dude in the plaid shirt.

"Why would he be dead?" Molly asked, really talking to herself, asking not just why would she present herself with a pantless dead man, but why the little grandpa and the bunny boy and why a talking tree? *I had the strangest dream*, she said to herself. *And you were there, and you were there, and you were there, too.* There were already midgets—über-midgets, actually, or under-midgets. She wondered if there would be flying monkeys, and if she would kill a witch and wake up whole of mind.

"Because something horrible is happening."

"I see what you mean," said the Tree. "Distinctive." He prodded the man with a foot. "Are you sure he's a mortal?"

"He is too ugly to be anything else," said Bunny Boy. "But special, I agree. In the worst way." He craned his neck down to sniff at the man's bottom. "There's something awful in there!"

"I think it would help me," said the dude in the plaid shirt, "if I knew somebody's name." He stuck out his hand to Molly and said, "I'm Will."

"I'm Eleanor Roosevelt," Molly said, not taking his hand, but two things happened before he could reply. Raccoons and squirrels started zipping through the clearing, all coming from the side Molly had entered on and then vanishing up the hill, and the weirder three of the six people now in the clearing all turned their heads at once to look back into the trees.

"Oh, no!" said Bunny Boy.

"We are not safe here!" said Tiny Grandpa.

"He's coming," said the Tree.

"That . . . thing?" said the dude in the plaid shirt.

"Inside! Inside!" said the Tree. "We can bar the door against him! Quickly! Quickly!" He was shouting at Molly while the other two dragged the unconscious man toward the cave. They had him by both legs and a hand, but their heights were too uneven to carry him smoothly, and he bounced on the grass. Molly sat down.

"I can't wait to see what's next," she said.

"Lady!' said the Tree. "Fly!" But Molly crossed her legs and looked to the trees. The Tree jumped up and down, looking like he had to pee. She started to laugh at him, until she saw what was coming out of the woods. It was just a black boy waving underpants over his head and shouting, which should not have been a terrifying sight, but she was terrified of him and was running before she had even decided to stand up. She was sure, in the portion of a second that it seemed to take to get into the cave, that this was the fastest she had ever run in her life. She registered the size of the cave—not actually a cave but a hall as big as a church—but had no attention to spare to marvel at it.

"Shut the door!" she said. "Shut the door!" They were already doing that, the man named Will helping to draw shut two giant wooden doors. She was positioned deep inside the room, but she could still see the boy, in the space between the closing doors, getting nearer and nearer. The man with no pants was just behind her; when she stepped back she stepped on him.

"Don't touch me!" he cried out, standing up as the doors slammed shut. They dropped a wooden bar down across them, but still the Tree was shouting, "The bar! The bar!"

"I've got it!" said Bunny Boy, holding up a large black button. The doors shook as if something considerably more massive than a little boy had hurled itself on them. Bunny Boy dropped the button, the doors shook again, and the left door cracked near its lower hinge. Tiny Grandpa picked up the button and stuck it on the door. The noise of the assault was curiously muffled, but two strikes later it was loud again and the right-hand door started to crack.

"Don't touch me!" said the man with no pants. He was fully awake now, backing away from Molly.

"We are going to die," said Bunny Boy. "We are not supposed to die!"

"Don't touch me!" the man with no pants said again, and tripped over a long bench. Molly reached for him, too far away to help. Something turned in her stomach as he fell; she almost threw up and had to sit down for dizziness. There was another noise at the doors, just a little thump this time, and when Molly looked back at them she saw the wood had become iron.

"Hooray!" said Bunny Boy, bouncing over to give Molly a hug. "Did you do that?"

"No," she said, sinking down to the floor and putting her hands over her ears to try to drown out the noise of Peabo knocking to come in.

"I'm flying!" Molly said.

"No, you're not!" Ryan called back.

"I *feel* like I'm flying," she said.

"*This* isn't what flying feels like," he said. It had been his idea to roller-skate across the Golden Gate Bridge. At first Molly had been pretty luke-warm about it. It was a long way from his house in the Mission to the Presidio, and there were some really enormous hills in between the two neighborhoods. Ryan rushed along without seeming to make any actual effort to go, and rolled down the hills with abandon, while Molly managed to trudge both up and down the hills, reduced to walking sideways down the steepest parts because she was afraid of the speed. She worried even more about Ryan, as he raced through the stop signs on the way down out of Pacific Heights, and had to swerve around a car coming through the intersection of Scott Street and Broadway. He was so fast, and he looked very much like he knew what he was doing, but that didn't stop her from picturing him with his head broken open and his brains glisten-ing in the lovely golden afternoon light he was always admiring. She would berate herself later for never putting together habits of speeding and dashing through stop signs, or pausing when they passed over the bridge to stare at long length over the rail at the water churning violently around the caissons, that time and every time, with a tendency toward sui-cide. The lesbian said the third key to surviving a suicide was understand-ing totally that there was nothing you could have done to prevent it, but Molly didn't believe that at all.

She had shown up at Ryan's house on Fourteenth Street on a pair of Rollerblades, which had made him laugh. "Rollerblades are for homos," he said, and rooted with her in his huge basement, which was full of bicycles and newspapers and empty suitcases, acres of detritus from the hoarding previous owner. There was a whole shelf full of skates, some so old they needed keys. She picked a seventies-vintage pair, red and white, slightly too big but possessed of lovely soft pompoms. She held her breath, looking around while Ryan beat the dust out of them. She liked his basement, though she found the house in general a little overwhelming. It wasn't the first surprising thing she had learned about him, that he lived alone in a five-story house with seven bedrooms and a fireman's pole that dropped into the basement from the third floor and a luxuriously overgrown courtyard garden in whose center grew a strange oak tree with golden leaves and silver bark that smelled like cinnamon. But it felt like the representative surprise, that he lived in a dilapidated mansion filled with a lot of garbage, some boring, some disturbing, and some delightful, that he would probably never sort through. She had spent time alone down there—taking the stairs, not the pole—while he was out or sleeping or distracted with work; she still didn't entirely understand what he did for a living, which was some kind of consulting work that involved the occasional business trip and frenetic periods of computer activity that punctuated his usual idleness at intervals of two or three weeks. He had bought the house when he came to San Francisco three years before. "Oh, I don't know," he said, when she asked why he had chosen it. "It just seemed like the right place. Sort of like where I belonged." When he told her it had been boarded up for fifteen years, it explained some of the time-capsule feel of the place, and when he told her what he had paid for it, she asked him why he hadn't gotten someplace nicer. That seemed to wound him a little.

"It *is* nice," he said. "It's interesting. It's full of history."

"I like it," Molly said hurriedly. "I didn't mean to sound like I didn't like it." That made him shrug and smile. He hadn't touched a thing since he moved in, though he allowed Molly very slowly to start making over a room or two. At first this only involved adding things, not taking anything away. "That has sentimental value," he'd said, when she tried to take away a lamp shaped like a tuna or an ashtray that neither of them ever used.

"But it's not even yours," she'd replied. "It came with the house."

"I know," he said. "But still." Eventually he relented a little and let her start to exchange things out of other parts of the house, or the basement, and she funneled the tackiest elements into two rooms on the second floor, concentrating the tastelessness there. Bigger than her whole apartment, the basement was mysterious and a little scary. She had a running game of trying to count all the bicycles when she was down there, and she never seemed to get the same number twice. There were walls filled with bottled preserves, with some pickled creatures set here and there among them, as if to trick the unwary into spreading fetal pig on their English muffin, and jars stuffed with leaves and herbs and roots. Molly had sniffed randomly at them. There was pot and hash mixed in randomly with sage and rosemary, and herbs she'd never encountered before, with smells she recognized but couldn't associate with any plant: old couch, cheesy feet, blood, warm television. He only shrugged when she asked him anything about the old owners, about why the house sat abandoned for so long, or why they needed dozens of bicycles, or why they bottled hamsters in their basement, or kept a cage and a spanking post and a pair of stocks. "It's San Francisco," was all he would ever say in speculation. "People do all sorts of things here."

He darted ahead of her on his skates and went around her in circles as she made her plodding way across the seemingly endless expanse of Crissy Field. There was a strong headwind coming through the Golden Gate; Ryan acted like he didn't feel it at all. It was something she wouldn't ordinarily have liked to do, skate-plodding into another county, but doing it with him made it a delightful use of her time. There were all sorts of these things she would ordinarily have found incredibly boring if not actually unpleasant, but which became fun in his company, and sometimes, looking back on what things were like before she met him, it seemed that her whole life had been an unpleasant use of her time and he had changed that. She had tried to tell him as much, but the closest she had come was saying to him, as they sat among the remains of a picnic lunch underneath the golden oak, was, "I'm having a really good time just sitting here with you." He was lying on his back with one arm around her; she was curled against his side; he was staring up at the leaves. He didn't answer in words but gave her a squeeze, which she took to mean what she wanted it to, that he was as happy as she was, though he seemed in that moment, and sometimes in others, to be more distracted than happy or sad.

Sausalito, it turned out, was rather a long way away, even with wheels on your shoes. She got tired, though Ryan pulled her along, or pushed her from behind, and they stopped half a mile or so from the bridge, trespassing in somebody's horse pasture. "Doing nothing with you is my favorite thing in the world," she said to him, and they lay about silently in the warm, scented grass, in a variety of positions, his head on her chest, her head on his arm, her heavy skated feet on his belly. After half an hour or so of rolling and sprawling, he suggested that they move along, and she said, "In a minute." Her head was very near his crotch—she only needed to turn her head to roll her face into his dick, which was not particularly obscured by his short shorts. It had been a long time since she had wondered, as she fucked somebody, what her father or her mother would think about it, but there was something about doing it in the open, and underneath the gigantic blue bowl of sky, which her father had once described to her as Jesus' big blue eyeball, that brought them to mind. It didn't bother her at all to think, as she suddenly did, that Jesus was going to run tattling to her father, or even to think, as she did next, of her parents gathered round to watch with solemn, disapproving faces. She even gave an extra little thrust here for her father, and dedicated a tickle of Ryan's balls to her mother, and said to herself and to them, This is what it's like to be really happy.

"What's the worst thing that ever happened to you?" she asked him at dinner. He was picking at a bowl of gray seafood stew. It was a limited choice of restaurants that would let them in on roller skates, and this place at least had a lovely view of the city, which was lit up behind him, so if she squinted it looked as if he was wearing the architecture of the higher hills like a hat.

"What sort of question is that?" he asked, looking up and frowning.

"I don't know," she said. "I was just thinking I don't know that about you." Actually, it was Salome who had thought it up. She had her own ongoing one-sided relationship with Ryan, conducted through the occasional conversation when he came to the shop and, much more significantly, through serial interrogations of Molly as she worked, exercises that always made Molly feel a little defensive, since they seemed intended as much to criticize her fund of knowledge about her beloved as to actually learn about him. "You don't know where he was born?" Salome had asked, managing to sound innocent and arch at the same time, and she was similarly surprised by Molly's ignorance of his sister's age, his grandparents' countries of origin, and the particulars of his job. "But darling," she'd said, "you've been dating for six months and you don't know him *at all*," to which Molly had replied that she knew what was important about him, he was a genuinely good person, and she'd known as much after only a few hours. Salome had made a face like Molly had a host of beetles crawling in her hair, and shaken her head solemnly, and said, "No, no, no, no, no." She'd retreated to the back room without another word, and returned an hour later with her desk-sized calendar, marked through the next month with questions of increasing significance for Molly to ask Ryan, in a four-week program. "How can you know if you love him," Salome asked, "if you don't really know him?" Molly didn't see what one thing had to do with the other, but it wasn't something she was going to argue about with lonely, neurotic old Salome, who was all theory and no practice. She took the calendar pages and used them to line her cat box. Still, the questions rattled around in her head, and she asked one every now and then, telling herself it didn't actually matter if Ryan answered them or not.

"Oh," he said. "I think it's probably this fish stew."

"It's a dumb question," she said. She quietly put her own answer—*my family*—back inside herself.

"Not dumb," he said, "just hard to answer."

"Too hard to pick one?"

"No. I just . . . don't remember. I have a hard time holding on to some stuff. It's probably for the best, right? Something you can't remember or describe shouldn't have any bearing on your life now. If it's already forgotten, it should be let go. Right?"

"Yes," Molly said, rather hesitantly. "Are you saying something happened to you that was so bad you can't remember it, or that the bad things were too trivial to remember?"

"No," he said, laughing. "I'm saying I'd rather pay attention to the good things. What's the best thing that ever happened to you?"

"Oh, that's easy," she said. "You, hands down." Now she was smiling too.

"See?" he said. "You too. Hands up, hands down, hands sideways, hands everywhere." He reached under the table and groped at her belly and her groin.

"Stop," she said, not actually wanting him to stop.

She fell asleep on the ferry back to San Francisco, nestled against him to hide from the wind on the outside deck. He kept waking her to look at passing marvels: the hulking dark blob of Angel Island and the lights of Alcatraz and a disturbance in the water that he swore was a whale and finally the approaching city. "Look at that," he said, again and again. "I *love* that."

"Yes," she said, half-awake, "lovely." She was half-drunk and half-sad, trying not to imagine a burden of secret sorrow for him but failing intermittently, heaving like the boat in and out of troughs of dispiriting fancy, wishing she could dwell solely on the nice thing he had told her. She slept again, not dreaming but aware in her sleep that she wanted the journey back to take a very long time, so she could stay curled up against him with her head in his lap, and she stayed groggy, rather willfully, as he led her off the boat and into a cab, as they rode along the Embarcadero and up Market Street, and even as he led her inside the house and upstairs to bed. She was sober by then, and not that tired anymore, but she let him undo her skates and take off her shorts and even undo the scrunchie from her hair, never opening her eyes until he kissed them.

"Hello there," she said.

"Good night," he said.

"I love you," she said, never having said it before, and the courage or daring or gall to say it might have seemed to come from nowhere, except that it was the perfect thing to say to his evasion, and to Salome's dissatisfaction, because that was a lady who would never understand if Molly told her she was saying it as much to what she didn't know about him as to what she did.

"I love you too," he said, with no hesitation at all, and then he turned out the light.

10

*H*enry was not an excitable person. It was a legacy of his old self that it still took a lot to get him worked up. In the past, that had been because nothing potentially upsetting had ever seemed entirely real to him, though he would never have described the situation to himself that way, back in the bad old good old days. Back then he thought he was just being careful not to follow his mother's example. She had spent the majority of her days in some sort of a tizzy and had developed over the course of her life a tizzy repertoire of abundant variety, from the black depressive tizzy to the anxious weepy tizzy to the more traditional furious tizzy, which almost always involved projectiles. Henry thought he had made a healthy choice not to be like her, in the same way he had chosen not to smoke or dabble in drugs, and it was a very late discovery that he was generally unflappable not because he was better than his mother but because he was his own special sort of monster.

Equanimity was easy, it turned out, when you were insulated from reality by a sustained assurance that nothing that happened could actually matter. His mother would have found it vindicating to hear that whatever had happened to him in the lost years of his abducted youth had in fact nearly ruined the rest of his life, that the still-unremembered trauma had kicked him out of the world to a place where he watched dispassionately as all the subsequent despairs and delights of his life passed by, somehow unfelt even as he experienced them, until Bobby came along, called attention to the arrangement, and disrupted it. The kindly therapist he'd engaged at Bobby's insistence had pointed out that it wasn't the unre-membered trauma but only his reaction to it that ultimately mattered, and it was not too late, after twenty years, to choose against his mother after all. And that was what Henry thought he had done, long after Bobby dumped him, when he finally realized that he would rather forfeit the hand washing and the bleaching and the constant guarding anxiety—to leave his state of comfortable dissociation, move back to San Francisco, and expose himself to whatever it was exactly that it was keeping at bay—than to live without Bobby.

So it was enormously dispiriting to wake up in a panicked state of ruin. Disoriented and knowing that something was horribly wrong, he opened his eyes, too upset to take things in except in pieces: an iron door, a girl, a handsome man in a plaid shirt, the great space all around them, a hall hung with tapestries he couldn't bear to look at.

"Don't touch me!" he said to all of them, standing up and falling down and standing up again. He stood up and realized he wasn't wearing any pants.

"If you didn't do it," said a boy Henry had failed to notice in his first look at the room, "who did?" He looked at Henry. "Did you do it?"

"Don't touch me!" Henry said, because he especially did not want to be touched by that boy, who should have seemed cute instead of terrify-ing, with his baby-blue shorts and red suspenders and fake rabbit tail and bunny slippers made to look like bunny feet, not bunnies. Henry hid his cock and his balls with his hands—for no reason at all he was getting a boner—and backed away toward the wall.

"No one is touching you," the girl said, and Henry started to cry, because he had promised absent, rejecting Bobby that he would never say those words to anybody ever again. He said them again and again as he backed up against the wall, understanding as he spoke what sort of cata-strophic backsliding it represented.

"It's okay, buddy," said the handsome man in the plaid shirt. "Nobody's going to touch you. Just take a breath. Something really fucked up is going on."

Henry took a longer look around the hall, appreciating just how big it was, and thinking as he looked of all the things that would fit inside it: elephants and cement trucks and hospital lobbies. He squinted at the tap-estries and looked away from them again. His eyes fell down to the people who were staring at him. They had all walked forward to surround him in a half ring, the little ones spaced between the big ones. He noticed the girl a little more distinctly, and recognized that she was kind of pretty, and noticed that the handsome man had taken off his shirt for some reason, revealing a beefy, hairy torso and a tattoo on his shoulder of some kind of spring tree in bloom. He got a better look as well at the boy with the fake tail, and the little man who, he realized now, had accosted him in the clearing, and the tall man with uncontrolled psoriasis. That one looked back nervously over his shoulder when the door shook again.

"Are you well?" asked the little man in the suit.

"Don't—" Henry started to say again, because it seemed to him that the whole half circle was leaning forward, about to get grabby, and this caused his panic to rise and rise until it crested. Then something broke in him, or a circuit tripped; suddenly the five of them seemed very far away, though the handsome man was leaning forward with his shirt held out, and the whole unfamiliar and confused situation, which a moment before had felt like a deadly crisis, didn't matter so much at all. He knew the feeling: the serene, dead detachment of a mind divorced from its feelings. It made him want to cry, because this was exactly the sort of thing that wasn't supposed to happen anymore, now that he had proven Bobby wrong and become, at long last, kind of a normal person. "I'm fine," he said, taking the plaid shirt the beefy guy was holding out to him and wrapping it around his waist.

"Take mine, take mine!" said the boy with the bunny tail, holding out a pair of blue shorts and suspenders identical to the ones he was wearing.

"I'm okay," said Henry.

"Did you do it?" said the boy.

"Do what?"

"The door, the door! I didn't do it. Lyon didn't do it. Who did it?"

"What?" Henry asked.

"Something fucked up is going on," said the beefy guy. "Maybe someone should start from the beginning. I'm Will." He pointed to himself, as if Henry was going to have a hard time understanding his introduction. The door shook again, and all of them but Henry shuddered.

"In the beginning," said the psoriatic, "there was the Beast. My Master bound him and then, in grief, my Mistress set him free. That is the whole story."

"Well," said the little man in the suit, "it's a little more complicated than *that*."

"I'm Will," said the handsome fatty, sticking his hand out to everyone in turn. "Will's my name." The boy with the tail took his hand and shook it enthusiastically but didn't say what his name was.

"My name is Lyon," said the psoriatic. "That is Oak." He pointed at Bunny Boy and reached out a hand to touch the little man in the suit. "This is Fell. We are all good servants of our Master, and therefore of our Mistress, and for these reasons we are trying to help you. You were in danger outside, so we brought you in. Our Master always bade us to escort mortals off the hill, if they wandered in. But there's no way off the hill tonight."

"I wouldn't normally be helping you at all," said Oak.

"Oh, I would have helped you," said Fell, speaking directly to Henry. "I don't quite know why, but I like you, my boy. I like you just fine!"

"What's your name?" Will asked Henry. He snapped his fingers right under Henry's nose, but they still seemed very far away. Henry felt like his head was floating up near the ceiling, and like watching everyone from above should give him not just a high perspective but a long one, and it should all make sense somehow.

"Henry," he said. "I'm Henry." He was floating but not floating, calling his name out from the ceiling and speaking it softly on the ground. He was there but not there, and that allowed him to act very calm. Funny, he thought, how often he had described his old self, to Bobby and his therapist, to coworkers and dates and even random tricks, as a dissociated creature, when he hadn't fully understood what that word meant until just now. He was in his body but above and around it too, and it felt not like he could do anything but like anything could be done to him without his much minding or noticing, which seemed its own sort of superpower.

"This is . . ." Will said, indicating the girl with his thumb. "What did you say your name was?"

"Tallulah Marie Jingleheimer Schmidt," she said. Henry tilted his head and frowned at her. "What are you looking at?" she asked him, which made him frown more. On closer inspection, she wasn't that pretty after all, but there was something pleasing about her to look at. He thought it might just be that she was troubled looking.

"What's wrong with you?" asked Will. "Why won't you tell us your name? And why are you being so hostile?"

"Why am I being so *hostile*?" She waved her arms around, indicating everything around them.

"Well, we're all in this together," Will said.

"Not really," she said. The door shook again, and they all looked at it. Will and the girl both shuddered again, and the three others all made a gesture, touching their thumbs and index fingers together to make a sign that looked to Henry like okay! but he could tell it was meant to ward something away.

"Somebody's knocking," Henry said.

"Can she . . . Can it get in?" Will asked.

"Maybe," said the three creatures. Looking at them a little more closely, Henry could not figure out a better word for them. They became more abnormal the closer he examined them. He noticed little details—string for skin, purple eyes, a knee that was jointed backward—which made it increasingly clear that they weren't actually human. *Of course they're not human*, he said to himself, and he could not understand why that was both a relief and a terror, or why he could accept it with a calm that was equal, in his new binary state, to the shrieking panic he was also feeling.

"Iron was a good choice," said Lyon. "I think perhaps it was my Master, watching over us in spirit. Who else would choose so wisely, and what other faerie is mighty enough to summon so much iron?"

"Master!" said Oak, running up to the front of the room and falling on his knees to prostrate himself before an empty high-backed chair set there on a dais. "Master, show your face!"

"Faeries," said Will, looking at each of the three in turn and walking backward away from Lyon, who was standing close to him.

"There's no such thing," Henry said.

"Of course not!" Molly said, shoving Will away violently when he backed into her. "They're not real. I made them up. I made *you* up. Do you know who that is out there?" She glared at him and then at Henry. "Stop looking at me!" she said, and started crying before she ran away down the long hall, her footsteps echoing off the stone walls.

"Wait!" said Will, and she called back, "Shut up shut up shut *up*!"

"Mortals," said Oak. "They always think they're dreaming."

"Maybe we are," Henry said, though what was happening felt unreal in a completely different way from a dream.

"I don't think so," said Will. "But I'm still waiting to hear what's happening. And shouldn't we go get her? Something might be dangerous in there." He pointed toward the darkness at the far end of the hall.

"Many things are dangerous there," said Lyon, "but nothing as dangerous as what lies in the opposite direction. We should all go her way. There's another door, down at the bottom of the hill, known only to my Lord's most trusted servants."

"Everyone knows that door," said Fell. "And who cares if we're eaten over the hill or under the hill? Eaten is eaten. Dead is dead. We may as well stay right here."

"Our Lord is coming!" said Oak, still prostrate before the empty throne. "He'll save us all," he added, very quietly. Henry had been wondering if the boy was capable of talking without shouting. He walked across the hall and up on the dais, and laid his hand upon the wood. It felt like an infraction to touch it, he didn't know why. He gave it a kick for no reason at all. "A great ass rested there!" said Oak, shouting again, and Henry shrugged. "But maybe . . ." Oak said. "Maybe you should sit." He leaped up and sniffed at Henry's bottom. "Is that what I smell?" He pushed Henry back into the chair, saying, "Look, the King is reclaimed by his throne!" and watched expectantly as nothing happened. It felt like a worse infraction to be sitting there, and there wasn't any naughty joy in it. Henry stood up. "You didn't change, my Lord," said Oak, and started to cry.

"Yes I did," Henry said. "But now I've changed back." Oak had already run to get Will. He dragged him over to the chair and sat him down.

"This is really uncomfortable," Will said.

"A mortal is a mortal," said Lyon. "These ones are no different from any others."

"Alas! Alas!" said Oak. The door shook again, and they all cringed, but Henry didn't cringe. He was protected, he supposed, from whatever regular capacity for feeling made them sensitive to the thing that was trying to get them. He tried and failed to imagine what it looked like.

"What does it look like?" he asked. "This beastie."

"Not a *beastie*," said Oak. "Haven't you been listening at all?"

"The Beast looks different to everyone who sees it," said Lyon.

"But is uniformly terrible to behold," said Fell.

"Can we get moving?" asked Will. "I think I just saw a bolt jiggle."

"I'll just stay," Henry said. "I've gone about as far as I want to." That was true. He found, when he thought about it, that he was a little more afraid of what lay beyond the hall than he was of what lay behind the door.

"You can't," said Will. "Look, we should stick together. We're all in this together."

"You keep saying that," Henry said. "But it isn't really true. I don't even know you. Or you, or you, or you."

"But we are all caught up in my Lady's mistake," said Lyon.

"Maybe she has a plan!" said Oak.

"And we are all going to die together," said Fell.

"I wish you would stop saying that," said Will.

"See you later," Henry said. He sat down and closed his eyes and decided not to open them again until they had left and the great room was quiet except for the periodic ringing of the doors. Then he would open up his eyes, and he would decide what to do. He understood the girl a little better now. A person needed a little solitude to know what to do in a situation like this. He could imagine following after them, when they were gone, deciding they had not been so annoying after all and that getting out from this place was worth the probable unpleasantness involved in penetrating deeper into it. But he could imagine, too, getting up after they left to see who was knocking so insistently on the door. He didn't know whether that was because he didn't believe these unbelievable creatures when they told him that a death-dealing monster was waiting on the other side of the door, or because he did believe them. He suspected they were all worked up for nothing—that they were trying to trick him—and if he opened the door it would be Holly Hobby on the other side, offering up a plate of cookies. And he suspected as well that there really was a monster out there, something that would rip him to pieces or crush his head or strangle him to death.

He was imagining what that would be like—his thoughts falling into familiar rutted tracks as he imagined a leisurely fade into suffocating oblivion—when he realized he was moving, and opened his eyes. He was being carried in the chair, moving backward toward the shadow at the end of the hall. Will and Lyon were ahead of him, Oak was hopping along behind, and Fell was nowhere to be seen until Henry peered over the side of the chair and saw he was carrying it on his back and shoulders. "We just couldn't allow it," Fell said. "It would have displeased our Master severely to leave you to die, even though you're just going to die later. But that's better than dying now! Mostly. It is! No, you don't!" He felt Henry standing, about to jump out of the chair, and called to Oak, who jumped up in Henry's lap, much heavier than his size suggested he would be and too heavy to budge.

"I told you not to touch me," Henry said.

"You're not the boss of me," Oak said, and gave Henry a hug.

Henry followed Bobby across the breakwater. They'd come to Province-town early in April. It was windy and cold, and it rained briefly upon them during the long way across the harbor. Henry walked carefully on the big flat rock slabs strewn in a jumble. It was not his first New England spring, but it was his first time in Provincetown, though he'd recently watched some porn set here, in which the protagonist made this same journey over the breakwater and then got a blow job and a fucking in the shadow of the Woods End lighthouse. Henry watched Bobby placing his feet on the upward- and downward-slanting faces of the stone slabs, thinking of how he had trod infelicitously, back in Cambridge, on a place in Henry's drive-way, marked with an oil stain in the shape of a bird, where a letter from Henry's mother had fallen to the ground. Cambridge was far away, sepa-rated from them by a huge expanse of cleansing water, and yet Bobby still had a taint upon his shoe. Henry deliberately failed to avoid stepping where Bobby stepped, which seemed like progress. He had measured progress against his obsessions and compulsions in much smaller incre-ments back then.

"Look at that!" Bobby said, pointing out a half-sunken rowboat in the tidal flats, where a little crab was standing with its claws thrust upward. "I did it!" Bobby said, throwing his hands and arms up spastically, aping the crab's gesture. Henry had a patient, a little girl with Down syndrome, who said those words and made that gesture at every opportunity, celebrating every triumph and mistake of her day, whether it was winning a bingo game or wetting her bed. Doctors in general and pediatricians in particular were not supposed to make fun of retarded children, but making fun of them, and deformed children and dying children and especially dead babies, was actually a staple of the training. Henry had trouble trusting pediatricians who couldn't laugh at a nice dead-baby joke; it suggested to him somehow that they weren't sufficiently traumatized by their common experience. He laughed, and threw up his hands too, in ridicule of that little girl but also in solidarity with her, because all his own triumphs seemed comparably admirable and pathetic.

He caught up to Bobby and lost his balance jumping over a gap in the slabs. Bobby caught his hand and kept hold of it. Provincetown was still largely abandoned. Three-quarters of it was closed down, and there was hardly a homosexual in sight, except for their ancient innkeeper and his rubber-panted gimp, but even in its most remote reaches the town felt like a place where it was okay for two men to hold hands. Bobby had worried a lot in his youth about God striking him down for being gay, and Henry had had a corresponding worry—not restricted to his youth, and never really abandoned—that nature, abhorring him, would do the same thing. Provincetown countered with a more pleasant delusion: all the gayness that had loitered there had rubbed off on the rocks and water and sand, so nature smiled on you when you held hands with your boyfriend on the breakwater, or made out with him on the moors, or even if you made a pornographic video on the beach. "I like it here," he said to Bobby.

"Me too," Bobby said.

"I mean, really," Henry said, meaning that he liked being there with Bobby.

"Me too. Really. A lot." Bobby didn't smile, but he was wearing his happy face, which was a different sort of troubled look from the one he habitually wore. That was so much easier to accept, and to believe, Henry found, than a big Donny Osmond smile would have been. Who could trust Donny Osmond, with his perfect teeth and his perpetually sunny outlook, fermented in a wish-fulfilling Mormon cosmogony that knew absolutely nothing of the terrible real world? Bobby had just come back from a difficult rotation in Lesotho, and that made his relative absence of frown more reassuring and uplifting than any ignorant smile would have been.

He had been gone for a month, which gave Henry a long time to miss him and to admit how much he liked him. He had been storing up affection for Bobby somewhat in secret, not just from Bobby but from himself. He was in the habit of ignoring alarming developments for as long as he could, and so he ignored the fact that he was falling in love with Bobby until he started to pine for him. Bobby took up residence in Henry's imagination, and Henry followed him through his African day, making up details to supplement the ones Bobby supplied over the phone: identical cowboy-print short-sleeved shirts for the twin orphan boys unofficially adopted by the expatriate staff at the hospital where Bobby was working, who were a mix of smarty-pants do-gooders and ne'er-do-wells hiding out from the stateside consequences of their laziness and incompetence; a collar made of paper clips for the skinny dog that followed Bobby every morning on the short walk from his dormitory to the hospital; bright red nails on the woman brought to the emergency room in seizures, poisoned by her husband. The absence of the real-world Bobby made it possible for him to date an imaginary Bobby and to fall in love with him; much later, post-breakup and post-breakdown, he would wonder if he would ever have fallen in love with the real-world Bobby without falling in love with the imaginary version first. It was something he would figure out only after Bobby dumped him: that his imagination was what made the real world, and real people, only barely palatable for him.

He wasn't thinking at all in those terms, that day on the breakwater, but he did notice how solid everything looked and felt, the water sloshing heavily against the rocks and the heavy pressure of Bobby's hand in his. He didn't think about whether or not he was afraid of the real world, or worry if he was ever going to find a way to live in it, but he did appreciate how far away California and his mother seemed, and he appreciated how being with Bobby felt like something he didn't deserve to have and wasn't *supposed* to have which had come to him anyway, by oversight or charity or blind dumb luck.

"I like it here," he said to Bobby again. "I mean, I like it here with—" He stopped walking and listed toward the left, though the slab they were on was quite flat. The odd solidity of things intensified, and he felt a little nauseated all of a sudden. He wanted to shield his face from the water and the sky, from the moss and the mussels on the stones, and he wanted to shield his face from Bobby's face, but he didn't. "I really like it," he started again. "With you, here. I—"

Bobby stared at him, letting him fumble for a few moments before he cut him off. "I love you too," he said.

11

It finally occurred to Will to wonder about his sanity when the girl ran away in a bitter huff. He supposed it was possible that he had suffered a psychotic break on the way to Jordan Sasscock's party, that the prospect of seeing Carolina was too much to bear, and that now he was lying on his belly somewhere in the real Buena Vista Park, gnawing on tree roots and eating dirt, or else locked up in the ER at CPMC down at the foot of the hill, drooling and babbling while some social worker tried to get him to tell her his name. It was possible, but hardly seemed worth thinking about—the heft of the little bunny boy when he had leaped into Will's arms, the texture of the golden leaves on the cousin of Carolina's tree, and the chill bite of the air in his nose were enough to make everything seem undeniably real, and he was secure enough in his sanity to think that when something seemingly fantastical appeared his first assumption should be that the problem was with the world and not with his mind. And he considered, walking after a man who looked like a tree into the secret darkness under the hill, that this catastrophe, if that's what it was, got him off the hook, in a way, with Carolina, and maybe that was ultimately why he didn't care to question whether or not it was real. As much as the lady in the tree had terrified him, and as much as he was frightened by the talk about being killed, he was in some sense as relieved as he was agitated by the crisis, because his first thought was how it would change things with Carolina. He had all sorts of reasons now to break their silence. Faeries and monsters and a tree that looked just like hers: one had to talk about such

things, and the other had to listen, no matter how vile a history of transgression lay between them. And while the existence of faeries and monsters was no reason for him to be forgiven, it had the potential to distract
her enormously from the memory of his crimes, and the existence of
magic, monsters, and faeries brooked other impossibilities—getting back
together with her seemed much less impossible than what he'd seen this
evening. So thank goodness there existed in San Francisco a boy with a
real bunny tail (Will had pulled it shortly after Oak had intercepted him
in the park and led him to the door in the hill) growing out of his bottom,
and thank goodness a monster in the shape of a middle-aged divorcée with
a bad face-lift was threatening to do something atrocious to the faeries and
to Will and that girl and Henry, who had lost his pants. Thank God
Henry had lost his pants, however it had happened, and thank God the
girl was such an anxious bitch. It had all happened just as it had to for
Will to find Carolina in the morning and say, "You're not going to believe
this!" And maybe, he thought, somewhere under this hill there was a
sapling, a baby golden oak that he could bring back to her, evidence of the
impossible and proof that they could start over.

"Where are we going, exactly?" he asked Lyon. They had passed from
the brightly lit hall into shadow, and walked until the room narrowed
around them into a dimly lit corridor. There was a brighter light in the
back behind them, and another up ahead, and Lyon raised an arm and
hand to point toward one.

"Down, and deeper," he said. Will looked at his arm, resisting the urge
to pluck off one of the little threads that were sticking up off his rough
skin.

"And there's a way out, farther down and deeper in?"

"Eventually," Lyon said, and sighed. "Probably."

"Probably?" Will said.

"There is a general trend toward a door being at the bottom of the hill
as well as at the top of the hill. More than that, I can't really say."

Will stopped and put a hand on Lyon's shoulder. "I'd really like a
straight answer about this," he said.

"Of course you would," Lyon said. "Mortals always do." Henry yelled
just then, and when Will turned to look he saw him heave himself to the
side. The chair tumbled off Fell's back, and Henry tumbled from the
chair, and Oak tumbled out of his lap.

"I told you not to touch me!" Henry said. When he got up he started walking back the way they had come.

"Hey," Will said. "Hey, don't do that, man!" Fell and Oak and Lyon watched him walking away and then calmly followed after him. "What are you doing?" Will asked. "That's the wrong way."

"It's become less wrong," said Lyon, "in the interim."

"I'm about to give up on you making sense," Will said. "And it's pissing me off."

"Giving up on that would be best," Lyon said, not breaking his stride as he turned his head around one hundred and eighty degrees to give Will a look that seemed both pitying and dismissive. "Piss away, mortal. Piss on me, if you please. Just because I'm saving your life doesn't mean I care about you, or care about your narrow little discomfitures, or have ever had the time, even in an eternity of ageless life, to explain things to you. Will you see the Redcap or the Bloody Falls before Under-the-Hill shows you a door? Who knows? I am not King under this hill, I only serve him, and I cannot straighten the paths you make crooked with your dreams. You mock me with your questions and should be careful, or I shall piss on *you*."

"I wasn't trying to . . ." Will began, meaning to tell him that he wasn't trying to mock him, and he didn't see how his perfectly sensible questions added up to a mockery, but then Lyon swiveled his head back around, and that was so disconcerting that Will fell silent. It would probably be perceived as a mockery, he supposed, to ask him how he did that, or to ask to examine his neck a little more closely, or to ask for a bit of the moss growing under his arms to look at later under a microscope. Will hurried up, passing Lyon, meaning to catch up with Henry and talk to him instead. The hallway was brightening, and the walls were opening up. By the time Will caught up with Henry he was standing by a set of doors other than the ones through which they had come in. Henry was standing before one of two statues on either side of the doors, a seven-foot-tall naked woman. A male statue stood on the other side of the doors, which were ajar. Will looked back, then forward, then all around, not bothering to say that he didn't understand what was happening. Oak ran forward and fell to his knees in front of the male statue.

"Master!" he said. "Put forth your hand. Save us!" The other two made flourishing bows to the statue but did not speak to it. Henry was cocking his head back and forth at the lady and the man.

"She's pretty," Will said, which was a serious understatement. He reached out and touched her belly, wondering too late if it might offend some part of the crowd in front of the other statue.

"It's our Lady," Lyon said, "and our Lord."

"I figured," Will said. "Are they going to talk?"

"No," Lyon replied. "They're only statues." But Oak had to be pried away from the feet of the male, and Fell climbed up the side of the statue and whispered something in its ear. "Onward," said Lyon, and gave Will a little push toward the doors. There was another, grander room beyond them, a cozier hall than the last, only about half as big, with grass on the floors and flowers on the walls, and a ceiling hung with hundreds of little colored lanterns. It was empty of furniture except for a table the size of a flatbed truck piled with food and surrounded by chairs of every conceivable size, and empty of people except for the girl, who had called herself Eleanor Roosevelt. She was sprawled in a chair with a bottle of wine in her hand.

"You all again," she said.

"What's your name?" Will called out to her, not understanding why it made him so angry to see her sitting there appearing to enjoy herself.

"Puddin . . ." she said, frowning at the bottle. She took a swig out of it, and said, "Molly."

"Well," he said, "Okay then. I'm Will."

"I know. But I don't know *why* your name is Will. Do you think that means something, that I named you Will?"

"I don't think you should drink that," said Henry. "Or eat the food." The three others—Lyon, Oak, and Fell—had fallen to the food on the table and were stuffing themselves.

"O sad feast!" said Oak.

"O Great Night!" said Fell. "O Last Night!"

"The wine is a little strong for mortal tastes," said Lyon, who had taken the leg of something that looked fancier than a chicken but was too small to be a turkey, and was licking it like a popsicle. "But eat up. This feast only happens once a year, and great care has gone into the preparation. Everyone is scattered on the hill, and most of them are too upset to eat now. It's all going to waste, which is not so terrible, since the Beast will put the whole world to waste come dawn, but it will lessen the shame of it all if you taste and enjoy. And how nice, anyhow, that the hill has chosen to feed you."

"I don't know if I would eat any of this," Henry said, but he was sniffing at a delicate-looking cupcake.

"Food," said Molly. "The apples mean something, and the dates mean something, and the pig means something, and wine means something else, and your names all mean something and Peabo means something. How am I supposed to figure all that out?" Will recognized a drunk girl when he saw one, but he didn't know how she could have gotten this drunk since they'd seen her in the hall. Her eyes were half-lidded, and she slurred when she said *figure* and *supposed*.

"Shouldn't we be moving along?" Will said. "I thought we were headed for the exit."

"That's all fine," said Molly, taking another swig of wine. "That's all perfectly fine, but I think I can't leave before I've figured anything out. I just figured that out right now. I'm crazy with a purpose, and when I figure it all out I'll be all better, and you will all be somebody else entirely."

"I think you've had enough of that," Will said, and took the bottle from her. She hardly had to stretch to reach another, which she took up and cradled to her chest but didn't open.

"I told you," said Lyon. "This feast is on the way and of the way. The hill would feed you, and the Great Night would have its feast." He threw a piece of the bird to Will, who caught it, then dropped it, and batted it to the table. It was piping hot. "You'll never taste the like again," Lyon added, "even if you're not murdered by dawn, even if my Master rouses from his slumber and saves us all, even if you live a fat span of bored and boring mortal years."

"It's a party!" said Oak, jumping from seat to seat.

"But not the one it should have been," said Fell, who had taken a seat at the head of the table in a chair that was too big for him, and sat balancing a bottle between his legs. "It's not a very great night. Or maybe it is great, in the way that last things are great. Just don't think," he said, waving a hand around to indicate the empty seats and the empty hall, "that it's usually like this."

"If you eat the food," Henry said, "then you have to live here forever." He was holding the cupcake a lot closer to his face.

"A myth! A myth!" said Oak, bouncing by him and shoving the cupcake in Henry's face. "It's a lie. You stay as long as we like you, no longer!"

"Or as long as the world lasts," said Fell, "whichever is shorter."

"Or until the way out is clear," said Lyon, sitting down. Henry was spitting icing out of his mouth and trying to wipe the cupcake from his eyes. Oak pushed him down into the chair, and for once Henry didn't say not to touch him. Will sat down next to Molly, listened carefully for the banging on those other doors, wherever they were, and heard nothing. He poured himself some wine but didn't drink it yet. He told himself he shouldn't be sitting down. There was too much to do: finding a way out of the hill, finding a sapling, finding a way out of the park, deciding how to break the crazy, wonderful news to Carolina. There wasn't time, really, even for a snack, but the food all smelled really quite nice—overwhelmingly delightful, in fact. As he turned his head he caught different scents. Something smelled like cardomom; something else like baked eggs. Any delay was ill-advised, but a snack seemed in keeping with what he was coming to think of as his very sensible reaction to the night's turn toward wonder and horror: he was taking things as they came and trying not to let fear or bewilderment compromise his appreciation of the extraordinary things all around him. He needed to pay attention, after all, to give a proper report to Carolina, because she might ask him anything. What color pants was the boy with the tail wearing? What sort of buttons did the little old man's suit have? Was Henry circumcised? Did the strawberries taste like strawberries? If he was going to tell her a coherent story, he needed to pay careful sustained attention and not skip over things in a headlong rush to the door. Thinking of the door, he thought again about their pursuer, but there was no noise in this hall except for the voices of his companions and the quiet rustle of paper on paper as the lanterns swayed in a gentle breeze that came, never twice from exactly the same direction, with the rhythm of breath. He took a sip of the wine, which tasted like whisky.

"Is that really my ultimate terror?" Molly asked, "a little black boy with limited opportunities?" She was slouching now, and he found his anger at her had dissipated with the first sip of wine, which seemed a little quick for it to be an effect of drunkenness. He was most certainly not going to get drunk at this table. It would make no sense at all to report back to Carolina that he had seen some wonders and then gotten supernaturally drunk, and have the story end prematurely in a blackout. It was more, he thought, that he could appreciate how drunk she was, and that made him better disposed to her. She seemed more sad than angry now, and more confused than belligerent. She looked like she was getting ready to cry, and that was a look he was used to running from, yet now it only engaged his sympathy, which was . . . swelling. There wasn't really a better word for what he experienced as he looked more closely at her, a feeling like someone who cared about her was standing up inside of him and stretching.

She held up both her hands, curling in her right thumb, then her pinky, then putting the thumb out again. She peered at her fingers, seeming to be fascinated by them.

"Maybe you should eat something," Will said, and proceeded to fix her a little plate, thinking it would help to make her less drunk. It was part of his sympathetic feeling toward her, that he didn't want her to make a spectacle of herself, and he sensed that was where she was headed—sentimental reminiscence would lead to more maudlin reflection, and shortly she would be crying.

"Stop!" Henry said. "Everybody stop eating!" His mouth was full, and even as he yelled at people to stop eating he took another bite of turkey. Will ignored him, and took up the plate in front of him, topmost and smallest of three stacked on top of one another. It was so light and thin he was almost afraid to burden it with anything heavier than pastry, but it held up under a brick of chocolate and a dense piece of something that looked like meat loaf but smelled like licorice.

"This is really good china," Molly said when she took the plate.

"I think it's edible," Will said, which made her roll her eyes.

"We are all in terrible danger," said Henry, holding up a spare rib and looking at it as if it might attack him. The three faeries—Will decided he was just going to call them that, and stop thinking about whether or not they were something else, occult species of man or aliens or something else for which there was no proper name—had huddled around Oak's chair and were muttering together. Then they were quiet for a moment, and they each threw out a hand into the center of their circle in a way that made it look like they were playing Rock, Paper, Scissors. They made three throws, and Fell gave a little cheer. Lyon boosted him up on the table.

"Listen, listen!" Fell said, stepping among the apples and the pork. "Listen, mortals! One thousand years ago our Master bound the Beast, and every year since we mark the day and night with a feast."

"Our Lady helped!" said Oak. "Our Lady helped to bind him too!"

"She helped *some*," said Lyon.

"Every year some honored faerie gets to sing the tale, already known to all, of that battle, to remind us of the struggle, and of what was almost lost, and remind us to cherish what's left to us, even if our kingdom is circumscribed by boredom, even if we are grown small in ways that have nothing to do with our size." He took a deep breath and stood straighter on the table and started to sing in a language that was not English.

"Is that French?" Molly asked. She had opened her new bottle without Will noticing; her lips were wet with wine. "I don't even know French. How can it be French?"

"I don't think that's French," Will said. It was musical and nasal and lispy and lilting. He would have recognized French, or Dutch, or even Chinese. This was something else. Every few verses it seemed that the man stopped singing, but his mouth still moved, and Will knew the singing was beyond the range of his hearing. Henry was covering his ears and singing *"La! La! La!"* to himself. Molly drank more wine and closed her eyes and seemed to sing along, except Will could swear she was singing *"Jesus Jesus Jesus."* He seemed to remember from his childhood, which was relatively impoverished of stories, someone—maybe a nun—telling him about Irish peasants who scared faeries away from their mischief by shouting out the names of saints, but she didn't seem to be frightening any of these faeries. Lyon and Oak had begun to eat in earnest. It seemed rude to the singer, to eat so voraciously and noisily, but Fell did not seem to mind, or even notice, how the others were stuffing. Molly was eating and shaking her head. Henry was eating in a weird, hesitating frenzy, pulling egg noodles hand over hand and shoving them in his mouth, and yet he took long pauses in between mouthfuls. Will was more reserved. He took the wine in sips, and the meat in carefully cut morsels, took time to appreciate what he was tasting, and took a few things for Carolina, a handful of nuts and a petit four filled with what he could only describe as intensely flavored air, a tiny saltshaker in the form of a sparrow, and a knife, the hilt of which was shaped like a woman with three breasts, which he put in his remaining shoe.

The song continued through Will's first glass of wine, and he became better disposed toward it as he finished the glass. In fact, he became better disposed toward the singer, too, and to the rest of his company at the table, and to the whole situation. "It's all going to be all right," he said, mostly to himself, because he suddenly believed that they were going to find the nether door and outrun or outsmart that lady (and the wine made Will think he had mistaken her identity; it couldn't be *that* lady after all) and escape the park, and they would all—it occurred to him as he looked first at Molly and then at Henry through the glass he had just refilled and sipped from again—become good friends. They would meet for lunch once a month down the street at Café Flore and reminisce about this strange night, about the wonders already come and gone and the wonders they had yet to experience. "Everything is going to be all right," he said, to Molly this time. And then he turned and shouted it at Henry. "It's all going to be fine!" It was strange, he thought, that he hadn't noticed already how nice-looking the man was. He looked back at Molly and was a little surprised by how pretty she was. And catching a glimpse of himself in a silver pitcher, he noticed that even his warped reflection was pretty good-looking, and with his shirt off he felt handsome, not fat. Without at all understanding why he was doing it, he raised his arms and flexed his biceps, watching in the pitcher while his distorted twin did the same thing. He smiled at Henry, who was staring at him, still with a fearful expression on his face. "Don't worry, buddy," Will said, and then something hit him in the side of the head. Fell had pelted him with a piece of rare beef.

"I am *singing*," he said, and then nimbly ducked a saucer-shaped pastry, which Molly threw.

"Who cares?" she said. "You're not even real! You're that time my mother said I was a slut!" She stood up and pointed at Lyon. "And you're the time my parents forgot my birthday." Swiveling in place, arm and finger still outstretched, she turned to Oak. "And you . . . what are you?"

"Hey," Will said. "Calm down. It's okay." He leaned toward her chair and put a hand on her shoulder. She shrugged him off.

"You think that just because you look normal you're any more real than those freaks? You're just a little piece of neurosis. That's all. That's *all*!" She had risen from her chair, the bottle of wine clutched in one hand and a pastry crushed in the other. Will rose too, then leaned forward and kissed her. It was *necessary* to kiss her, because she was so pretty, and because she was angry, and because it made sense, in that moment, that he might pass along a little of the hopeful peace the magic wine was causing him to feel. It was cheating, he thought—the first time he had cheated on Carolina since she broke up with him—and yet he didn't stop.

"Maybe we should skip right to the toast," said Oak. Without taking his lips away from Molly's, Will peered to his right and saw Oak climb on his chair and raise his glass. Molly was not kissing Will back, but she wasn't pushing him away, either. "To kisses!" said Oak.

"To death!" said Lyon.

"To the Great Night!" said Fell, standing on the table with two glasses raised. He kicked food at Molly and Will, and though an éclair hit them in their joined face, neither of them pulled away until Henry, with a resonant groan, threw his chair over the table. It fell on the grassy floor with a muted thud. Will was almost afraid again when he saw the look on Henry's face—it was such a despairing face. But still he thought, *How handsome* and *He needs a hug.*

"What sort of toast is that?" asked Fell. "You mortals are all so *rude!*" In answer, Henry put his hands over his face and crouched down on the floor, looking like someone was about to hit him.

"It's okay, dude," Molly said. She was pale, and her face had begun to sweat. "None of this is real."

"Yes, it is," Henry said from underneath his hands. "Yes, it is!"

"Don't you all understand?" Will said, practically shouting it. "Everything is going to be fine!" But as soon as he said it they all heard a giant noise: a gong and a clang and a thud. Will didn't ask what it was: the noise put into his head a perfect little movie of the iron doors toppling from their hinges.

"Uh oh!" said Oak.

"Oh, my!" said Fell.

And Lyon shouted, "Run!"

Will and Carolina went to movie night at Dolores Park. It was Will's idea. Carolina said she preferred books to movies, and she didn't even have a television, but she liked the idea of being outside, and Dolores was one of her favorite parks. Will didn't usually like people who didn't like movies, though he agreed that there were lots of stupid movies (though not necessarily fewer stupid movies than stupid books), and he tended especially not to like people who made a fuss about liking books better than movies. But it was ostensibly true as well that he didn't like girls with short hair, or broody women, and people who didn't have to work for a living, and Carolina was all of those. These were all separate issues that had no impact at all on how much he loved her, which was a surprise; he never would have guessed how little he ever could have anticipated of the shape and the character of the person he had fallen in love with. But then again the whole experience of her had been a giant surprise.

The surprise was more lovely than not, but sometimes it was terrible, or at least terrifying—every now and then he was seized with a panicked *what am I doing?* feeling, but whenever that happened, when he was disturbed by thoughts of Carolina while he was at work in someone else's garden, or waiting in line for a sandwich, or laboriously pedaling his bike up a steep hill, it was thoughts of Carolina that soothed him again. It was all very weird and very wonderful and felt ill-deserved somehow, which he told her repeatedly. "I don't deserve you," he'd say, long before he had started doing things to make that a true statement, and she would reply, "Sure you do. Everybody deserves to be in love."

"What makes you so sure of that?" he asked her during a picnic conversation under the tree, and she looked at him like he was from the moon.

"Everybody deserves to be happy," she said, like she was walking him through a math problem. "Everybody needs to be in love to be happy. Therefore, everybody deserves to be in love."

"Maybe not everybody needs to be in love to be happy. And does everybody really deserve to be happy?"

"Absolutely," she said. She lay on her back with her feet on the tree, her hips bent almost at ninety degrees. Will sat cross-legged at her head, staring down at her face.

"Everybody? Genghis Khan? Dracula?"

She sat up and took the knife from her plate. "Everybody," she said. "For a little while, anyway. I'll write it down, so you won't forget." She started carving letters into the silver bark with a knife, but Will stopped her. "That's bad for the tree," he said.

The movie was *Soylent Green*, which Will had never seen before, even though a drunk girl had run naked through his dorm one night in college screaming that Soylent Green was people, so his interest was piqued and he always meant to rent it. But the best thing that could be said about it, he decided, was that it was enormously dispiriting, and they both decided they would have been better off never having seen it. "That was a bad movie," he said to Carolina later, "but not a badly made movie." That led them to a discussion about whether a movie could be bad for a person or generate ill in the world. Will said he didn't like it when art did nothing but make you feel bad, and Carolina replied that she thought that was weird, considering how relentlessly depressing his stories were.

"That's different," he said, though it was hard for him to articulate exactly how. "I didn't write those stories on purpose," he added. "I mean, I did, but they're not designed to make people sad. They're not supposed to increase the total sadness in the world. They're *supposed* to do the opposite of that." Though that wasn't exactly true either. He thought it would be most accurate to say that they were supposed to make him feel better and worse at the same time, and that he couldn't really speak for anything they might do to someone else. But he didn't say that. Carolina kissed him and said again how much she thought Ryan and Sean would have liked each other. Sometimes she talked about how much they had in common, anxiety and dissatisfaction and a troubled relationship with their parents and even being dead, in a way that made it sound like they belonged together even more than she and Will did.

It was a dispiriting movie but not a dispiriting evening. The weather was not traditionally lovely, but it was the kind of evening, cold and just foggy enough to put golden halos around the streetlights, that Will really liked, and the whole enterprise of giggling at an earnest depiction of dystopia, snuggling in public while vendors sold popcorn and hash cookies and mushroom cordials, seemed like something that would only happen there. He felt very lucky to be lounging in this city and in this park and with this woman, which was part, he supposed, of feeling like he didn't deserve any of it.

"This movie is making me hungry," she said. Will got her some popcorn, and when the lady came walking along the slanted edge of the hill, stepping carefully between blankets and towels and softly calling out, "Special cookies! Special cookies!" he ordered two. That made him a lot better disposed toward the movie, and it seemed okay, after the cookies and three beers from Carolina's backpack, that Soylent Green was people, that women were treated like furniture and old people were euthanized, that they put down Burl Ives as gently and ruthlessly as a dog.

There was a feeling in him that misogyny and food riots and cannibalism and Charlton Heston's despair did not preclude the existence of justice and beauty in the world. Mr. Heston might run off the screen and, seconds after the movie ended, run into a girl with a Monchhichi hairdo who could demonstrate that it didn't matter at all to your happiness what was happening five minutes ago, or five years ago, or fifteen. In fact, she might be running from the opposite direction, having just discovered, in another factory, the terrible truth about Soylent Green (which he was suddenly drunk and stoned enough to realize was the truth about *life*, the horrible open secret that everyone thought they had to ignore to be able to plod through one more day), which was to say it was people, it's hard to be good, and brothers die. She knew this as well as he did, and she was running from the truth as spastically as Mr. Heston, and yet when they ran into each other she would tell him, very sincerely, that despite all that, despite *everything*, everybody still deserved to be in love.

The movie ended, and people applauded. Will and Carolina had switched positions; now her head was in his lap, and she had fallen asleep.

He sat watching her while everyone around them shook out their blankets and gathered up their bottles, while they let the air out of the blow-up movie screen and it wilted away, and the audience—everyone but a few scattered snoring homeless people—was gone from the park by the time he woke her to tell her that he loved her.

12

*T*itania had always had a habit of taking a mortal lover after an argument with her husband. He did the same thing. It was soothing and distracting, a response to sadness or strife that was as natural as tears. So she ought to have taken one after he left her, and because it was the most terrible argument they had ever had, she ought to have taken a terribly good lover, or a terribly large number of lovers, or a lover who manifested a terribly extreme sort of mortality—an old man on his deathbed or a consumptive youth. When she imagined Oberon rutting his way through the city, forgetting her and their Boy in thrusting increments, she wanted to do it, too. She wanted to sweep down the hill in a rage and capture the first man she saw, and use him up, as she had done a thousand times before, leaving remnants that were more or less ruined, depending on the intensity of her rage and the intensity of the argument with her husband. So this time she considered, sulking and ruminating on her throne, that she could become a sickness among the men of this city, and take them by the dozen every night, until she had burned them all out, leaving them useless for life, if not dead, and still not exhaust her anger at Oberon or her grief for their Boy.

All her courtiers thought it was a good idea, too. It would reassure them for her to ride out on a horse made of fog and bring back a mortal to use, and the faeries tasked to carry away the man's trembling bones would sigh complacently at one another and say, "At last she's behaving *normally* again." This was before she cloistered herself on the hill for fear of encountering a child in the street. A few faeries went ahead and tried to set her up, taking it upon themselves to forage among the houses and apartments that surrounded their hill for someone interesting or pretty. Some foraged for the sake of an anticipated reward, and some just out of fondness and concern for their afflicted Lady. They brought back images caught in water, which they held cupped in their hands for her to see, or caught on silk, to make waving flags for their cause. Oak came hopping up the hill with a stolen tennis shoe, which he held up for her to sniff. "His feet smell like peanut butter," he said. "He is *distinguished*!"

The mortals all looked equally boring to her, equally plain, and looked to be equal wastes of her time. She had never thought before of anything as a waste of time; she had an eternity of time to spend and could afford to be profligate with it. But she went down the hill anyway, on three different nights, to meet three different men. The first was the youngest, a boy in his twenties. She found him on her own, passing down the sidewalk near the corner of Noe and Henry streets. He was about to go into his apartment. It was early in the evening, but the moon was high and full. Its light caught in his hair just so, and that was enough. She revealed herself to him.

"Come here," she said, after he had stared for a while. He came down the steps, abandoning his key in the lock, and stood on his toes to kiss her. He tasted like sugar and ashes—the flavor of mortality common to all men which she usually found deeply arousing—but this time her tongue felt wooden in his mouth. *What's his name?* she wondered, and then she asked him.

"Ralph," he said breathily, speaking it against her lips and then against her neck and her chest. "Ralph, Ralph, Ralph."

"That's *ridiculous*," she said, because it was a ridiculous sound, a cough, a hairball, a bit of puking. Why did she care what his name was, or whether there was someone waiting for him in his apartment, or if he had a child, or had been a child himself once? She had never cared about any of these things. Mortal men, never to be told, asked her name, begged her name, died to know one letter of her name. She did not ask for anyone's name.

She left him there to make a solitary spectacle of himself, laid out on his stoop and coming in his pants. He was barely ruined at all. He would recover, and forget about her, and be satisfied with mortal women, and never be troubled by her again except in deep dreams.

The second was older, a man in a suit. Lyon said it was a nice suit, though it was not made of smoke or dew or spider legs, and that he had picked the man for her largely on account of its quality. "Fine suit," he said. "Fine man." He was taller and darker than the blond boy, and he talked too much. She allowed him to talk; she had decided, reflecting on the experience with the blond boy, that it would be best to take her fill of his story before she took her fill of his body. And maybe, she thought, if she heard enough, if she drained his story out of him, she could enjoy his body without wondering about which portions of his life were given over to joy or to sadness, whether he had cried today, or whether he had a mother who had loved him when he was a child. "Your name is Minna," said Lyon, who had taken it upon himself, rather boldly, to orchestrate the whole thing, and made the introduction through a computer, sending fake pictures over the wire in an internet café on the corner of Seventeenth and Sanchez. It was a proper date: Titania met him at a restaurant in his neighborhood, the Marina, and sat at an outside table.

"I'm the youngest person ever to head up my department," he said. "In the whole history of the company, which has been around for like fifty-five years." He paused to let her comment.

"My name is Minna," she said. That was all she said to him all evening long, but he heard in it whatever he needed to. Maintaining this little glamour was easier than actually having to talk to him, and left her attention free to wander a little while he emptied himself out. She was considering how flat and treeless this neighborhood was. It ought to be one big beach, she thought.

"It's hard work," he said. "It comes home with me a lot, which is okay. There's still time for fun. And when I have fun, I have *fun*. You know what I mean?"

"My name is Minna," she said.

"Exactly!" he said, and started to tell her about his boat. She picked up a pea from her plate and breathed upon it to turn it into an acorn. She shook the acorn in her hand, and it divided with every shake, until she had a handful of them, which she tossed over her shoulder. They rolled away down the sidewalk, still dividing, in search of someplace to plant themselves. It cheered her a little, to think that there would be an improvement in the neighborhood. She sighed and watched her date. He had the rib of a pig in his hand. He wasn't talking about what he was supposed to be talking about. She didn't know anything about his previous experience of love, or if he had ever killed anyone, or if he liked sometimes to be cruel. He hadn't mentioned his mother even once: it was possible that he didn't even have one, and she thought for some reason that that would make him entirely useless to her. She could make him talk about those things. She could take away the nasal quality in his voice and make it more pleasing to hear. She could change the shape of his face, or grow him a beard as thick and luxurious as Oberon's, and scent his hair like flowers, or even turn his hair into flowers. She could improve him, but she declined to improve him, though she had experimented on mortal men and women in the past, changing them, for their own good or to their detriment, but always to her amusement. Sitting there, watching his lips, glistening with pig fat, flap away in the gentle golden light of the early evening, she conceived the spell to change him but then let it go, because her Boy came to mind, the way the color of his hair changed from light to dark as he grew, and the way she could never tell which word he would learn next, and even the way she could never, in his last days, predict what new pain or trouble he would have—all his surprises ruined any satisfaction she might take in making someone to delight her, because those sorts of surprises were beyond the reach of her craft.

She was enormously patient with the man. She listened (or at least half listened) all through dinner, waiting and waiting for him to say something of substance, and then walked with him down Union Street while he looked into shopwindows and told her about the things that he owned that were similar or dissimilar but always superior to the things on display, and she even walked with him down to the end of Scott Street to have a look at his boat. She felt progressively weary as they walked down toward the marina; by the time they arrived she was exhausted. That seemed curious to her, since she had exerted practically no physical or magical effort all evening, until she realized that it was her little-exercised faculty of patience that was wearing her out. Just for a moment she was proud of herself, and then she was angry for thinking that nostalgia for her Boy's lost delights compelled her to suffer the prattling of a mortal fool. "There is nothing in you," she said to him as they stood on the boat slip, interrupting his discourse on the Volvo Penta engine. "No grief, no sadness, no rage. Shame! Shameful excuse for a mortal! Where are your tears?" She stood up higher as she talked—she had been hunching under the disguise all evening long—and he goggled. His stupid uncomprehending eyes were round and black; they looked like a crab's eyes. "What do you have to say?" she asked him. "What do you have to say to me?" His mouthparts bubbled but he didn't make any words. She turned him into a crab, because of those eyes, and when he scrabbled out of his fine suit, she kicked him into the water. She made herself into a bird, and took his tie in her beak before she flew away, taking the long way home, so people marveled at the snow-white crane with a bloodred tie in her mouth as she winged her way over Crissy Field and the Presidio and Seacliff. Back home, she handed the tie wordlessly to Lyon, who knew, from the look she gave him with it, to hang it with barbs and flagellate himself until dawn.

She tried one more time, with Oak's peanut-butter-footed gentleman. She waited for him on a bench in Duboce Park. It was dusk, and the fog had followed her down the hill to muffle the barking of the dogs at play. They ran aimlessly and brought back toys and balls not thrown for them. A dog approached her, a black Lab with a collar of silver spikes, and sat down at her feet.

"Milady goes a-whorin'," it said. She kicked at it, and it wagged its tail.

"If I showed you what was in my heart," she said, "it would burn you to a cinder."

"I've tried to burn you similarly," it said, "but you never even noticed when I opened up my chest."

"Go sniff out your Master."

"I've searched all day," he said. "He's not—"

"Fetch," she said, picking up a stray ball and throwing it, because she was in no mood to listen to Puck's litany of failure, which was to say she was in a relatively good mood, her recent romantic misadventures, for whatever reason, not weighing heavily on her just then. She threw the ball clear over the city; it bounced once outside the Ferry building and splashed in the bay. Puck barked once and trotted after it, and not long after that Oak came along, leading a dazed-looking man by the hand. He sat him down on the bench, gave him a hug, then bowed to his Mistress and hopped away.

"Goodbye, Arthur," said the man.

"Goodbye, darling!" said Oak.

"That was my nephew," the man said. "I think."

"A charming boy," said Titania, shaking her head because Oak had brought her a homosexual again. Not that it ultimately mattered; the man would see someone he wanted, but she sighed over it nonetheless. The man sighed as well, which made her laugh.

"Are you laughing at me?" he asked, tilting his head. He was confused, still charmed by whatever song Oak had used to draw him down from his apartment, and she could tell that his desire had not yet cast her into a definite form.

"Yes," she said. "Shall we go to dinner?"

"I know a little place," he said, and then sucked in his breath when her image settled. "But are you sure you want to go there with *me*?" She examined his perception of her: a stocky bearded youth whose handsome legs were shown to lovely effect by his soccer shorts.

"Of course," she said, taking his hand. The little place he knew was a sushi restaurant across the street from the blond boy's apartment: Titania half expected to see him still coming on his stoop. The staff in the restaurant let out an insincere cheer when they walked in, but the waitress, a middle-aged woman who reeked of death, seemed genuinely happy to see Titania's date.

"A friend!" she said. "You have a friend! No lonely sushi combo to-night!"

"This is . . ." her date began. "This is . . ."

"Joe," said Titania. "My name is Joe." The lady pumped Titania's hand. Titania raised her nose at her, the better to smell her. The odor of death was interesting, and not all that unpleasant, but a deeper sniff told her a cancer death was in store for this lady, and she was transported back to the ruined little room in the hospital.

"I'm sorry," said her date when the woman went to fetch them tea. "She's . . . enthusiastic. I live around the corner, and I come here all the time. I got food poisoning here once, but I still come here all the time. She's my sushi aunt. She makes fun of me and she always offers to set me up and asks if I'm lonely. Which I'm not. Alone is not lonely. I can say that in Japanese." He barked the phrase at her. "Are you all right? Did she upset you?"

"My name is Joe," she said, and he smiled, and leaned back in his chair. He shifted his leg under the table, and their knees collided. Neither of them drew away. Their tea came, and the waitress withdrew again with a giggle, and he looked at her coyly from over the steaming cup. His eyes were round and bulged a little, but not unpleasantly, and they sparkled as he looked her up and down.

"What shall we order?" he asked.

"Whatever you desire," she said, settling her chin in her hand to look at him. She barely moved again for the rest of dinner, though the sushi came in an increasingly exotic procession, as the waitress tried ever harder to surprise them, and the chefs and all the other staff, intoxicated by her presence, shed their fake sushi cheer and became genuinely delighted with their patrons and showered them all with fine fish. Titania didn't eat a thing but drank the sake, impressing her date when she lifted the brimming box to her lips without spilling a drop. The strongest mortal liquor was weak compared to faerie wine, but she thought it might be affecting her because she was feeling very well disposed toward the situation. Though there was no delight for her in the mortal art of arranging fish cleverly upon a plate, and the great common happiness in the room—the very good time being had by all—seemed as futile and hopeless as any mortal happiness, Titania was happy to be there.

That was different, of course, from being *happy*. She was as unhappy as ever, in the pervading absence of her husband and her Boy, but there was something about her present situation that deferred the pain of it, made the unhappiness temporarily acceptable. This was a rather mysterious surprise, the felicitous blame for which she laid upon the shoulders of her date. She didn't know why exactly this was, and it did not bother her particularly not to know. As wise as she was, as many mysteries as she kept, there were many things she didn't know or understand because she was not interested enough in them to bother to understand them. But here was something she was keenly interested in, and yet she did not get it. What was so special about this middle-aged homosexual that he had captivated her over a meal of dead fish served by a dying woman?

She considered this question through the remainder of their evening together. It wasn't his sparkling googly eyes, or his rounded biceps, or the stark veins standing out in his forearms, or the little cowlick of gray and white hair that curved down over his forehead. It was nothing about his physical presence, but neither was it the nervous way he flitted from topic to topic in the one-sided conversation he was having with her. They went dancing, but it was not the way he danced, shuffling in place and boxing with unseen enemies in a crowded upstairs club on the corner of Eleventh and Folsom. She didn't exactly choose to intoxicate the already drunken drag queens and hipsters and costumed freaks, but neither did she withhold intoxication from them. It was a by-product of her mysterious temporary contentment, how the fake beehives hung from the ceiling became real beehives, and the fake stars set on the ceiling brightened and the ceiling became a night sky, how the chubby hipster in a fuzzy bear-eared hat became an actual bear, hopping on his hind legs and stuffing his paws in his mouth for joy. She naturally presided over any dance; the whole club circled them round and round, and a few of the weaker ones swooned into attitudes of frank worship upon the floor. Her date had stopped talking, so she knew it wasn't his words that kept her suspended between being heartbroken and being heartbroken.

They walked back to his place silently, hand in hand. Actively looking forward to the sex, she conjured a wind to hurry them along, and lift them here and there over a busy intersection. She was sure the fucking would reveal the source of her engagement with him, and though she anticipated that orgasm would put an end to her transient satisfaction and return her to the gloomy depths of her brooding nostalgia, she wanted to get there, so she started kissing him as soon as they got in his door.

"Are you sure you want to—?"

"Oh, yes," she said.

"But I'm—" She didn't let him finish. It wasn't the words, or the stories he told, or his oddly shaped little body, or the clumsy motion of his tongue inside her mouth. It wasn't his round little arms, or his firm belly, or even the heft of his penis in her hand, though at last she discovered what it was when they were standing naked before his bed. She left him then, absent an orgasm, and went home to the hill. She let him watch her depart unobscured, a gift, because she was fond of him despite his being the occasion for another terrible discovery. She went up the hill in the skin of a lion, with antlers on her head and a single floppy wing on her back and a heavy blunt dragging tail. She had been gone long enough that her courtiers presumed the evening must have been a success, and they prepared a feast, chocolate cocks and marshmallow pussies set upon a table on the top of the hill. They started to sing as she approached, ignoring her defeated form, until she grabbed one of the smallest of them and, ignoring its cries, reshaped it, molding its head into a pair of lips a little larger than human-sized and pulling its body into a hollow tube. She made it a pair of wings and, cradling it in her palm, said, "You are made to a purpose." Then she breathed on it, and set it winging back down the hill. She sat down at the head of the table, and said nothing else to anyone for the rest of the night.

All this to say she knew right away what was happening when Puck mastered her effortlessly and gave her over to the absurd mortal in the long green coat. The lesson of the peanut-butter-footed man was that it was everything and nothing about him that put her misery in abeyance. By dumb wild luck, Oak had found her someone whom it was possible to love, though that possibility was so remote there existed no measure sufficiently broad to describe it. She'd never again find a mortal lover to destroy in spirit of callous fun. Her realization was ridiculous and obscene, and she ought to have punished her date, not sent him a blow-job faerie magically equipped to suck out some small portion of his loneliness, but she was fond of him even in her despair and found that she couldn't hurt him. She considered, in her long silence, while her courtiers nibbled agitatedly at their chocolate cocks, that it ought to have pleased her to know she could feel fondness for any creature after the disastrous departures of her husband and her Boy, but the possibility only felt like a looming, destroying threat.

Puck defeated her with startling ease, and then he punished her with startling intuition, creating a hell for her out of material at hand. When he shoved the candy ring upon her finger, she felt it right away, that same fondness she had felt for her lonely little date, but this was only the beginning. Shortly the rest of it came crashing over her, leaving her not enough of herself even to scream. She smiled and put herself hand in hand with this ridiculous—ingenious, alluring—man and said, "What is your will, my love?"

Huff flexed his finger, which was sore, and considered the situation. The Mayor had departed, running away at top speed waving a pair of underwear in his hands, which seemed like an extraordinary stroke of good luck. And he had married Huff to the lovely woman before he left, which was extraordinary, certainly, though it remained to be determined whether it was lucky or not. Huff had been married before, the first time when he was only seven years old. That had been an informal but not unserious arrangement with an older neighbor girl named Julia. He had decided to show her his penis and when he asked her if she wanted to have a look she said she could only do that if they were married. So he got down on one knee and asked her to be his wife. She squinted at him a moment, and flattened her lips together, and finally said, "I suppose so." He was going to get his five-year-old brother to come be the preacher, but she said, "Stupid. That's not how you do it." She'd fetched a broom and they each jumped over it three times. "That's how the slaves used to do it," she said proudly. She liked to remind people that her family had owned them as recently as one hundred years before. Huff could remember her pale face very well, a lingering effect, he supposed, of their marriage, fleeting as it was. She had a wide nose and full lips that she seemed always to be trying to eat, chewing at them with her snaggle teeth or folding them up like she did when she was thinking hard about something. They honeymooned out behind her toolshed, where he showed her his stuff. "It's nice, isn't it?" he asked her, because he had just that morning noticed how nice it was, and that was why he suddenly wanted to show it around. She said, "It's okay." They divorced later that afternoon after she brought him the certificate she'd drawn up. *Hereby*, it said, *I do divorce you.* There was something to be savored, he thought much later, about how brief and entirely to the point it had been, and the near-total absence of rancor in their relationship was its own sort of pleasure. There had been rancor galore in all the subsequent marriages, to Sylvia and Natalie and Carla and Allison and D'Artania.

All that to say he had been married extensively enough to know what it was like, and to know how a person could seem magical and intriguing, like the answers to your prayers and your problems, and then later, twenty minutes or two weeks or three months or a year, have become, while you looked away for a moment, something or someone else entirely. The magic went away, they became bored and boring, and all they cared to notice about you anymore were your many flaws. "You," D'Artania had told him, for example, in her valedictory address, "are the most selfish person I have ever met."

If anyone was going to be different, though, it would probably be this lady, who came somewhat refreshingly to her wedding dressed in armor and carrying an ax. Most ladies didn't bring the ax out until well after the honeymoon. He thought this must mean she was holding her tenderness in reserve, which seemed like a better arrangement overall than to use it all up at the beginning of the relationship—he had always been a person who liked to get the hard part over first. And yet she was looking at him very tenderly already, from beneath her helmet, and her ax was discarded in a tree.

"Well," he said. "He didn't ask us, did he, if we would take this woman or this man? And yet I think it was lawful, him being the Mayor and all. He has always liked to marry people, and now he's done it to us."

"What is your will, my love?" she asked him again, and looked at him expectantly. The whole population of the field was looking at him expectantly, the big people and the little people, the ones shaped like trees and the ones shaped like furniture; even the very abstract-looking ones, whose eyes were not immediately to be identified, leaned forward and bent their forms at him expectantly. Huff drew in a breath, but he didn't know right away what to say. It was a complicated matter, after all, to ask someone what he wanted, and an even more complicated matter to ask it and sound, as she did, like you really wanted to know the answer. He might say *I don't know*, which would be true, because it was his deepest, truest, and hardest-won piece of wisdom, that he didn't really know what he wanted, that he was driven by an inchoate desire, and that the secret to becoming a serene person was not, as some people advised, to give up desire but to realize you could stop there and just accept that what you really wanted could never actually be described. So he might turn to her and say, *I want*—and demonstrate the object of his desire with a little dance or a gesture or a good fucking, which was really the closest approximation he had to express what he meant, since all his grunting and groaning and especially his ejaculation articulated it just the way it should be articulated, without words and sincerely. His copious, forceful ejaculations were the most sincere thing about him.

But it was too early for that degree of sincerity. He had only known her half an hour, and only been married to her for five minutes. It might scare her away, and it would certainly upset the weaker souls in their audience, all of whom were staring more and more intently. Some were stepping closer: the circle of eyes (and eye stalks and empty sockets and waving sensory filaria) had contracted a little. It would be forgivably misleading, he thought, to be specific about what he wanted. Still, there was a whole continuum of things that he might mention, from world peace, on the one hand, to a sandwich, on the (far-flung) other. He wanted nice things for his friends. There were dead people he would like to return to life, and living people whom he'd like to thrust into death. He wanted a home.

"Are we dead yet?" asked one of the dwarves. Huff peered at him and frowned, understanding that he didn't have all night to answer the lady's question and suddenly able to prioritize.

"I want to stop the Mayor," he said.

"The whom?" asked the lady.

"The Mayor," he said. "That handsome man who just married us."

"The Puck? The Beast?"

"Oh, yes," he said. "He is a beast. A beast and a fuck. A great, terrible fuck."

"I hate him," she said. "But I am in his power."

"Well, that's what everybody thinks," Huff said, knocking gently with his free hand on her helmet. "Everybody thinks, *I am in his power,* and everybody says, *There's nothing I can do* about how handsome he is or his negligent attitude toward the schools or his policy of enforced cannibalism, because he is too powerful, too intelligent, too ambitious, too *mayoral.*" He looked around at the crowd, registering the frightened looks on their faces and pseudo-faces.

"My Lady," said one, a chair. "While the Beast is distracted, we should flee."

"To the west," said a very large bee with the head of a Vietnamese lady.

"Or to the center of the earth!" said another.

"To the moon!" said a round bubble of fur.

"There is no way out," said a tall one, who looked like a librarian made out of leather. "The walls of air hold us all here, and death is our only escape!"

"Hear, hear!" said Huff, knocking louder on the lady's helmet. "Order, order! You are all suffering from a delusion! You are thinking just what he wants you to think!"

"Knock softly, my love," said the woman, catching his hand.

"Excuse me," said Huff, surveying the nervous creatures again as they gathered closer. He squinted at them, and saw them not as furniture or bee people but as Furniture and stagehands and a chorus. "Do any of them," he asked the lady, "belong to the Mayor?"

"They are my people," she said. "And my former husband's people, but he is gone. Only the beastly are with the Beast, and only those who love death would serve him."

"So they can all be trusted?"

"They will all serve you," she said, "because they serve me. What is your will, my love? There is time for us to delight you, before the Beast returns to consummate my defeat."

"Defeat? Don't talk like *defeat,*" Huff said, stroking her helmet now. "Don't talk like *death.* Don't talk like any of that. Does this come off?" He chucked her on the chinstrap, and she lifted a hand to undo it. The helmet fell softly on the grass and rolled—not like a head, he thought. Like a luscious apple. "I want to bring down the Mayor," he said, catching a handful of the lady's hair and cradling the back of her head and zooming in for a kiss. "And I want you to help me." He kissed her, and the murmuring crowd fell silent. A little man came running forward when

Huff did that, waving a sharpened twig, and though he was very small, Huff still cowered from him, raising his arms up over his face. But before the blow could fall, the lady bent swiftly, picked the little man up by his neck, and held him up at eye level. "I thought you said we could trust them," Huff said.

"He thought you were disrespecting me," she said, and frowned at the little man, and gave him a shake. His tiny head was turning purple where it poked out of her fist.

"I meant no disrespect," Huff said.

"I know it, my love. Kiss me again."

"I'd like to," Huff said. "But the time for kissing is past. In a little while, I'll kiss you again, but until then, there's work to do." He turned his attention to the purple-headed man. "Listen, you," he said. "Your loyalties are all confused. You don't want to be working for the Mayor. He's bad, through and through, and whatever he promised you, he won't deliver. Did he say he would make you tall? Was that it? Did he promise you a tiny lady? A hundred tiny ladies? A thousand tiny virgins? My man, he's just *talking*. But look, there's always one more chance to be good. Will you swear him off, and swear us on instead?" The lady squeezed him a little tighter, but still he managed just barely to nod his head. "All right, then," Huff said. "What's your name?" The lady put him down, and it took him a few tries to gasp it out.

"Bench," he said.

"Okay, Bench. I've got a job for you. Will you do it?"

"As my Lady wills," he said.

"That's the spirit," Huff said. "And here's your job. It won't be easy. The park is very big, and you are very small, but I need you to find somebody for me. I need you to find my friend. If we can't find her, the Mayor has as good as won. She's about this high, and her hair is gray and curly, and you'll probably find her sitting like this." He dropped to the ground and splayed his legs like Princess did. The lady settled down gently next to him, very softly even in her long coat of mail.

"I smell her on you," the little man said.

"There you go," Huff said. "Can you find her? Forgive me, but is it too *big* a job?"

"Even if the Beast has mauled her, I'll bring the pieces," he said. He made a curlicue gesture at Huff, bowed to the lady, and scampered off.

"One down!" said Huff, to everybody, and then to the lady, "but there are three more, and I need three more helpers. Who else do you trust?"

"I trust them all," she said. "They will all obey me unto death."

"Well, that's an extreme arrangement," Huff said. "How about you pick us a few who are obedient just about *up* to death? Let them hesitate, and wonder if the cause is just, before they do anything drastic." She cocked her head, and signaled without looking to three more to come forward, a puffball and the bee and the librarian. "Names, please," said Huff.

"Nemnaut," said the puffball.

"Kusaka," said the bee.

"Nilo," said the librarian.

"Gentlemen," he said. "Here are your assignments. Bob: about so high, he frowns a lot and he's wearing a plaid shirt. Hogg: nothing like a pig, long brown hair, big shoes. Mary: sometimes contrary, more often quite agreeable, her bottom is *huge*. Have you got them?" They all sniffed at him, and bowed, and then they were gone. "Away you go!" he called after them. "Now what?" he said to the ones who remained. He took the lady's hands—they were much larger than his, but much softer, though her nails, he noticed, were serrated like the edges of steak knives. "Now comes the hard part. I'm sorry everyone, but I'm afraid we've got a lot of work to do, if we're going to turn things around. I know it seems like the Mayor has us right where he wants us, trapped with him in his own private Disneyland, but in fact he's the one who's trapped. Well, not yet— but soon!" He made the round of eyes again, smiling at them all in turn, even at the mouthless ones who couldn't smile back, and though he felt a little dispirited, he didn't show it. Such a motley crew, and probably none of them had ever acted before, or even seen the movie, and they hardly had the time or the resources now for a screening. The seconds were ticking away. Huff knew from experience that you could distract yourself with a pair of underwear for only so many hours, and they had weeks of work to cram into this night—the shortest one, as it happened, of the whole year. He sighed expansively but made himself smile wider at them, though the effort hurt his face. "We are going to trap him, you see"—he had turned his strained smile to the lady, and her face distracted him—"with his own conscience . . ." She was staring at him both lovingly and blankly, a combination Huff had never seen in any of his previous wives or girl-friends. "With music." He started suddenly, realizing that he was holding her hands. "Soylent Green, you see, is—were you going to say something, Ma'am?"

"I love you," she said. "My liege, my own mortal joy."

Will didn't notice the lady until she had moved almost to the head of the line. He was piling up a sundae for one of his classmates, a fat boy with diabetes who was enormously popular despite his two social hits of obesity and disease. Craning her head around his classmate's bulk, the lady peered at Will impatiently, and looked at the fat boy like he had no right to be ahead of her in line and no right to eat ice cream. Will tried to ignore her. People stared all the time, as if that would make you serve them faster, though more than half the time the ones that glared the hardest at you still had no idea what they wanted when they made it to the head of the line. As he scooped Butter Cookie on top of Oscar's Wilde on top of Deadly Chocolate Orgasm for his classmate, he caught glimpses of her as she stared at him, and noticed her orange lipstick and too-smooth forehead and very soft-looking hair. These were elements common to a particular type of lady in his town, a wealthy, spiritless suburb of Orlando, and when his classmate shambled off and Will turned to take her order he was expecting her to be nothing special, the sort of facelift on top of a Talbot's dress that he and his coworker Lauren made fun of in the back all the time.

"Crepuscular Rays," she said. "Really?"

"Pardon?" Will said.

"That's the gayest thing I've ever heard," she said.

"Our owner is a latter-day Willy Wonka, " Will said, because that was what they were supposed to say anytime anyone remarked on the names of the ice cream, though Thom, the owner, had in mind when he trained his employees that people would be saying that the names were creative and fascinating instead of stupid or pretentious or twee, which they were.

"This town," the lady said, shaking her head and setting her earrings to jangling. Will had her pegged for Deadly Chocolate Orgasm because that was what all the middle-aged ladies ordered, but she settled on plain strawberry after tasting Crepuscular Rays and making a face. When she took the ice cream she made a point of touching him, which a lot of the middle-aged ladies did, laying her fingers on the inside of his wrist before she drew her hand back to capture the cone and bring it immediately to her lips. With ice cream on her face, she handed him a hundred-dollar bill and told him to keep the change. Then she walked away, out of the store and onto the street, not looking back at all, though the middle-aged ladies usually did that too when they came in alone for ice cream, throwing a glance over the shoulder to see if he was watching them leave.

Lauren scrutinized the bill after they closed, holding it up with both hands to the fluorescent light and even touching a corner of it to her tongue before pronouncing it real.

"She only tipped you like that because she wants to fuck you," she said, when he proposed that they split it. "I don't want any part of that. Fuck money is bad luck."

"Don't be stupid," he said. "She didn't want to sleep with me."

"They all want to fuck you," Lauren said, explaining as they cleaned up that she meant not just the poor little rich ladies of Winter Park but the whole adult world. She wasn't any older than Will, and was almost as friendless at school, and her prospects weren't any brighter than his—like him she was a junior with middling SAT scores and grades barely good enough to get into college at Gainesville—but she liked to lecture him at closing time. She thought he was naïve, and said all the time that he would come to a bad end if he didn't do something about his optimism and trust in strangers.

"I hate everybody," he said.

"No, you don't," she said. "*I* hate everybody. You're just a poseur." She didn't protest anymore, though, when he offered again to split the tip. With the rest of what was in the jar they each had seventy-eight dollars.

He stole a pint of Cookie Galore for his mother before he locked the store. He might have paid for it if Lauren hadn't talked her shit; he wanted to show her that he hated Thom and the way he strove for excellence in his ice cream and the way he took sprinkles as seriously as the plague. If there were a way to craft them individually, millimeter by millimeter, Will was sure Thom would do it. As it was he ran them through a colander several times a day to eliminate the clumps, saying every time, "No one wants their sprinkles to look like cat litter."

"I waited up for you," Will's mother said when he got home. It was hardly after ten, but she never finished drinking until after midnight. His father was flying a trip to San Diego and would be gone for two days because of the layover. She hadn't eaten, so Will made her a sandwich and sat with her while she failed to eat it. "What do you suppose he's up to?" she asked, because his father hadn't answered when she called the hotel.

"Probably out having a sandwich," Will said, pushing her sandwich closer to her. "It's dinnertime in San Diego." His mother always accused his father of having all sorts of wild fun on his layovers: erotic massage from small-footed Asian ladies in San Francisco, Donkey Shows in Tijuana, and naked hot-tubbing with the stewardesses in Chicago. His father denied it all, and had confided to Will that he didn't dare even go out to dinner with the crew most nights for fear of raising his mother's jealous mistrust.

"She ruins everything," he'd said. "Even from three thousand miles away, she ruins everything."

"She really loves you," Will had said, because his mother said that to Will, just as his father said the same thing during his own drunken complaints and confessions, and Will thought they loved each other more than they detested each other because it was the love that came out, in blubbering tears, in their very deepest drunks, and Will believed that people were most honest when they were most drunk.

His mother dialed his father again on the cordless phone, letting it ring and ring for the course of half a cigarette, while her eyes got heavier and heavier until she closed them and seemed to be sleeping, with the phone still chirping mutedly at her cheek and the cigarette ash lengthening at her mouth. "Asshole," she said finally, opening her eyes and hanging up and putting out her cigarette. "Why does he have to be such an asshole?" she asked Will directly, setting her face in a way that made her look as sad as she was angry. Will tried to reproduce it sometimes, staring in the mirror and raising his eyebrows while he frowned. When Sean caught him doing it once he told Will his face was going to get stuck that way if he wasn't careful.

"I don't know," Will said, though in fact he knew that the answer was the same to the question his father asked him, on equivalent nights, in the equivalent situation, "Why does she have to be such a horrible bitch?"

"Then what good are you?" she asked, which wasn't really an insult because it was what she always said when he answered that impossible question. "There was something I was going to tell you," she said. She strained visibly, then relaxed back into her grimace. "Nope," she said. "Now it's gone."

"That's all right," Will said. "Tell me later."

"It'll come," she said. She wobbled when she stood, so he helped her into bed and stayed downstairs only long enough to make sure she didn't light another cigarette and fall asleep with it. He took the Cookie Galore up to his room and lay in bed eating it with a big spoon and staring at his television, which was turned off, but he liked sometimes to imagine that he was watching his whole day again on the gray screen. He skipped right to the interesting part, and watched the lady hand him the hundred-dollar bill, and then watched her walk back to her Jaguar and drive it to her million-dollar home on the lake. She stood on the step to finish her ice cream, and wiped her mouth carefully before she went inside, and then he was too tired to imagine what it was like on the other side of the door. The Cookie Galore was all gone and he was too sleepy even to put the empty carton on his nightstand. He fell asleep with it tipped by his pillow.

He woke up a few hours later, not realizing a noise had startled him out of sleep until he heard it again: someone was moving around downstairs. His mother almost never woke until morning, and he wondered if he had locked the front door. There wasn't a lot of crime in the neighborhood, but his mother lived in terror of a home invasion whenever Will's father was away; she had a handgun in her dresser, and she made Will keep a baseball bat underneath his bed. He fished the bat out and crept downstairs with it, thinking he would see his mother gazing confusedly into the fridge, but it wasn't his mother sitting and smoking in her customary chair at the kitchen table. It was his brother, who was supposed to be far away, living a life that had nothing to do with any of them. "I've come to take you away," he blurted out, when he saw Will looking at him.

"Did you buy yourself something nice?" the lady asked when she came back again the next night. She mocked a few more flavors and then ordered another strawberry cone.

"It went into the college fund," Will said, which wasn't true. When Sean heard about his tip he insisted on taking him shopping, so that day, before their mother woke up and before their father got home, before any of the evening's arguments about what Sean was doing or not doing with his life had begun, the two of them took a walk up Park Avenue and went browsing in the fancy shops for something that cost seventy-five dollars. Just taking him shopping wasn't what Sean had meant when he said he was going to take Will away, but he wouldn't say anything more about it just yet. "I've got a plan," he said, "but I'm still thinking of the right way to sell it to you." He nodded his head slowly in the way that he had, moving it very slowly at first but then faster, as if he were convincing himself as he spoke. "Yeah, I shouldn't even have mentioned it yet, but I was so excited to see you." He gave Will a hug. That was uncharacteristic, so Will asked what was wrong with him. "Nothing!" he said. *"Everything."* He led Will along by the wrist. Will pulled away and put his hands in his pockets, but followed his brother out of the house and down the street.

Most of the town's pretension was concentrated in five blocks that ran alongside a park full of magnolias and azaleas and monuments to William Flagler: the stores that clothed and jeweled the rich ladies, the fancy restaurants where lunch was served to them on artfully arranged plates, and the boutique hotel where they had the occasional assignation. Sean hated it all, and made fun of every store they entered, and everyone who worked in those stores, and yet he insisted that Will should get something nice for himself. "They never get you anything nice," he said, meaning their parents. "What's wrong with them?"

"They got me a car," Will said, though technically they had only gotten him half a car—he had gotten the other half for himself out of years of savings.

"That thing's a piece of shit. Try this on." They were in a fancy men's store, a place where all the shirts had distinguished logos at the left breast. Will's ice-cream-loving classmate shopped there, and came to school every day in a different pastel-colored shirt, which Will now saw cost sixty dollars, whether they were tent-sized or normal-sized. He pulled the shirt on over his T-shirt. Sean folded his arms and stared at him. "That's *gorgeous* on you," said a salesgirl hovering nearby.

"It's not quite right," Sean said. "If you're going to spend sixty bucks, it really needs to be perfect." He said the same thing about six more shirts, about a pair of shoes three stores down, about a series of wallets, and five different colognes, and finally a pair of golf pants.

"We've run out of nice stores," Will said, because they'd come to the end of Park Avenue. Across the street there was a gas station and a muffler shop and then the Rollins College campus. "Mission not accomplished," Will said. "Oh, well." He hadn't really wanted to spend the money anyway.

"One more store," Sean said, and crossed the street to the college campus. Will thought they might be going to the bookstore for a sweatshirt, which he was going to say was not a very luxurious item, but Sean kept going past the bookstore to a dorm on the lake. "They might be closed," he said, but the door he was looking for was wide open. There was an exchange that Will didn't totally follow—it involved some hugging and a complicated handshake and the two of them saying *Dude!* a few times, and then Sean was asking Will for his seventy-five dollars and exchanging it for a large bag of pot. The kid shook Will's hand, like he had won something, and then Sean took him down to the college boathouse, where they sat under the dock near the edge of the water and got stoned. "I swear I wasn't planning that," Sean said. "I just thought of it all of a sudden. And I knew it wasn't something you'd ever do for yourself."

"Thanks," Will said.

"You like it?" he asked.

"It's good," Will said, though he wasn't sure that he really knew how to judge whether it was good or not. Pot tasted the same to him regardless of how people exclaimed or apologized over the quality, and it all made him feel the same: quiet and sad and detached. They sat without speaking for a while, passing Sean's pipe back and forth. Will tapped his toe at the edge of the water, which seemed to be coming farther up the sand, tiny wave by tiny wave. "Do lakes have tides?" he asked.

"Sure," Sean said. "A glass of water has a tide. How are you doing?"

"What, with the pot?"

"With everything. How are you doing? How have you been?"

"I'm okay," Will said.

"Just okay?"

"Okay does fine," Will said. "How are *you*?"

"I totally suck," Sean said. "It's complicated. But we don't have to talk about that. I didn't come here to shit all over you, little brother. I came here to take you away from all that."

"From what?"

Sean opened his mouth as if to answer, but then he just shook his head. "From all the shit," he said finally. "You don't see it yet, and that's the whole point. You should get away from it before you do."

"Where would I go?" Will asked, already feeling quiet and sad and detached from Sean's mounting agitation.

"Do you remember when you were like three and I read you this Richard Scarry book?"

"Who's Richard Scarry?"

"You know. Busy world. Cats and worms and badgers. Except the badgers are anesthesiologists and lawyers."

"Sounds awesome," Will said, closing his eyes.

"There was this one story. The cat makes fudge and it gets completely out of hand. The fudge comes out of the oven like it's *alive*. Like it's the blob. It comes out of the windows and the doors and the cat is stuck on the roof with fudge seeping through the shingles around his paws and then the worm comes by in a little helicopter and saves him. You remember that?"

"No," Will said, but then he thought he could remember the tiny helicopter at least, a one-seater that held the slim body of the worm, and he remembered that the worm wore a single shoe.

"It's like that," Sean said. "But you're the cat, and I'm the worm, and *it's not fudge.*"

Will burst out laughing and couldn't stop, thinking of cats smeared with shit, and worms in boots, and of Sean in that one-seater helicopter swooping around their house with his knees shoved up against his chest.

"It's not funny!" Sean said. "It's not funny at all!" But he was laughing so hard he was crying.

"I didn't give it to you to waste on your *college fund*," the lady said. She paid for the cone with a twenty and held out her hand for the change. "I don't make the same mistake twice," she said. That made him laugh, partly because he was still pretty stoned, but partly because he thought she must be kidding. "I should make you give it back," she said, and then he thought she was genuinely angry at him, and for the next twelve customers or so he imagined the conversation he would have with Lauren as they closed about how crazy the lady was. But then she was there again in line. "I want another one," she said.

"Sure," he said. "That last one wasn't very big."

"What's that supposed to mean?"

"Nothing," he said. "You got a kiddy scoop. Those are small. That's not enough for me. That's not really enough for anybody."

"I want a tub," she said.

"Really?"

"Why would I joke?" She pointed at the chalkboard behind him advertising the price for the take-home tub. It was twenty-three dollars and ninety-five cents with tax. She put the nickel in the tip jar and stared at him when he heaved the tub on top of the counter. "I think I'm going to need a little help with that," she said. He lifted it by the flared plastic handles near the lid, but still his hands were chilled and aching by the time he got to her car, a red Mercedes convertible. He dropped it in the back and a bit of frost fell off the side to land on the leather seat. He stared at it, not sure if he should try to pick it up, and when he turned to apologize to her she had moved much closer to where he was standing. He was sure she was going to try to kiss him, and while he didn't pucker up, he got ready for it, lifting his head back and narrowing his eyes and doing something that felt necessary with his tongue, like getting it primed. She reached out swiftly, but only touched his ear, measuring the distance from his earlobe to the hole in his head with her forefinger and thumb. "Such big ears," she said. "We should talk sometime." Before she got in her car and drove away, she handed him a card and said, "You can call me whenever you want."

Will stood outside his house, home from work but not ready to go inside yet. It was lit up as if a holiday were being celebrated inside, but Will figured that was probably just because everyone was home, and they had spread out to every corner of the house, each of them trying to put a maximum distance between himself and the other two. He cocked his head and squinted at the house, imagining fudgy shit pouring from the windows and spouting from the chimney, but it wasn't funny anymore. He still felt a little slow and sad from the pot, and he sat outside for a while in the backyard, turning the lady's card over in his pocket, waiting for some of the window lights to go out, but they never did go out. He went inside.

"*There* you are," his mother said, patting the chair next to her. She had a story for him that was partly about his father and partly about her own father and partly about Sean, how all three of them had let her down in the same way. She kept saying how clear it was, like crystal or the water in the pool just after it had been cleaned, or like her vodka, which she held up for him, flat and still in the heavy round tumbler she drank from—like *this*, she said, but Will couldn't make much sense of it. He nodded and drifted a little, wondering what the lady had for dinner instead of asking his mother if she had eaten. When she finally mentioned that she was hungry, he poured her a glass of milk.

"I'm not hungry like that," she said, so Will drank the milk while she explained that people needed more than food to thrive, and that what she was missing would be more nourishing than milk, when she finally got it. She was a very particular sort of drunk that night, one that Will was usually grateful for, because instead of complaining about how her husband didn't love her or how he didn't deserve her love, she talked brightly about her new plan for happiness, which was the same as her old plan for happiness, the one she conceived in hopeful tears on nights like this but then forgot in the following days. It involved travel and divorce. She would move away from Florida, back to Washington, D.C., which was a much more civilized place than Orlando or Winter Park, and was where her family abided. She would learn to be a sign language interpreter, or she would go back to being a real estate agent, or she would open a flower shop. And Will would live with her, in a room that she still described to him in the same terms she had used when he was five, but now the idea of having an observatory bubble in the roof, or a horse post at the end of his closet, or a hot tub in his bathroom, was only remotely appealing. She was being easy and happy, but it was harder for him to sit there tonight, for some reason, than when she raged in tears. When the milk was done Will put her to bed.

He passed by the living room on the way to the stairs up to the second floor, and his father called out to him from the couch. "Hey, buddy." He didn't pat the couch next to him, but Will sat down next to him anyway. "I feel like I haven't seen you for days," he said.

"I guess you haven't," Will said, and his father told him that he should come along on a trip sometime. It would be free for him to fly, after all, and he could probably even sit in the jump seat, if he wanted. Those trips never seemed to happen, and that had been a disappointment, when Will was ten and daydreamed of sitting in the jump seat or maybe even getting to fly the plane for a little while, if the engineer and copilot should be overcome with food poisoning and his father needed another hand at the controls. But now he had no particular interest in the jump seat, or flying, or San Diego, or going anywhere but to work and to school. "I don't think I could miss work," Will said.

"It's just a thought," his father said, waving his hands as if to dismiss the notion as silly, but he added, "It's not like the ice cream will all melt if you go away for a few days."

"I guess not," Will said. His father offered him a beer, holding up the half-depleted six-pack that he'd brought with him into the living room. Will took one and opened it and had a sip, which was what he usually did. His father talked for a few sentences about San Diego before he said, "I just want to make one thing clear." There was always something that he wanted to be clear about, that he loved his wife or that he thought Will was special or that it was in everybody's best interest when Sean moved out of the house or that getting married was the worst thing that could happen to a person or that it could be the best thing. That night he wanted it to be absolutely clear that he absolutely did not go out drinking until five in the morning with his copilot, who happened to be a lady. "Maybe it's inappropriate for her to be in the cockpit *at all*," he said, "but that doesn't mean there was any inappropriate *behavior*." He scowled at his beer can. "Certain *people* can think whatever they want." He went on for a while about how it said something about you if you could never trust someone, and how you could drive a person to do exactly the sort of thing you accused them of, how mistrust could make an innocent person guilty just from the force of violent spite, and wouldn't that serve you right, if it did? Wouldn't it serve the hater right, if it did? Will nodded, but it was even harder for him to pay attention than it had been with his mother.

"Are you going to drink that?" his father asked, and Will handed over his beer can. The empty plastic rings were at his father's feet.

"Sorry," Will said.

"Just don't want to waste it," his father said. "I think I'll watch some television, now that certain people have gone to bed."

"I'm pretty sleepy," Will said, when his father asked him if he wanted to come, and they parted ways at the stairs, Will suffering his father's hug awkwardly because the embrace brought a thought to Will's mind in a heated rush and he wondered what it would be like to hug the lady.

Sean was sitting on Will's bed upstairs, surrounded by a small collection of kitchenware and decorative statuary. In his hand he held a meat mallet, blond wood with a shiny, wicked-looking head of corrugated steel. "There you are," he said.

"Are you going to hit me with that?" Will asked.

"Do you remember this?" Sean said. "Or this or this?" He held up a garlic crusher and a solid plaster statue of the Infant of Prague, chipped on the head. "Or how about this?" He reached behind him and produced a croquet mallet.

"What are you doing?" Will asked, because their mother had made a weapon of everything on the bed, at some point over the years hitting their father with it or throwing it at him. "Starting a museum collection?"

"I'm showing you," Sean said. "I'm showing you what I mean, since I can't just tell you, not in the right words. There's still blood on these," he said. "There's still blood all over the place in this house."

"I thought it was shit," Will said.

"You know what I mean," Sean said. "All of these"—he waved the croquet mallet around—"have been put to *unnatural* uses. You can't just watch that. What I'm trying to say is that there are consequences, and that's why you have to come with me."

"I'm *really* tired," Will said.

"You're not listening to me. Now you're just tired. Now you hardly think you notice it, but later it's all you can think about. And the only thing that makes it any easier is the thought that you can take somebody else out of it. Nobody could take you out of it, but you can do it for somebody else? Do you see what I mean?"

"*Really, really* tired," Will said. Sean sighed and started to gather up the statues and mallets and trivets and heavy spoons. As he walked by he thrust his hip out to Will, drawing his attention to a piece of paper in his pocket.

"That's a note," he said, "to *them*. It explains everything. I'll leave it tomorrow night, after they go to bed, and then we'll just go. We'll just get going, and everything else we'll figure out later. Okay?" Will moved away and pushed the croquet mallet under his bed. "You don't even have to answer now. You just need to know I have a plan."

"I don't care," Will said, not turning around. "I don't want to go anywhere with you." Sean dropped something—Will heard the impact on the carpet—but didn't say anything. Will waited till he was gone before he turned around. Then he sat on his bed.

He took the lady's card from his pocket, lay back, and held it up to look at it. It was the size and shape and stiffness of a business card, but all it listed were her name and her number, as if her name was all there was to her job, or just being herself was her profession. It was after midnight, but she had said he could call anytime, and he chose to believe that. He listened for a moment to the dial tone, unreasonably afraid that his mother might be listening in, and then he dialed the number. She picked up almost right away.

"Hi," Will said.

"Hi," she said. "Who is this?"

"Will. From Thom Tickle's. The ice-cream shop."

"I knew who it was," she said. "That was a joke."

"Oh," Will said, and tried to laugh but only managed a cough.

"Are you sick?"

"No," Will said. "How are you?"

"I'm good," she said. "I'm pretty good. I was hoping you would call."

"Really?"

"Sure."

"So am I. I'm glad I called."

"Well," she said. "Then we're on the same page."

"I guess," Will said. Then she didn't say anything for a while. Will might have been afraid she had hung up, but he could hear her breathing. He wondered if he had said something wrong. Maybe he should have said *definitely* instead of *I guess*. "Anyway," he said.

"Do you want to come over?" she asked.

"I bet she has syphilis," Lauren said. "You can't go around fucking every soda jerk in Central Florida with no consequences."

"Nobody has syphilis anymore," Will said. "It's like leprosy."

"It's on the rise," Lauren said. "None of that bad shit ever really goes away. Anyway, you better wear a condom."

"It's not going to happen," Will said. "I don't want it to happen. Haven't you been listening to anything I've said?" He had told her about the phone call, and then wished he hadn't. He hadn't gone over, but before Will hung up they had talked for another twenty minutes about what might happen if he did.

"She has spots on her palms, I saw them. I'll buy you some condoms, if you're too embarrassed." Before Will could reply, Thom came up with a hot towel and told Will to polish away the frost on the ice-cream canisters.

Fancy-looking ladies came and went, but Will's lady stayed away. They closed at ten, but because Thom was there it took a little longer to finish cleaning up, because he hovered over every spot and smudge, though he never actually cleaned anything himself. Sean had told Will that he wanted to leave at midnight, and had offered to help him pack that morning and sneak his bags past their parents. Will had just shaken his head.

"Do you need more time to think about it?" Sean had asked, and Will had said, "Maybe."

"Take all the time you want," Sean had said. "Take all day."

"Okay. I don't think I want to go anywhere."

"You say that now," Sean said. "But will you say that at midnight?"

It was eleven when Will left the store, and though he started toward home, he took a detour to 813 Old England Avenue. It wasn't totally out of his way, and he told himself convincingly that he just wanted to see where the lady lived. At the end of their phone conversation she had said he could come by anytime, exactly how she had said he could call anytime. Still, he was only going to stand in the driveway. It turned out to be a guesthouse set back away from the road, and long sweeps of Spanish moss hid her windows from the sidewalk. Will walked down the driveway, meaning to leave as soon as he had counted her windows, but he knocked on her door instead, and it didn't occur to him until after he had knocked to worry that she might have a family.

"There you are," she said, and seemed to appraise him as he stood in her doorway.

"I guess," Will said.

"You look better out from under those fluorescent lights."

"Thanks," Will said. "You too." That made her laugh. She turned around and walked inside.

"Do you want something to drink?" she asked him as they passed her kitchen.

"I don't think so," he said.

"Me neither," she said, and took his hand. They passed through the rest of her tiny house to get to her bedroom, but she wasn't giving him a tour. In brief glimpses he saw her little living room and dining room before she led him upstairs. Her bedroom took up the whole second floor, and her bed, king-size and strewn with green and blue pillows, was the biggest piece of furniture he had ever seen. She let go of his hand and lay down, turning to face him as she raised her hands over her head, stretching and sliding in a way that made him feel like he was watching her at the bottom of a pool. "There you are," she said again.

In his fantasy it seemed like the right thing to do. There, he imagined a moment when, inside her, he paused to consider that this was how things were supposed to be, and he made a point of enjoying how nicely they fit together, how something or someone in charge of them both had engineered things such that they fit together. He imagined himself thinking, *This is perfect.*

The actual fucking left him little time to think, or really enjoy it, though it went on a long time. He came right away, while she was still nosing around in his groin. She surprised him by shoving her tongue in his ass, and more than pleasure he felt the most immense and startling surprise: at the narrow, suspicious look on her face, at the way his cock arched and bucked without being touched, at the fountaining geyser of semen and the discrete noise it made when it fell on her pillows, a rapid series of soft tip-taps that sounded like some fleet little creature had just run across her bed.

"Is it over already?" she asked, but he wasn't done. He put away all thoughts of his fantasy, because he hadn't really imagined any of it correctly, and they did things that he probably couldn't have imagined, because he thought it was disrespectful to imagine such things. He stopped thinking altogether, and just did what he was told and when they were finished he continued not to think, but lay away from her on the far side of the bed, silent since his third big shout, which was only a peep compared to hers. He stared at her, not holding an opinion one way or the other about her or what they had just done, until she made an odd noise, a burbling sigh the sort of which he'd never heard come out of anyone's mouth. When she did it again he realized it wasn't coming from her mouth but from between her legs. It broke the silence and his unthinking reverie and seemed like the greatest and suddenly the worst surprise of the night, and for all that it was just a meaningless utterance of air, like the beginning of a regretful conversation he would have with himself for the rest of his life.

"I have to go," he said.

"Of course you do," she said into her pillow, half-asleep. "But don't stay away too long." Will picked up his clothes and dressed on the stairs, and started to run as soon as he was out the door, not really understanding why it seemed like such a good idea now, after all, to get in the car with Sean and drive and drive and drive, but knowing it as certainly as he had ever known anything. It was hardly a mile to his house from hers and he was home by twelve-thirty. The house was brightly lit and his mother and father were both waiting up for him, but his brother was long gone.

Part Four

13

*A*s she ran, Molly heard her mother telling her it was too soon after eating to exercise so vigorously. When she heard the noise of the iron doors falling down, she had sprinted out of the feasting chamber through the nearest door and hadn't slowed down since, running at top speed down a featureless gray corridor that opened every few minutes into another marvelous room, but she knew it would be stupid, or even deadly, to stop to see the sights. The more she ate, the hungrier she had felt, and even though she had gravy on her lips and pudding in her hair, she felt very light on her feet and was sure she could run a mile, or swim two, if she needed to. She went along with a bottle in her hand, sure she could feel the threat behind her as an actual pressure and heat against her back and her bottom. When she finally paused for breath, she took a long sip of the wine.

The more she drank, the more clearheaded she felt and the more coordinated she became. As she ran, everything was feeling for the first time like it was making sense: she was lost in a cathartic dream of instruction, peopled by incarnations of her neuroses, and the deadly threat behind her was nothing less than the roiling mass of her feelings for her dead, abandoning boyfriend. She neither knew nor needed to know why those feelings should take Peabo's form in the same way that she didn't need to worry anymore about whether or not what was happening was real. It was real enough to demand that she deal with it, and sometime very soon she was going to need to stop running and turn around, but not quite yet.

The lesson of the meal she had just left was that there is always room to enjoy yourself, and always something to appreciate, even when you've lost your mind and lost all hope and have clawed your way down not just into the slough of despond but beyond it into the subsequent sloughs of despair and please-kill-me-now. She hadn't meant or wanted to enjoy that unexpected feast, but she had, and it made her feel big in her soul, how she could delight in the texture of a crispy bit of chicken skin at the same time that she mourned her lost boyfriend and her lost mind, and she didn't have to choose between delight and despair: she could experience them both to their fullest simultaneously. She didn't know whether that was progress or just a detour on her road to suicide-survivor recovery, or if this double capacity for feeling might dissipate when she turned around to be rent by monster-Peabo. But she was going to enjoy it for a while. If she was drunk, this was the best drunk of her life, and she wanted it to go on and on. She sped up, sure she could be sprinting down a balance beam as easily as a sidewalk, and gave it a try, fleetly placing one foot in front of the other, and then leaping imaginary candles perched along the imaginary balance beam, and then stepping through tires set at intervals between the imaginary candles on the imaginary balance beam, and wondering, just before she tripped and fell, if she could see the tires and the candles so clearly, why they didn't just appear, here at the approaching bottom and climax of her allegorical recovery dream adventure?

She felt like she'd been running as fast as a car, and she tumbled along, rolling and spinning, as far and as fast as if she'd fallen out of one, finally coming to rest seated with her legs splayed out on either side of her and listing so far to one side that her hair swept the ground before she righted herself. She kept her eyes closed and patted herself on the head and arms and legs, feeling for fractures and bruises, but her bones and her muscles felt pleasantly numb all over, as if she were touching someone else entirely. She straightened her hair and cleared her throat and opened her eyes, half expecting to be back at the feasting table or face-to-face with Peabo, but she was in another giant room, this one not quite empty but filled with portraits.

The corridor that had brought her here was nowhere to be seen: it might have ended here, except that she remembered having seen it shortly before she tripped, stretching featureless and gray into the distance. Now the darkness all around was broken only by puddles of light thrown upon the wall at regularly spaced intervals, lighting up pictures of boys. They stretched to her left as far as she could see, until the puddles of light shrank to specks. To her right they ran to a wall in the far distance, where a brighter light fell down upon some kind of sculpture. She didn't like museums; they made her feel sleepy and overwhelmed, and though she considered that in her dream of transformative drunkenness she might have an opportunity to change that, she didn't care to feel any differently, and she just wanted to get out of there. She walked toward the sculpture, hoping to find a way out, glancing at the portraits as she went.

Somebody really likes little boys, she thought as she walked along, because none of them was older than eleven or twelve, and some were only fat little toddlers. The pictures were executed in every different style, and some of the boys were clothed in beads or feathers or scraps of cloth or little swarms of bees, but they were all very pretty, and they all shared an expression, a vacancy to their smile that made them look mildly dissatisfied and a little drugged. She felt sure, in her state of heightened drunken genius, that she knew the point of them and the point of the gallery: they were an installation of lost boys who were iterations of her own lost boys. It would not have been a surprise for her to see Peabo there with a 3D Jesus poking out of the painting. "Now you are getting obvious!" she said aloud to her subconscious, when she came to the portrait of the tan boy with the crew cut. It was Ryan, of course. It took her a moment to recognize him; she wasn't sure she would have known him if she hadn't been expecting to see him. What she couldn't understand was why his picture was just one of many, not the last in the row and not elevated to a position of honor, and why the picture next to his—a brown-haired boy with enormous ears—had a black X painted over his face. She pulled at Ryan's picture because it felt like the right thing to do, to move it forward in line. It came easily off the wall and was much less heavy than the thick wooden frame made it appear. It was another twenty or so portraits—blond boys and buck-toothed boys and freckled Tom Sawyer types and a minority of minorities, a black boy and an Indian boy and a mestizo boy with a heavy Frida Kahlo unibrow and one weeping toddler—to the front of the room, to the sculpture, which she now saw depicted a dead boy on a funeral bier. There was indeed a door there, on the far side of the sculpture, but she didn't go through it yet. First she tried to hang Ryan's picture on the wall, but there were no nails, and though it stuck briefly by itself, it wouldn't stay. She decided to put it on the sculpture, since that was a sort of pride of place, too, that would be different from the hundreds and hundreds of other pictures. She didn't know what the significance might be, or how moving pictures around in a dream might make her real life and the real world bearable, but it felt necessary and right, and she half expected, as she set the picture down, balancing it against the very lifelike sculpture of the reclining boy, that she would wake up.

Instead she heard a voice. "What are you doing?" There was someone in the small space underneath the bier.

"Nothing," she said.

"Are you the Beast, come in a fair form to lure me out? I command you to answer truthfully."

"I'm not," Molly said. "Who are you? Are you stuck?" She didn't particularly care if he was.

"*Poodle! Poodle!* There's still some power in that word, and I command you with it! Are you he? Are you my enemy, come to eat me? Answer!"

"I'm just a girl," Molly said, "and I don't know what you're talking about." Though she did. It made a certain sense that everyone in her breakdown dream would be afraid of the same thing. Dreams and lunatic minds were spendthrift in their creativity, and yet their economies dictated only one villain per drama. "Okay," she said. "I know who you're talking about. The black boy."

A foot emerged from under the bier, stepping out of the darkness, followed, somewhat hesitantly, by a second foot, and then a little limboing body, shoulders and head dragging on the ground. When he stood up the little man only came halfway up her shin. "Black boy? I suppose, if that's how you see him. He's anything and everything, as long as it terrifies you. Myself, I generally see him as a large brown boot, except when he's trying to trick me." He reached under the bier and removed a wooden knife. It was long as he was tall, but he hefted it easily onto his shoulder.

"Don't give yourself a splinter," Molly said, wondering who he was supposed to be or what he was supposed to represent, what message she had packed away for herself in the form of this little man with a big knife. As if to answer her, he jumped up and touched his tongue to the skin of her knee.

"Just making sure," he said, licking his lips. "Just a girl! What are you doing here, Just a Girl?"

"I got lost in my dream," Molly said, because that seemed like the best way to describe the whole adventure. "What are you going to do with that knife?"

"It's for my Lady," he said, "so she can bind the Beast in blood once again. She didn't think I would find it, but it was obvious where it would be. She hides everything important here. Lost in a dream?"

"Exactly," she said. "I'm stuck in a dream, or something like that. Or I'm crazy. Locked up somewhere. Dreaming. Deluded. Drugged up. You're just a figment of my imagination, but you mean something." It made perfect sense when she heard herself explaining it to him. "What do you mean? Is it cheating, if I just ask you to tell me?" She laughed and took another sip from the bottle. At the taste of the wine, she thought of her dinner companions again, Henry and Will. She missed them suddenly. Such companionable figments, she thought. Such handsome delusions. The tiny man was squinting at her.

"Lean close," he said, "and I'll tell you, for I'll not shout a secret." She bent at the waist, halfway to the floor, but he said, "Closer," so she knelt, but he said, "Closer still," so she lay down on her stomach and put her face close to his face. His ears were covered in soft golden fur, and his breath smelled like rosemary. "Now close your eyes, the better to listen," he said, so she did that; she almost felt like she ought to purse her lips. Finally, she thought, this dream is starting to cooperate! He didn't keep her waiting long, but with a thin little shriek cut her cheek with a swipe of the knife. She rose swiftly to her knees, raising one hand to her face and knocking him sprawling with the other.

"You could have put my eye out!" she shouted, the first thing to come into her head.

"The better you would see, then!" he shouted back. He was already on his feet again, making a wobbly threat with the big knife. "Mortals! Always it's a dream. Maybe *you're* the dream. Away! Away! I've got more important things to do than babbling with a fool!" He ran off down the long hall with the knife clasped against his chest. Molly thought of a few different things that she could have called after him: *You little shit!* or *I'll cut you too!* or *You're supposed to help me get out!* or *That's even more dangerous than running with scissors!* But she couldn't quite find her voice. She stood looking at the blood on her hand, touching her face again, then looking at the blood again. The blood made her feel unbalanced all of a sudden, as if she were about to slip and fall within herself. She clung tighter to the bottle for support and leaned against the stone bier and the sculpture of the boy.

"And who are *you?*" she asked him, meaning *What do you represent* and *What is your name* and *What are you doing here*, but it was so hard, looking at him, to think he represented anything but a dead child. *It's so lifelike*, she thought, though that seemed like the wrong word for a piece of art that perfectly represented the state of human death. She looked a little closer—the lights in the room seemed to brighten as she did—and understood why he was deathlike, that he was not a triumph of some sculptor's art, but some undertaker's. A voice in her head shouted, *Don't touch him!* Of course it was the very same sort of voice that used to say such terrible things about her family—she heard it in the very same way—but now it sounded solicitous and panicked instead of snarky and sarcastic and she wondered if it had always meant to look out for her. *I won't*, she told it, but she did, and then she ran away too, bouncing against the walls in her unsteady haste. There was a door beyond the bier, after all.

She slammed the door behind her, and stood pressing her back to it to keep it closed, as if the dead boy was going to chase her in here. She looked around. *Someone has destroyed Cher's bedroom*, she thought to herself, because the room was in luxurious tatters, and it really looked like the sort of place Cher might sleep, if it weren't all cut up and smashed. There were jeweled tapestries on the walls, and the furniture was made of lustrous exotic wood, and thick, intricately woven rugs lay three deep on the floor, but the place looked like the lady had erupted in a rage, and wreaked havoc on her luxurious nest with hammer and scissors and ax: the tapestries were in shreds and the furniture was in splinters. Molly walked to the bed, carefully appreciating how white were the sheets and how fluffy were the pillows where they weren't torn asunder—she had abundant attention to spare for everything but the thing she was trying so hard not to think about. She sat down crooked on the bed—it stood on a single leg, the upper right—and ran her hands along the sheets, marveling at how soft they were, and wondering why they ended abruptly in the middle of the bed. "Oh, no," she said softly, feeling a shift underneath her, and the remaining leg gave out. The bed crashed to the ground. She kicked her legs out, and bounced once on the mattress. It felt like something shifted and fell inside her at the same time, and she could not ignore any longer how real it felt when her face was cut, and how the little boy's body had felt hard and dead in a way that nothing, not even her grieving trickster mind, could fake. She cried because that boy was dead, and because children died of neglect and accident and disease and because Ryan had died and because she really had become lost trying to make any sort of enduring sense of why he was dead, and become lost in pursuit of any sort of enduring peace over him, but now she could guess, if the dead boy was real, and the ugly little man was real, and faeries were real and magic was real, and threatening monsters in the size and shape of little boys were real, what Ryan's picture was doing in that gallery.

Molly threw Ryan a party for his birthday. The planning was slightly complicated by the fact that he seemed to have no friends. She had lost a few herself, in the time that she had been dating him, overly sensitive types who thought silence could only indicate antipathy and who couldn't understand that when you were in love you were allowed to ignore everyone except for your beloved, at least until the honeymoon was over. And if the honeymoon seemed to go on forever, then they should just be happy for you. She didn't have enough friends to fill up his gigantic house, but when she included Salome and some Root and Relish co-workers, there were enough to make his garden look full, and even post a person here and there in the first- and second-floor balconies, ready to cast down handfuls of compostable Norwegian confetti of which Salome, in a spasm of generosity, had made Molly a gift. Ryan's peculiar sister, who looked and acted like his twin even though she was two years older than him, was there too. Arranging for her to come had felt like a coup, since she always seemed at least mildly disapproving of Molly, getting her to return a call or e-mail had been a challenge, and she had reminded Molly three times during their negotiations that birthdays just weren't that important for their family. "But they're important to me," Molly had replied, and not realized until much later how lame that must have sounded. She had meant they were important to *us*, though she understood that she was throwing the party as much to make that true as to demonstrate that it was true.

"Where could he be?" Salome asked, when Ryan was only ten minutes late for his surprise. She thought tardiness was rude, and it was especially unforgivable to be late for your own party, even if you didn't know it was happening.

"I'm sure he's on his way," Molly said, though he hadn't replied to the three texts she'd sent him so far. She had formulated a not-very-sophisticated ruse to get him home on time—dinner with Salome, to whom he had taken an unexpected and persistent shine. He said he liked to listen to her because she made him forget about his own troubles. To Salome's delight, Molly had finally discovered that he was a troubled person (Now you're really getting to know him! she said). Part of the reason that it took so long was that he wasn't troubled in exactly the ordinary sense of the word. He had more money than he seemed to know what to do with, and a large strange and spooky house; he loved his family in what seemed like a very straightforward and uncomplicated way; and, remembering and reviewing her training in psychology, she couldn't really place him on any spectrum of disorder known to the DSM-IIIR. She had been trained in psychology only enough to recognize drastically maladjusted parishioners and to refer them for help if their problems were beyond her limited scope of impotent pastoral practice, but she certainly knew enough to recognize a lunatic, and Ryan wasn't a lunatic, for all that he sometimes had unusual things to say about the moon. When she evaluated him through the lens of her former profession, she saw a person unable to find a home in his happiness. It wasn't that he didn't appreciate what he had, or feel lucky to have it—he made it plain to her every few weeks or so how much he appreciated his house and his city and, yes, even his shiftless, mildly overweight girlfriend—but she had the sense that none of this was quite enough.

He never actually said it in so many words, or even indicated it in so many actions, but here and there, month by month, he dropped a hint, and by the end of the year he had given her a lot to reflect on. Some of those hints were a little more concrete than others. "See the moon?" he asked her one night as they walked along the Embarcadero.

"Sure," she said.

"That's not the moon," he said. "There's another moon—a *better* moon—behind that one." It was bloodred and pumped up grotesquely, just coming up over the bay, so she thought he meant there was a regular moon, calmer and prettier and looking less like it should shine over a battlefield, but that wasn't what he meant. "It shines on a whole different world, where you can do things you can't do here." They were both pretty drunk—or at least she was; no matter how much Ryan drank he never slurred or stumbled—but their conversations often got weirder after he had been drinking. So she was content not to know what he was talking about and just guess at his meaning. Whenever this happened, whenever he talked in a way that only appeared to invite a reply from her, she thought how nice it was still to be with him, how handsome he looked when he was wistful, or how his eyes sparkled when he looked like he was about to cry, though he never did cry. It was easy to distract herself that way when she was drunk, and when she was sober she never dwelled on these conversations until it was too late to extract a useful lesson from them about the character of her boyfriend. "Do you know what I mean?" he asked.

"No," she said.

He sighed. "The other moon shines on the better world."

"And on the better people?" she asked.

"Exactly," he said. She tried to imagine that better world, that better stretch of the Embarcadero and the better Ryan and Molly who inhabited it. Ryan was not so different, but she imagined herself as someone who didn't have to flee her profession, and imagined the different, better past that had shaped her.

Then there was the physical evidence, less what he said and more what he made or did. It didn't always substantiate her theory that she was somehow not *enough*; more often it was only evidence that he was kind of weird, but sometimes the weirdness was part of a general tendency to lay his attention in strange places, and this was a process in which she never could participate, because he did it secretly, or at least he thought that he did. She found notes scattered around the house, pieces of paper torn from notebooks or scraps torn from cereal boxes, the blank side covered with a list of flowers and fruit: *Buttercup, Radish, Acorn.* There was a door in the cluttered basement that he told her led to a room where he kept his "art projects," but when she looked inside one day when he was gone she only found one picture, drawn in chalk on the stone floor, of a round wooden door, meticulously detailed down to the shining highlights on its brass doorknob, the whole thing stamped on and smeared as if he'd been angry at it. She woke sometimes to find him missing from the bed, and looking out the window she watched him standing naked in the garden, staring up at the moon, or peeing on the plants, and once leaning with one arm against the gold and silver tree while he used his free hand to masturbate. He had a tendency to hop every now and then as they walked, even in the absence of any obstacle, and she never totally understood what he was doing until she saw him one night in the garden doing the same thing, step-step-hopping from one end of the garden to the other, throwing up his arms with the hop and arching his back, and—recognizing the motion from her own dreams—she realized he was trying to fly.

This was all okay with her. Eventually, she came to think it had been too okay. She ought to have called down to ask him what he was doing when he appeared to be having sex with his tree. She ought to have asked where he was trying to get to through the door in the floor, and asked what was so special about the word *Doorknob* that he should feel compelled to write it down a hundred times on the blank side of a torn-up cereal box. But it didn't seem like her business yet, to pry out all his secrets when he wasn't yet inclined to volunteer them to her, especially since he had secrets that were as hidden to him as they were to her. Never mind that she already felt like she had volunteered all of hers. She didn't imagine that such confidences, beyond the easy ones, were currency to trade with each other in achieving intimacy. And anyway, mysterious drawings and list-making and even semi-public nocturnal emissions were all clues that pointed someplace strange but not disgusting, weird but not illegal. She hadn't found a limb in the basement, or a pair of bloody panties under the mattress, or even stray traces of lipstick on his collar.

And she hoped, anyway, that he would come to find what she had found, and feel what she felt, which was that there were always going to be intimations from the world that there was more to be had, something different and something better, beyond what they were sharing together. It was his loveliest gift to her, and one she was trying as hard as she could to give back to him, the special and certain knowledge that those intimations were just life trying to fake you out again, when in fact it didn't get any better than this. It didn't get any better than the two of them.

Waiting to surprise him, she thought, *This is going to be the first day of the rest of your life*, and that was the real surprise, not the fact that your sister and Salome and a few friends and a few more acquaintances were lurking in your garden waiting to shout at you. Surprise! Everything is actually okay. Surprise! You can stop looking for more. Surprise! I love you so much. That was the biggest surprise of all, the depth of inexhaustible feeling for him that she had in her, and when he walked in the door and she looked at him she would have that feeling she had every day, of being perpetually startled by it.

"Maybe you should give him a call," Salome said, but he didn't answer when she called, then or in the seven times she called in the following hour, and he didn't come home until after the last guest was long gone, even his sister and the unexpectedly faithful Salome, who stayed and worried with her after Carolina took her casual leave from them, saying, "He's a flake, and birthdays aren't important in our family. Don't take it personal." Salome drank so much white wine that she departed at last as well, curling up beneath the picnic table Molly had rented for the party and placed underneath the golden oak. Molly sat with her head in her hands, eventually not worrying anymore about whether or not Ryan was safe, and not caring anymore about all the wasted expense of food and alcohol and premium confetti, and feeling almost, by the time Ryan finally came home, walking through the gate wheeling his bicycle at his side, like she didn't care about anything at all, like if he had been just five minutes later, she would never have cared about him, or be hurt by what he did or didn't do, again.

"What did I miss?" he asked, looking around at the food on the table and the balloons on the banisters and the ribbons in the tree, and Molly burst into tears.

14

Will was starting to enjoy being lost, or at least he was starting to get so used to it that it didn't really bother him. He found that he could enjoy the continuous surprises more than he worried about them. The farther he ran, the less he felt pursued, and at last it was more the pressure of his mission to find a sapling for Carolina's garden that drove him forward than fear of the monster who was chasing him, and as he penetrated into the deeper chambers of wonder beneath the hill, be began to take time to look around. His drunkenness served both to insulate him from the strangeness and to sharpen his appreciation of it. And the drunkenness brought tears of concern for his lost erstwhile comrades, lovely Molly and handsome Henry and the three dear horrible little elves, but the tears were intermittent, and sometimes he wept with awe instead of sadness.

He went through rooms he named as he discovered them, and which he hardly had time to appreciate before he'd flung open a door at the far end and plunged through—the Sparkling Gullet and the Panda Market and the Jade Toilet and the Mushroom Cathedral, he paused in each one only long enough to verify that they were empty of trees of any size or age, and then his mission pushed him onward. But at the Warm Frozen Waterfall he slowed, and in the Hall of a Hundred Little Windmills he paused, and in the Library of All the Same Book he actually stopped to examine a few of the volumes, all titled *Various*, that lined the shelves. He thought they were translations of the same book into countless languages—none of which he recognized—until he found seven in a row in English, but none of them had the same first sentence. He half expected to read *then Will picked up a book in the curious library and began to read* or *Make a wish, Bastien!* but they were ordinary sentences about animals setting off on an adventure, a mole in one and a badger in another and in yet another a girl-pig named Davida. He kept that one, a souvenir for Molly to add to the others he had gathered for her. Molly! he thought. That wasn't who he meant at all, and it seemed a worse crime than kissing her to imagine, even if only fleetingly and mistakenly, giving her the gifts that were meant for Carolina. He paused to imagine, firmly and concretely, Carolina's face when he came to her with a little box containing the little tree.

He had found the door on the other side of the library and was reaching for it when it opened forcefully, as if kicked, knocking books to the floor when it slammed against the shelves. Before he was quite aware of what he was doing, Will found himself trying to hide behind the book he was carrying, his terror of the pursuing monster suddenly as fresh as when he had first seen her in the park. He recovered his dignity enough to lower the book even before he heard the voice. "Are you?" it began, and then the little man to whom it belonged snorted. "No, I don't even have to taste you to know. Another mortal! Who let you all in?"

"A boy," Will said, and then, "A little man," which seemed like the wrong thing to say because of the bristling anger this little man radiated and the outsized knife he carried. "A tree person."

"Well, it's a fine night for tourists!" the little man said, punctuating the statement with a vigorous thrust of the knife toward Will's face. He was a good ten feet away, and five feet down, but Will still flinched.

"Would you like a drink?" Will asked him, holding out his bottle of wine and thinking it might help him be less angry and antagonistic.

"There's no time for *that*," he said. "Is that how you're making yourself useful in this crisis? Where is that killjoy high-handed mortal seriousness when it might actually be appropriate? Eh? Eh?" He poked again with the knife, and Will said, "Hey, there. Settle down, little man. I'm on your side!" That made the tiny fellow howl and do a spastic dagger dance, swiping and stabbing at the air all around him. "Sorry! Sorry!" Will said, backing away.

"Oh, but you will be sorry, you ridiculous *delay*, if I don't get this knife to my Lady in time. Now out of my way!"

"I didn't mean—" Will began, but the little man was already running by him, swiping at Will's feet as he passed. Will did a skip and a jump, and called after him, "Sorry!" and "I'm actually looking for the nursery!" but the angry creature was already gone. "A tree nursery," he added softly, "not a baby nursery." He cracked the door and peaked outside before he walked through it.

Will stayed longer at the Marble Pool (an Olympic-sized pool filled with marbles instead of water) and with the Singing Ferns, and then the fun part was over. He came to mildewed chambers that felt like they must be at the very bottom of the hill, because all the time he had been fleeing alone Will felt like he had been going down, and now there were no more carved pillars or mirrored ceilings or floors carpeted in tiny flowers but just rough wet stone and moss and coarse grass and danger, at first no more seriously threatening than the little mannikin with the wooden knife, but deeper down, more significant. They were a totally different category of danger than the thing he was running from, more ordinary sorts of extraordinary that called to the brave parts of him instead of commanding the craven parts, and made him want to stand up and face them instead of shitting in his pants and crying and lying down and giving up on everything. He started to get the definite feeling that the way out of the hill was guarded by challenges, that a person needed to demonstrate some kind of fortitude in order to find it. He imagined, as he fought his way through the snake vines and then pushed past the mud people and waited patiently (finishing his wine) for the three-eyed watcher to take a nap, that he was blazing a trail for the others and making it easier for them by his effort. And he imagined, of course, that he was fighting his way back to Carolina, since the way out was the way back to her, and there was something in the attack of a mud person and the bite of a snake vine and the stinging, sleeping slap of a three-eyed watcher that felt like it imparted an earned virtue to him that he felt sure would be apparent to anyone who saw him when he eventually emerged, battered and bruised, from under the hill. Certainly Carolina would see it, and it did not boggle belief to think there might be, at the end of this winding, challenge-strewn path, which he ran with an intermittently waving sense of terror at his back, a little golden tree whose roots were carefully bound inside a burlap sack, waiting for him to take it back to the place that could be his home again.

He had the sense, too, as the challenges intensified, that he was getting closer to the exit, and when he came to the last rock chamber, and his internal bathymeter told him he had gone as low as he could go, he felt ready to face a dragon, though he was armed only with a salt shaker and a book and an empty bottle and a very small knife. But what he saw in the chamber looked like a waving sea of thick flesh-colored anemones, until they got close enough—as soon as he entered the chamber they started hobbling toward him—for him to see it was a sea of disembodied penises, softly shambling toward him on variously sized testicle feet. He was drunk enough and not drunk enough to be afraid of them; they were less uncanny than they would have been if he was sober, and yet he was sober enough to remember how awful the thing chasing him was, and realize that they were comparatively innocuous. They nuzzled around his ankles, and he waited apprehensively for them to become erect and monstrous as they rubbed against him and each other, but they were as harmless as a roiling basket of puppies. He didn't know what the challenge in them might be, unless it was to avoid stepping on one, and he was thinking that the hill was giving him an odd sort of goodbye present. He wondered if he might dare put one in his pocket for Carolina, since despite the awkwardness involved in making her a present of a detached penis the gift would prove beyond any doubt the truth of his story, when he heard a rustling far above his head, followed by a noise that put him in mind of a yawning cat, a stretched-out mewling that faded to a breathy sigh. He looked up to see a swarm of bats that were not bats. He never got a really proper look at them, but the situation told him it must be a swarming flock of vaginas that flew all around his head, biting him toothlessly on his ears and his cheeks and his neck. He ran then, heedless of the gentle sluglike cocks that he squashed, and felt blindly along the opposite end of the cave for the way out. It was there: a tunnel only a little taller than him, that narrowed as he went, so he had to stoop and then crawl, a flapping vagina harassing his bottom until the passage became so narrow that he had to crawl on his belly and it could only bump at his feet. His panic was rising again when he felt a little air move on his face, and he started to slither in champion haste when he caught sight of a light at the end of his tunnel. He wondered if it could be dawn already, and then he was sliding the last few feet and tumbling out into the lushly appointed wreck of a room. Molly sat weeping on a ruined bed not twenty feet away.

Mrs. Perkins lived in a big pink house in Russian Hill with a garden out back. She was a familiar type among Will's clients, though not a common one: a lady whose great wealth made her eccentric instead of crazy. She became interested in her garden for a period of a few weeks once or twice a year and kept Will occupied moving plants and trees to make room for a pond or a little temple to her first husband that had to go just here or there. In the intervening months Will would make his regular visits, but only see her from a window, and it was her current husband, much younger but still a little pickled-looking, who brought Will his check. But when she was interested she was very interested, so it wasn't unusual when she came out while Will was working. Usually she stood around with her hands over her eyes or pressed against her forehead, her two poses of active imagination in which she made rearrangements in her head before she commanded Will to execute them, but that day—which Will marked later as the beginning of the end of his relationship with Carolina—she sat down near him in a redwood chaise, flipping languidly through a book with a joint hanging out of her mouth.

"Mmm?" she said, which he knew from experience meant she was offering him a drag off the joint.

"No, thanks," he said. "Might make me water something too much." She threw back her head and laughed. She was wearing a fancy muumuu and a turban, with a crystal dangling above her eyes. The crystal sparkled when she tossed her head and then bonked on her forehead in a way that looked quite painful, though her smile didn't falter at all. Will had never hated her before—she was a harmless lady who took good care of her plants and whose only crime was being obscenely wealthy—but just then there was something about her laugh and the way she tossed her head and the ridiculous turban that made him want to hit her in the face with his shovel. He leaned on it instead, and sighed, deciding he was a bad person for thinking such a thing, and considered that there must be something wrong with him, a thought that had been occurring and recurring to him, in yards and gardens all over the city, for the past few months. He might not actually be a terrible person, but there was certainly something wrong with him. He thought he ought to be able to describe it to himself better, but when he tried all he could do was make lists in his head of episodes of real and imaginary bad behavior: he wanted to hit harmless Mrs. Perkins in the face with a shovel; he was cruel to his clients' plants and actually hurt a lemon tree in Bernal Heights, pruning at it furiously and unnecessarily until it was reduced to such a violated nubbin that he moved a fern in front of it to hide it from the owner. And just that morning he had looked up at Carolina at breakfast and found her not very attractive.

That was a surprise every time it happened, though it happened more frequently all the time. It felt like a crime to find her unattractive, or at least like some sort of aberration—he was aware, even as he looked at her, that *other* men would find her quite attractive, in that moment when he could take her or leave her. Something always snapped back into place and then she was as lovely as ever, and his return to his senses was usually marked by the special boner he had only ever gotten for her, an entity he wasn't sure he had ever actually convinced her was real, but it was true that there was a different quality about it when he was with her, which went beyond ordinary stiffness. "A hard-on is a hard-on is a hard-on," she'd said to him when he first told her about it, though she said later, not entirely jokingly, that it was the first time she had ever been touched emotionally by a penis. He wanted to ask her what was wrong with him now, but she was the last person in the world he could talk to about it.

Mrs. Perkins toked ostentatiously and made satisfied noises while Will worked, and neglected to offer any opinions about the garden. Will was waiting for her to say something, and was getting preemptively angry at her uninformed opinions and her inability to make up her mind, but she remained quiet. He continued working, escalating his imaginary argument with her until he couldn't stand the silence he would ordinarily have appreciated. He turned toward her chaise and saw that she was reading a book.

"Have you read this one?" she asked, showing him the cover. It was his collection of short stories.

"I heard it wasn't very good," he said.

"It's written to a particular taste," she said. "But I wouldn't say it's bad." She closed the book and rubbed it against her cheek, a weird gesture, and one that Will always thought should have inspired him to flee from the garden and Mrs. Perkins's orbit and influence. But he only leaned on his shovel and stared at her. "I had no idea you were an artist," she said. "You ought to come to my salon."

"I'm really more of a gardener," Will said, which was what he always said when people asked him what he did for a living, because nobody knew what an arborist was, and the one time he had told some girl he was a landscape architect she had asked him where he went to school to be one and then caught him when he lied about it. If he was still a writer he was the kind that didn't really write anymore, and to say that was his profession would have been like saying he was a kindergartener or a virgin. When he sat on a pillow in Carolina's sunroom, ostensibly working on a story while she worked on a painting, he usually ended up just describing what she was doing in a dozen different ways—she mixed her paints languidly or anxiously or she attacked or stroked her canvas or the light made a triangle on her back—but nothing he wrote about her painting or her life or his life or the life they shared ever added up to a story.

Mrs. Perkins made as if to throw the book at him, and he flinched. "Oh, please," she said. "It's every Wednesday afternoon at three. I'll set a place for you."

"Is it lunch?" he asked.

"Of a sort," she said.

"All right," he said. "I'll bring my girlfriend. She's the real artist."

"No guests," she said. "Until you are a senior member of the salon. But promotions are easy and I have a feeling you'll go far and fast." She lay back on the chaise with the book on her chest, face down and open to the place she'd stopped reading. She closed her eyes and adjusted her turban before she folded her hands over the book. "Such dispiriting stuff," she said. "I need to take a little break."

He ignored her for the rest of his stay in her garden that afternoon and didn't say goodbye or even ask to be paid. It bothered him that Carolina wasn't invited, and it bothered him when people said his stories were dispiriting—he thought they were as hopeful as anybody could reasonably expect from a collection of stories about dead brothers—and he was thinking all the way home about how the salon, which he imagined to be a circle of dried-up pretentious people stuffing Fabergé eggs up one another's asses all afternoon, could go fuck itself. He almost told Carolina about it, but she was in a sad mood when he got home, and he didn't want to make her any sadder with news of a rejection, no matter how inconsequential. At first he considered the invitation strictly as a rejection of Carolina, and he couldn't understand how anybody could fail to invite her to anything.

But he got a little more curious about it as the week passed, and when Carolina scolded him for peeing all over the bathroom he had a moment of small resentment in which he very privately cherished the invitation that had excluded her. It passed in an instant but came again and again; she happened to be particularly scoldy that week. The anniversary of her brother's death was approaching, and she seemed to get angry at everything during that time. At first it seemed a fascinating contrast to the way he got sad and retarded around the anniversary of Sean's death—everything seemed to slow down and he felt like he wanted to sleep for the whole week that preceded and followed the eighteenth of April—but now she was starting to seem shrewish. It had to be its own special sort of crime, he thought, to withhold sympathy from the person with whom, of everybody in the world, he ought to sympathize the most, and when he tried to hide his annoyance from her he ended up acting sullen, which only angered her more. He started to dread breakfast, because again and again her beauty seemed to fall away over a plate of scrambled eggs or pancakes or the grapefruit he had prepared for her, carefully cutting out the triangles of flesh so she could lift them out with her spoon. He had put half a maraschino cherry in the center of the grapefruit and was waiting for her to say it made it look like a boob, but she only picked it up, squishing it with her thumb and forefinger, and put it aside. It was an unlovely gesture, and she looked particularly unlovely doing it. "What?" she asked, because she saw him shaking his head. "I don't like cherries."

"Nothing," he said. He squeezed his eyes shut and opened them again.

"What?" she asked again.

"Nothing," he said. "Belly trouble." It was the first excuse that came into his head. He went and sat on the toilet, considering everything else he could have said, and remembering what he had said a few months before: that he wished he could give her brother back to her. He had told her that when she started crying one night the previous year, apparently for no reason at all as they lay cuddling in bed waiting to fall asleep. He had said it almost without thinking about it, the exact right thing, and that night, despite the fact that their brothers were dead and so much else was wrong in the world, everything had felt right between them in exactly the way that everything now suddenly felt wrong.

He went back to Mrs. Perkins as much to stay away from Carolina as for any other reason, considering that it was probably naïve to think there was only one right thing to do for her on the day her brother died, and it might be as right to leave her alone for a little while as it was to hold her while she cried. If he felt like a failure as he made his way up and down the hills on Broadway in his truck, maybe that had more to do with him alone than with him and her together, and maybe a little time spent in the company of pretentious fools was just what he needed to make him appreciate his girlfriend again. It was better, anyway, than going off to drink alone at a bar, something he felt pulled to do as well, and it even seemed better than drinking with a friend, because his friends had all been her friends first, and he was sure it would be very hard for him to explain, and harder for them to understand, how there was something wrong with her, which was actually something wrong with him.

"Follow me," said the butler at the door. It was the first time Will had rung the front doorbell since he had come to the house; he usually let himself into the garden through a side gate. The butler loped through five different rooms—Will barely keeping himself from aping him even though he hadn't said "Walk this way"—each of which seemed perfectly serviceable for hosting a salon. They passed through the living room and dining room and library and some sort of parlor full of cat sculptures and finally the kitchen, where the butler held open a door that Will at first thought led to the pantry. The stairs behind the door led both up and down but the butler pointed down. "Thanks," Will said, but the butler only blinked at him.

Funny place for a salon, Will thought, though he had figured out, after only a few steps, what sort of party it was. With one foot still on the stairs he had a look at what was happening, and looked long enough to take it all in, and yet when he tried to remember what he saw it only came in pieces: a girl in a feathered Indian headdress down on her knees in front of a fat man wearing a Minnie Pearl hat, someone's hairy butt thrusting against the sort of vaulting horse that the Mary Lou Rettons of the world were always colliding off of, and Mrs. Perkins, naked except for a pair of Groucho Marx glasses, complete with nose and mustache, seated on a wicker throne smoking from a hookah and watching over it all. He walked slowly back up the stairs. It seemed like bad manners to run, and also he didn't want ridiculous Mrs. Perkins to think he was afraid.

He planned the conversation with Carolina in his head: *You won't believe what I just saw!* Yet he never managed actually to have it with her. There was some minor degree of culpability even in having only seen that flash of thrusting buttock and Mrs. Perkins's droopy breasts, and he felt guilty already for having gone to a party to which she was expressly not invited, even if the party he thought he was going to had turned out not actually to exist. It was a little too complicated to get into at the moment, but it was too good a story not to tell, and so he only delayed the telling, and delayed it again. At breakfast and lunch and at dinner and in bed, he failed again and again to tell her what he had seen, and he told himself that he kept thinking about the salon only so he could better describe it to her. It was vile and silly, he would say: a vile, silly scene. He didn't admit to himself that he thought it was just plain interesting until it made an at-first unwelcome intrusion into his mind as he was masturbating. He was having a nostalgic whack on the HMS *Pussywillow*, someplace he didn't return to that often, though he had been retreating to the bathroom to masturbate more and more in the past month. The *Pussywillow* was a little degraded from its former glory, or else he just saw it differently now: the curtains on the portholes shared a dingy quality with the petticoat chaps that Carolina wore, and he found himself noticing how dusty everything was, and how dark. It would be better, he thought, to do their fucking up top against a cannon or the ship's wheel, yet he could not make the exertion of imagination to move them there. Instead, the room got even darker, and rocked less and less, and there was a smell, like cat litter and mothballs and cedarwood, that he recognized from the basement, and the orgy theme from *Conan the Barbarian* started to play. All of a sudden it was Mrs. Perkins whom he was fucking in her petticoat. He dropped his cock, and let out a little yell, and slipped on the toilet, and waited quietly for Carolina, who was sleeping outside in the bedroom, to say something, but there wasn't a sound besides his frantic labored breathing.

He crawled into bed with Carolina, who didn't stir even as he put one arm around her belly and wriggled another awkwardly beneath her shoulder, but when he placed his fingers lightly around her bellybutton and moved them very slightly to and fro, she said, "What are you doing?"

"There's a jellyfish on your belly," he said.

"What are you *doing*?" she asked again.

"Nothing," he said, not moving his fingers anymore but not letting her go, either.

It was a Wednesday morning and the anniversary of Sean's death. He declined to make breakfast, but she didn't remark on it, quietly pulling cereal from the cupboard, getting an extra bowl for him but not a spoon. He did not fetch the milk, either.

"I think I'll take the day off," he said.

"Not me," she said, holding a hand up high over her head with her wrist flexed to ninety degrees. "Work up to here."

"We could go for a bike ride. Or a museum."

"Up to here," she said, straining higher with her hand.

"A movie?" he said, and she only grunted, dropping her hand and raising her bowl to the lips to drink the gray dregs of milk. He went outside when she went into her studio, and sat for a while underneath the grand, weird tree, pretending to read. The orgy theme kept playing unbidden in his mind, and he found himself thinking at length about Grace Jones, even though she wasn't in the orgy or even in that particular Conan movie. He thought about the outfit that she wore and the fierceness of her haircut and how at odds it was with the surprising, furry tail that hung down from the straps of her loincloth. "Want to take a break?" he asked Carolina inside, as he opened an uncharacteristic 2 p.m. beer.

"Sorry," she said, cutting a giant picture of Ryan into confetti-sized pieces. "I think I'm on to something here."

"Alrighty," he said. "I'm going to go pedal around for a while."

"Have fun," she said, but none of it was really fun, not the laborious bicycle ride over the many tall hills between the Mission and Russian Hill, or the way it felt like he was pedaling his mind around and around on the same circuit of thought—that it was poor taste for her to be concentrating so devotedly on her dead brother on the deathiversary of his—or any part of the silly vile spectacle at Mrs. Perkins's, the masked girl in the sling or the game that was like Whack-a-Mole with blow jobs or the sixteen-hand massage. He didn't have fun, though he participated with a focus of attention that felt requisite to enjoyment, and nothing frightened him off, not the bad music or a smear of poop, blithely ignored by her, on Mrs. Perkins's leg, or even what appeared, in the dim light of the backmost back room, which everyone called the treasure chamber (as in, "Haven't you visited the treasure chamber yet?" or, hands hefting his cock, "Here's one for the treasure chamber!"), to be a man (or woman) in a strap-on poodle, nuzzling and shoving at the ass of a man tied to a whipping post.

When he came home, Carolina had dinner waiting for him, a meal made up entirely of foods that Sean had liked, that they could enjoy together on his behalf, the menu assembled over the past few months from questions she'd asked so subtly that he had no recollection of answering them. She handed him a note that said *Surprise*, because it wasn't the sort of occasion where that should be shouted out, or to which one invited guests, and yet she had wanted to surprise him with something nice. "Well," she said, lighting candles all down the table, "nice is probably the wrong word, but you know what I mean." And taking his hand as she sat him down she said, "You are probably the only person who knows what I mean." He nodded at that, though he didn't think it was true—weren't there countless millions of bereaved brothers and sisters out there who would know just how it was pleasant and unpleasant in exactly the right way to sit down to such a feast on the anniversary of a death, to not exactly celebrate the death and not exactly mourn the life with carrots and Pop-Tarts and mashed potatoes and Mississippi Mud Pie? But maybe he only wanted it to be untrue, because he didn't deserve to be so distinguished, and did not deserve this gesture of something related to but much, much better than sympathy, and was not worthy of anything of hers, not her beauty or her generosity or her home or her wonderful tree or even, eventually, her woundedness, her fury, her disgust.

15

Henry took extended refuge in Bobby's apartment, though they never quite officially moved in together, Henry having always maintained a separate residence even when he spent almost every night in Bobby's bed. The closest they came was living next door to each other; they had planned to share both apartments but the breakup sundered their bachelor households before they could really be joined. Bobby's continued closetedness and Henry's continued terror of invisible filth made actually moving in together complicated: Bobby needed someplace that could, with the push of a button, become a straight man's apartment should his parents come to visit, and Henry needed someplace where he could mop and scrub to his heart's discontent in his continued losing effort to eradicate the invisible contamination still radiating from his mother and from the West.

He rented his new apartment from a pleasant muttering gentleman named Bilbo, who was shy and retiring but not short or hairy-footed. It was the first home Bilbo had owned with his wife, a seventies love nest whose chocolate brown carpet had been replaced and whose burnt orange walls had been repainted, but there was still something about the place—a three-story loft with a floating teak staircase and track lighting even in the bathroom—that always made Henry feel like he should prance around it in a caftan. It had twelve hundred square feet of moppable wood floor, some of which was quite old, and the whole apartment was kind of dingy. Henry scrubbed and mopped and bleached all day when he moved in, a complicated process because his old apartment had become contaminated by a sixth- or seventh-degree touch from his mother, so he scrubbed each object that made the five-block journey between apartments with the aqua regia of his obsession, a mixture of ammonia and water with a teaspoon of bleach (just enough to increase the disinfecting power of the solution without generating a deadly gas) and three dashes of rosemary shaken from a spice bottle. He didn't know why the rosemary was required, though it made as much sense, or nonsense, in its way as the ammonia and the bleach, since he wasn't concerned at all about bacterial contamination. Bobby had pointed out that he routinely left food to rot on his counter, and he ate from moldy dishes and drank spoiled milk. But if he happened to leave out the rosemary, or even failed to count how many dashes he'd shaken into the bucket, he'd have to clean everything all over again.

He started on the bottom floor, with two buckets, one for the mop and one for the sponge, wiping the walls and doors down and then mopping himself backward to the stairs. The first floor was just the foyer, a couple of closets, and the door to the basement. He had swiped here and there in the vestibule but not tried very hard to make it actually clean: he shared it with another apartment, a studio where Bilbo's frail aged sister lived, whose spotted claws would be all over the mailbox and probably the ground outside, thence to touch the walls and mirror as she leaned and heaved, breathless after the five steps from her threshold to the stoop. She might even lean on his door or try his knob in confusion, so it was useless to try to make any of those common surfaces safe to touch; he'd have to clean them again as soon as they had come and gone from his sight. He polished his inside doorknob with the sponge until it dripped.

"Let's get a dog," Bobby had said, a few months before.

"That's a terrible idea," Henry said. When he saw how Bobby's face fell, he added, "I mean, it's a little soon. Maybe when I'm better. Or more better. I'm getting there." He said something about how it would be unfair to make the dog wear shoes when it went outside, or a surgical mask to keep its sniffing nose from ever actually touching the ground.

"Maybe," Bobby said, "the dog would *make* you better. Like if you loved it enough, all this stuff wouldn't matter anymore. Because it would get a pass on the contamination, you know? Like it would have happiness on its paws instead of dirt."

"I don't think that's how it works," Henry said, though of course that ended up being exactly how it worked. "I do love dogs." That was true: he loved them as a category but was scared of them specifically, mostly because their adorable paws were always on ground that was trod by postman's shoes that were contaminated by dropped letters and the elixir of filth that had dripped from his old mailbox when a letter from his mother had stewed for days in rainwater. His Cambridge mailman had become his archenemy. Henry tried to avoid him, but every now and then he got caught on the street and scolded for never emptying his mailbox of circulars and flyers and the occasional bill that slipped through. "No, thank you," Henry said, as if to decline the mailman's anger, or as if the mailman were the manifestation of whatever agency sought to connect him back to his mother and the whole great contaminated state of California. Just before Henry had moved to Bilbo's, the mailman had accused him of hiding his mail cart, because it disappeared just as Henry was walking down the little garden path (surrounded by reaching hedges that he had become skilled at dodging), trying to avoid being noticed and talked to because there had already been an exchange that week and an ultimatum given, which hinted at dangerous depths of postal rage. There was a dog, a friendly and dumb-looking black Lab, sitting where the cart had been, as if someone had exchanged them one for the other. Henry worked himself into a tizzy of worry that the mailman might touch him, a finger to his chest or a shove against his head, or that the dog, watching and wagging his tail, would come over and put his paws on him. But as the mailman closed on him, actually shouting now, the dog growled and leaped for him, not bothering Henry. He chased the mailman down the street, not seeming to mind at all the backward puffs of mace that came like toxic blinding farts from the vicinity of the mailman's ass. Henry hurried away and moved soon after out of that delivery zone.

"It's too soon, I think," Henry said to Bobby, standing with him next to a bench that neither of them was allowed to sit on, in a park full of frolicking dogs. "But maybe not much longer. I'm getting better, right?"

"Right," Bobby said, though he wasn't, really, or at least he was getting better in such infinitesimal increments that he appeared to be standing more or less frozen on the road to recovery. He made the occasional visit to his psychiatrist, separated sometimes by weeks or months, and all they had really worked out in a year and a half was that Henry had a complicated relationship with his mother, and the unmemory of his lost child-hood was ruining his life in exactly the way she foretold that it would. They never got to the part where they decided what to do about it; Henry's truancy generated a lot of false starts, though it felt to him that just showing up was brave effort, and talking repeatedly about things he already knew was progress.

He went up the stairs, sloshing the mop back and forth as he vacated each step, and washing the banisters as he went. When he got to the second floor he pushed the bucket in steps with his feet to the windows, where he paused to sponge the glass and the sills, picking up real filth now in addition to the imaginary kind, watching children at play in the playground across the street. It was late in July, and a series of holes in the ground spewed water into the air in rhythmic intervals, the noise of the water and the delighted screaming of the children sounding like a conversation. It was cheery work, for all that he was laboring in the service of his miserable obsession; cleaning made him happy and having someplace that could be made clean made him happy. He thought he understood how Snow White could have gone so cheerfully about her work, though her situation, when you gave it any amount of thought, was terribly grim.

"Let's have a party," Bobby said, and Henry said, assuming it would be a party of two, "That's a great idea. What are we celebrating?"

"Nothing," Bobby said. "Our friends."

"Maybe we should wait for an occasion," Henry said, thinking of all the people crowding into Bobby's small apartment, the hands everywhere that might have been touching the ground or the mail. And their friends were all Bobby's friends; it might make more sense for him to celebrate them by himself, someplace else, one of their houses or perhaps even in a rented hall. "My birthday," Henry said, "is only a few months away." At which time he could, if he wanted, ask for a cancellation as a present.

"That's a terrible idea," Bobby said.

"No, it's not," Henry said. "People have been having birthday parties forever."

"I mean the waiting," Bobby said. Henry shrugged, and they continued to negotiate, but a few weeks later they had a dinner party. It was just a few people, and Henry won the right to ask them all to take off their shoes and leave them in the hall when they arrived, a precaution that turned out not to be enough, since some of them trod on the porch in their socks and then walked inside, and anyhow who knew what they did in their socks at home? Henry did a bad job with the minuscule portion of hosting that was allotted to him, and he was sullen though he didn't mean to be sullen. But there was such a high pitch of anxiety abuzz in his brain that it was hard to listen to what people were saying, and hard to care if they had recently become engaged or gone to Morocco or treated a sassy child for diabetes or found a lovely purse at a garage sale. He only had attention for their feet.

Bobby was furious after they left, unreasonably so, Henry thought, since he had warned him he was likely to fail at this and he had tried, in his way, to appear normal. "I'll just go out if you have a party," Henry said, very reasonably, "and mop when I come back." Bobby could not even reply to that until he had finished washing the dishes, at which point he started in on a familiar course, saying very carefully before he offered any criticism how much he loved Henry, how he thought Henry was the best thing that ever happened to him, and how the vision he had for them, with which Henry consistently refused to cooperate, was a vision of happiness for both of them, not just for himself. There followed a discourse about guests and friends and the recipe from an African cookbook and orphan children who might one day be adopted by them as a couple, children who would roll on the floor and put shoes in their mouths and probably run to give the postman a hug regardless of whether he was delivering bad news or good. You and me and a bottle of ammonia, he said. It's fine for now. It's fine for now, but what about the children?

"Maybe I'm too crazy to be in a relationship," Henry said, which was his familiar response to Bobby's familiar discourse about the future. It felt like a grown-up thing to say, and like a difficult concession, and what he meant by it was *I am trying as hard as I can and it's not enough for you* or even *Why can't my weak eccentricities be adorable to you, as yours are to me?* But Bobby always heard it as a conversation stopper, childish and easy and glib.

Henry swabbed the living room floor in broad strokes with feelings of piratey good cheer. He stopped and crossed to the kitchen, then worked back from there to the foot of the stairs up to the third floor. Bobby had seen the place already—he'd helped him pick it out—but Henry had an ascending sense of excitement, as he mopped and mounted the stairs, over having Bobby here when it was properly clean. He had been living for weeks at Bobby's, and it was going to be lovely to have him as a guest in his house and his bed. The long sojourn at his apartment had made Henry feel like he was a guest in Bobby's life, when they should really be taking turns visiting each other's lives. He had tried to explain the notion to Bobby, but he didn't really get it. "But we're not just *visiting*," he said.

"Of course not!" Henry said, but when Bobby asked him what he meant exactly, he'd changed the subject. "Let's go somewhere," he said. Taking a trip was something Bobby had been asking about. Henry had already consented to going camping, though it meant sleeping on the ground, because postmen didn't go into the wilderness, and if he was careful about his packing, and if they were both careful about where they stepped on the way to the car, they might actually leave the larger part of the contamination in Cambridge, and Henry would be relatively normal for the trip. Bobby wanted to go out to Yellowstone, but that was too close by far to San Francisco. He pushed a finger across the map that Bobby had spread out on the table, but try as he might it would go no farther than Nevada. So they settled on Zion, and Henry, demurring and delaying, postponed the trip for months, and Bobby stopped asking about it until Henry brought it up again that day.

They were on their way within a week, Bobby having finalized the travel arrangements before Henry could change his mind or think of a convincing reason to delay. They changed their shoes in an airport bathroom, Henry wrapping away the Cambridge shoes in layers of insulating plastic, then stowing them in their own special bag. That feat of enabling accommodation put Bobby in a foul mood for the long drive out to the park, but he was soon cheered by the abundance of natural wonder and by Henry's increasing ease. San Francisco seemed far enough away, and all the old filth of his life seemed adequately contained and controlled, so Henry took a vacation from his compulsions. He still didn't like the floor, and there were some rituals to be observed in their little cabin, but walking up the Narrows with Bobby, hand in hand on the empty stretches, it bothered him not at all to be wading in river water that flowed over other people's shoes, in which they walked through lives that might or might not have taken them through the Cambridge post office, or even through San Francisco. Some of the unseen upstream hikers might even be postmen, but he declined to even think about that and was able to appreciate instead how nice it was to go step by uncertain step over the slippery underwater rocks, and push against the current, and come through a tight canyon, the sides of which they could touch with their outstretched arms, into a clear sunstruck pool under an expanse of limitless blue sky.

Henry swabbed the third floor, from the bathroom (the tub had been incubating in straight bleach all morning) in the back, to the bedroom in the front, wiping the windows again and contemplating the high view, church spires sticking up here and there above the full trees, and all the leaves looking very shiny and full in the late-afternoon heat. He mopped carefully around and under the bed, suddenly afraid that he was missing places, spots that might border on microscopic and yet still be big enough to contain a leaven of taint sufficient to ruin the whole apartment again. He briefly considered going downstairs and starting again, watching carefully this time to make sure the mop was always heavy and always wrote wide, confluent lines of solvent across the floor, but with an effort he smothered the worry. That was what he meant when he told Bobby he was getting better, that he didn't have to do this twice, and that he understood, even if understanding did nothing to set him free, that all the ritual and care were for nothing and did nothing to address or ameliorate what was actually wrong with him. In a few more passes—stylish, now, but careful—he had mopped himself into the enormous walk-in closet and finally into a half-moon of dry floor in the corner. He unslung a pair of brand-new house shoes from around his neck and stepped into them carefully on the clean part of his floor, then picked up the old shoes with one hand and finished the mopping with the other. Something settled in him as the last bit of floor was covered. He took a deep breath, and meant to sigh, but the fumes made him cough instead.

His mother called just after he had taken a shower, and he slipped and slid on his bleached feet as he hurried to the phone, not to answer it—it would be a terrible idea to talk to her now, just when everything was finally all clean—but to place a bowl over the phone to contain any emanations that might escape from it as she left him one of her long voice mails, enumerating the days that had passed since they talked last and giving an interim account of her life, not always in synopsis, which Henry never deleted without playing, though sometimes he let the message play under a pile of clothes, or from within a cabinet, so he could say with some degree of honesty that he had listened to it.

There were still a few steaming puddles on the floor when Bobby came up the floating staircase and dutifully stepped out of his street shoes into the house shoes, black rubber clogs that Henry had bought new especially for him, Bobby's eyes were watering despite the open floor-to-ceiling windows. They sat at a new glass dining room table which wasn't very big, but Henry had set places at its opposite ends, so Bobby felt very far away, and it was a long journey for the soy sauce for their take-out sushi when they passed it back and forth. Bobby slid it across the table to Henry and it toppled and rolled off, not shattering but leaking drops that mixed with a little puddle of aqua regia. "I have another," Henry said, using his napkin to pick up the bottle and throw it away, but he didn't actually have more. "It's bad for you, anyway," Henry said, and Bobby agreed, but then Henry began to miss the soy sauce more and more, and he only stared at the glistening heap of fish on his plate, from which he'd carefully dissected out the rice, which he'd eat later.

"I have some next door," Bobby said, and Henry said, "Great. Would you mind terribly?"

"Nope," Bobby said, and there was nothing aggravated or cranky about the way he folded his napkin and laid his chopsticks down on top of them. He took a little sip of wine and got up, pausing by the head of the stairs to swap out his shoes. But then he turned and looked at Henry again, and Henry always thought that he ought to have noticed something, something to make him panic and pull the save-this-relationship alarm, and say right then that he loved Bobby regardless of whether or not he wore house shoes, and that he loved him more than the aqua regia, and loved him more than the idea of being able to lie in bed at night and feel entirely untouched by all the things that made him feel dirty.

"Are you okay?" he asked Bobby.

"Fine," Bobby said. "I'll be right back." But he left in his house shoes, and he never set foot in that apartment again.

Henry fled much less hastily than the others. Half a moment after Oak said, "Run!" the feasting room was empty and Henry was alone with the chicken bones and the empty glasses and stained napkins. He listened, thinking he could hear a heavy sound of feet falling in time to his own heartbeat, which was loud and quick in his ears. He was terrified and calm in equal measure, which was how he had been feeling all night, but the liquor inflected his feelings a little, so there was something a lot more leisurely about his backsliding breakdown, with the odd taste—foreign and familiar—of faerie wine in his mouth, than there was without it. Something shifted in him, and now he was sliding instead of falling—still backward, though—to old habits of mind and being, but taking with him the regret and the different sort of sadness he had learned as an individual who had been reformed by love and for the sake of love. If he had eyes in the back of his head, he thought, taking another long drink from his glass, he might be able to see where he was going and where this was all going to end up. As it was, he had a feeling that the backslide was going to be epic—maybe it was more of a hope than a feeling—and that his slide would carry him so far backward it would wreck and reshape him even more dramatically than the way forward had, and personal atavism would look even more like progress than progress did.

He flicked the edge of his glass and set it ringing, and a flock of pigeons started from roosts in the walls. They ought to have bumped against the high ceiling, which was painted crudely with stars, but instead they vanished into it, getting smaller and smaller as the stars lit up in groups and the ceiling became an actual sky. Henry looked away, at the multitude of doors all around the table, but he didn't get up and choose one. *Backward and backward*, he said to himself, and thought he should catch himself before he slid right into the extraordinary misery of the past year. He held on tight to the arms of his chair but didn't slow and thought of the long parade of dead children and grieving parents whose awesome sadness he managed to conflate with his own sadness—small and ludicrous by comparison—all year long. Eat up, he said without speaking, imagining them, in reverse order of death, popping into place around the table and falling to, hungry spirits at a bounty. The last was a lovely nineteen-year-old girl who brought coolers of trout with her when she got her chemotherapy, which she caught flycasting in between admissions, to hand out in abundance to the staff, a whole fish for anyone even tangentially involved in her care. The first had been a little trailer-park boy, whose white-trash parents (the mother was called Trudy, a classic trailer-park name, and he could never remember the father's name) had made Henry perpetually uneasy. They made him want to bleach himself, though he never succumbed to the temptation, even on the day the boy died, when they seemed most dirty and uncanny and unbearable. It had been mere death, he had decided, that had sent him fleeing from the hospital to run all the way home—through this very park—crying the whole way for the death of the boy and the death of his relationship with Bobby. It felt like gross intrusion, to weep like that for the boy—even trailer-park people probably had better manners and minded better boundaries—but he couldn't stop himself. He came down the hill picturing the boy clearly in his mind, imploring him not to die, but when he blubbered and spoke aloud it was to say, "Please don't leave me, Bobby."

He could never properly recall what exactly he was thinking once he got home and was actively preparing to kill himself. He had gotten a gun during one of the deeper downs over Bobby, but it had stayed in his closet the whole time, sending forth invisible rays of comfort. He hadn't seriously thought he would ever use it, since the most attractive thing about it, aside from the dark burnish of the metal, was how nice it was to think that he *could* use it, and though it was calming to think sometimes about blowing off his head—even down to particulars of bullet trajectories and splatter patterns and mysteries like whether or not he would hear the gun go off—he shied away from any considered or sustained reflection on being dead. Now, all of a sudden, suicide was all he could think about. He wept and snotted himself into a flash of insight, a whole string of thoughts coming together at once and weaving together effortlessly into a stark truth: Whatever death was, he belonged to it, and wherever it was, he belonged there; now that he had finally really noticed how much it hurt that Bobby was never going to come back, it became a very sensible thing to do; the entirely unbearable world in which countless little children died from cancer and countless ruined parents died to happiness was no place to live, and the unbearable world in which Bobby didn't love him anymore was no place to live. And running through the center of this weave like a shining silver wire was the sudden unbreakable conviction that there was someplace better, where such things simply never happened, and though death was probably not the way to get there, suicide would express his solidarity with that place.

Even without having practiced, he was quick to assemble and load the gun. He knelt by the window in a crooked rectangle of moonlight. Through his window he could see the park and the hospital, and he stared at them, unblinking and unthinking, as he put the barrel in his mouth, shoving roughly against his palate and pulling the trigger. It only made a sudden tickle in his mouth, which quickly grew frantic. He spit a bug onto the floor, an enormous beetle that shone as if it were made of ink as it crawled leisurely away. Henry threw away the gun—it seemed as disgusting all of a sudden as the bug. He spent the next hour throwing up in the bathroom, too miserable to spare much thought for how strange it was that a beetle had taken up residence in his gun.

Still feeling like he was moving without moving, he slid gratefully past that night, to other terrible nights and days; they went by in such a quick and comprehensive succession that he wondered if he was about to die and asked himself why the agency in charge of such things was declining to show him any of the happy times in his life. The backward way became more and more slippery, and he moved faster and faster, falling toward the misery that was the most spectacular of his life, even if the terrible things that had happened to him in it were all presumed. He risked a look back at last and saw the city rushing toward him, and then the park. He started in his chair as if he had just fallen into it from a height, and spilled his wine. There was a far-off crash, barely discernible.

"Why are you just sitting here?" someone asked him, breaking his reverie. There was a little man standing on his plate.

"Where did you come from?" Henry asked him. "Are you dessert?" The little man poked at his face with a knife, and Henry flinched and ducked. "Don't touch me," he said, not very forcefully.

"What are you even doing here in the first place? Who let you in? Never mind!" he said, when Henry started to answer. "I already know. Are you waiting here to die?"

"I don't know," Henry said. "Why are you yelling at me?"

"Mortals!" the little man said. "Mortals everywhere. Isn't it enough that the world is ending tonight? Did you have to come in and pollute everything with your smell?" He drew back his knife and sniffed aggressively at Henry, making a disgusted face that was shortly mitigated by curiosity. "What have you been eating?" the little man asked, sniffing all up and down Henry's arm.

"Chicken," Henry said. "I think."

"Liar!" the little man said. "Liar! Why am I standing here listening to your *lies* when my Lady is waiting for her knife? Why are you trying to distract me?"

"Why are you so angry?" Henry asked, shying away sideways from the swiping knife.

"Because everything is so *horrible*!" the little man said, and ran off down the table and out of the opposite end of the room.

"You're going the wrong way!" Henry called after him, but there was no answer except for another far-off crash and a faint roar. Henry picked up another bottle of wine and left his chair. He examined the abundance of doorways leading from the room, some just arches over darkness, some rude holes, and some closed with heavy curtains or richly carved doors. He picked a door, dark oak carved with a pair of faces, one laughing and one crying, like theater masks but exceptionally detailed and lovely faces, a man and a woman. The door mirrored his state of mind, since he felt very much like he contained opposites, and yet he thought there could be no illustration of the dissociation in which those opposite emotions were suspended in him. He didn't really know what that face would look like.

The door opened directly on the lushly appointed wreck of a bedroom. The room was the size of a small house, the boat-sized bed floating in pieces in the middle of a giant sea-blue rug. It was more of a cave than the other rooms he'd seen—the walls were hewn stone and the floor, where not covered by rugs, was mossy—yet it was grander than all the other rooms, despite the fact that the paintings and hangings were slashed and trampled. The single occupant wasn't grand at all, though. Molly, the girl who kept saying nothing was real, was sitting slouched on the foot of the bed, her face veiled by her hair, crying into her lap. Across the room, from a hole that looked hardly big enough for a dachsund to wriggle through, Will the handsome pudge came slithering out to collapse in a pile on the floor.

Henry knew what was going to happen before it happened. He saw what was coming, and chose not to stop it. Before he sat down on the bed on Molly's left and Will sat down on her right, before Will looked at him and then lifted the crying girl's chin with his hand, before he kissed her and then turned her face to Henry so he could kiss her too, he saw it all happen, and knew—or rather *remembered*—that it was the faerie wine and the faerie bed, in addition to whatever regular drunken horniness they might each contain, that was responsible, though how he remembered that about wine he'd never drunk before, and a bed he'd never snuck into before, he was still just barely choosing not to know. In a twirling flash of images the montage of fucking came and went, before anybody removed their clothes, or tasted skin, or pushed with their hips, or came. And yet it all happened just as he saw it, because of magic or because these two lovers were bound to his will or because of luck, but it was for a different reason that he knew how it would end, because he could feel the monster moving in time with his heart, getting ever closer though the sympathetic hill tried to thwart it with mazes and dead ends and chambers of carnivorous toads. So when they were done, and when they had all woken from a brief nap, it was no surprise but no less of a terror to see the black dog standing at the foot of the bed.

"There you are," it said, and leaped at them.

The boy walked out of Buena Vista Park not knowing his name or where he was from or why he was crying. He didn't know if he had forgotten this information or if he had simply never known it at all. Standing on the steps into the park, it felt like the first time he had thought about such things, and it was hard to keep such questions—*Who am I? Where am I going?*—in his head. His thoughts were crowded with the image of a weeping dog, a black Lab puppy with enormous brown eyes crying giant, perfectly formed tears. He knew dogs didn't cry, just as he knew that a boy should know his name, yet what bothered him was not how strange it was that a dog should cry but that the dog was sad. Somebody ought to be cuddling it to make it feel better. Maybe that was why he was sad, he thought: because the dog was sad. But whose dog was it?

He looked back at the park. A stiff wind was blowing down the hill, and as he thought of going in to look for the dog it gusted all of a sudden, strong enough to push him down a step and cold enough to draw his attention to the fact that he was wearing pajamas that were far too small for him. He thought of the dog, of the tears as round and rolly as marbles coursing down his snout, and turned away. It was a clear day: he could see the whole city laid out below, house after house all down the hill, and other parks in squares and circles here and there all the way to the bay. It occurred to him to go to one of those, since he suspected that he belonged in a park, and that he might find the dog in a park, even if the wind wouldn't let him go back into this one.

He started down the hill, noticing that his feet were bare as he placed them on the steeply slanting sidewalk. High up the hill, the streets were empty, but Castro Street was busy. He crossed against the light, not paying any attention to the cars, and barely missed getting run over by a large yellow Cadillac.

When he reached the corner of Noe and Duboce he discovered a park, mostly treeless but covered in grass and full of dogs, who all ran over to circle him in prancing leaps that looked a lot like dancing. That made him laugh, but also brought to mind the sad puppy. It seemed there was every sort of dog in this park except a black Lab, and there were no puppies, and the absence of trees bothered him greatly—it was a wrongness much worse than not knowing one's name, though not so great a wrongness as a weeping dog. Having walked only a few paces in, he went out again, briefly pursued by the dogs, whose owners could not see what they were so excited about.

There were trees on Noe Street, an abundance of them shading the sidewalk, so that was the way he took. People kept running into him or nearly running into him, seeming to notice only at the last moment that he was there, and crying out "Oh!" as if he had appeared from thin air. As he approached the intersection of Noe and Market, he started to wonder if he had taken a wrong turn, and tried to ask a lady if he was headed toward the big park near the church. She didn't reply but only swatted around her head, as if she were being harassed by a bee. He even shouted at her, but that only made her run away. He sighed, and sniffed the air, and thought he caught a rich hint of grass blowing from the other side of the street, so he crossed, nose up, again not giving a thought to the traffic. This time he surprised a woman in a long blue Volvo, who noticed him only when she'd nearly run him over. She turned aside sharply and ran into an oncoming streetcar.

The boy stood in the middle of the street, suddenly afraid to move, and afraid of all the attention that the accident attracted. The woman in the car was looking all around for him, insisting that there had been a boy in the street, while the streetcar driver asked her loudly what she was smoking. The accident drew a crowd into the intersection, people who shook their heads over the wreck; none of them were looking at the boy, and no one had asked him if he was okay. But amid all the noise he heard someone shouting "Hey, you!" and "Hey, kid!" and looked across the street to see another boy, about his own age, who was plainly staring at him, along with a fat man with a big beard. They both were straddling bicycles, and wore identical blue T-shirts and caps.

"Come over here," the man commanded, "and watch out this time." The boy crossed the rest of the way, still not looking where he was going, but the traffic was stopped. He stood before the man and the other boy, who looked him up and down. The other boy reached out to run a hand across his cheek, then held his fingers up to the sun.

"He's covered with it," the other boy said.

"What's your name?" the man asked.

"Henry," said the boy, because to be asked his name was suddenly to remember it. In that moment he knew some of who he was, and some of where he was from, though he had no idea in the world where he was going, or what he was going to do, given what he had just lost. He wept with the dog, then, and heard it howling in his head, a terrible noise totally out of proportion with the form of a puppy.

"Henry," the man said, putting a hand on his shoulder and squeezing gently. "Henry, Henry, Henry. It won't be all right, not exactly, not *ever*. But it will be a little better soon."

"Wash him good, boys," the man said. "He's *covered* in it!" His name was Mike, and the other boy's name was Ryan. They had taken Henry to an enormous green house on Fourteenth Street, loading him on the back of Ryan's bike for a quick, swerving ride through a treeless neighborhood, going by the park toward which Henry had been walking. Henry tried to jump off the bike as they passed it, a grassy hill punctuated here and there with palm trees, but Mike, pedaling alongside, reached out and grabbed his arm. "It's just a park," he said. "It's not what you're looking for—trust me!" The two bikes wobbled toward and then away from each other and then steadied. Henry didn't try to get off again. "Be careful," Mike called out to Ryan as he sped ahead. "With him on your bike, they won't see you either!"

"Nobody touches me!" Ryan shouted back. He darted through the traffic and swerved on and off the sidewalk, passing so close to some of the pedestrians that Henry brushed them with his shoulder. He hung on tight to Ryan's waist and pushed his face into his back to keep his head steady, because his neck was starting to feel too long and his head too wobbly, and because he had started to pay more attention to the people they passed. They were all starting to look very strange—they looked wrong, even monstrous, though he wasn't sure why, and he didn't want to see them. And he liked holding on to Ryan. He liked the smell of his shirt and the way the round bones in his neck felt when he pressed his nose against them. It reminded him of something.

They skidded to a stop outside the house. Henry might have fallen over if Mike hadn't leaped off his bicycle, letting it clatter to the ground, to catch him. He set Henry on his feet and said, "Steady there. You've still got too much of their stuff on you. You'll feel better after your bath!" He walked behind Henry, steadying him with his hands on his shoulders, pushing him when he slowed and bearing him up when he stumbled. Instead of climbing the steps to the front door of the house, they passed through a silver gate set in the wall underneath and to the left of the door, down a dark, damp hallway. A set of stairs at the end of the hallway led up into a square courtyard garden surrounded by high porches on three sides and a high wall on the fourth.

The porches were full of boys, all of them older than Henry, but none by more than a few years. More came out of the house as he watched, climbing out windows or jumping through doors. He looked from face to face to face, and they all started shouting down to him at once, but Mike cut them off.

"There'll be time enough for introductions, boys! Right now he needs his bath!" He marched Henry toward a gazebo in a far corner of the garden, covered in thick dead vines that nearly hid the hot tub inside. The boys poured down the porch steps—the ones on the lowest porch jumped—and crowded around him, hands reaching to grab at his too-small pajamas and pull them off. They pulled hard, and tore the fabric, but Henry didn't protest. "Hey, boss," Ryan said. "He's got something in his hand." He held up Henry's left hand, which was clenched in a tight fist, for everyone to see. Henry hadn't really been conscious of having his hand in a fist, and he didn't know what might be in there. Ryan didn't ask him to open his hand, but peeled his fingers up one by one to reveal a silver and brown acorn sitting in the middle of Henry's palm. He had been holding it so tightly it left a deep round impression in his skin.

The boys took a collective step away when they saw the acorn. "They don't let nothing go," said a boy with long blond hair. "How'd he get *that?*"

"Time for questions later," said Mike. He plucked the acorn from Henry's hand and put it in his pocket, then took off his shirt before he picked Henry up and dropped him into the hot tub. The water was cold and very dirty, covered with leaves and a thick layer of brown scum. It stank like moss and mildew. When Henry stood up, Mike grabbed him with his big hairy hands. "Welcome to the real world!" he said, while Henry gasped at the cold. Ryan was holding up a hefty bar of white soap, which Mike seemed to pray over a moment before Ryan threw it in the water. Then Mike held Henry still while the boys, now all shirtless as well, leaned over and started to soap him up. "Don't miss an inch, boys!" Mike said, and they didn't. They stuck soapy fingers in his ears to wash there, and turned him on his head to wash his bottom, and they paid special attention to the spaces between his toes. They washed him four times before Mike pronounced him sufficiently clean.

Mike dipped a finger in the water and tasted it. "Oh, that's spicy!" he said. "How long were you under that hill, anyway?" Henry only stared at him. The bath had made him feel very strange, nervous and sleepy and hungry and nauseated, and the fact of his name weighed on him very heavily all of a sudden.

"My name is Henry," he said, as if saying it might lighten the load of it, and he started to cry.

"Michael is my name," said Mike, smiling but making no move to comfort him.

"Ryan," said Ryan.

"Peaches," said the boy with the long blond hair, and then the others said their names, striking their chests and smiling warmly, though still no one moved to touch him where he was shivering amid the piles of brown foam heaped up on the surface of the water. "Greg," "Jeff," "Miles," "Jim," "Mateo," "Alan," "Eric," "Niall," "Mark."

"Peaches?" Henry said, because somehow that funny name was the only thing that seemed curious or out of place just then. Peaches scowled. "Can we drink the water now?" he asked, pulling out a ladle from his pants.

"Carefully, Bubba," Mike said. "He's made a potent brew."

"Wait!" said Ryan. "I have an idea." He leaned over to Mike and whispered something to him that made him throw back his head and laugh.

When Mike shared the idea with the rest of them, and they passed the acorn around from hand to hand, everyone but Peaches voted to do it.

"But I want a drink," Peaches said. "I want to get drunk. I want to fly!"

"Then be a bird," Mike said, flipping the acorn off his thumb and catching it in his mouth. He spat it into his palm. "But you can still have the dregs." Some of the boys ran off to fetch buckets, while the others ran to the middle of the garden, where they fell on their knees and began to turn up the earth with their hands. Ryan cupped some water in his two hands, and Mike dropped the acorn into the water Ryan held, and then Ryan ran madly to the hole in the ground, launching himself the last few feet to reach it before the water ran out from between his fingers. He dropped the acorn in the hole, and they all cheered. The boys with the buckets started dipping water out of the tub and taking it to the hole, which shortly was covered over. Mike kicked off his shoes and stamped down on it.

Still naked and shivering, Henry watched as they took the water, by bucket and glass, from the tub to the middle of the garden, which was getting to be more and more of a muddy mess. Only when the water had fallen below Henry's ankles did Mike seem to remember him. He lifted Henry out and wrapped him in a thick, dirty towel that smelled worse than the water had and gave him a long hug. "It's worse than you think, Bubba," he said, wiping at Henry's tears with the edge of the towel. Peaches slipped past them to get into the tub and started to lap and suck at the shallow remnant of water that was left. All the other boys were wrestling in the mud and laughing raucously.

"Everyone falls asleep after their bath," Mike said. "Why are you still awake? Is there something different about you, Bubba? Is that why they gave you a souvenir, while the rest of us only ever got dirty feet and a handful of dust?"

"I don't know what you're talking about," Henry said, but the words brought an image to his head, the black puppy trotting up to him with the acorn held carefully between his oversize, unpuppyish teeth.

"We're going to have a party!" Mike said. "We always do, whenever my elbow itches in a special way and a new boy comes out from under the hill. Pity he can never attend, what with the sleepiness and all. But we lay him down, and dance around him, and wish him well, and we don't talk about the bad news. The abundance of bad news! The bushels and bushels of bad news! That can wait till tomorrow. Are you feeling sleepy, Bubba?"

"No," Henry said, but really his lids felt very heavy. He didn't want to close them—he was sure he was going to miss something terribly important if he did—but he couldn't help it. Just before he did close his eyes he thought he saw Peaches float feet-first out of the hot tub. "Boss!" he said. "Look at me!" And Mike replied, "Flying like that is *vulgar!*" Henry fell forward into Mike's arms. Turning his head as he fell, he was sure he saw muddy animals sporting where the boys had been before, dogs and cats and raccoons and a beaver and possibly an alligator. Then his face was pressed against Mike's hairy chest, and Mike's arms had closed around him, and all Henry could think about was how nice it was to get a hug.

"It's all right, Bubba," Mike said. "Go to sleep now. You're home."

"I have served my Lord one thousand years tonight," the dog said, "and he has made me a gift of you. Come away with me." It sounded like both a question and a command; Henry found himself sitting up in bed without quite having wanted to. Suddenly he knew he wasn't dreaming, and he wasn't scared, though he thought that he should be. He looked over at his parents, sound asleep on the other bed in their hotel room. They'd come up from Carmel for a visit in the city.

"Never mind them," said the dog. "Already I love you more than they love you, and I will only love you more and more as the hours and days and weeks and months and years and decades and centuries pass and pass until I stop them." He slapped his paw on the ground but smiled very gently. "Come away, my new friend. Come away."

"I'll get in trouble," Henry said. His parents were both snoring soundly.

"Come away with me, my puppy," the dog said. "What's here for you but trouble and grief? I'll make you king of those. Come on. Take my collar. Come away."

Henry looked at his parents again. "Just for a little while," he said.

"Forever," the dog said, but Henry went with him anyway.

"You are a changeling," Mike said to Henry. "They stole you from your parents, and kept you as a toy, and thrust you out when they tired of you. You're supposed to forget about it. That's what passes for mercy with them; they put you back into a world where you don't belong anymore, because of what they did to you, because of what they showed you, and then they make it so you can't remember *why* you don't belong. Ha!"

They were standing in the garden, on either side of the tiny silver sapling that had sprung up where the acorn had been planted the night before. Henry had woken in a giant bed full of muddy boys, some curled like dogs, others stretched out in any direction with their head or feet resting on or against Mike's gigantic bulk. Henry had been the first to wake, but he stayed where he was, listening to Mike's rumbling snores, until the boys began to stir, all at once, as if they were sharing the same troubling dream. Together they began to wake, one of them opening an eye on one side of the bed and then another opening one on the other side of the bed, until, eyes wide open, they all sat up at once and stared at Henry.

"Hi," he said.

"The lesson of this house," Mike said to him in front of the tree, "is that forgetting is perilous. We who live here never forget what happened under the hill, though we don't entirely remember, either; nobody has the specifics, you see. But now look what you've brought us—a reminder!"

"But I don't remember," Henry said, which was mostly true. He had his first name, but not his last, and he had some brief scenes involving the creature who had taken him from his family, but not the whole story of what had happened with him, and when he closed his eyes he could see the faces of his parents and his sister, but he didn't know their names. He didn't know where he had lived before he came to San Francisco. He didn't even remember his birthday. He told that to Mike.

"It will come. In the meantime you'll just have to live as if every day is your birthday. Happy birthday, Henry Whoozie. Happy birthday!" He picked him up and carried him around the garden, singing "Happy Birthday" to him. Then he took him inside where the other boys were seated on and at a long table in the kitchen, having cereal and cookies and, here and there, a beer for breakfast. "It's his birthday, boys!" Mike shouted. "Sing him a song!" They put down their bottles and spoons and joined in enthusiastically, but the bored look in Peaches's eyes made Henry think they did this for everybody on their second day.

Ryan took Henry to the basement to pick out a bicycle. He had already split his clothes with him, because of all the boys they were about the same size, and Henry had his own "Mike's Messengers" T-shirt, which he would wear while he was working. "Everybody works," Ryan said.

"Some harder than others, but we all ride. You and me, we should only be working when school's out."

"We go to school?" Henry asked.

"Fuck no," Ryan said. "Or not like you think. But we can't be out on the street when the cops think we should be in school."

The basement was not just full of bicycles. There were piles of newspapers and old magazines, and decaying papier-mâché sculptures of animals attacking each other, and canvases stacked face down up to Henry's shoulder. Henry lifted one up and could just make out the contents: a painting of the park surrounded by fog. Ryan pushed it down. "Those are Mike's," he said. Henry followed him, passing through a room piled up with what Henry thought at first was exercise equipment until he got a closer look: there was a wooden post as thick as he was and twice as tall, with a pair of manacles dangling from it, and a couple of wooden tables, and a toilet seat strung on a wicker chair but not actually attached to a toilet, an iron cage big enough to hold three or four large dogs, and a set of stocks, like the Pilgrims used to have in their town squares. Henry suddenly remembered getting his picture taken in a pair of those, in Williamsburg, and he remembered very clearly that he had only been visiting Williamsburg. That wasn't where he was from.

"Do people get punished down here for something?" he asked.

"Belonged to the previous owner of the house," Ryan said. "Weirdos. I can get out of that cage in ten seconds, though, and the stocks in thirty. Here you go." They had come to the bicycles, lined up in a rack as long as the whole wall. There was every sort of bicycle there that Henry could think of, ten-speeds and motocross and beach bikes and even a little purple-framed girls' bike with a bright yellow banana seat and tassels on the handlebars. A little license plate on that one said, LORRAINE. "Mike says the bike chooses you. You close your eyes and touch them and you know when it's one that wants you. But it's not always sized right when you do that." Henry closed his eyes and ran his hand along the bicycles, touching fenders and tires and seats. He felt nothing the first time he went down the row, but when he had come halfway back there was a feeling like his hand was immersed in flowing water, and the texture of the wheel he was touching felt suddenly different.

"I think I found it," he said, and opened his eyes. There was a little pony staring up and breathing softly at him where the bicycle had been.

His hand was placed high up on its nose, just between its eyes. It huffed and changed back into a bicycle. Henry stepped back, feeling both alarmed and somehow reassured at the change: it was at the same time one of the strangest and most ordinary things he'd ever seen. He and Ryan both stared at the bike, a little green ten-speed that had seen better days, but it didn't change again.

"Well," Ryan said. "*That's* never happened before."

The black dog led Henry out of the hotel and up the street to catch a streetcar. It stopped for them, but nobody looked at them when they got on board, and the driver didn't ask them for a fare. The dog sat quietly as the train trundled up Market Street, so Henry did the same. He wasn't inclined at all to ask lots of questions about where they were going or ask the homeless person sitting in front of them for help or to run away. All he could think of was how nice it was to ride on the streetcar and how pretty the rain was against the windows and how lovely the neon looked reflected in puddles outside the run-down theaters they passed. The homeless woman in front of them had bugs in her hair, flat gray lice the size of pencil tips that crawled in loops all over her head. Henry imagined that they were in a circus, doing tricks on and under the lady's big filthy top. He leaned forward to watch more closely. The dog stood up. They had come to the last stop, near the corner of Market and Castro streets.

It was one-thirty in the morning, but Castro Street was pretty crowded: there were men holding hands, men in pants but no shirts, or shirts and no pants, men dressed like women or space aliens, and men dressed like men but carrying dainty parasols instead of umbrellas. Henry stared at them, but none of them stared back.

They crossed Market Street and climbed up the hill, away from the crowd. Henry looked back as they went, then stopped altogether. "Say goodbye," the dog said.

"Huh?" Henry said, but the dog only pulled on his hand with his mouth and led him on, higher up the hill, which grew so steep eventually that there were steps cut into the sidewalk. Henry wanted to go up them on all fours like the dog. They climbed past houses that got fancier and fancier as they went higher. The wind shifted and Henry could smell the trees just before they came into view over the crest of the hill. "They smell like soap," he said, because his

sister kept eucalyptus shampoo in the bathroom they shared at home. It occurred to him that his sister was going to wonder where he was. "Wait a minute," he said, as the dog tried to pull him up the stairs into the park. "What's your name?"

"I have many names," the dog replied. "You can call me whatever you want." Henry was standing in the streetlight, but the dog was standing in shadow, and Henry could hardly see him at all. His own arm seemed to disappear where it entered the shadow.

"I think I want to go home," Henry said.

"But you are *home," the dog replied, and pulled him along up the stairs. Henry did not exactly resist, because he wanted to follow the dog into the darkness under the trees as much as he didn't want to follow him. The part of him that didn't want to follow was just starting to pull away, and he was thinking of how much his parents would worry when they woke and found him missing, when he heard a lovely noise of bells. They were walking on a winding path, not entirely alone; Henry could see the glowing tips of cigarettes gliding through the dark on other paths to his left and to his right.*

"What's that noise?" Henry asked.

"Music. Come along. Come away. We are so much the same, you and I!" He walked faster now, dragging Henry along the path, which ended suddenly at a flat stretch of grass, soft and oddly warm under Henry's feet. The grass ran up to a dark expanse of rock, where even as they looked at it a door was opening in the side of the hill. Light spilled out onto the grass, along with a louder noise of bells and laugher.

"I don't want to go in there," Henry said.

"Yes, you do," the dog said. "You have always wanted to go in there." Henry looked back again, but there was nothing to be seen of the city, just grass and trees and flickering lights in the darkness that he didn't think were cigarettes anymore. He was already forgetting what he was supposed to be getting back to beyond the trees, but he still pulled one more time. The dog led him into the light and the music and Henry went along, experiencing the curious sensation that he himself was a bell and that he was starting to ring in sympathy with the music he heard. The light became brighter and brighter, until he couldn't see anything anymore, but he could hear, amid the laughter and the bells, a rising cheer.

———————

Henry said he didn't need anybody to teach him how to ride a bike or deliver a message or a package, but Mike made him Ryan's student anyway. "You listen up, Bubba," Mike said, putting a "Mike's Messengers" hat on Henry's head and turning it around on his head a few times before he settled on a position, cocked a few degrees west of Henry's nose. "You've got talent, but baby boy here has got skills." He waved goodbye to them from the tall stoop of the house on Fourteenth Street, standing there until the last of the boys had pedaled away with a roomy messenger bag slung around his shoulders and neck, empty except for one of the sandwiches that he made the night before, carefully folding lettuce and cutting away crust, and wrapping each one lovingly in wax paper, upon which he wrote the day's motto, a different one for everybody. "Are we taking these somewhere?" Henry asked, reading his sandwich: *You are just as special as you think you are.* Ryan said, "Just try to keep up."

That wasn't hard. Henry's legs were not as strong as Ryan's, but his bike was light and fast, and though it never turned into a pony again, he didn't always have to pedal it to make it go uphill, and Ryan took him up some big ones. They went up Steiner and passed within view of Buena Vista Park. "Don't look at it," Ryan called back, but he stared too at the pile of trees at the top of the hill, and barely missed wrecking when a man opened his car door in front of him. "Asshole!" Ryan said, and pedaled away furiously up the steepening hill. He spared no attention for Alamo Square Park, though Henry almost paused to admire the giant cypresses and galloping dogs. When he stopped at last in front of a huge house on the corner of Broadway and Steiner, Henry couldn't tell if Ryan was pleased or displeased at how well he kept up. He seemed to be both smiling and scowling. "Wait here," he said, and left Henry on the front walk with the bikes while he hopped over a garden wall and disappeared around the side of the house. Henry wondered if he was supposed to ring the bell, and if Ryan had something in his bag to deliver here. He looked around. A sparrow rose from the garden and flew into an open window on the side of the house.

Shortly after that Ryan opened the front door. "Come on," he said, after he had put the bikes behind a bush. "Nobody's home," he said. "I've been watching to know when they come and go. You'll learn how to do that."

"How'd you get in?" Henry asked, looking around at the marble foyer and the fancy chandelier.

"You know how," Ryan said, and started up the stairs. "You can do it too. You just have to remember."

"Remember what?" Henry said. But Ryan was gone; a gray cat was racing silently up the stairs. "Remember what?" Henry said again, running up the stairs and stopping at the top. A long carpeted hallway went left and right. Henry walked to an open door at the end into a cavernous bedroom. Ryan was rifling through the drawers. "I've been in this house before," Henry said.

"No, you haven't," Ryan said. "That's just you trying to remember the wrong thing." He shook his bag at Henry. "Come on," he said. "Fill 'er up." Henry went farther into the room, into an alcove off the bathroom, and sat on a plump velvet stool in front of a gold and white table. He looked through the drawers. They were full of makeup and jewelry. "Look at this," he said, holding up a heavy diamond necklace.

"Too fancy," Ryan said. "It needs to be stuff Mike can sell at the shop."

"Shop?"

"I'll show you. Keep looking." Henry put the necklace on and looked at himself in the mirror. A wave seemed to pass over the glass, and he looked away, down at the surface of the table, and picked up a brush and smelled it. That made him think of his mother, and how she always said she was going to put on her face when she did her makeup. It made Henry believe when he was very small that her face was detachable, and he had always hoped and feared she might take it off for him. Without Ryan telling him so, he knew he was remembering the wrong thing, and he looked up again at his face. This time he saw the wave move across it, though he didn't feel a thing. The mirror cracked.

"You're useless!" Ryan said. "We're not here to break stuff." He came over and started emptying the drawers of their jewelry and told Henry to take off the necklace. But he only hid it beneath his shirt.

Henry's bag was only half-filled when Ryan said it was time to go. He told Henry to stuff underwear around the watches and bracelets and earrings to keep them from jingling and then criticized him for using too much packing. "We're not here to steal underwear," he said. They left through the front door and rode away on the bicycles.

The stealing didn't particularly bother Henry. He had stolen things before; he remembered putting candy and paperback books down his pants once at a drugstore on a shopping trip with his mother. He hadn't really been hungry for candy, and the book, an overheated romance novel, had been interesting only because the man on the cover was wearing a kilt and no shirt. He had taken the things just for the sake of taking them, to see if he could do it. He couldn't remember if he stole often or never again after that, and either way it didn't matter now. The whole day had collapsed into this pedaling moment; the morning and the evening felt so far away he was sure they had never happened and would never happen. And his priorities had collapsed so that only a few things mattered: his bicycle, his new friend, and one other thing he could not quite name. He was smiling as they coasted down into the Marina, crossing Lombard Street just as the light was changing and swerving through the traffic. "What are you so happy about?" Ryan called back, and Henry said he didn't know.

They went to the beach, leaving their bikes at the edge of a cliff in the Presidio and scrambling down a crumbling path that wound through small groves of eucalyptus and patches of waist-high purple flowers. Henry slid the last fifty feet and ended up on his back in the sand. Ryan skated over the same fall of rock and sand, throwing his arms out like a ballerina and landing lightly at Henry's feet. He dropped his bag and told Henry to do the same thing. Henry asked if they wouldn't be stolen, though they were in an isolated cove and the stretch of beach was empty except for them.

"Come on," Ryan shouted. "This is important!" He took off running. Henry chased him down to the water. "Come on!" Ryan shouted again, not turning around to say it, but Henry heard him very clearly. "Come on!" Henry almost had him—he reached to grab the edge of his shirt and pull him down into the water—and then he was gone. A sleek tan greyhound was running in his place. When Henry tripped, he thought at first it was out of surprise, but he understood as he fell that what felt like surprise—swift, sudden, and shocking—was actually delight, and he was glad he had tripped, because the little accident seemed to provide the momentum he couldn't provide for himself. He fell forward and felt at last that he had caught up with his friend. A wish was a change: a boy fell and rolled in the shallow heaving surf, but a dog straightened himself out. A black Lab in a diamond necklace shook out its fur and took off after the greyhound.

"How are we different?" Mike asked. He was seated at the head of the long table in the dining room. Henry was staring at the hole in the floor. A fireman's pole dropped through two bedrooms upstairs and a downstairs par-lor before it stopped in the basement. The former owners, Ryan explained again, when Henry asked. He had slid down it already, over and over until it was boring, and now he wanted to slide down it as something other than a boy. But no one could leave the table before Mike excused them, and changing wasn't allowed during dinner anyway.

"How are we different?" Mike asked again. His eyes met Henry's eyes, and Henry worried that he was supposed to answer the question. He blushed, and didn't know what he would say, but Mike looked away, down the table to where Peaches sat at the other end. That seat was a rotating place of honor, but Henry didn't know how it was earned. The table was heaped with food and heaped with loot, which they would sort after they ate, cash and jewelry and small electronics and here and there wallets standing up on their edges so they looked like tents and in the cen-ter of these a bird in a golden cage, brought back by Peaches from a man-sion on Russian Hill. He said it was a macaw.

"We're smarter than anybody," Peaches said. Mike gave him a thumb-up, then pointed with his other hand at Mateo, seated on Peaches's right.

"We've seen magic and we can do magic," he said.

"One man, one reason, Bubba. But you're right to suggest a difference between the lesser magic we do and the greater magic we've seen. If that's what you were doing." He pointed at Eli next, and the answers proceeded clockwise around the table. Henry wasn't sure if they were bragging to one another or saying grace, but it turned out that Mike required a moment of serious collective reflection every night before dinner. "At least he didn't make us all hold hands tonight," Ryan said later. Henry tried hard to think of a reason of his own, but Mateo had taken the obvious one, and then every other reason he could think of—*we are fast* or *we are a team* or *we watch each other's backs*—got used up as his turn came closer and closer. He thought about the beach, of running on all fours in the surf with Ryan and sitting on a rock with him with waves pounding all around them. There was no way to describe what he felt, but it had to do with the way Ryan teased him about the necklace, and snatched it from his neck, then stood up with it shining in his fist, the heaving waves around his feet making it look like he was standing on the water. He threw the necklace into the ocean. Henry almost dove after it, but Ryan caught him with a hand on his arm and an arm around his bare chest. "There are a hundred

more where that came from!" he shouted. "And we can take them whenever we want!"

"Bubba?" Mike said. He was staring at Henry, but he only blushed
again and shook his head.

"It's all right, Bubba. First one's free. I'll do it for you. But you're
going to have to learn to pull your weight." He cleared his throat and
folded his hands in front of his chest and raised his eyes to the ceiling like
a choirboy looking to heaven. Pitching his voice high, he said, "We all
belong someplace else."

*"Master," said the dog, "I have fetched myself a gift, just as you permitted.
Here he is, a dear friend for me for life." He bowed and, still bent at the waist,
pulled with his mouth at Henry's shirt to make him bow too. They were in a
long hall before a set of stone chairs in which a terribly fancy-looking couple
was seated. Stone columns, thick at their tops and bottoms but tapered pencil-
thin in the middle, lined the hall, and creatures that were not people were
gathered in all the spaces between them, bouncing on their haunches or standing on their hands or clinging to the stone with their claws or hovering in the
air. Henry was able to pay them very little mind, not because they weren't the
strangest and most interesting things he had ever seen in his life, besides a talking dog, but because his attention was commanded by the extraordinary majesty
of the man and woman on the chairs. Sitting down, they looked about the
same size as his parents, but he suspected that when they stood up their heads
would scrape the top of the cavernous chamber. When he straightened up they
were both staring at him intensely, which made him blush, and he danced
from foot to foot because his feet were suddenly itchy.*

"Hmm," said the man. "There's something wrong with it."

"It's mortal," said the woman.

*"More deeply than usual, I mean," said the man. "There is a deeper sort of
darkness in it." He looked at the dog, who had straightened up as well and was
beaming proudly next to Henry. "Old one," he said, "you chose unwisely."*

*"Oh, no," said the dog. "I chose well! A friend for the ages. There is a
sameness in us!"*

*"It's rather overripe," said the woman, and she leaned forward to poke
Henry in the belly with a long finger. That gave him a funny feeling, as if he
had to pee and poop and laugh all at once. He smiled at her; she frowned*

back. *"I think it will be rotten in a day or two,"* she said. *"Why didn't you choose something fresher?"*

"Yes," said the man. *"Take it back. Go choose another."*

"A promise is a promise," said the dog. *"I chose my choice, and you must let it stand."*

The man gave him a hard stare, and the dog stared back, and Henry had the sense that the man and the dog were both holding places for other things entirely, things that wouldn't just stand to the ceiling but would fill up the whole chamber. The man smiled, then the dog grinned, and they were diminished.

"So it is," said the man. He sighed and stood up and wasn't any taller, after all, than Henry's father. The lady followed him, and all the other creatures in the hall flipped off their hands, or rose higher on their haunches, or drifted down to the floor. The man turned to Henry and stared down at him, kind and stern and a little sad. Henry noticed for the first time that his beard was full of flowers. *"Human child,"* he said, *"do you forsake your mortal life, and your mortal cares, your mortal loves, your mortal family, and do you swear to live by our laws, which are few, and obey your Lady and your Lord, and cater to their whims, which are diverse, and not to be comprehended by your like? Do you swear?"*

"The answer is yes," the dog said, when Henry didn't answer right away. He wanted to say no or to say, *Tell me more about what it means to agree to all this,* but the man's face was not a face to which he could say either of these things.

"Yes," Henry said.

"And do you swear to be my friend," the dog said, *"forever and ever and ever?"* He wagged his tail and took Henry's hand in his mouth.

"The answer is yes," the man said, shaking his head sadly.

"Yes," Henry said. The dog was squeezing his hand much too tightly. *"You're hurting me,"* he said to the dog.

"Nonsense," said the dog. *"Friends don't hurt each other."*

"Kayd Meela Falchaa!" said the lady, and raised her hands to the assemblage.

"Kayd Meelah Falchaa!" they said. *"Welcome, child of man, no longer a child of man! Welcome! Welcome!"* The woman yawned hugely and walked away, and a dozen of the creatures followed after her, worrying at her train and her hair and sweeping the ground before her with their furry, feathery bodies.

"Old enemy," said the man, "you must only promise me one thing: Do not teach this one any magic."

"Oh, yes," said the dog. "I promise."

The tree got bigger every day. In two weeks it was a gangly sapling as tall as Henry; in four it reached as high as the third-floor porches; in six it had started to fill out. The trunk was as thick as Henry's leg, and though it grew in the exact center of the garden you could stand on the porches and almost touch the golden leaves. Mike said he thought it would bloom before the middle of summer. It looked like it had been in the garden for years, which seemed right somehow to Henry, since he felt as if he had lived for years at the big green house. It felt like he had been sleeping for years in the big bed, and eating dinner every night at the big table, and listening for years as Mike reminded them every night that they all belonged someplace else, and feeling every night despite that that there could be no place else he belonged. The memories he had of his mother and father and sister seemed infinitely remote. He wondered sometimes if they had ever even existed; they were more unlikely, somehow, than the faeries who had kidnapped him, and there was no proof beyond his memories, while the faeries' gift transformed every day.

They had a picnic around the tree one Sunday, which was their day off, since people generally stayed in their houses that day. They covered the grass with half a dozen quilts and bedspreads. Ryan and Henry sat on a *Star Wars* quilt, and because of the picture it displayed Henry could not keep himself from picturing Peaches with his hair done up in double Danishes clinging to Mike's leg as Mike held a turkey leg aloft. He told Ryan about it in a whisper and they laughed.

"What's funny?" asked Mike, seated cross-legged on a Ziggy blanket.

"Everything," Ryan said.

"Nothing," said Henry.

"There are no secrets in this house," Mike said. It was a rare hot summer day, and he had been drinking in the heat for an hour, so he sweated and slurred.

"This house is made of secrets," Ryan said. "Have you looked in the basement lately?"

"There is a difference," Mike said, "between what is not known and what is not shared." He frowned and belched. Henry, afraid that an argument was brewing, reached over to Mike's blanket and turned a can into a bottle. "For instance," Mike said, sticking a finger in the bottle and lifting it to point at Henry. "For *instance*. How did you do that, Bubba?"

"I don't know," Henry said, which was almost true, so he added, "A dog taught me." He knew there must be more to it than that, but much as he wanted to tell them why he could do something the rest of them couldn't, he didn't know how; they could all change themselves, but changing something else was beyond them. It seemed like a comparatively boring trick to Henry—he could only do it with small things, and whatever he changed never strayed out of its type, so a can could become a bottle and a bike could become a pony but a knife could not become a pen, and the changes were never permanent. But Mike was wonderstruck and some of the boys were jealous.

"That," said Peaches, "is the stupidest thing I've ever heard." It was what he always said when Henry talked about the dog.

"It's all I remember," Henry said. "A dog. A black dog."

"I remember your gay lover," said Peaches. "That's who taught you."

"Hey," said Ryan. "Fuck you."

"Fuck you right back, fag," Peaches said, and Mike stood up, stepping on plates and kicking bottles and wobbling a little before he settled his back against the tree. He looked down at them with his face flushed and sweat shining in the roots of his beard.

"What's wrong with you?" he asked. "Don't you understand what you've got to do? Haven't I taught you a thing? You've got to be *good* to each other, because nobody else is ever going to understand." He turned to Peaches. "One of them took a shine to him in there, and you think that means he's lucky now? That just makes it harder. I keep telling you. I keep *telling* you. The tricks are wonderful, but listen, they're not enough. That other thing—I can't even think of the name for it!—is more horrible than the tricks are wonderful, and you know what that means!" He didn't ask it like a question, so none of them tried to answer. "It means you have to be good to each other forever. It means you have to be good to each other or else you won't have anybody to remind you what happened and tell you what's the matter with you, and nobody to keep you from getting—all stretchy, you see?" He turned and bent, wobbling, and put his face close to Peaches's face. "You get all stretchy, you see? Like a rubber band. Tighter and tighter until—" He raised a finger and a thumb to his temple—

"Blam!" They all jumped. "Anyway," Mike said, "you have to be good to each other. That's all I'm saying." He slid down the tree, sat with his knees drawn up to his chest, and started to cry. The noise of his weeping mixed with the strange ululating call of Peaches's rare bird, which had taken up residence at the top of the tree as soon as he let it out of the cage, but the boys were all quiet until Ryan moved forward on his knees and gave Mike a hug. "Cheer up, boss," he said, and the others all did the same, not one after the other but all at once, so they made a heap.

Much later, after Mike had sobered up and directed them in a set of games where gerbils and hamsters raced the perimeter of the garden while he played the theme from *Chariots of Fire* on the kazoo, and a little herd of cats swarmed in the tree, trying to touch Peaches's bird with a paw but not hurt it, after another meal and other games inside, after Mike had become drunk again, not just on beer it seemed to Henry but on their good behavior toward one another, and after they had all fallen asleep in the big bed, Ryan woke Henry up.

He put a hand over Henry's mouth, and led him by gestures into the basement for their bikes and then out of the house, and didn't speak until they were out on the street. "You can't tell where we're going," he said. "We'd get in so much trouble with Mike. You have to promise." Henry promised, and followed him as he pedaled up Seventeenth Street, not slowing until after it crossed Castro, and then only because the hill was so steep. He turned off at Roosevelt, where Henry was distracted by the spectacular view as they rode along the edge of the hill. He had figured out where they were going by then, but instead of thinking about it he added the view to all the other views of the city he'd stored up in his head. As they rode around for work, Ryan was always stopping them to take in some vista of the city, from the top of Alamo Square or Twin Peaks or just as they were about to plunge down into the Marina, and he'd say the same thing every time: "This whole city is ours!" He meant there was nowhere they couldn't go and nothing they couldn't take, but half the time, in half of the incredible sweeping views, Buena Vista was the obtrusive exception.

They walked their bikes up the last part of the hill, which got so steep that Henry thought his bike was about to turn upside down. There was no wind coming down the Duboce Steps, but they walked by them. Henry closed his eyes, trying to pick up another scent beneath the eucalyptus and cypress, but he couldn't. Ryan left his bike in the bushes a few hundred yards past the steps and then started up the hill on foot. Henry followed him without being told, sometimes hauling himself up hand over hand and thinking that four legs would be better than two but not making the change. After five minutes of climbing, Ryan stopped at a flat rock in the shape of an arrow and pushed it aside. He slipped into the tunnel it was hiding, but this time he had to call twice before Henry followed him. It wasn't very long, but it was wide. At the end of it they could almost lie shoulder to shoulder. Ryan had a flashlight, which he waved around, now on the earth or a root and now on his face or Henry's face. "I've been working on it for a year," he said. "You're the only one I ever showed, but I figured you could make it easier. I know I'm headed the right way, but who knows how deep I'll have to go. It could be *forever* deep, you know? But I thought you could make it easier. You know what I mean?"

"Yes," Henry said, because he could picture himself touching the earth to make it sand, or even making a door at the end of the tunnel that would open onto the place that Ryan could go.

"When we're done," Ryan said, "we could go back for the others and let them know. If we wanted to."

"Okay," Henry said, but at first he didn't want to because he was scared, and he thought that might be why he failed. Mike said it was okay to be afraid of what was under the hill, and Henry *was* afraid, but much more than he was afraid of the place he wanted to go back to it. There was suddenly no way to measure how much he wanted to go back. He remembered a noise of bells, so clearly that he looked to Ryan to see if he had heard them too, but he was still just staring at him with the flashlight under his chin, looking spooky and expectant and hopeful.

"Magic is change," the dog said. "Do you understand?"

"No," Henry said.

"Observe," the dog said. He leaned close to a teapot in the center of the room, an isolated chamber they'd come to only after an hour of walking under the hill, and barked at it. It became a vase full of flowers. He barked again, and it was a swarm of bees, hovering in a globe that shaped itself now as a dog and now as the image of Henry's face. He barked again and it was a baby elephant. He barked again and it was a rough piece of stone. "Now do you understand?"

"No," Henry said again.

"Well," the dog said, leaping over the stone and jumping up to lick Henry's face, "you will. I'm an excellent teacher, and we have all the time in the world for you to learn."

In the middle of the summer they all celebrated the Great Night. The boys talked about it for weeks before it happened. "It's like Christmas but better than Christmas," Ryan said, and Peaches said, "Christmas is so fucking lame." Mike seemed continually overjoyed in the days leading up to the feast. "Forget everything you know about holidays," he told Henry, which wasn't that hard to do.

It felt most different from the holidays that Henry remembered because nobody else celebrated it. The windows in the shops on Castro Street looked the same way they always did, and nothing special hung from the streetlamps on Market Street, and no one Henry saw on the street exhibited any holiday cheer. More than ever, coming home to the house on Fourteenth Street felt like walking into a different world, because the whole house was hung with decorations, braided flowers and glass beads and birds in little cages that Mike kept catching in the garden. The garden was the last part of the house to get decorated. Henry helped Ryan hang ribbons on the tree. Henry passed ribbons to Ryan, who stood on a ladder to reach the highest silver branches. Warm days made the tree smell, which tended to attract them all to it, and an 85-degree afternoon might find them all standing around it taking deep, low, sniffing breaths through their noses. Henry rested his head against the trunk, breathing in the odor of the tree. He could smell Ryan, too—something like pickle juice and the warm inside of a car.

"Want to go for a bike ride?" Henry asked.

"Later," Ryan said, a little harshly. He was up in the tree, tying long silk ribbons to the branches. They had gone to the hill the night before, and aside from a little mundane digging, Henry had failed once again to help Ryan with his tunnel. Henry frowned.

"Are you mad at me?" he asked.

"Don't be stupid," Ryan said, and asked him to hand up more ribbon. Henry climbed up with it instead, and they decorated together, tying ribbons as carefully as you would into a little girl's hair. They went high in the tree, and the leaves were thick enough now that you could hardly see through them to the house. Henry pretended that he and Ryan were not just the only people in the tree but the only people in the house, that they lived there together with nothing but the garden and the furniture and each other for company.

There was more work to do even after every branch was done, but they snuck away instead of helping Mateo where he was coloring the water of the hot tub or Greg where he was carefully wrapping a chain of flowers around the gazebo posts. They took their bikes and rode for a while in widening circles around the house, a few pacing laps before Ryan broke away and sprinted up Fifteenth Street. On the other side of Market they took Sanchez to Steiner, and then went up Fell to the Panhandle, riding against the traffic and ignoring people when they honked and cursed. They stopped a few times on the way to the park for random robberies. They all had the whole week off, to get ready for the holiday, so what they stole from one house they left in the next, and they took what was interesting or pretty without any thought for its value or whether Mike could sell it: they took a stuffed owl from a tall narrow Victorian near the corner of Lyon and Fell and left it perched on a toilet in the house next door, and they transferred all the linens in that house to a condominium down the street.

Despite its size and the variety of diversions it contained, Golden Gate was an inferior park. It was boring for the obvious reason, and also because it wasn't off limits. Henry liked passing through it better than anything else, taking his bike off the paved roads and bumping over roots and rocks that would have popped the tires of any other boy on any other bike, and he liked ending a ride at the sea because it felt like they had raced to the end of the world. They met the incoming fog halfway through the park. It was high, and looked as solid as a wall, and Henry wondered if he could make it be a wall. He restrained himself but made Ryan stop to be buffalo, because of the way they looked in the fog, and they shuffled about for a while and mingled with the other gray shapes. *I'm looming*, Henry thought, leaning forward and sideways and forward again. Ryan, quickly bored, was a boy in the center of the herd, staring down a shaggy bull. Henry knocked him over with his enormous head.

It was getting dark by the time they came to the beach, and they wondered to each other if they were going to be in trouble for skipping out on the work of decorating; there were whole floors of the house where no ribbons or crepe or flower chains had been hung, and whole hallways that Mike had said must be carpeted in sod, and now with night falling they had barely twenty-four hours until the celebration would begin. They hurried back but still stopped at the hill, which could be construed to be on the way home, and dug. Henry tried a new trick every time they came, but nothing was really any more helpful than digging with a spoon: if he made a door it only opened on more damp earth. They had made a lot of progress, but Henry went back to undo their work every day they did it, because now he was afraid of how disappointed Ryan would be when they dug clear through to the other side of the hill, as he thought they must. And he didn't want the digging to end.

The tunnel was wide enough now that they could dig side by side, and high enough that they could kneel next to each other as they worked, but it was still cramped. Henry could feel Ryan's shoulder working against his shoulder as he scraped at the dirt.

"I think it's getting late," Henry said. "Maybe we should go."

"In a minute," Ryan said. "I've got a good feeling all of a sudden."

"Okay," Henry said. And after a few more strokes with his spoon he said, "This is nice."

"Huh?"

"This is nice," he said again. "The digging."

"Yeah," Ryan said. "And necessary." Henry turned his head and tried to kiss him. Ryan pushed him away, but in the cramped space he didn't go far. "What was that?" Ryan asked.

"I don't know," Henry said. Ryan was flushed. In the light from the flashlight he looked orange.

"What was *that*?"

"I don't know!" Henry said, because there wasn't any way he could put it into words, and then he became something that wouldn't have to answer the question because it couldn't talk. A black rat fled away down the tunnel.

"Bring me a peach," the lady said.

Henry kept walking through the hall, hoping she was talking to somebody else. He tried to stay away from her, because she scared him. She was around all the time, but she wasn't hard to avoid; you heard about her or saw her somewhere every day, but it was like seeing the president on television or hear-ing about what he was saying or doing, and most days talking to her was a similarly remote possibility. He was beneath notice.

"Boy," she said, just before Henry made it to the door out of the hall, "are you deaf? I want a peach."

"Yes, ma'am," Henry said. The peaches, large and round and soft, were piled on a table much closer to her than to him, but he didn't complain. He selected one from the top and took it to her, staring at his feet as he approached. She was sitting in her high-backed chair. He saw her bare white feet, and noticed how different they looked from his, which were filthy, and how nice her toenails were, perfectly rounded on the edges and painted with mother-of-pearl. She grabbed his face when he was close and raised it to hers, but he did not look her in the eye.

"What's this?" she said.

"A peach," he said. "Like you asked for."

"Not that," she said. "This." She slid her fingers down his chin and drew them to a point just beneath his chin, catching something there and then plucking it out. She showed him the hair.

"I don't know," he said. "A hair."

"I said you were ripe," she said. "And now you're spoiled. Puck can choose another slave."

"I'm not his slave," Henry said. "I'm his friend."

"You are a slave. Puck has no tender feelings. It's time to throw you back, little fish."

"What?" Henry said.

"I don't repeat myself," she said. "Ask the stones, if they listen better than you do." She got up and swept away, her bare feet sounding very loud in Henry's ears as they fell on the stone floor.

"What?" Henry said. "What?" He threw the peach at her, not staying to see if it found its mark, and ran away calling the name of his friend.

Henry was the guest of honor at the Great Night celebration. "*Guest* is the wrong word, of course," Mike said. "This is your *home*. But tonight you are the most special boy—tonight you *matter* more than anyone else." It was because he was the youngest and the freshest, the most recent of the exiles in the house on Fourteenth Street. That meant everyone was supposed to be especially nice to him, and hug him every time they saw him, and contribute a present to a pile that had formerly sat on the feasting table but now, in a brand-new tradition, sat under the tree. But when Ryan saw him that morning, he didn't even talk to him, let alone give him a hug, and the other boys avoided him too. Only Mike embraced him, and he did it so often and so vigorously that it started to feel oppressive. Henry spent the whole afternoon out of the house, walking around in the Castro, playing a game with himself of stealing various items from stores and then returning them to the shelves an hour later. It was something he thought Ryan would enjoy.

He came home barely in time for dinner. That was rude, since it excused him from all the final preparations, but then again, as guest of honor, he wasn't actually obligated to help today. No one seemed to mind that he had been gone; they smiled and wished him a happy day, and Peaches told him he could hardly wait to give him his present. Ryan didn't talk to him, but he didn't scold him either. Still, Henry found he couldn't enjoy his seat of honor at the banquet, and he wasn't hungry enough to do more than poke at the jelly beans and toast and popcorn on his plate. He watched Ryan, who was the only person, besides himself, who didn't look like he was having a wonderful time, but Ryan, clear down at the other end of the table, never looked back at him.

"How is this night different from all other nights?" Mike asked, and the answers started to roll from around the table. Ryan had told Henry that no one really knew: the celebration was something that Mike had remembered from his time under the hill, but he never could remember what it was about, only that there had been a great feast, and music, and the exchange of gifts. "It's fucking stupid," he had said. Henry had taken him to mean the curse of forgetting, and not the holiday they aped in ignorance, but now, watching Ryan frown and pout over his plate, he thought the celebration disappointed Ryan, so he let it disappoint him too. The talk of why the night was special became once again talk of why the boys were special, and Henry wanted to raise his hand and ask if he could have a holiday from being special, because that night he didn't feel lucky at all to be that way.

"The rest is a mystery," he said, when his turn came to speak. It was what Mike had told him to say.

"But not forever!" the others all said in chorus, and they raised their beers in a toast to Henry and the Great Night. Then they marched out to the tree and danced around it once in a ring before Mike said it was time for Henry to open his presents, which were really, he reminded them, everybody's presents.

"Best for last!" said Peaches, holding his back from the rest. The others gave him a black feather, a shirt made out of tiny flowers, a stick stripped of its bark, and a variety of other natural curiosities that were more or less interesting. Henry sat on the ground to open them, and placed them carefully to his left or right. Ryan hung back, and while the other boys shouted out in turn to identify their gifts, he was silent. Finally only Peaches's gift was left. Henry opened the box and lifted out some fruit, a banana and two oranges glued together; it took him a moment to understand what it was supposed to look like, but the other boys were already laughing.

"We thought you would enjoy peeling that banana!" Peaches said, in between guffaws. Mike stared about, confused. Ryan was laughing too. He wasn't laughing very hard, and he was doing it without smiling, but he was still laughing.

"What? What? What?" Mike said, as Henry ran away into the house. Mike chased after him but Henry was faster, and he made use of the fireman's pole to get to the basement and his bicycle and then to the street. Mike was in the upstairs doorway flanked by boys and shouting something at Peaches. Henry pedaled away, but found before he had even crossed Valencia Street that he couldn't go fast enough, so he left the bicycle in the road and ran as a rat, a dog, a rabbit, and a pony all the way up to Market Street. When he got there he was a boy again, and he looked like any other messy child sitting on the sidewalk crying into his sleeve, unusual only in that kids like him rarely wandered out of the Haight. He was thinking of them all dancing around the tree without him, as dogs and cats, as mice and chickens and voles, as alligators and crocodiles, as otters and bears and wolves, the colored streamers dragging on their fur. He wanted to turn them all to stone, or cheese, or air, to make them all go away, but though he pictured his furious will arching over the neighborhoods between here and there he knew he couldn't touch them. He hardly thought of Ryan at all in his anger, though that wasn't because he was spared, in the dozen plans of violent revenge he conceived and dismissed as he sat crying on the corner. A voice intruded on a vision of the tree in flames.

"Hey, kid," it said. "What's going on?" It was a lady cop, short and wiry and fast, even though she was old, from whom Henry had run a few times before when he'd been stealing in the Castro.

"Nothing," Henry said, wiping his nose on his sleeve. But he told her everything.

They all said goodbye to him together, just as they had all said hello to him together. Henry was too upset to register all the faces and almost-faces that stared at him, but he caught sight of a few as he was marched down the aisle toward the door out of the hill, faces with whiskers around the eyes or tentacles around the mouth, or noses that looked like they were made of broccoli, or eyebrows that looked like a child had drawn them with crayon. The dog walked next to him, pulling at a chain that was fastened to his silver collar. The lady's husband had put it on him after he complained about Henry having to go— complained *wasn't actually strong enough a word for what he did. The conversation had started out civilly enough but quickly escalated into a shouting match, everyone in the hall covering their ears and closing their eyes, though nobody ran away or chose not to listen. Henry thought his friend would have won; he was getting bigger and bigger as he shouted louder and louder, and his argument—that a promise to him was being broken—seemed rock solid to Henry, but just when he thought his friend would fall on the lady's husband and cover him and his objections up forever, the lady produced the chain from under her skirt and clipped it on him. That made him shrink.*

"Goodbye," the lady said to him, on the grass outside the door.

"Goodbye!" said all the rest of the host.

"I want to stay," Henry said. "Why can't I stay?"

"You were never here," the lady said.

"You were never here!" said the host.

"I want to stay!" Henry said, and only realized, when he started crying again, that he had stopped for a little while.

"It's not allowed," the lady's husband said, and Henry's friend rose up snapping at him, jumping at his throat. But the lady pulled his chain tight, and he fell on his back.

"Down, dog," she said, and he rolled on his belly, a puppy now, crying fat tears, and Henry thought how dogs cry not just when they're sad but when they're angry.

"There is no magic," the lady said. "There never was. There is only mortal life and mortal cares and death to take them both away. You were never here!" She waved goodbye at him, and everyone else waved goodbye, and the dog howled. They were waving him away, some of them vigorously, some of them halfheartedly; a few, like the lady's husband, just held up a hand. But the waving hands put a pressure on him; he was going away.

"Something horrible should happen to you!" Henry said, not sure whether he was talking to all of them or just the terrible lady.

"You were never here," she said again. From very far away he saw her turn her back on him, and all the others followed suit except his friend the black dog, who watched him mournfully over his shoulder as he was dragged along, and then they were gone, and Henry was standing at the entrance to the park, not sure why he was crying.

16

A-one," said Huff, "and a-two!" A tiny man, dressed in a paper bag and a monocle, was still running to hit his mark. "Don't make me count to a-three!" Rehearsals were under way, and though time was short (there had already been two false alarms about the Mayor's return), the players were all industrious, and the addition of the Mayor's ever more numerous defectors was a piece of edifying good fortune. They did whatever the lovely lady told them to, but Huff wondered whether the grand necessity of the project didn't also command their loyalty. It had seemed grander by the hour: the additional players made it possible to perform a much more complicated entertainment. Now there were more songs, and more scenes, and more things happening in every scene, and Huff felt like a hundred little tentacles had erupted from his head, each one topped with an eyeball and equipped with a clever little satellite brain, because it felt like he was doing a hundred different things at once, writing dialogue or lyrics or humming out a theme or choreographing a new step, and yet the whole time he was sure as well that he could never take his eyes off the lady.

Princess had her jai-alai baskets back, and the industrious defectors had copied a dozen more pairs and added to them hulking costumes of straw and grass to turn the largest among them into fair semblances of backhoes and bulldozers. Now they danced in blocky mechanical steps and leaps, squaring off in a musical confrontation that the fleshly were destined to lose. It was a sad scene in a sad play, but Huff explained, carefully, when the little man he called Mr. Peanut (because of his size and the brown color of his bag and his monocle) said he was accustomed to singing happy songs and didn't see why there couldn't be one or two in this production. Happy songs, Huff said, were not going to move the Mayor to vulnerable, regret-stricken tears.

"You may as well try to wring tears from a stone as from the Beast," said Mr. Peanut.

"Faith! Faith!" Huff shouted at him. He shouted it a lot, all through rehearsal, because, impossible as their task seemed, he was feeling better and better about it and had confidence in the power of artfully executed musical theater to change a person's soul. Six hours ago, before he had met his lovely lady friend, before the world (and the musical) had become peopled with strange creatures, little and big, before his crew had been gathered and become outfitted with a new enthusiasm, before things had suddenly started to fall into place, he had been more of a doubter. He hadn't liked to admit it, but he knew it was possible that they might be arrested or killed or turned into stew before the first transfiguring bar was sung, and that the Mayor might be deaf to their effort and unchanged by it—they might all be wasting their time, just distracting themselves before they became burritos. "But you might say that about anything," he said to the lady. "You might say that about life in general, that we are all just distracting ourselves before we become burritos."

"I don't care for burritos," she said.

"I don't like them either, those burritos of futility and despair," he said. "Though I have eaten them, over and over, down to the last bean and stale tortilla nubbin. But people who believe that it's all for nothing deserve to have it all turn out for nothing."

"But it *is* all for nothing, my love," she said. "We've already lost, and there's nothing left but this lovely delusion. I am reduced, and you are dead already."

"Enough of that talk," he said, and stopped her mouth with a kiss. They retreated behind a bush to make out more discreetly, though not for very long. The clock was ticking the seconds away to the Mayor's return, and there was barely time to properly rehearse, let alone make out, and yet it was necessary to explore the boundaries of her mouth with his tongue, since they might be in prison or worse when morning came. "Come away, my love," she said, pulling at his belt and beckoning him behind deeper bushes.

"Duty calls, my lady," he said, and led her out to the next scene. Short on time but long on players, they were rehearsing multiple scenes at once, five cells scattered around the field waiting for Huff to come inspect them or participate, since he had taken the part of Ty Thorn for himself. So when they had walked a few yards down from where the scoops were dancing aggressively around the food rioters, he joined Princess (who'd put down her baskets and put a rose in her hair) for their pas de deux around a corpse, Hogg in a suit stained with bloody berry juice. "Excuse me, my lovely loon," he said to his lady, and fancy-stepped over to Princess. They joined hands over the body and released, each of them turning away and kicking a heel up backward just as they brought hand to mouth to bite the knuckle, then they each threw up their hands at the sky and threw back their heads as they stepped lightly on the balls of their feet, circling the body and singing.

> There's been a murder here, a murder!
> Mr. Fancy Feast is dead.
> Murder most foul; murder most fancy;
> Who killed him?
> Was it you or you or *you*?

Huff blinked at the sky, open above the walls of fog and full of stars, and then brought his head forward to point with his eyes as well as his fingers. You or you or *you*—that was just a preliminary motion, meant to tenderize the listener a little before the sharper jabs came later. He and Princess pointed accusatory disco fingers, now at the crowd and now at each other, and Hogg rose up to join them for a dramatic three-person tango, sternly (and somewhat sexily) charging them both to solve the mystery of his death.

> Before the day is gone, baby,
> Before the play is done, honey,
> Find the truth!
> Find the truth!

Then he lay down again on his back and put his arms and legs in the air and shook them vigorously before he let them drop with a thud.

"Don't shake like that," Huff said. "You look like a bug. But turn your head to your side, and make your eyes bug out, and put out your tongue. A little more to the side. Precisely!"

"A lovely dance, my love," said the lady. "Such grace! How can it be tolerated, on the hill or under it?"

"I dance in my head all the time," Huff said. "When I'm trying to fall asleep. As a bit of flame, or a tampon on the wind, or a pony. And tonight it's as easy to do it as to dream it."

"Well," she said. They retreated to the bushes once again, to nibble each other's nipples for a while. His were brown and fat, but she praised them sincerely. "Such beautiful buttons, my love," she said. Hers were so perfectly formed and such a lovely shade of rose he could hardly believe his eyes when she parted her dress. He brought out a penlight, the better to see them with, and stuck it under her breast, looking to see if it was real. "Do you wish for them to glow?" she asked, and then they both did, with a light that was so warm he could feel it on his face.

"Forgive my doubting, lovely lady!" he said. He put his face between them to make a joyful little speedboat sound. He had almost been arrested, once, for lurking in a Laundromat to press his face into the piles of warm laundry, and now he knew what he had been seeking when he did that, the ideal experience of which that, pleasant as it was, was only a degraded iteration.

"Do pinch them," he said muffledly, of his own nipples, raising his hands up on either side of her and snapping his fingers like a pair of castanets. He looked up to see her smiling down benevolently on him. "Perfect!" he said, because she was pinching just hard enough and no harder, and who can ever do that at first pinch? But even through the perfect pleasure he heard strains of music and voices arguing. "Duty calls us," he said, and bowed three times, once to the left breast, once to the right breast, and once to her face. "Shall we have a part two?" he asked her.

"And three and four," she said. "We would have endless days and nights, my love, if this weren't the last night. But pleasure has a way of lengthening the hours."

"I've always found it shortens them," said Huff. "And cold nights are longer than warm ones." He closed her dress, and took her hand, and led her from behind the bushes in a dance, so everyone would think they were merely rehearsing back there.

Mary and Princess were arguing nearby. "Feather step, feather step, feather step!" Mary said.

"Do-si-do!" said Princess, and did just that, circling Mary but keeping her eyes on Huff the whole time. "Right, boss?" A small crowd, drooping streamers in their hands, surrounded them. Bob and Hogg, dressed respectively as a chair and a couch, were sitting on the ground quietly talking.

"You can't just make it up as you go along," said Mary. "That's not *choreography.*"

"You're just jealous of my moves," said Princess, and struck Mary with her hip. It was obvious that she meant it in a friendly way, but Mary pushed her. Huff sighed, and thought of all the things he could say, that this dance was very important, that its intricate geometries were meant to hypnotize the Mayor and make him more receptive to the subtle lessons that would come later in the play, that the delightful irony of Furniture dancing with furniture would cause him to let down his guard so the more serious ironies yet to come could strike home. He shook his head, and drew in a breath to scold them with, but caught sight of his lady's face before he spoke and had a different idea. He held out his hand and she took it. Without speaking, they started to dance, and with their feet and their hips and their jiggly necks showed the quarreling girls and the lazy boys and the crowd of limp-ribboned extras exactly what he meant. They all fell into step, the furniture and the Furniture, following him through the steps he had created, the high-grass kick and the lawnmower and the jack-in-the-box and the yoga-master-taffy spin. It wasn't effortless, but it was so easy he started to cry.

"Why tears, my love?" asked his lady, spinning her hand round and round above her head, so all the little people danced in a ring and waved their ribbons.

"For happiness, of course," he said, which wasn't exactly why, so he tried to dance it out, instead, how wonderful and overwhelming it was to want something and to get it.

"Happy or sad," she said, wiping his tears away, "I cannot bear them." She drew him away from the crowd, now a self-sustaining choreography, and they went behind another bush.

"What rank delight," she said, before she blew him.

"Your mouth," he replied, "is like . . ." But he could think of nothing to compare it to, and then it seemed rude or ungrateful to try. The lesson of the dance, that words were not necessary, or not enough, was still with him, so he answered her with a moan and a giggle and a deep gurgling sigh, and then went nosing under her skirts, to give her a reciprocating thank-you, but the way seemed very long, from her ankle to her crotch. Her skirts were white and transparent, layer by layer—initially he could see her white leg aglow with a special mixture of moonlight and starlight and torchlight—but the world beneath them darkened as he nosed upward, until he was navigating only by touch and smell. Even the way up became notional; he wasn't entirely sure where his arms and hands had gone, and his head seemed to be floating sideways and down as much as up. Then there was a faint light in the dark, and a soft wind blowing a scent against his face—something like rosemary and gourmet cat food— and then he had arrived. He gorged himself on her, eating with his lips and tongue but also somehow just as much with his cheek and nose and eye, and pressing his eye to her as if to a keyhole he thought he saw the source of the light, flashes of lightning deep inside her.

When they emerged again from the bushes she was riding on his shoulders, having ascended there somewhat accidentally. Without her armor, she was very light, and he pranced merrily to that portion of the field where Bob lay on a bier of sticks and stones while the wonders of the lost world were projected, shadows on a white sheet held up by taller defectors, for his sad, dying, benefit. There was disagreement about how the images should be sequenced, and Mary was complaining that there was no color in them, and Princess was calling her a snob and a colorist.

"Black and white was good enough for everybody for hundreds of years," she said. "Hundreds of years!"

"Is it time for me to sing?" Bob asked, staring at the screen with his head cocked to the side and an empty glass in his hand.

"*Garçon!*" said Huff, snapping his fingers at one of the little people walking about with a bottle on his head. He took the bottle and poured for Bob, then took a swig for himself, careful to balance his lady by holding more tightly to her leg with his other hand. "It's time," he said to Bob, not bothering to hush Mary or Princess.

"I don't know if I've had too much or not enough," Bob said, sniffing at his glass.

"Drink up," said Huff. "It's good for your voice." When they tried the song earlier it had not been plaintive or sad enough. Bob had sounded like

James Cagney singing "You're a Grand Old Flag," and Huff had told him to take a break, and a few more drinks, and to reflect on sad things. Now he just looked confused, and Huff thought of pinching him again a few times to get him in the right frame of mind. The scene and the song was meant to convey Sol's great weariness—he felt *constantly afflicted*, Huff had explained, pinching. He just wants to *get away* from it all. "I get it!" Bob had said, slapping away Huff's fingers, but now Huff realized he had forgotten something. With his lady on his shoulders, it was almost as if he could borrow a little of her being to think with, and now it was stunningly obvious that Sol was as nostalgic as he was despairing and believed death would somehow bring him back to the good old days. He wanted to explain that, but Bob was already singing:

Take me home, my friend,
I want to go home, my friend,
It's no good here, anymore, my friend.
All the good things have gone away, even strawberries:
Strawberries and peaches and apricots,
Compassion and empathy and fellow feeling, where did they go?
Take me home, my friend,
O thin sharp pokey needly friend, take me home!

Listening, he realized that he had understood the form but not the substance of Sol's nostalgia, and now here Bob was singing it back to him in explicit detail, while the shapes of sunflowers and peach trees and buffalo and tall stately giraffe stretched and leaped and pranced upon the sheet, first in stark black and white and then in shimmering color. They all started to sing along with Bob, even though it was supposed to be a solo number, and Huff swayed in time with the music, which came from everywhere and sounded very full, though the string section played on crickets' legs and the horn section blew blades of grass between their thumbs and the largest of the tympani was a paper cup. Huff swayed too far and unbalanced his lady, who fell to the right. She turned in midair and landed on her feet, but Huff fell on his side, transported by the images and the song. "Cover my eyes!" he said, and she threw a veil over his neck and face and led him away once more behind the circling bushes.

Now they fucked in earnest, which seemed like the right thing to do. The glorious success of Bob's rehearsal seemed like permission somehow.

He hadn't said *Take five, everybody,* but he beamed it at them now, wishing they could all find as refreshing a pastime as he and his lady had. "No more tears, love," she said as he blubbered on her, but he couldn't stop, not even at the thought of mistakenly impregnating her with his sadness, and not even at the thought of what fruit such a union might bear. *A child constitutionally incapable of being happy,* he thought, and part of him watched it, as he sniffed and licked and thrust, as his cock darted and bucked, as he rolled himself on her and off her and poked her now from the front and now from the back and now from the side. It wailed in its cradle and pouted in its high chair and frowned in Santa's lap, and everyone and everything disappointed it because it had been born sad to live sad. Tears were its nature and formed its lot, and though it never asked for any of the terrible things that befell it, it luxuriated in them just the same, mistaking cynicism for bravery and despair for reason. "I'm crying because it's all so *beautiful,*" he said to it, but it didn't listen; it thought deafness was a virtue.

"No more words, my love," his lady said, so Huff didn't speak to it anymore but tried to show by gestures what he meant, and it felt like he was discovering what he meant by and through this marvelous fucking, like he had never, in all his days of being wise, sometimes pretending and sometimes not, actually understood anything about suffering or joy until this very moment, which encapsulated and recapitulated the named and nameless struggles of his whole life, the outcome of which he was both breathlessly creating and breathlessly waiting for, not actually knowing if it would be triumph or defeat until he came, standing, with both hands thrown up high over his head and his lady lifted to the stars on his impossibly stiff, impossibly eloquent cock. He came and came and came and fell backward, as if through a mile of air or a lifetime, to land on the soft grass with a noise like his name, feeling like he was saying his name properly for the first time because for the first time he knew who he was and what he was all about and what he really wanted, which was precisely this. He had nothing left, not will or energy or expertise, with which to venture from the bush and offer to his friends and co-conspirators, though he heard them rehearsing the last song ensemble and unsupervised: *People,* they sang. *People who eat people are the loneliest people in the world!*

"Bravo!" he called out, the words muffled by his lady's breast. "Bravo, everybody. Well done!"

I'm going to die, Titania thought, *in the grip of this delusion of love.* It wasn't the real thing, but it numbed and distracted just like the real thing. As she promenaded through the dell with her new husband, inspecting the rehearsal scenes and improving them with her magic, she considered how this false love was a lot like what she had once felt for Oberon—intense and consuming and passionate but still light as air, compared to what she felt, then and now, for her Boy. There had been no real suffering in her passion for Oberon until after she drove him away, she realized suddenly, gazing at the candy jewel on her wedding ring. That's what made it feel like a cousin to this false love.

Now she had suffering galore, of course. She suffered for her husband, and for her Boy, and for her subjects, and for herself. Death, about which she knew so little, even after becoming familiar with it in the hospital, was coming for her at dawn, and underneath the fatuous devotion to her new husband, she was more frightened now than relieved. Yet when she thought about it, what she feared more than anything was that her own death would evoke her Boy's death. She had heard mortals say that they lived their whole lives again in the instant before they died, a consolation, as they described it, though it sounded dreadful to her even before she realized that it meant they relived every death that ever befell them. She didn't want to go back into that hospital room, or listen to her Boy's labored, rattling last breath, or feel his skin cooling under her hand to the temperature of a graveyard stone. Once was more than enough for all that.

Furthermore, oblivion had lost its allure. She had thought for a while that that was death's great magic: it ruined everything and then made it all better; it took away the pain it gave you, because even though she didn't want to die it was already a relief to be dead. But then it had become obvious to her, in the quiet bubble in her mind within which she reflected on things even as she pranced around the dell, that when she died her memory of her Boy would die as well, and that seemed unbearable, because she realized that eventually everyone who ever remembered him, faerie or mortal, would die as well, and then even the memory of him would be dead. What her dead mind might do, she couldn't know, though somehow she felt sure it would do nothing at all, that death would be such a total state of being that it would leave no room for the exercise of memory or longing or love.

These thoughts would have inspired her to rage, if she hadn't been bound by Puck's spell and powerless to lift it. The candy ring throbbed on her finger, but she couldn't remove it, and she likewise could do nothing but smile and fawn on the mortal fool, and waste her last few hours, and her people's, catering to his folly. She might have spent her remaining time chopping away at the earth and the trees, and reduced the whole hill to a scarred lump, but instead of destruction she wreaked a particular sort of creation for her new husband's sake. There was something mildly interesting about that, she thought within her bubble, and something mildly appealing about rehearsing a nonsensical play while extinction loomed. Some of her people seemed to have entered into the enterprise in that spirit; they danced and sang and capered in a way that seemed insane and carefree compared to the ones who were doing it only because she told them to. And scene by scene, she tried to sympathize with them more, and to sympathize with her carefree self, the Titania outside of the solemn, angry little bubble. But it seemed too much like something Puck would approve of, for them all to mutter nonsense and do handstands until he came to kill them, and she decided she wanted no part of nonsense right now, no matter what her mouth might be saying or her body might be doing. It was a distinctly mortal attitude, which she understood a lot better, now that she was herself convincingly threatened with death; she wanted it all—her life, her losses, her death—to mean something.

She might do what the mortals did, and strain to convince herself that the death of her Boy and the loss of her husband had happened for some reason, that some restitution would be made for her, that she would be paid for her suffering with a truer and more tolerable understanding of the world, but she didn't think she had the muscles for it. Just thinking about it made something—the body within the bubble—ache, and made her want to lie down and sleep. So she did magic instead, scene by scene, working a sort of dual cosmesis upon the players and the play, so the mortals sang more sweetly and their voices and feet were linked to the faeries in such a way that the song and dance became ugly vessels containing real beauty, and she made it so the play would show whoever saw it not just the dancing backhoes and prostitutes and singing corpses and dwarves juggling wafers of green plankton, but also whatever was most frightening, exultant, and pathetic about their own lives. It was a crude and subtle piece of magic, and the more deliriously the exterior Titania giggled and fucked, the more industriously the interior one worked it out, even though she knew what she would have caused herself to see, when the music was over and the play was done.

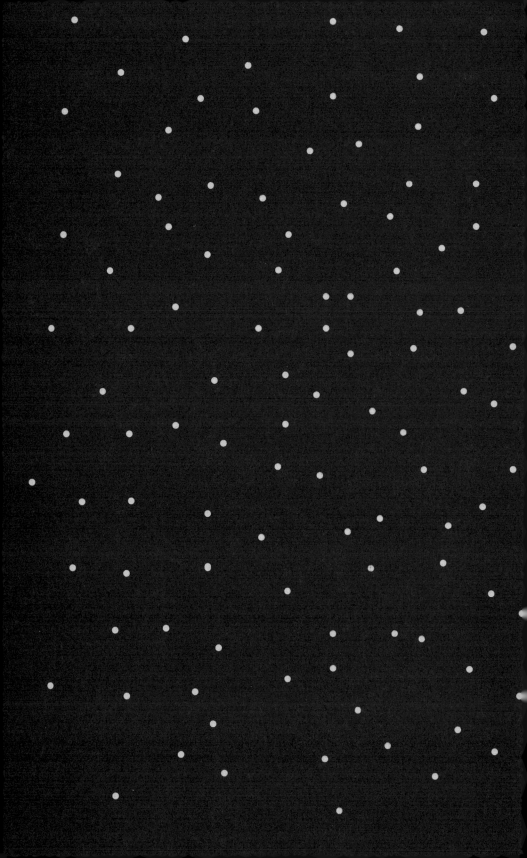

Part Five

17

*A*fter her Boy died, Titania stayed in bed for weeks. It seemed like the right place to be, since she deserved a rest, and since her employment as a mother had come to an end. She vaguely remembered what she had done with her days, before the boy had come and before he had fallen ill, and she had no interest in any of it. She had a dawning sense of what her new occupation was going to be, and she was in no hurry to take up the post. Better to stay in bed, even if she couldn't exactly sleep.

Oberon stayed with her, at first. He seemed to know better than to say anything, but he pursued her around the bed, always seeking to hold her, which was fine when she was sleeping but annoyed her when she was awake, as did his tears, which thankfully came in smaller and smaller daily volumes as time passed. "It's all right," he said at last, when a week had gone by. "You don't have to get up. You don't have to do anything. You can dwell here, in his memory, for as long as you wish." She didn't snort out loud, and her face was hidden in her pillow when she rolled her eyes. It wasn't his memory she was seeking there; in the first few days after he died, her mind recoiled from images of his as if they burned. She wasn't seeking anything. She was doing just what it looked like she was doing, lying about, half-awake and half-asleep, passing the time and waiting for something to change. Because it seemed very clear to her, in those first few days, that what she felt was so intolerable that it couldn't possibly last, and if she did nothing to distract herself from it, she'd use it up, and then she'd be able to get up, and move about, and care once again about her duties to her people, about her constitutional obligations to dancing and singing and feasting and praising the movements of the stars. She didn't consider at all—she didn't dare to consider—that the sources of grief inside her might be inexhaustible.

When Oberon rose and left her it felt like a betrayal, but it also gave her hope that her tactics were sound. It had already happened for him (of course, because he had always, after all, felt less for their Boy than she did), which meant it might happen for her. He retreated in degrees, keeping a vigil at first on the edge of the bed, and then in a chair, and then lounging about the room, and finally just poking his head in now and then to check on her, so she felt the pressure of his eyes and pulled the blankets over her head. One evening she looked out from the blankets and saw a creature in the chair her husband had vacated.

"Good morning, Lady," said Radish.

"It is nighttime, pixie," she said.

"Whenever you wake and whenever you rise, that is morning. Then we'll count the days and months and years again, a whole other eternity beginning in that very moment. Shall I fetch your slippers?"

"Where is my husband?"

"Reigning and raining," said Radish, standing on one leg on the chair and miming her meaning by placing an invisible crown on her own head and tracing tear tracks down her cheeks. "Over half his—" Without sitting up, Titania backhanded her and sent her bouncing off a far wall, then turned on her side and drew the covers over her head again.

There were other visitors, faeries tall and small and round and narrow, who came to sing to her or bring her treats or weep at her bedside, as if it were she who was dead. She stole their voices and ignored the food and threatened to tear them to pieces if they didn't stop singing, and yet they still came, sent in one by one, she suspected, by Oberon, who came himself, now and then, to sit silently in the chair, or put his bare foot under the covers to touch her, which she tolerated, though she wouldn't take his hand when he offered it, for fear he would draw her from the bed. "I'm not done yet," she said, though he never asked her for an explanation.

"I wish *I* could sleep all day," said Puck. He was her last visitor. She lifted the covers for a glimpse of him, then wished she hadn't. He was wearing her Boy's form, naked and thin with a heavy silver chain around his neck.

"Take off that face," she said.

"I put nothing on," he said, "and can take nothing off. I've only come as commanded, to tell you a feast has been prepared. I forget what the occasion is."

"Come closer," Titania said. "I'll pluck off your nipples, and put out your eyes." That made him laugh, and when he saw the damp spots blooming on the thin blanket that lay over her face, he laughed harder.

"I remember crying once," he said. "Did I look so funny to *you*?"

"I'll kill you," she said, a threat they both knew was empty, but he was gone. She wondered when he had ever cried, and wondered if he was lying about a feast, and wondered what the occasion could be, though there was no vigor in her wonder. None of it mattered. She wasn't done yet, and she couldn't leave her bed. She had a new notion, not completely formed, that the bed was carrying her somewhere, and sometimes in the dark she peeked over the edge of the bed, imagining dark heaving seas. It was as naïve and useless a notion as thinking she could exhaust her sadness with continuous grieving; there was nowhere any vessel could take her where she would feel any different. She got up not very long after Puck's visit, though not because she had mastered her feelings or become wise to a way to make them bearable. She began to wonder if the face Puck had worn had been her Boy's real face. In the space of an hour she became terrified that she had forgotten what he looked like, which seemed like a terrible insult to him, one he wouldn't forgive her and one she could never forgive herself. When she became convinced that she *had* forgotten, she sprang from bed, nimble and fleet despite the weeks of indolence, and hurried to him, running through her changeable kingdom under the hill, which showed her the way to the dining hall before it showed her the way to his bier. Countless faeries cheered when she appeared at the door, and Oberon lifted a glass to her, but she raced by and brooked no more detours from the hill. She tore the door to the crypt from its hinges and raced to him as if he were in danger she could save him from. He lay where they had left him, surrounded by the portraits of his foster brothers and sisters, uncorrupted and unchanged, the very picture of her memory of him.

She checked on him after that not because she ever thought again that she had forgotten what he looked like, but because a notion hatched in her mind that he had come back to life. It started quite suddenly. At a joyless meal with Oberon, she felt her heart skip a beat and knew with absolute certainty that he was alive again, and she went running off once again to the crypt and threw open the door to find him as dead as ever. Next she was sure he had come back to life and died again waiting for her to come to him, so she brought a chair to sit in and wait for him. "What?" she asked Oberon, when he came to stand by her and scold her silently. "What do we know of death? Can you really say he might not come back? What do you know?"

"They do not come back," Oberon said.

"What do you know?" she asked again. "What do you *know?*" He left her alone to wait, and she waited and waited, until she became distracted by another plan. Another idea hatched in her mind: she would go back and have vengeance on the hospital that had killed him. She put on her armor and took out her ax, and gathered up a hundred bellicose faeries to march with her. But little Radish tattled to Oberon, who commanded Puck to steal her ax.

"You have robbed me of my satisfaction," she said to Puck.

He shrugged. "I'd ruin all your happiness, if I could," he said.

"Oberon sent you on an errand. Now I'll send you on one too." She told him what she wanted, and he laughed. "What fun," he said, and yawned. But within an hour he'd been to the hospital and fetched Alice the social worker back to the hill.

"Trudy," she said. " Trudy Trudy Trudy." Her eyes were glazed and her heart, when she pressed herself against Titania and clutched at her back and her neck, was racing. "How are you all holding up?"

"Not very well," she said hesitantly.

"Of course not," Alice said. "That's normal. That's normal! Are you taking care of yourself? Are you being good to yourself?"

"What's that got to do with anything?" Titania asked.

"Everything, honey. Everything! It's your time now, don't you see? Nobody else matters now. You worked so hard—it's time for a rest."

"She slept for a month," said Puck.

"Of course she slept for a month! A month?"

"Tell her how it gets better," Puck said. "You have a friend. You have, say, a love of your life, and then they go away, and you forget about them, and everyone else forgets about them. Completely."

"Oh, no, Grandpa. No, you don't. You don't forget. You never forget.

How could you forget? But it gets better, honey. You can't imagine that it ever will, but trust me, it does. I've seen it happen again and again, and it's never okay. How could it ever be okay? But it gets better."

"See?" Puck said. "It gets better!" And he laughed and laughed. Titania stepped close to Alice, and put a hand behind her neck to draw her in close enough for a kiss, and whispered, cheek to cheek, "Tell me the truth." She wanted Alice to tell her it would never get better, that she herself was as dead as her Boy, and what was left for her to live now seemed hopelessly estranged from a real life because it was. "You've just got to give up, honey," Alice said. "Nothing could ever happen to make this any better. Why would you ever pretend otherwise?' She was weeping, not in awe this time but because of all the baseless rumors of hope she'd spread in her time.

Oberon found them weeping together while Puck grinned and played a fiddle. He didn't scold her this time for overwhelming a mortal but just said it was time for Alice to go home.

"You are not suited to sadness," Oberon told her, and that was as close as he ever came to criticizing her for grieving too exorbitantly for the child or ignoring the burden of sadness that he carried. She was waiting for him to do that. She had plans of battle prepared more intricate and more violent than anything she had drawn up when she was prepared to invade and destroy the hospital. She was sure he'd lose the last protecting shred of her love, if he had criticized her forcefully, or complained that she was ignoring him, or asked, What about my grief?

But he expressed his impatience by courting her, instead. He came to their room in a wagon, drawn by Puck, a giant dog. "Let's go for a ride," he said, but it was twelve visits before she consented, and he didn't talk for the first three times they went out. "I got you something," he said eventually. They were always small gifts, dark baubles to suit her new mood, a raven or a piece of shale or a bag of beetles. She tolerated the courtship and made herself alone on her side of the bed, examining her insides every night to determine what portion of love the boy had drawn after him into death and always deciding that he hadn't taken everything, after all, just most of it, the best part.

At last—she had no idea at all of how much time it took him—her husband brought her a sunflower.

"What's this?" she asked.

"Marry me," he said.

"We are already married."

"Marry me again," he said. "Marry into our new life. We'll be diminished from our former selves, I promise you that. We'll not forget what we lost, but not neglect our future joys. Can you imagine it?"

She looked at his flower but not at his face. "No," she said.

"Ah," he said. "Come along with me, Titania." He held his hand out to her, as if there were someplace else to go, except where they were. It summed up in a sentence how wonderful he was, and how furiously she wished to destroy him and destroy his love for her just then. Even a month later, she'd wish she'd said, *I do not understand how to love you now*, or *I do not wish to love you anymore* or *What can it possibly mean to love you now?* but instead she said, "I do not love you. I never loved you." My husband, my friend, my life, I do not love you. I never did.

18

A-one," Huff shouted, "and-a-two!' He remembered to sing just as the Mayor arrived, so Huff was singing "A-three!" as he pulled up in his obscene royal wagon. He wasn't alone: there was a man at his side, whose hand the Mayor was holding very tightly, and his cart was pulled by another man and a woman, both naked and dazed-looking. Three more creatures—Huff had ideas for three more characters when he laid eyes upon them, a Soylent Bunny and a tall barren tree to dance with Mother Nature and a little man to physically represent Thorn's atrophied ambition—came behind, dragged along by chains attached haphazardly to their ankles and wrists. It was too late to add them in, and too late to add in the naked man and the naked woman, who would have made a handsome Soylent thug and a lovely piece of Furniture. He could do nothing for them now but sing, so that's what he did.

It felt like magic, to wave his arms and wink and wiggle his nose, subtly conducting the music as he danced and sang. It would have been no more startling to point at a tree and have it erupt in flames as it was to point at Princess and have her erupt in beautiful heartbreaking song. Everything was so much worse than he had ever imagined: the state of San Francisco in 2022, the plight of a woman whose body was bought and sold with the apartment she lived in, the debilitating nostalgia for jam, the pain of hunger and the memory of how far the world had fallen and had yet to fall. And it was all—the music and the words and the enraptured faces of his cast, and even the nostalgia and the hunger and the secret ingredient in Soylent Green—lovelier than he could bear. He wanted to say to his lady, "Look! Look! It's a miracle!" But he was afraid to break his concentration even for a moment.

They came to the final number, the revelation that Soylent Green was people, and Huff put it in his singing, though it wasn't in the words, that the secret was out and could never again be put back in. The lovely last few bars (where half the cast sang "Up with people!" while the other half sang "Soylent Green *is* people!") rang softly over the clearing. It was a tactical decision to end on a gentle, plaintive note instead of an abrasive, accusing, and militaristic one—Huff decided, at the very end, that he would take the great risk of appealing to the mummified little portion of humanity in the Mayor's heart, rather than trying to bully him into doing the right thing. He kept his focus almost all the way through, but lost it in the last bars of that last number. Tears obscured his vision and he lost sight of his cast members. Still singing, their stationary forms melted into something else altogether. He waved his arms, trying to make it stop, but if he had ever had any control over the play, he had none now. The pretend smokestacks blew real smoke and the lovely singing gave way to a high continuous whine of machinery and the odor of grass and sweat and eucalyptus and rosemary was replaced with something else, sharp and brittle and sickly sweet all at once. It was the odor of Soylent Green. Something had gone horribly wrong: singing about a thing had made it so; now they would all be meat, and it was just as terrible, after all, as it was delightful, to want something and to get it. He covered his hands, and wept, and failed to notice that the Mayor was weeping too.

It was curious, Molly thought, during the little orgy, how she didn't begin to behave like she was dreaming until she became convinced she wasn't dreaming. She had conducted herself with a pretty respectable sort of propriety, aside from drinking very freely from that wine bottle, when she was sure that she had diverged in the woods of the park from the real world, and that everything happening that night was a drama enacted as a byproduct of the meltdown of her tortured subconscious. Now she knew she actually had diverged from reality somewhere in those woods, but not in a way that impugned her sanity, and now she knew that everything she did in this unreal world would have real-world consequences, and yet here she was trying to get two dicks in her mouth at the same time, something she never would have tried even in her dreams.

This was what it was like, she supposed, to reach the end of your rope and then let go. It would be no surprise to her mother, she was sure, that saying no to Jesus would eventually mean saying yes to two dicks in your mouth in a topsy-turvy kingdom of little people under the ground. *You say that like it's a bad thing*, she said to her mother, not meaning that this double fellatio was exactly a virtue. What she meant, and what she wanted to tell her mother, was that everything was suddenly a lot more complicated. The two dicks were merely representatives of the fact that she felt suddenly like she could do anything, and her free fall had more in common, she thought, with what happened when you let go of the rope swing than what happened just before you hit the bottom of the well.

She didn't have much of a clue as to why this should be, why everything shouldn't have gotten even more confusing or horrifying when it all turned out not to be made up, until Peabo showed up at the foot of the bed. Her first reaction, beyond surprise at how suddenly he appeared and horror at the menace that seemed to radiate from him, was relief. He really was black, but he wasn't really Peabo. And in the instant that she understood this, she understood as well that she hated him, and she wanted to do him a terrible harm. Anger overcame her horror, and she leaped to intercept him as he was reaching for one of her boys, thinking, in midair, *You did it to him. It's not my fault, it's yours!*

What that meant exactly remained to be puzzled out (though it wasn't really much of a puzzle) during her subsequent captivity. Peabo plucked her out of the air like a balloon, or he popped her like a floating bubble, or he batted her aside like a shuttlecock—it felt like all those things. She did what he told her and watched mutely with Will at her side as he had his tender, horrible reunion with Henry. *That,* she would have said, as she watched Henry shrink against the head of the bed, trying to avoid the reaching touch of the boy. If she could have spoken, she would have said, *That's* what you did! You made his whole life like that! Because Henry's weeping gyrations had the character, she thought, of Ryan's whole life with her. She watched as the sheets rose up and attacked the boy, as the air over the bed became a wall of mist and then a wall of wood and then a wall of iron, as black birds detached out of the darkness above them to swoop down at him. The sheets burst into flame when they touched his skin; he walked through mist and wood and iron alike, and he ate all the birds in one bite. Then he had Henry, still weeping, in his arms, and he was saying, "There, there. I've got you now. My own dear friend, I've got you forever."

Let him go! Molly kept thinking, though she knew she should be thinking *Let me go!* But, though she was shortly bridled like a horse and he was sitting on a golden pillow, Henry's captivity felt more onerous than hers or Will's. *Let him go!* she shouted again inside herself, not just at Peabo and Henry but at whatever spirits of the air had tortured and confined Ryan, and she wept bitterly, even before the horrible musical began. She wanted someone to do something, and couldn't understand at all, when they ran into their former supposed guides and guardians, why none of them tried harder to overcome Peabo, or, when they encountered the whole otherly population of the park, why they chose to sing and dance instead of scream and fight.

Somebody should do something! she thought, struggling mightily with her bonds, though to anyone watching it looked like she was just standing there watching the ridiculous musical. She hated musicals. There was no worse waste of time on the whole planet, and though she knew there were worse tortures than to be made to sit through one, it still felt like an exquisite misery to be stuck there with invisible toothpicks holding her eyes open. This is what you missed? she asked Ryan. The lyrics were asinine, and the action was stupid, yet she found herself moved, inexplicably at first, but then it was obvious why she was crying, since the action had suddenly veered from futuristic San Francisco to Ryan's garden. *Don't go in there!* she shouted, not making a peep, to the fat homeless lady who was playing her part, but she went through the gate and walked down the hall and came out in the garden, singing something about how hard it was to get out of bed every morning, and doing a little dance, leaping and twirling on point beneath the tree until a man in a moon costume, whose face shone like white gold, was hoisted on a pole and lit the tree and the garden, revealing Ryan's body where it had been swinging the whole time, a purple-faced slouch-shouldered dance partner. Homeless-lady Molly dropped to her knees, arching her back and putting her fist in her mouth and staring at her lover with eyes that seemed to leap out of her head on coils, and sang a fist-muffled aria.

Molly wanted so much to be able to move, to throw something at the players, or rush forward and cut Ryan's body down from the silver tree, or tear out her hair, or at least speak, but when she found her voice again she could only shriek and weep in conversation with Ryan like she had when she had found him, two years ago and two miles away. But back then she was asking *why, why, why?* and now she was asking *for what for what for what?* For this stupid musical, and this unbearable hill, and these monsters? For that lady with the terrible hair? She felt she ought to be able to destroy the whole scene with the noise of her voice. Even when she admitted to herself, really and finally, that there was magic in the park, she was no less angry, she judged no less severely, because she knew, by a process that might have looked as quick and miraculous as magic if she hadn't suffered for it in the most profoundly slow and mundane way, that what she had been offering Ryan was better than all of it.

Will was thinking of Carolina as the action unfolded in front of him in the amphitheater. He could almost convince himself that the musical was being staged for him, because of the way it seemed to be staged *at* him, with the singers and dancers and the parts of the set that were made of living bodies darting so close, and curving around him. Yet they were all looking just past him, at the thing in the back, the terrible lady who contained such a density of terror, who looked like his ice-cream-loving divorcée, until she touched you, and then you knew she was somebody else, somebody worse. Even without seeing her, Will still felt a pressure on his back that made him want to run, the force that made the buggy go. The only thing stronger than that force was the lady's admonition to stop, so Will stayed stopped, and felt like he would stand there forever if the lady didn't ever tell him he could move again.

As he watched the musical, Will thought of the last time he'd seen *Soylent Green*. He thought he should feel guiltier than he did, since he had once again gone to a sex party of sorts, something he had sworn never to do, and the fact that it was an entirely impromptu sex party, one he had stumbled into accidentally in the course of the strangest night of his life, seemed like no excuse. But he felt quite at peace with the sex party and found he did not regret one poke or thrust or jiggle; there was nothing he regretted having put in his mouth or touched or tasted, and he felt quite pleasantly disposed toward weird, weeping Henry and toward Molly, though she had said nothing to him to make her seem any less anxious or bitchy. None of them had said much of anything together, the potentially awkward postcoital conversation having been abbreviated by the arrival of the monster who now held them all in thrall. He should feel horrible about what he had done, and feel revulsion toward the people he had done it with, and yet that thought was as remote somehow as the nostalgia he felt for that other night in that other park when he'd watched the other version of this despairing futuristic cannibalism with Carolina. It seemed very far away, and she seemed very far away, and though he was worried about what was going to happen next—he was chained, after all, around the neck, and something or someone whose awfulness he could only barely understand was holding his reins—he was quite content to stand and watch this wonderful, ridiculous show until the action started to change.

A tree was growing in the dell. My sapling! he thought at first, but in moments it was too big to carry without a truck. The stage had been full of people moments before, singing what had to be the closing number— Ty Thorn had found out the secret of Soylent Green and announced it to the world—but though Will still heard the voices, people were nowhere to be seen until a single figure, dumpy and awkward-looking but dancing very gracefully with a silver ax in her hands, came spinning into the dell and danced around the tree, her wild spasms contrasting with the irenic strains of the music. Though he couldn't understand the words of the song anymore the message was perfectly clear: everyone deserves to be loved and everything is going to be okay, and it was all plucking harps and deeply reassuring overtones even as the dumpy lady sank the ax in the tree, and chopped wildly, bloody sap spraying her hair and dress and skin, so she looked just as crazed and scary as Carolina had when she had done the same thing, nonmusically, after showing him the pictures Mrs. Perkins had sent along to the house, and telling him they had never really dated anyway, and she had never loved him. All this time it had been their dead brothers who were dating, and they had just been along for the ride. *Don't do it!* Will shouted in his head, crying as if the ax were falling on him instead of on the tree, but she chopped and danced and howled until the tree fell, striking the earth in a shower of sparks that leaped furiously to the sky.

Though he had never seen the movie before, Henry knew when the end was coming. Enough people had died, and the not-so-surprising secret had ripened sufficiently to be revealed, and the music was increasingly becoming dominated by strains of the overture, and, most importantly, he knew it was almost time for him to do something. That knowledge had come as certainly as had the lost memories of who he was and what had been done to him, and though he didn't totally comprehend the plans his terrible childhood friend had for the two of them, he knew he bore some responsibility to stop them. He stood very stiffly next to his friend, who was now a large handsome black Lab, and now Bobby's spitting image, and now a thin wild-eyed man whom Henry knew was Ryan twenty years later. Henry could tell he was amused by the musical even though his face was impassive.

It was very strange—much stranger than being lost in the park, or discovering that it had once been his home, and stranger even than remembering there was such a thing as magic, and that he had lived with it and used it and been good at it and suffered for the lack of it, and even stranger yet than the strangest and most wonderful discovery of the night, that it was something as lovely as it was terrible that he had been so afraid of—to feel so powerful and so helpless. He knew how to turn a tree into a house, and bacon into a pig, or a pig into a cop, or cop into a penny—and yet he didn't know what to do to stop his friend and make things better.

The answer came from the musical—or, rather, one of the players, the tall lady with cobwebs in her hair, whom Henry recognized from his time under the hill, and for whom he still felt a twinge of hatred, though it was very small and very much overpowered by the pity he felt for her, since her glamour fell away now in his memory, and he knew her from the hospital as well. She was brandishing a silver knife and threatening to kill herself for love, and throwing herself on the dirty homeless-looking man who played the lead, who told her over and over that there was no room for love anymore in a world that contained the horror of Soylent Green. The rest of the cast—all the population of the hill, it seemed—came walking in procession onto the stage to sing about people who ate people, how lonely they were, and how sad, but they had so much more to say about them than just that. Henry strained to listen, but the words escaped him, not because the music and voices weren't loud, but because new voices had jumped in to confuse the lyrics. At the same time he saw Bobby weeping as he broke up with him, while Henry patted him dumbly and numbly on the back. He saw the boys of Fourteenth Street scattering in the police raid, ocelots and raccoons and fleet foxes sailing over the wall and between the legs of the policemen to run free in the city, only to wake within days like Henry, remembering less and less of who they really were and where they had been until there was nothing left at all. He saw Mike raging in the form of a bear, then fleeing to his room under a barrage of bullets, and dying there in his bed in his own form, and Ryan, wearing the form of an angry boy, punching a policewoman in the face. And he saw a black Lab puppy, sitting still but not quiet in the middle of the stage, weeping and howling.

It was Ryan but not Ryan, an actor who wore Ryan's face upon his own as if it were projected there, and every scene was excruciatingly clear, though they were laid on top of each other and within each other. "Why are you doing this to me?" Henry asked the lady with the cobwebs in her hair, because it was obvious to him that this was her magic. He spoke very quietly, but he was sure she heard him. She shook her head, singing and dancing and smiling faintly. A little brownie came running up to her, and bowed, and exchanged her silver knife for a wooden one. "Why are you doing this?" he asked again. "Are you trying to make me feel guilty? I didn't ask for any of this!"

"Hush," said the black dog next to Henry. "Here comes the good part." The lady knelt before the dog on the stage. Her eyes met Henry's a few times before he understood that she was trying to tell him something, before he saw that the way she was swinging her knife was an invitation to him to fight alongside her, and her eyes, which remained open, and dulled so convincingly after she fell on her knife that he worried she might actually be dead, stayed locked on his as she lay on the ground. So he stood very quietly as the show ended, as the last animal ran into the woods, and Bobby closed his door on him, and the puppy lay down on its belly and put its paws over its muzzle.

"What, Titania?" said Henry's friend. "Did you want to remind me of something I never forgot?" He was crying, but smiling fiercely. He took away his hand, releasing his hold on Henry, and wiped his eye. Henry jumped as a rabbit, and sailed through the air as a slim black ferret, and landed as a dog before he stood before her as man.

"I'm ready," he said to her.

19

Titania's attention wandered as she danced and sang. It was supposed to all be on Puck, focused there by the terms of the spell she was under, since her new mortal husband had commanded her to *sing her heart out* at him, and she would have done that, anyway, since the crude and complicated spell that she had woven into the song and substance of the play required her voice to come to fruition. He stood, at first impassive and unaffected next to his companion, who commanded more and more of her attention until he had all of it.

"How is he today?" he'd asked, just barely inside the door of their room, looking at the floor instead of at the child.

"How does he look?" she would always reply, and he would mutter something and wander out. "You are the worst doctor in the world," she had told him at one point, in answer to some inane question when the boy was in his last days. She had noticed how he had a boy's face in his face but had not remarked that it was one she knew. Is that what this is all about? she wanted to ask Puck, but her words were all taken up in song. You have forgotten why we quarreled a thousand years ago, but you want to kill us all because we took away your toy in 1988? She wanted to laugh, but then she let out a sob that stopped the music briefly: she weaved it into the spell, sadness and chagrin and a dawning glee, which she tried to squelch.

Dr. Blork had haunted her grief the whole past year, and she had come to hate him for failing to save her child, in ways it had never occurred to her to hate him before her Boy had died. She did not wonder how she could have failed to recognize him as someone who had lived under the hill: recognizing former changelings was the farthest thing from her mind in the hospital, and this one, like so many of them, used the magic that was left to them to hide what they were from themselves. She remembered how disdainful she had been of him, and what a poor choice he had seemed, though nobody had expected Puck to pick a changeling for his beauty or sweetness. What had been so distasteful about him, she understood, as she watched him weeping with ghosts in his eyes, was not that he was ugly or mischievous or smelled bad, but the huge capacity for suffering that had been so appallingly evident in him. Now that she really saw him, she thought she could remember the vast empty chambers she had seen in him when he stood forth with Puck, chambers that could be filled with only one thing. How odd, she thought, and how horrible to see them still there, slosh full of tears and regret, but no more capacitous, and perhaps not as full, as her own.

Oh my, she thought, watching Puck cry next to Dr. Blork, and understanding what she had to do when Doorknob came running up furiously, looking certain to stab her with the rowan knife until he knelt and presented it to her, taking her silver knife in exchange. She took a moment to regret her decision, but not very long. As certainly as she knew what to do to save her people, she knew her husband wasn't coming back anymore than her Boy was coming back, that she had waited as long as she could for both of them. She knew those facts would never be anything easier than a great gnawing sadness, and she knew it would always be true, even as she lived day after day into eternity, that she couldn't live without them.

Dr. Blork held her eye and nodded at her and even seemed to wink once: he came to her in one fluid changing leap. And he told her, as if in benediction, when he landed: "I'm ready."

"So am I," she said, and as gracefully as he had flown to her she stood and stabbed him in the heart with her wooden knife.

20

Henry already knew that it took forever and no time at all to die. He had watched children die over weeks and months; some died over years, dying from the moment they were diagnosed with the incurable diseases that he and his colleagues handed out. And yet at the same time they were, eventually, alive one moment, and dead the next. But it was still a surprise how much time seemed to pass between the moment he was stabbed and the moment he hit the ground, and from that moment until the sun came up and darkened his sight forever. In that time he had the opportunity for all sorts of reflection, and a variety of action, and in a flash he considered everything he might do before he died, because he felt sure he could do anything in that short eternity. Except not die, of course—that was as solidly unavoidable as the wooden knife in his chest. But there was time, he felt, to undo his old forgotten friend, and he felt just about magical and mighty enough to do it, as capable as he had been incapable a few moments before. He had the certain sense that death would grant him that wish. *It's too bad I have to die*, he thought, *but it's probably worth it*. With a particularly clarified vision he saw what his friend would do if he was left unrestrained, and then his death seemed like a small price to pay. *Clever lady!* He thought of Titania, whose hundred thousand names he suddenly knew as well, and he pitied her and he hated her.

But his friend was already vastly diminished, and swarms of faeries were molesting him cruelly, clawing at him with their nails and biting him with their teeth, hacking with little axes and swords, gouging black gobbets of flesh from him and swallowing them without chewing. He fought back, but his sadness dominated his rage and made him weak. In no time—or was it forever?—they had bound him with a necklace of bones, and the snarling black dog was a black Lab puppy with a mouth full of milk teeth. They might have been the bones of their fallen comrades, plucked from Puck's gullet, or they might have been Henry's friends' own bones, or they might have been Henry's bones. At the end he sat meekly at Titania's feet amid a pile of faeries, some dead and some mangled, and a fog of golden blood hung in the air, and there was dancing and song and a noise of bells.

A number of things happened next, though Henry paid only partial attention to them. Titania began to call out names and issue orders; she named every faerie still living, and told them to fetch what was precious to them because they were leaving, abandoning the hill and moving farther west. "Wake the horses," she said. "We will ride on the sea until we come to a new home." *How interesting!* Henry thought. *I want to see what their new home is like.* But he didn't, really. There was something more important he should be thinking about, and yet, ridiculously, for another eternal moment what it was escaped him. At some point, before this or after this, Titania told Molly and Will and all but one of the other mortal cast members to go home, and they all did, turning and marching, naked or clothed, down the hill and through the morning fog, out of the park and back into the world. *How interesting!* Henry thought. *I hope Molly and Will start dating!* And yet he didn't hope that, or else there was something he wanted more, and it seemed like a betrayal that they passed by without saying goodbye to him, though he knew—in fact, he could literally *see*— how they were bound by Titania's words to do just as she said, and he knew they might forget everything that had happened that night and might invent other reasons to explain how they met or why they fell in love. To her remaining mortal cast mate, the male lead, whose name was Whoosh or Puff or Snuff, Titania said, "Goodbye." Those words represented something terribly important, Henry knew—it came with knowing all her names that he knew her heartbreak as well, though he had known it anyway, when she was poor Mrs. Trudy Doolittle, whose son had died like everyone else ever born into the world—and yet he suddenly cared least of all about that. It was the thought of Molly and Will walking home naked together and then falling in love—real love, not the lust and obsessions borne of faerie wine—that made him remember.

Bobby! he thought. *Forgive me!* He meant, most immediately, *Forgive me for forgetting you,* and yet he also meant *Forgive me for everything else,* and yet also just as soon as he said it he realized it was not what he meant to say. Or rather, there was something more important to say to Bobby and not much time to say it. He tried to hurl himself across the country, but his body wouldn't budge, and he tried to fling himself there as a whispering wind, but that was too hard, too. Maybe impending Death was fickle with his gifts, or maybe he was too close now to actually dying to manage it. He needed a messenger. Everyone seemed so busy. The faeries were packing, and Puck was still weeping, and Molly and Will were shambling down the hill. It seemed unfair, anyway, to make them carry his message; they had their whole lives to get on with. He considered Titania briefly, and though it would have been satisfying to make her deliver his message—as his murderer she owed him something, he was sure of that— he knew she would ultimately be too hard to convince. It would take too long, and he didn't really have forever until he died. It only felt that way.

He settled for a squirrel. Its brain was small and its will was weak, but it was changeable and so he changed it into his messenger. *Listen,* he said to it, *you must go tell Bobby the good news.* And Henry told it, in rather a hurry, what it should say. The faeries had mounted their wagons and their chariots and their steeds, and Puck was sitting all alone by Henry's body, weeping silver puppy tears that rolled like marbles down the hill, and Molly and Will and the others had nearly made it through the fog.

There is magic! the squirrel said.

Exactly! Henry said. And then: *No, no . . . there is love! That's what I mean to say.* Or did he mean magic? *Just tell him the whole story!* he commanded, not knowing if the squirrel could do it, but wanting so desperately that it would. *There it is,* he thought. *The last thing I want!* He knew it was his mightiest moment as a magician, and he very carefully failed to want anything else while his fellow mortals found the steps out of the park and the faeries began their wild ride to find a new home, leaving behind a host of treasures under the hill, and leaving the body of Titania's boy, which began very subtly to rot, and leaving Puck to weep as long as he would next to Henry's body and then be free to harass the park and the city with muted mischief, but taking with them the secret word that might unbind him so it would never be spoken again.

Henry died just at dawn, and did no more magic in the world. From the west side of the park a host of faeries streamed down Waller Street, and birds fell out of the sky, and cats danced on garbage cans, and early rising widows fell down at their windows, blinded by the glorious glowing sight of them, and they rode faster and faster, so by the Outer Sunset those who witnessed their passing saw them as a wind full of color. They passed onto the ocean and were gone. From the east side of the park the mortals spilled out: Molly and Will, naked and hand in hand, just above the Duboce Steps, where they were quite startled by the lovely sunrise over the city; Princess and Huff and Mary and Bob and Hogg a little higher up. "I got one," Princess said, because she had stuffed a faerie in her pocket, but when she brought it out she saw that it had been replaced with a bunch of sticks and a little grass. And from the north entrance a squirrel ran out and paused on the sidewalk on Haight Street, standing up on its hind legs and sniffing the air a moment before dropping to all fours and starting the long journey to Boston.

ACKNOWLEDGMENTS

Many thanks to Eric Chinski, Eric Simonoff, Nathan Englander, Cressida Leyshon, and Deborah Treisman for the use of their wisdom and intelligence to improve this novel, and to the John Simon Guggenheim Memorial Foundation for the means to complete it.